D0965923

The Heavenly World Series

A Half Century of Praise for Frank O'Rourke

"Cannily displaying the intricate complexity of baseball, adroitly clarifying and reducing it to a human level, and balancing the throbbing pathos of individual achievement against the universal mystique of a shared endeavor, this sterling collection . . . represents the best work of a venerable mid-century master of baseball fiction. Harking back to a more naïve time, it is also a valuable repository of a style of American popular fiction. . . . From the whimsical title story to the moving and brilliant drama found in 'The Last Pitch,' 'Flashing Spikes' or 'One More Inning,' the tales are a fine sampling of O'Rourke's consistently excellent control of language, style and composition. His sturdy players come off the page with such vividness that readers can almost smell their sweat, feel their heat, share their triumphs as well as the bitterness of their defeats. In the longer stories, particularly 'The Catcher,' this collection meets the challenges of making a single player, a single sport, into something immeasurably bigger. . . . It should occupy a revered place in any collection of sports fiction or, indeed, of American fiction from the last half of the 20th century."

—*Publishers Weekly*, December 3, 2001

"He has come up with a raft of sports fiction that is marked by a special, endearing quality. That is his ability to capture the authentic flavor of the dugout or the diamond or the pressbox or the locker room, places which comparatively few people get to visit but which the reader comes to know first-hand through O'Rourke's words."

—Red Smith, from his introduction to
The Saturday Evening Post Book of Sports Stories

Flashing Spikes, 1948

"Worthwhile . . . for the good baseball and the excellent picture of a ballplayer's life on and off the field." —*Library Journal*

The Team, 1949

"No youngster could read this book without gaining real understanding of the complex nature of bigtime baseball."

—*The New York Times*

Bonus Rookie, 1950

"Frank O'Rourke's byline on a baseball yarn is invariably a guarantee of good reading. This is no exception."

—*Chicago Sunday Tribune*

Football Gravy Train, 1952

"Vigorous, forthright treatment of a difficult problem."

—*Christian Science Monitor*

"A timely, knowing and dramatic book by one of sportswriting's top practitioners."   —*The New York Times*

The Catcher and the Manager, 1953

"Pair of excellent stories."   —*Chicago Sunday Tribune*

The Diamond Hitch, 1956

"A story of the West that will become a classic in its field."

—*Oakland Tribune*

The Last Ride, 1958

"A work of art."   —*Boston Sunday Globe*

The Far Mountains, 1959

"*The Far Mountains* belongs among the lasting novels of the Southwest."

—Walter Havighurst, *New York Herald Tribune*

A Private Anger and Flight and Pursuit, 1963

"The heroes of both these finely carpentered escapades are the sort favored by Simenon."   —*The New York Times*

"Two excellent novellas. . . . High creativity with Steinbeck flavor. Powerful." —*Boston Sunday Globe*

A Mule for the Marquesa, 1964

"A brilliantly conceived chase that never flags for a single hoof-beat and is inventive even in its paradoxical conclusion. Truly magnifico!" —*The New York Times*

The Swift Runner, 1969

"O'Rourke's novel is one of the bright spots in this year's list of new releases—a supersensitive narrative of the dying Old West." —*Sacramento Union*

"Mark Twain would have admired it." —*Tulsa World*

The Abduction of Virginia Lee, 1970

"Ingenious!" —*The New York Times*

"Frank O'Rourke has a positive genius for creating an impossible situation and making the reader believe in it." —*Sacramento Bee*

Burton and Stanley, 1993

"A children's adventure that is comfortable on high ground." —*The New York Times*

"Harks back to the simpler world of such classics as Stuart Little." —*Publishers Weekly* (starred review)

"A gem of a story." —*Boston Globe*

Ellen and the Barber: Three Love Stories of the Thirties, 1998

"Surprisingly wonderful trio of love stories."—*Kirkus Reviews*

"Powerful, posthumous novel . . . reminiscent of both John Steinbeck and Eudora Welty." —*Library Booknotes*

The
Heavenly
World Series

Timeless Baseball Fiction

Frank O'Rourke

Edited by Edith Carlson

Introduction by
Darryl Brock

CARROLL & GRAF PUBLISHERS
NEW YORK

To the editor

Philip Turner

THE HEAVENLY WORLD SERIES
Timeless Baseball Fiction

Carroll & Graf Publishers
An Imprint of Avalon Publishing Group Inc.
161 William St., 16th Floor
New York, NY 10038

Book design by Michael Walters

Pages 327 and 328 represent a continuation of the copyright page.

Library of Congress Cataloging-in-Publication Data is available.

ISBN: 0-7867-0950-2

Printed in the United States of America
Distributed by Publishers Group West

CONTENTS

THE BASEBALL WORLD OF FRANK O'ROURKE

As a boy I read them all: Duane Decker, Ed Fitzgerald, Dick Friendlich, John R. Tunis and many more—a galaxy of sports-fiction writers. Frank O'Rourke stood out from the rest. His characters possessed quirky depths and seemed to inhabit larger, grittier worlds. They included pressure-plagued managers pacing their hotel rooms at night, end-of-the-road veterans fleecing rookies in high-stakes card games, scouts perching on splintery bleachers and eating greasy food in hash joints. O'Rourke's ballgames typically were warlike affairs, strategy-driven conflicts, whether waged on rural diamonds or in smoke-grimed big league ballparks. Moreover, his fictional players sometimes faced "real" stars—Maglie, Musial, Robinson—in situations echoing actual pennant races of the time.

Frank O'Rourke's realism derived from two sources: his playing experience and his intimacy with the major leaguers he portrayed. During the 1940s, he and his wife Edith spent their winters in Florida, and in the fall of 1948 rented a house on the beach in Clearwater, Florida, site of the Philadelphia Phillies training camp. The following spring, through an accord between Phils' management and *The Saturday Evening Post*, O'Rourke worked out with the pros each day until the club went north—the first writer ever allowed such an opportunity.

"Frank was in very good shape," Edith remembers, "better than some of the players. At six feet two he was physically imposing, with an athlete's body." A shortstop on the sun-baked rural Nebraska diamonds of his youth, O'Rourke described

himself years later in a letter to Jack Knarr, a newspaper colum-
nist, as "the cornfield Babe Ruth in my neck of the woods."

> I played with my hometown team, and hired out to
> other towns for special games (that was in the '30s, the
> time of depression and drouth; the only thing people
> had was baseball, and the big games during the fairs
> and holidays were the best of all because both towns
> spiked up with hired players). I usually got ten bucks and
> expenses to play a game. Got to know all the good play-
> ers in three states. Many were former American Asso-
> ciation and Western League pitchers [and] others were
> college boys, like myself. . . .

A decade later, in the late 1940s, he still played and managed
small-town summer ball in Minnesota. Although he hit over
.500 each of those years (once over .600), he readily acknowl-
edged his inability to cope with big-league curve balls. Still, did
he secretly aspire to making the Phillies squad? "Good God,
no!" he said, decades afterward. "I [had my] own locker in the
clubhouse, and absolute entry anywhere . . . I worked out with
the team, got to know everybody, and most important, gained
their confidence."

"He ran track," Edith recalls. "Played pepper games, caught
[Coach Benny] Bengough's fly balls....The idea was to suit up,
do the workout, not interfere with the actual play, shower with
them, sit in the dugout. This made him part of the club in a
way that simply circulating among them as a sportswriter
would not have done."

The extent to which he was accepted is symbolized by the
special copy of his novel *The Team*, autographed by players and
coaches, and inscribed, "To Frank O'Rourke, the father of the
team, from his kids, the Fighting Phillies." The club's management gave him the red-trimmed wool Phillies uniform he
worked out in. Notes made with Jim Konstanty for a book on

pitching, never completed, currently reside with other of the O'Rourke papers in the Special Collections of the Marriott Library in the University of Utah.

"It's been thirty-five years or more now, and those men are still my friends," O'Rourke said in a 1985 *Contemporary Authors* interview. "I used them as my fictional team. I called them the Quakers and I changed the names phonetically." Many of his baseball books involve those Quakers, and in them the Whiz Kid Phillies are easily recognized: Richie Ashburn is "Robbie Ashton," (who even claims Ashburn's hometown of Tilden, Nebraska); Robin Roberts is "Robbins" or "Ramsay," (Eddie) Waitkus is "Watkins," (Andy) Seminick "Semik," (Granny) Hamner "Hammett," and so on.

The stories in this new collection first appeared in *The Saturday Evening Post, Collier's,* and *Esquire* in the late 1940s and early 1950s. They bring baseball history alive, from turn-of-the-century cow-pasture games to the small-town fever of the Thirties, and on to the major leagues of the Forties and Fifties. When read now the stories and novels take on a marvelous time-capsule quality. "I'm tighter than a dollar watch," one character exclaims. "I've unloaded on everything but income tax and President Truman." Players bunk in swaying Pullmans on road trips and toss their gloves on the grass when they come in to bat. Fans tune in Mel Allen and Red Barber on the radio at World Series time, and we see Joe DiMaggio again, portrayed as Duke DiSalvo in the story "Moment of Truth," " . . . making his run for that invisible circle within which the ball and his glove would come together as if by magic."

Juxtaposed with such contemporary flourishes, O'Rourke's narrators, usually old-time players or sportswriters, frequently harken back, like baseball itself, to earlier times. A prospect isn't merely promising, but "the hottest pitcher since Chief Bender and Bullet Joe Bush came out of the jackpines to make history in a bygone day." Another delivers fastballs down the middle "the way old Dizzy used to pull himself from holes." A skipper contemplating using an untested rookie hurler in the World Series can't avoid ruminating back two decades on "the most daring, magnificent gamble a manager ever took," Connie Mack's choice of washed-up Howard Ehmke to open the '29 fall classic.

Mack himself, whom the O'Rourkes met at a St. Petersburg luncheon, makes a cameo appearance in the novel, *Bonus Rookie*. Edith remembers him as a tall, slender, alert man wearing an elegant pinstriped suit, vest and starched white shirt, "no longer his high collar, but it made you think it was," whose courtly manners and reserve set him apart. Her husband sketches this ballpark portrait:

> . . . wearing the dark suit and high white collar and string tie that were throwbacks to another age . . . the Old Gentleman seemed touched with the lasting ivory yellow of eternal youth. He had known the greatest victories and the worst defeats; he was the living bridge between the present and a forgotten generation of ball players, a relic of time in one sense, yet conqueror of all time. He sat unmoving in the dugout shadow, holding great moments of ten thousand past games in his mind, watching the young men and thinking. . . .

There is abundant time in the stories for such sidelights, for referencing the past, as when we revisit Grove vs. Ruth in a climactic 1928 confrontation, or learn Paul Waner's technique for suckering pitchers, or see how a 1950s catcher's stance differs from that of old-timers like Cy Perkins.

The most haunting among O'Rourke's historical figures appears in the story "Flashing Spikes," an aging shortstop on a barnstorming team that challenges local nines at county fairs.

> . . . he moved with great deliberation, field-ing easy ground balls and tossing them care-lessly to first. But his face made me look time after time; it was

> browned and seamed and filled with some old, old
> knowledge. . . . It was a tired and resigned look as if
> he didn't care who won the game or how he played.
> He had a big nose and a wide mouth and I could tell
> that his fingers had been broken and were bent and
> gnarled like an old-time catcher's.

The young shortstop opposite him (essentially O'Rourke himself) eventually recognizes the notorious "Dane Bjorland, of the old Black Sox." In "Flashing Spikes" Bjorland becomes an important mentor figure, and also appears, in altered form, in the novel *Never Come Back*, which deals sympathetically with an alcoholic player's struggle to return to the top. Of the latter's composite nature, O'Rourke wrote, "There's a little of a right-handed pitcher who came up with the Cubs back in 1932, had a helluva half season, came back the next year and set the league on fire, and was out of baseball by 1935 already a complete drunk, [and also] a little of a shortstop who was banned from baseball, pushing forty, looking fifty, and unforgettable."

Unforgettable indeed: a transparency of White Sox infielder Swede Risberg.

In his most whimsical creation, "The Heavenly World Series," O'Rourke expands his historical scope to otherworldly dimensions. God, besieged by John McGraw [Muggsy in Paradise?], reluctantly allows an all-star contest to settle the issue of which league, National or American, is superior. The respective squads are managed by McGraw and Miller Huggins; starting pitchers are Christie Mathewson and Walter Johnson. Judge Landis is on hand, Bill Klem umps at home plate, and all of baseball's immortals—literally—up to that time (1952) are eager to play. Studying the lineups, God Himself, obviously a fan, remarks, "It seems the Americans have a preponderance of hitting power." Nonetheless the contest is tied after 26 innings, when it has to be called due to recurring uncelestial behavior by the opponents.

"Frank had a baseball aficionado do some research for him," Edith recalls, "and one player he suggested was Big Ed Walsh. After the story came out in *Esquire*, a friend of [Walsh] wrote Frank to say that Big Ed was still very much alive and delighted to know that he would be a star in the afterlife, too."

But it is in his evocation of this baseball realm that O'Rourke is most impressive. Through his free-ranging pages we visit dressing rooms from Florida training camps to Yankee Stadium, taking in their sounds and scents ("hot and sweaty and slightly moldy in a faint tropical way, not so much from body odors and rubbing solutions and sulphur water, as from the smells of ambition and hope and pride and age"), and are ushered through old-fashioned grandstands with their steel pillars and wooden seats, up to smoke-palled pressboxes where typewriters clatter.

And of course we are on the diamond. O'Rourke's flowing use of detail renders his action passages gripping yet free of cliches so characteristic of this genre. A squeeze bunt, for example, from the story "The Impossible Play":

> He saw Randy Miller running faster than a man had a right to move under any condition, go headlong to the right of the plate, diving in a streak of twisted, blurred features and dust and spikes gleaming in the slanting sun, left hand stabbing out and slapping the white rubber as the Redskin catcher caught the chest high throw and lunged for him with the ball...and then [they] were rolling together in a mad ball of arms, legs, and faces, covered with the swirling dust as [the umpire] was sheared from his own feet and rolled with them, all three stopping and lying completely still for one last breathless moment.
>
> Billy Lawson thought, If it is my time to die, let it be now, and waited.

The spring training experience yielded a cornucopia of close-up detail, and O'Rourke's early novels are virtually love songs to the Phillie organization—not only the players, coaches and manager, but also groundskeepers, scouts, traveling secretary, publicity director and office staff. Marshalling exhaustive minutia, he describes the inner workings of a big-league club: 17 trunks crammed with uniforms, equipment, towels and soap; 110 dozen balls for spring training (300 dozen more for the regular season); a dozen bats for each regular; $70,000 total training camp costs. We are given the precise dimensions of the vintage Clearwater ballpark, and learn that a new underground watering system has been installed. We see the trainer at work with his infrared and sine and diathermy machines, and are favored with an item-by-item inventory of the 60-odd medicines and supplies on his shelves. O'Rourke even provides sample days from a two-week travel itinerary as the club breaks camp and heads north.

In the novel, *The Team* (1949), Phils' real-life owner Robert Carpenter becomes Bob Chambers, a young man "with a sincere love for baseball, topped by a shrewd mind and the ability to understand [that] there was no easy shortcut to a pennant."

> He told all of us that he did not expect the impossible;
> we had set fourth place as our goal for that season and
> if our young men came through we might do a little
> better. . . ."

The Phillies did indeed do better in 1949. So did the fictional Quakers—and O'Rourke's reputation as a crystal-ball gazer was launched. Writing six months before the actual outcome, he has his youthful players spurt to a third-place finish, 87-67, two games behind the Boston Braves, one behind the Dodgers. In real life the Phils, too, rode a late-summer surge to end in third, albeit sixteen games behind winner Brooklyn. O'Rourke's Quakers top their league in fielding (the Phils were sixth) and he projects some of their final batting averages: Ashton .345 (Ashburn actually would log a modest .284); Hammett .287 (Hamner .263);

Del Anderson .310 (Del Ennis .302); Semik .262 (Seminick .243). In one instance he hits it on the nose, Quaker first baseman "Watkins" duplicating Eddie Waitkus's .306.

O'Rourke's powers of prognostication reached an amazing zenith the following season, with pre-publication serialization of the novel, *Bonus Rookie*. Beginning July 29, 1950, it ran for three weeks in *The Saturday Evening Post* and provoked enormous reaction—over fifty thousand letters, the magazine's record to that time. Even the Phillies, who happened to move into first place that very week, took note. "On Wednesday," claimed O'Rourke, "the day the *Post* hit the stands, they were all there after breakfast to grab their copies and read, and find out what they were supposed to do that week!" Some of the Whiz Kids took to kidding each other, the *Post* later boasted, with their fictional names, "Sipler" for Sisler, etc.

Here is the closing scenario of *Bonus Rookie*, which, as the actual season drew to an end, appeared to form an uncanny script: The Quaker City club, with catcher Semik sidelined by an injury to his right ankle from a collision with a Giants player at the Polo Grounds in the final week, cling to a two-game lead over the Dodgers with two games remaining. As fate and the schedule mandate, they meet Brooklyn head-on to decide matters. The Dodgers nail down a victory in the first game with three runs in the eighth inning. Facing Don Newcombe in the next day's finale, his other pitchers exhausted, the Quaker manager goes with young bonus hurler Ramsay, a fictionalized version of Robin Roberts. The game is tied after eight, both starters going the distance. Brooklyn loads the bases in the ninth, but Ramsay whiffs Hodges to end the threat. The Quakers score dramatically and win the pennant.

On the final Saturday of the '50 season, O'Rourke was sitting in the dugout box at Ebbets Field beside Robert Carpenter, thinking, he said later, "about the hundreds of letters Dodger fans had written...saying that if O'Rourke was in their ball park those last two days, they'd kill him."

Perhaps the Brooklynites had cause. Except for minor varia-
tions (it was Seminick's left ankle he sprained against the Giants
on September 27 and played on anyway, learning later that he
had a bone separation; Hodges flew out in the ninth against
Roberts with the bases jammed) all the things capsulized above
occurred as O'Rourke had projected, and the Phillies captured
their first flag in 35 years.

A pinnacle, in fiction and reality. Afterward came a different
story. In 1951 the "Fizz Kids" sank to fifth, finishing 25 games
out. Seminick was traded in December. Third baseman Jones
was fined $200 the following spring for "conduct detrimental to
the club," and Hamner was relieved of his team captaincy. Manager Eddie Sawyer was fired 63 games into the '52 season, his
club in sixth, the timing of it ironic, for earlier that day Curt
Simmons had blanked the Giants on three hits.

Sawyer, who remembers Frank O'Rourke as "a wonderful
man," when asked in a phone interview why he was let go after
the shutout victory, replied, with a hint of testiness, "Ask
them." However, *Dell Baseball Annual 1953* quotes Sawyer as
saying, "They got fat-headed on me. . . . They knew everything. I just had to get tough." The Dell reporter offered this
summation:

> A kindly, gentle, wise, understanding and fatherly man
> by nature, Eddie had stepped out of character by his
> crackdown and his Whiz Kids could not forgive him
> for it. They got worse and worse. . . . Finally Carpenter
> read [them] the riot act in an unprecedented meeting.
> It failed to nudge them. Regretfully and reluctantly, he
> fired Sawyer.

O'Rourke's last baseball creations, two companion novellas, *The
Catcher* and *The Manager* (1953), included in this new collection,
explore certain anomalies of baseball's establishment. For one
thing, the players have changed, softened. As his narrator says:

I've watched ball players who gave everything for their team, men who went out on the field with injuries an ordinary man could not bear. They played ball in that way long ago, but it doesn't happen often today. DiMaggio had it, and a few others, but today they scratch a finger on the beer-bottle opener and yell for the trainer and a doctor.

It becomes clear that this is due in part to management's failure to reward loyalty and endurance. The old-style catcher in the story, traded by his team and come back to face them in a crucial contest, is portrayed as thinking, "You ran, and fought, and gave everything for your team; and last year, nursing the bad ankle, you wanted more than ever to help them come back, for you loved that team. And they traded you for that!"

As for O'Rourke's hard-pressed manager, he nods to his Giants counterpart before what proves to be his final game, and reflects:

He—Art Cassidy—was wrong because he'd come up the old way, then changed with the supposed times and tried to play this new kind of baseball that everyone said was so necessary, what with the different players and so forth. But Durocher hadn't changed, not a bit, no matter what the papers said about softening up. Durocher came up the hard, rough, no-quarter way, playing every game for keeps, trusting no man and fighting every man. Durocher still played it that way, unchanged, and he'd never change. They'd piled the hard knocks on old Leo's skull until the scars and bumps covered even older scars and bumps, but he hadn't faltered. He'd wrecked one team, getting his kind of club, and now he had it and that team was playing ball. Sure Durocher took his lumps. He couldn't keep his mouth shut, but at least he spoke his mind. He was a ham, the worst kind, with that third-base hokum and the folded

arms and the big jaw shoved up the umpire's ass; but
never once had he broken faith with himself. . . . What
[Cassidy] should have done was pass among his prima
donnas with a pisselm club and a blacksnake whip, and
instill a little pride and guts in their hides. And go to
the front office, take that general manager by the wattles, and let it be known that one man ran this team,
and he was that man.

But the system, with its pampered players and front-office
politics, defeats him. Cassidy is fired that day, his team mired in
sixth place, after his Blues shut out the Giants 4-0. "The first law
in baseball," he postulates ruefully, is "watch your own skin."

While O'Rourke's old-timers deplore certain contemporary
trends, it is clear that modern players, too, are victimized. "He
felt that owners never shared fairly in profits," Edith says. "He
saw that baseball had become a business, inevitably so."
O'Rourke himself later wrote, "I felt strongly about the way
baseball players were treated in those years just before and after
World War II, the way they were forced to fit into and stomach
a system in which they became chattels."

Ultimately, he concluded, "I simply stopped writing
about baseball. I had gotten too far inside. I had
become involved much too intimately and knowingly
with too many players who were, first of all to me,
human beings. . . ."

Yet even in the relatively bittersweet final stories, the game
itself retains its powerful grip on those human beings. Strapping
on his protective gear, his worldly-wise catcher, Bill Malloy,
thinks, for the thousandth time,

Each day you went out in the sun and felt the strain on
your legs, all the old scars and cuts and sprains and bro-

ken bones, and you knew that just once more you were
good for one more time. You didn't hear the crowd
roar because that was part of your life, heard and
absorbed from the very beginning, down the gone, lost
stairway of the years that climbed upward toward today.
You felt the shin guards against your bones, the elastic
straps holding those red plastic shields in place. You
hitched up the serrated chest protector that lay snug
and hot on your body, the long tail sliced off years ago,
for you didn't need the tail with these modern inventions guarding you so well. You lifted your right hand
in the gesture people knew by heart, pushed the mask
atop your head until the steel bars peered emptily at
the sky and you smelled the acid, wet odor of your own
sweat and dirt and grease just above your ears in the
thinning fringe of gray hair. . . . You took the pitch and
then the tenseness shattered—you were on the way,
the game was moving and nothing could return it to
the unfilled pages of the scorebook where your name,
this day, was written on the visiting side; or return it to
the home dressing room, the home dugout, where you
would not sit again. The game would run its course,
and you with it, for no matter where you played, the
game was everything.

Baseball, then, as a metaphorical tide sweeping its practitioners along with it. As it did Frank O'Rourke in the years after
World War II, when it provided so vivid a focus for his artistry.

—Darryl Brock
Berkeley, California
December 2001

Home Game

Whenever I see my father's lumpy fingers and flattened, crooked nose it takes me back fifty years to his youth and his last summer of hometown baseball before he went up to the Cubs. His hands and face are eloquent testimonial of baseball's evolution from those bare-handed days to the present era of trap gloves, manicured infields, and high salaries. Dad has a tintype of his hometown team taken that last summer, ten sober young men sitting self-consciously on the post-office steps in their homemade uniforms. Their faces are caught and frozen on the metallic texture of that old tintype, moustaches and sideburns etching stern, dark lines of false age against the youth of their faces. At their feet are two bats, three gloves, and one grass-stained baseball which comprised the whole of their equipment. They are echoes from another age and live only in forgotten pictures and reluctantly told tales of men like my dad. The story of his last game with Hopkinsville against Burnside seems to personify the strong, bold spirit of baseball in those days.

Baseball was different then in the small towns. People turned out in large numbers and cheered good plays and booed the umpire much as today, but transportation facilities limited the traveling range and the lack of financial backing made almost every town team one hundred percent simon pure. The Hopkinsville players were all local boys and because the town was so small they did not play more than thirty miles from home. They bought their own equipment and paid their own expenses. The manager might pass his hat each spring and collect ten dollars from the merchants to buy a new bat and two baseballs, but that was the limit of their spending power. Balls cost a dollar apiece and it was the usual thing to make one ball last a full nine-inning game, even if it was necessary to call time and search the weeds for a foul fly while the sun dropped an hour in the sky. Bats were seventy-five cents each and it was not uncommon for the players to make their own from ash wood, carving them out with a draw knife and polishing them with pieces of glass.

The Hopkinsville diamond was west of town in Brubaker's cow pasture. The baselines were not chalkmarked but hazily identified by two red bandannas tacked on sticks thrust in the ground. The bags were burlap sacks stuffed with hay. Home plate was a block of wood cut and smoothed to the correct shape and pinned into the earth with three long carriage bolts. The infield was coarse, thick grass splotched with darker, thicker grass growing well above the general level. The outfield was pocked with gopher holes and water-soaked after a night's rain. Right field lifted up a side hill and left field ducked abruptly into Spring Creek some five hundred feet from home plate. Center field was limitless, extending half a mile into the rolling depths of the pasture. People tied their teams well away from the field and stood or sat along the baselines to watch the game.

Ready-made uniforms were far beyond the reach of young men like dad, working for thirty and forty dollars a month, so they made their own suits. They cut overalls off below the knee and at the waist and sewed on belt loops; and they wore blue work shirts and stenciled the town's name on the shirt front in red paint. They wore railroad engineer caps of blue-and-white pinstriped material, and most of them used tennis shoes, although dad and the pitcher nailed spikes on the soles of old work shoes. They did not wear sliding pads because it was dangerous to come into a base on grass infields any way but headfirst. They made their own gloves and mitts from cotton flannel work gloves, sewing padding in the palms to suit their individual tastes. Half of the boys played bare-handed. Dad's catching mitt was a cotton flannel husking mitten padded with one-half inch of bunched underwear material. He made his chest protector from burlap sacking stuffed with goose feathers. He caught without a mask or shinguards, directly behind the plate.

When they traveled to other towns or rural communities, the team drove buggies and wagons, and occasionally a big three-seater buggy owned by the mail carrier. They had to start early in the morning, depending on the distance to go, and always took a lunch and coffee along. Traveling was easier between towns on the railroad. When they played at Burnside they took the morning passenger at ten and returned after the game on the westbound at six o'clock. Dad remembered one year when the game went into extra innings and the conductor held the six o'clock in Burnside for half an hour until the final out.

Dad was living at home and working in the lumberyard for Mr. Grimes, who managed the town team. Dad was twenty that summer and people described him as the last size of man next to an elephant. He was the best young catcher in the state and was considering an offer from the Cubs, pending certain decisions at home. Old-timers have verified, as do official records of his eighteen years in the majors, that he could peg to second from a full squat and kill his pitcher if that man didn't leap quickly toward third base. Dad hit a long ball with tremendous lift and power; and in those days of dead baseballs and unfenced dia-monds, his record of eight home runs the previous year spoke for itself.

Dad wanted to play professional baseball but his parents and other friends were dead set against such an idea, for ball players in those days were considered the worst type of roughnecks.

Dad's only boosters were the children. They seemed to have vision of better things to come in baseball, as children sometimes do when their elders cannot see beyond their noses. The children collected pictures of big leaguers from Fatima and Sweet Lotus cigarette packages and helped, in their small way, to bolster Dad's arguments with his parents, friends, and his girl, Sarah Goodhue, who lived in Burnside. Sarah wanted no part of a ballplayer's rowdy life, even though Dad pointed out that he could earn two hundred dollars a month, maybe more in time, and still keep his lumberyard job in the winter. Dad knew he had to make his decision that summer.

Burnside was ten miles east of Hopkinsville on the railroad. A natural rivalry existed between the towns in all forms of sport and business. Hopkinsville's four hundred population was barely half that of Burnside's, but Hopkinsville managed to hold fairly even in everything. That spring the Burnside businessmen imported two ball players to assure them victory over every team in the region. They hired a pitcher from Iowa named Dinty McDougal and gave him a job as night watchman in the grain elevator; and they got Rabbit Baranville, the fastest out-fielder in the state, from Penderson, and gave him a job in the Harding Skimming Station. Burnside could afford to do this, Dad explained, because their businessmen were great sports and also they charged fifteen cents admission at their home games to help defray expenses.

Dad drove over to see Sarah Goodhue once a week in his parents' spring buggy and team; and one Saturday night in April he found a competitor on the Goodhue front porch. Rabbit Baranville had arrived in Burnside that week, met Sarah at Wednesday night Bible class, and was losing no time in getting his share of front porch lemonade and cookies. Sarah giggled nervously and introduced them.

Dad towered over Rabbit when they shook hands and eyed each other appraisingly. Rabbit was eighty pounds lighter and a full foot shorter than Dad, but made up these physical deficiencies with unlimited spunk and a generous veneer of big city polish. He was a year older than Dad and already well known through the state in sporting circles.

Dad had heard about Rabbit, just as Rabbit knew all about Dad. They sat on the front porch and talked baseball, ate cookies, drank lemonade, and tried to outwait each other for the privilege of saying the last goodnight. Dad wasn't angry because he realized Sarah couldn't sit home six nights a week and wait for him to pay a call; but the idea of a scrawny little runt, and a baseball player with professional leanings, getting encouragement from her, was a blow to Dad's conceit. Rabbit made no bones about his opinion of towns like Hopkinsville being small potatoes in baseball; and that Burnside, with him and Dinty McDougal leading the way, would win every game that summer.

"I got an offer from the Giants last winter," Rabbit said casually, grinning at Sarah. "That big city is where I want to be."

Dad was shocked to see Sarah act as if she thought professional baseball was wonderful. Dad said, "The Giants are all right, I guess. I'm thinking of signing with the Cubs this fall."

"Yeah," Rabbit said. "They ain't bad."

"Yeah," Dad said calmly. "That's true."

"The Giants offered me three hundred," Rabbit said.

Dad knew that was a bare-faced lie. He said, "I'll be lucky to get two hundred if I make the grade."

"Well," Rabbit said smugly. "Catchers are like streetcars. There's another one along every ten minutes. But you sure got the size."

"I reckon you're pretty fast," Dad said honestly.

It was strange, their talking on a front porch in a quiet, little town, two young men with the same dream. Dad and Rabbit often laughed about that conversation in later years when they played against each other in the majors. Dad admitted that in eighteen years of catching against Rabbit, he had more trouble with the little center fielder than any other base runner. But that night in Burnside, with their future still unknown and the present all important, they thought of nothing but impressing black-haired, blue-eyed Sarah Goodhue. Dad finally gave up. He had to drive ten miles while Rabbit was only two blocks from his boarding house. Dad said goodnight and drove away, and that was the beginning of the hottest summer in baseball between the towns.

Bad feeling was prevalent long before the season started. In other years Hopkinsville and Burnside had played three games, but that spring Burnside loftily refused to play more than one game. They explained that due to their improved team, they were scheduling better ball clubs up to seventy-five miles away. Mr. Grimes and the Burnside manager exchanged hot words and parted with an agreement to play one game on the last Sunday in August. Mr. Grimes refused to play in Burnside, so they tossed a coin, and that was the only solace. Mr. Grimes won the toss and the game was scheduled at Hopkinsville.

Dad practiced after supper with his pitcher, Fred Luterman. Fred was a right-hander with great strength, speed and a fair curve, but little control. Fred farmed just outside town and walked in three nights a week to practice with Dad. They labored until darkness on those long summer evenings, trying to improve Fred's control and get a sharper break on his curve by experimenting with emery dust, tobacco juice, and other abrasives commonly employed in those days. Dad knew they couldn't beat Burnside unless Fred pitched steady baseball. The Hopkinsville boys wouldn't hit Dinty McDougal very hard, and Dad foresaw that one run might decide the game.

The hot summer days arrived and Burnside piled up easy victories all over the region, while Hopkinsville struggled through their schedule against other small towns and rural teams. Dinty McDougal was pitching three- and four-hit games every Sunday. Rabbit Baranville was making circus catches commonplace in center field and hitting over five hundred and stealing bases on every catcher in the region. Worst of all, Rabbit not only escorted Sarah Goodhue to various social functions, but seemingly had changed her mind about detesting ballplayers with professional inclinations, for twice he took Sarah and her father to Sioux City on the train to see Ducky Holmes' Western League team play ball in Mizzoo Park, where the games were enlivened by a great deal of tobacco chewing and a proclivity of Ducky Holmes for climbing into the stands and exchanging blows with insulting patrons. Those were the days of the old Western League and the two men and the rowboat stationed behind the short right field fence in the river, to retrieve the home runs and foul balls; and if Sarah and her father enjoyed that rough and ready baseball, then she had done a complete about face. Things finally came to a head one night in July. Dad drove over to see Sarah and her father informed him that Sarah was attending a dance with Rabbit and had not mentioned a visit from Bill Martin.

Dad said, "I thought she didn't like professional ball players."

"She knows her own mind," Mr. Goodhue said stiffly. "Besides, you ought to be in bed Saturday nights. You can't stay up late and play baseball."

"What about Rabbit?" Dad asked.

"Rabbit don't smoke or drink," Mr. Goodhue said. "He sleeps late Sunday mornings."

This was a direct insult because Dad touched nothing but an occasional glass of beer and chewed tobacco only while playing to keep his throat moist. He said, "Seeing as how I'm such a rounder, I won't bother her any more," and went home. Dad did not call on Sarah again.

The summer seemed to melt away and the big game was only two days distant. Hopkinsville had won ten games and lost four. Burnside had won twenty straight and added insult to injury by decisively beating the four teams that previously whipped Hopkinsville. Nevertheless, interest ran high on the game. The Hopkinsville fans stirred from their torpor and accepted bets from the Burnside sports, and all indications pointed to a record crowd that Sunday. Dad spent Saturday evening talking with Mr. Grimes and Fred Luterman, and they decided that Fred would be better off if he stuck to emery dust in the beginning and only used tobacco juice as a last resort. Tobacco juice made a ball sail and skitter in unchartered fashion, and it was too easy to walk hitters if they waited a pitcher out. Other than a certain scheme which Dad kept to himself, they made no plans for the game.

The Burnside team and rooters arrived early that Sunday afternoon and overran the ball diamond. Dad estimated the crowd at fifteen hundred people an hour before game time. Teams and buggies overflowed the back pasture and were tied to the fences along the road to town. The Burnside fans sat and stood in a solid line, ten deep, from home plate all the way up the side hill in right field. The Hopkinsville rooters were on the left field side, behind the home team's bench, and made up for inferior numbers by their yelling. Burnside had brought their town band along, and popcorn salesmen and lemonade stands had sprung up magically on both sides of the field. There were even a large number of fans from Bent Fork in evidence. This proved how much interest was reflected throughout the region, for Bent Fork was the big city with a fine ball club of its own.

The Burnside team was sporting new ready-made suits, red pants with a criss-crossed pattern of white piping sewed up the front of each leg, red shirts with white lettering, white socks, and bright red caps. Their wealth of equipment made Hopkinsville look shoddy. They had half a dozen balls, ten bats, and complete catchers' equipment. They also brought an umpire and this caused the first argument.

It was the custom for the home team umpire to work the game alone from a spot behind the pitcher, but the Burnside manager refused to sanction this arrangement. After twenty minutes of wrangling, Mr. Grimes agreed to both umpires, trading off on strikes and balls every two innings. Dad thought it was a good idea but didn't say so openly. He watched the Burnside team take infield practice, looking professional in their fine uniforms, scooping up grounders and whipping a brand-new ball around the bases. Dad warmed Fred Luterman up slowly and when the Hopkinsville umpire announced the batteries and Dad stepped behind the plate, the Burnside players started razzing him about his size. Dad gave them a cool look and stopped the talking. They knew that Dad was slow to anger, but hell on wheels once he got under way.

Rabbit Baranville was the Burnside leadoff man. He stepped jauntily to the plate and tipped his hat to Sarah Goodhue, sitting behind the Burnside bench, and grinned at Dad. Rabbit said, "How's the boy, Martin?"

"Pretty good," Dad said. "Nice suits you got."

"Passable," Rabbit said grandly. "I hate to dirty my pants, stealing bases."

"Maybe you won't need to," Dad said. "You got to be close before you slide."

"Yeah," Rabbit said. "I'll be standing on second when you let go of the ball."

Dad squatted down and gave his signal for the first pitch. Fred Luterman threw a fast ball, inside and high, and Rabbit choked up and poked a single into center field. On the next pitch, Rabbit streaked for second. Dad seemed slow getting rid of the ball, and Rabbit went in standing up with a big grin on his face. The Burnside fans booed Dad and Mr. Grimes looked puzzled, but Dad just squatted down and called for the next pitch.

Dad knew exactly what he was doing. They retired Burnside without a run and the game moved along rapidly. Dinty McDougal used tobacco juice and threw a spitter that wobbled and sailed and was almost unhittable, but Hopkinsville played inspired ball in the field and came up with good plays to back Fred Luterman's steady throwing. Dad hit cleanup and singled his first time, was walked the next, and had the only hit for his team through the first six innings. Rabbit Baranville singled in the fourth and again stole second on Dad. The tension mounted as the innings marched by, and it was a scoreless ball game until the eighth.

Burnside got a man on second with two out and Rabbit Baranville singled him home for the run. The Burnside rooters screamed and waved their hats, and gloom settled heavily on the Hopkinsville baseline. Dad had expected a Burnside score, and on the next pitch Rabbit streaked for second, to find Jim Beason waiting with the ball. Rabbit was out by fifteen feet and when he trotted out to center field, he turned and waved at Dad. He knew what Dad had planned, and worked. Dad had let him steal twice on purpose, and when the chips were down, Dad really cut loose with a peg. It was smart baseball and Rabbit was more than man enough to approve.

They had to score in the last of the eighth or lose the game. That was the situation and everyone knew it, for the Hopkinsville leadoff man, Jim Beason, was the first hitter. Dad squatted beside the bench and hoped somebody would hit and get on and give him a chance with men on the bases. He had two singles and a walk, and Dinty McDougal was wary of him.

Dinty McDougal got too much tobacco juice on the ball, lost control with a three-two pitch, and walked Jim Beason. Fred Luterman was a fair hitter for a pitcher, and this time swung on the first pitch, sending a clean single to center field. Rabbit held Jim Beason on second, but the spark was ignited and the Hopkinsville fans were whooping for a score. Dinty McDougal was calm on the mound. He spat contemptuously in the grass and whipped across two strikes on Bill Preiss; and then put too much tobacco juice on the ball. It sailed in and up, hitting Bill Preiss in the ribs and filling the bases. In the sudden stillness that followed, Dad picked up his heavy homemade bat and walked to the plate.

Dinty McDougal couldn't walk him on purpose this time, with the bases full and only a one-run lead. Dad was confident and eager, facing the big right-hander. Dinty took the signal and started his windup, and far out in center field Rabbit edged backward, playing him on line. Dad knew it was a straight ball and he swung from his heels and met the pitch with all his power at the last possible moment. He knew, dropping his bat and digging for first, that he had never hit a ball as hard before.

The base runners were racing around the bags toward home and Rabbit Baranville was a flying speck in the distance, his back to the infield, running like an antelope into left center field. The ball was high and traveling on and on, Dad said, the longest ball he ever hit in his life. Rabbit looked up and over his shoulder, gauged the ball, and Dad, coming into second base, had a sinking feeling in his stomach. He knew that Rabbit was going to catch that fly ball; he felt it in his bones.

Rabbit turned at full speed and threw up his gloved hand. The ball dropped and Rabbit made the catch, a beautifully timed one-handed stab while completely off balance; and then Rabbit disappeared and did not reappear.

Dad was the only man who kept his head in that impossible moment. The base runners were home or nearly there, all of them liable to be doubled off base for a triple play. Dad ran on around second base, cupping both hands over his mouth, and shouted at them above the roar of the crowd:

"Jim, Fred, Bill! Get back on base and tag up. Go around and touch every bag in order!"

They heard Dad's stentorian bellow and turned, two of them across the plate and Bill Preiss halfway in from third. They stared wildly at Dad and began running backward around the bases with Dad urging them on, while the crowd and both teams waited for Rabbit to get up and make the throw in that would turn his wonderful catch into a triple play. Dad tried to watch the base runners pounding desperately in reverse and still keep an eye on the spot where Rabbit disappeared. After an eternity, Bill Preiss reached first. Fred Luterman returned to second, and Jim Beason was on third; and still Rabbit did not show himself.

The Burnside left and right fielders were running frantically toward that spot now, and Dad roared, "Come on, boys! You've tagged up!" and waved them home.

Jim Beason crossed home plate with the tying run as the ball appeared in deep left-center field, thrown high and hard, in fact, just far enough to drop behind the Burnside outfielders rushing to Rabbit's aid. The ball bounced and rolled dead a hundred feet from the infield. Fred Luterman crossed the plate; Bill Preiss came pounding down the baseline, red-faced, breathless, and dived headlong across home with the third run just as the Burnside shortstop reached the ball and made a belated, desperation peg to the plate.

Rabbit Baranville reappeared at that moment, supported by the outfielders; and the crowd immediately understood what had happened. In the excitement of the play they had forgotten about Spring Creek with its slick clay banks and muddy bottom. Rabbit told Dad about it in later years. He had made an impossible run to catch the ball and had to whirl and make his stab while off balance, without looking ahead. He caught the ball and the earth vanished beneath his feet. He somersaulted into the center of Spring Creek, down a fifteen-foot clay bank, and lit headfirst in two feet of water and five feet of mud. Rabbit held the ball and struggled to get loose and climb back on the field, but the mud retarded his progress. Actually it was only a matter of seconds but it seemed like years to him. Finally he clambered out of the water, got halfway up the bank, and slid back down. Then he made his throw, sight unseen, and was horrified to see the puzzled faces of his fellow outfielders appear over the bank, in time to watch helplessly while the ball soared above and beyond them.

Dad ran out to meet Rabbit who limped between the two outfielders. Rabbit was all mud and water, his fine suit ruined. Dad said, "That was the best catch I ever saw, Rabbit."

"Thanks, Bill," Rabbit said, spitting mud and water. "That was the hardest hit ball I ever hope to see."

Dad put one arm around Rabbit's shoulders and the Burnside rooters misunderstood the gesture. The fight started with instantaneous fury. Dad and Rabbit grinned at each other and quietly edged back and stood together, watching the Burnside and Hopkinsville rooters engage in a fine old-fashioned donnybrook that raged all over the diamond for fifteen minutes. Horses reared and ran away, dragging broken reins and buggies behind them. The umpires were rolling in the grass behind home plate, even the other players were swinging, and some of the ladies, overcome by excitement, scurried about the battlers, waving their arms and shouting words of moral support to their men.

The game was never finished. Dad and Rabbit sneaked away and walked to town and took their baths and changed clothes at Dad's house. Rabbit had to go back and take Sarah Goodhue home, and for that he never forgave Dad. Rabbit always swore that Dad deliberately aided and abetted Rabbit's marriage to Sarah, and in future years enjoyed the spectacle of Sarah taking the paychecks and doling out spending money to Rabbit, while Dad and other single ballplayers, during their first years in the majors, chewed tobacco and stayed up late any time they so desired. But one thing remained clear and good in their memories; the game itself and the picture of people crowding a crude, grassy diamond while two teams of young men played the game as it has been, and will always be played in this country, so long as they have that spirit and will to win. The homemade uniforms and cotton flannel gloves and tennis shoes were all part of that forgotten spirit, and Dad still has the best part of it all in the old tintype of the sober young men sitting self-consciously on the post-office steps.

Flashing Spikes

I don't know what happened to most of them, and it was sheer luck that I saw Dane Bjorland playing out his long, lonesome string on a sweltering hot August afternoon in a little town. This was back in '36, long ago, but the memory returned today when I read a column about one of his former teammates. It was written by a friend of mine, a wonderful sports writer, and told how this teammate of the Dane's had been a kind but illiterate gentleman who didn't realize, even after he accepted the bribe, what he had done to his own life; and the saddest part about this is that that man was truly a gentleman and one of the greatest ballplayers who ever swung a bat. And reading his story again, after so many long years, made me think of the Dane, for he, too, was one of the greats. It sent me back nearly twelve years to a hot day in August at our county fair, with the main attraction the ball game between our town team and a crack traveling outfit.

Really to understand, you have to see the town and the fairgrounds and the crowd moving sluggishly among the exhibits of cakes and needlework and prize sows and ears of corn; and the grandstand facing the half-mile race track, with the free-act platform just across the track in front of the grandstand, and behind it, the ball diamond. To see the ball game, the dyed-in-the-wool fans crossed the track and lined up behind the restraining wires stretched along the base lines, where they could drink pop and warm beer, and yell their lungs out.

You can't know how it is to play ball on a diamond like that unless you have seen one, or, better yet, felt one under your spikes. The infield was skinned, raw dirt and the outfield was mowed grass pocked with gopher holes and rough spots. They stuck two white flags on the base lines about three hundred feet down each one, and home plate was just ahead of an over-hanging screen which trapped all foul balls and kept them from going back over the track into the grandstand. They ran a few horse races and had the free acts, and then it was three o'clock and time for the ball game; and if you were lucky you found a place in your own dugout when you came in to hit—if the rooters from your home town hadn't already moved in and taken over. That is how it was, and still is, at those ball games.

I was playing shortstop on my town team that year. I was still in college, and considered one of the best hitters and fielders in our part of the state, with a good chance to make the grade in professional ball; and I was chock-full of the old college try and fight that made me give everything on every play with all of my two hundred pounds. Our team was composed of boys like myself, young and tough and full of vinegar. We'd licked every-thing in our part of the state, and after this fair game with the Carry-Carriers, the traveling outfit, we were heading for the state tournament. We knew they had a ball club made up of old pros who had slowed down too much for double-A ball or better, but who made more money with this traveling team than they could in any kind of ball from Class A down.

That was the situation on a hot August afternoon. We fin-ished our batting practice before the Carriers came from their bus and took over the other dugout and loosened up their arms. While the crowd filtered across the race track, we sat in our dugout and watched them warm up and take their batting prac-tice. They looked like old men to us, and maybe they were, in a sense. They only hit four apiece, mostly easy taps and bloopers onto the short grass. They finished batting in fifteen minutes and walked off the field; and we grinned knowingly at one another, and I remember how we said, "Oh, brother! Will we tie the can on these has-beens!"

We took a snappy infield workout, burning the ball around the bases, scooping up the grounders, yelping at one another and looking like a million dollars; and when we finished and their turn came, their manager, a wrinkled man in a dirty, over-large suit, walked to the plate, and their infield trotted out and started the workout. Their manager hit easy grounders with handle hops and they fielded slowly, missing half, barely making their pegs good from base to base. They looked terrible, worse than cow-pasture ball, and the crowd behind us growled that old refrain about "What kind of punks did the fair board get to play our boys? This won't be no game. We'll beat 'em fifteen runs."

So they finished their infield practice, and while we waited for the tumblers to end their free act, and the managers conferred with the umpires, I placed the Carrier players in my mind, trying to remember how each one had hit and fielded.

Being a shortstop, I had particularly watched theirs work out at his position. He was a big, broad-shouldered man with small hips, and legs that looked fragile, but were really full of knotty muscle. He wasn't young; there was gray in his hair under the cap, and he moved with great deliberation, fielding easy ground balls and tossing them carelessly to first. But his face made me look, time after time; it was browned and seamed and filled with some old, old knowledge that, to me, was beyond anything I could understand. It was a tired and resigned look, as if he didn't care who won the game or how he played. He had a big nose and a wide mouth, and I could see the small white scars around his ears and along his jaw. His hands were big and wide, and, looking closely, I could tell that his fingers had been broken and were bent and gnarled like an old-time catcher's. I watched this big man labor through infield practice and tap four balls in hitting drill, and I told myself that I had him whipped all around the board.

We took the field and the umps called the batteries and the game started. I played a deep short, and on this fairgrounds diamond, because the infield hadn't been skinned back deep enough, I played a good eight feet on the grass. I was fast and could charge a ground ball in plenty of time, and besides, I could go either way and back for those short bloop Texas Leaguers they'd been hitting in practice. The second baseman was another boy my age—nineteen—and we knew each other completely, or so we thought, and he was playing very deep too. We had a lefty working for us, and he toed the rubber and took the sign, and we got under way.

Five minutes later I had learned the first of a great many lessons. Those old men, in their slow and seemingly bungling way, had fooled us nicely. Their lead-off man tapped at an inside ball, and it dribbled lazily toward me. I charged the ball, made a fast pickup and burned a perfect peg to first. That old man beat my throw by two feet. He wasn't so slow. So I went back to deep short again, and the second hitter did the same thing, and they had men on first and second, and that was when I slowly realized that they were playing me for a sucker. Those men could lay a ball where they wanted it, off pitching like Lefty's, who was hot stuff in our neck of the woods, but just another busher to them. And then the other shortstop came up, slouched back from the plate, and I edged up to the skinned line and told myself, *Let him lay a slow one at me.*

Lefty took the sign for his hook, and in all honesty, he did have a good curve that broke fast and cut downward with a nasty spin. This big gray-haired man didn't swing until I thought the ball was in our catcher's mitt, and then he seemed to explode that black bat, and the ball was a streaking bullet going over second, going on a line between our right and center fielders. I backed up second, and the long peg came in to Tommy, but this big man had rounded second and beat the short peg to third with a beautiful inside hook slide that showed me a quick, dust-filtered picture of him going in, legs perfect, and suddenly standing on his feet, all slouched over, dusting his pants with those big hands and staring with sleepy, half-closed eyes at our third baseman, who had missed him three feet with the tag.

We held him on third. The next two hitters flied out to short center, and the third out was a topped grounder to Lefty. I tossed my glove back on the grass and met him coming out from third. He gave me a level, unsmiling look and spoke in a soft voice that had no feeling or lift to it; it was just a voice, but somehow I remembered every word. He said, "Kinda slow infield, son," and went around me and picked up his old, dried-out, ragged glove and forgot me.

I played through three innings before I knew what he meant, and if he hadn't spoken to me again when we came to bat in the fourth, I would not have caught on. They seemed to fold up after scoring two in the first, and from then on hit fly balls and ground balls and we got them out. But we didn't score, and in the fourth I played up close and threw out two of them on those dinky ground balls. But the third man came up and swung his bat in a long end hold, and I edged toward second because I figured he'd swing late. Lefty took the signal for his fast ball, and the big man, coaching third, called in that expressionless voice, "All right, Doc!" and as Lefty delivered, the hitter shortened his hold and chopped the ball to my right, between me and our third sacker, where I should have been if I hadn't tried second-guessing. The next man flied out, and as he passed me, the big man said softly, "Your catcher crossed you up, son," and went on by with that sad, old look.

Then I understood. He was trying to help me play the game. He had stolen our catcher's signals and was giving voice relay signals to the hitters, and the hitter had taken the signal, watched me shift, and crossed me up. Then I began to understand that this big quiet man knew more baseball than I would ever learn, and I was a fool if I didn't listen to him.

I knew they were playing with us, making it a close game for the benefit of the fans, just as the Monarchs and Globe Trotters and the other fast traveling teams played when they came through our county, so that we would invite them back the following year. I caught a slow curve on the outside corner in our half of the fourth, and stretched it to a double when the ball bounced in a gopher hole on the right-field line and their fielder juggled it momentarily. I made my slide and stood up, slapping dust, and grinned at the big man.

"I caught that one," I said.

"Good hit," he said evenly. "How'd you guess it?"

"He wiggled his glove," I said. "I watched him three innings. He does when he throws that slow hook."

"Good eyes," he said, moving back to position.

I felt pretty cocky and took my lead and the pitcher turned off the rubber and grinned at me; and then the big man moved with deceptive speed, cutting in behind me, took the underhand flip from their second baseman and tagged me out by five feet.

"Watch the ball," he said tonelessly. "Don't start no jaw act when you're feeling so good."

I walked off the field without answering. My pride was hurt. I had been a sucker for the oldest gag in the game, the old hidden-ball trick. He talked to me and I forgot the ball, and their second sacker held it until I had my lead, all fat and dumb and happy, and then they lowered the boom. I was a prime hick from Podunk.

When I reached the third-base side line and tried to ignore the scorching yells from my hometown fans, I turned and looked at him. He was crouched so easily at short, not smiling, and I thought that any man who knew baseball as he did was wasting his time in the bush leagues.

The game went along smoothly, and they gave the fans double their money's worth. We scored in the sixth on a single, a sacrifice and another single by Lefty, our pitcher. By that time I had got his name from our scorebook—Bjorland—and was over my anger at being caught off second. Each time we traded positions he had something to offer me, always sober-faced, even-voiced, and as the game went on, there seemed to be something else on his face, a kind of fine-drawn fear of some old memory that threatened to come out and bother him.

We came in to hit in the last of the seventh, and while we wiped sweaty faces and sucked lemons and drank from our water bucket, and the fans talked in a loud hum all around us, I saw one of the old-time baseball fans in the county come running on his short legs. He ducked through the crowd and under the fence, and stood beside our manager, talking a blue streak, waving his short arms and glaring out at Bjorland, his face red and sweating with righteous anger. I walked over, wondering what had got his goat, and heard his words tumbling out: "—didn't know till I went over and saw their lineup! Then I had to watch him for three innings! Sam, that's the Dane Bjorland, of the old Black Sox! I tell you, that's him!"

Then I knew. Every boy who played and loved baseball knew the Black Sox, knew how they threw the World Series a long time ago and almost ruined baseball, and were kicked out of organized ball forever. I had first read about them when I was a ten-year-old kid playing midget ball, and I knew their names by heart, and here for the first time, like an old ghost from the forgotten past, playing out his string on a dusty, bumpy small-town diamond was one of those great men, a man who led his league in fielding and hitting, a man who threw away a magnificent career for a few dollars he never received. I turned and stared at Dane Bjorland, and every man on the team heard the words passing along the fence, and turned, mouths open, to see a ghost walk.

I thought, *And he has the guts to tell me how to play baseball.*

I was young then—younger than I knew—and I had yet to read my American history and temper it with the hidden wisdom of the truth. But I was young, and I burned up. And I stared at him.

Along the fence line the murmurs began, and then someone

yelled, "Start riding them! We can lick this bunch of has-beens!" Then the same voice rolled into a harsh shout, "Where's your black socks, Bjorland?"

That was the beginning. I watched him when the yelling started, because there was a difference between these shouts and the ordinary razzing you hear at any ball game. This had an ugly, deep, angry tone, and he knew it. He had to, but he didn't turn that big head or make a move. He just settled back and waited for play to start.

Their manager came around the catcher and stood beside ours and I heard him say, "Took you longer to recognize him than I expected, Mr. Ronson."

Sam said, "He's not supposed to play baseball."

"Organized ball," their manager said, speaking as if he had an old and well-used speech to give. "Not bush league."

"All right!" Sam said harshly." But you get this, buddy: I've got a bunch of fine boys on my ball team, and I don't want him talking to 'em, you hear, or even coming close to 'em."

"I understand," their manager said. "I just wanted to get it settled now."

"Yeah," Sam said nastily. "We've got three innings left, mister. Maybe we ain't got it settled."

Their manager looked at Sam for a moment and then went away.

Someone behind the wire yelled, "That's the way to tell 'em, Sam! We'll fix him!"

We didn't get a man on in the seventh, and when I ran out and passed him, he looked at me and didn't speak. But I was young and righteous, and I knew what was right and wrong.

I said, "Thanks for the advice, Bjorland."

He said, "That's all right, son."

"Yeah, thanks," I said. "I'll be damned sure I don't follow it . . . your way."

He turned and stared at me, and I saw that old pained look touch and gray his face, and for a moment I felt very small. Then someone yelled, "Don't take nothing from him, Bill! Clean his plow for him!"

I was our state's intercollegiate heavyweight champion too. And I knew it, how I knew it then. I guess he understood, for he looked at me, and then turned and went across the field to the third-base coaching box. I threw my practice pegs, and all the time I could hear them giving him unadulterated hell from that fence, a few short feet back of the coaching box. I knew that it took courage to stand out there and take it, when he could go to the dugout, but he stood there and ignored them.

Our second baseman took the peg and tossed it to me, and we ran up to the pitcher's mound for our pep talk.

Our second baseman said, "We'll get that baby, Bill. What he's trying to tell you?"

"Nothing," I said. "Now."

They scored another run in the eighth and led us three to one. We didn't score in our half, and they failed in the ninth, and we came in to do or die; and when we passed each other between innings, he didn't speak. But he looked at me. That same even, gray look. It made me boil over. I was the first hitter in the ninth, and the fans were yelling for a rally.

I went up there to hit or else, and they dusted me off. I hit the dirt and got up, moving for their pitcher, and then I knew that was childish, because I had asked for it, showing my eagerness to hit so boldly. I stepped into the box and tried to calm my nerves. I could see him at short, waiting for the pitch, big and quiet and ready. I took a strike and a ball, and then I knew what I was going to do. I hit the next pitch on the nose, a long liner into right center, and took off.

I rounded first and saw their center fielder just getting the ball, and I dug for second. He was waiting for the throw, straddling the bag and giving me plenty of room for my slide. The peg was coming in and I saw him there, so damnably cool and capable, and I went into him with my spikes high, aiming straight for his legs. I felt the spikes hit his stockings and then flesh, and I made my grab for the bag and caught it as I drove him off his feet on his side in the dust. The ball hit his glove and bounced off, and I was safe.

I jumped up and waited for him. I was ready for anything, and I could hear the crowd roar, and I knew they were all with me; it was a strange, furious feeling.

He rolled over and sat in the dust, and I saw the blood come out on his torn stockings and run down the outside. He looked up at the base umpire and said "Time," in that even voice.

Their pitcher came over, and their infield gathered around him, and he said, "Get the kit."

One of them waved at the dugout, and their manager ran out with a big first-aid kit. He rolled down his stockings and the inner sweat socks, and I looked at his legs and saw the criss-crossed, thickly laid scars and welts and bumps from a thousand spikes biting into his legs over the years, and then I was sick in my stomach. I turned away and crouched on the bag.

He sat there in the hot dust and poured the disinfectant on his legs and cleaned them, and wrapped the clean white bandages on them, and got to his feet.

Their manager said softly, "Okay, Dane?"

"Okay," he said. "Okay."

Their manager said, "Not so bad this time," and went back to the dugout.

I had to turn then, for play was starting. I saw him walk straight, but with great pain, to his position and turn, crouching down. The blood came through the bandages and caked fresh on his socks; and I looked at it and then at his face, and understood a great deal. The crowd was roaring, enjoying every bit of it, and I wondered how many times he had gone through this same inevitable sequence: starting a game and being recognized, and then waiting for the spikes at second base . . . and never backing up. Those number-less scars told how much he had ever backed up.

I looked at him and said, "Mr. Bjorland, I'm sorry."

He looked at me, and I saw something flicker behind those gray eyes—something warm and real. He said, "Why, son?"

"I—" I said. "I don't know, Mr. Bjorland. But I am."

"Forget it, son," he said evenly. "Some things never get paid for."

Then we started play, and our second baseman singled to center and I had no time to tell him. I came home standing up, and the crowd roared at me, and I sat in the dugout and felt miserable. Everybody was yelling "Good boy, Bill!" and "That's the way to show him, Bill!" and I wanted to go home and cry.

Then that little red-faced fan who found him out came over and patted me on the back and said, "That's showing him how we feel, Bill. Just wait till the game's over. We'll show that crook how we like guys like him playing with decent boys."

I looked at him, and then I didn't dare talk. I got up and went to the water bucket and watched the game.

Their pitcher walked two men and the bases were full, with no one down, one run to tie and two to win. Our next hitter flied out to first base. I turned and watched Bjorland, and he moved to his left a little and spoke to his pitcher in that soft, low voice. I could see the blood on his stockings, bright and red, and I wondered how he could stand up. Then their pitcher delivered, and our hitter, the catcher, laid plenty of wood on the ball.

It was a white streak past their pitcher, heading for center field, a sure hit and the ball game. But he was there, waiting, all the time. He made a long dive, and the ball hit and stuck in that ragged glove, and he rolled over and trotted two steps and doubled our man off second. The game was over, ended by the finest kind of baseball, the kind you never see at the county fair or on the little-town diamonds, the kind that means the best. And then the crowd started to growl.

I have always been proud of that afternoon—at least that part of it. I ran across the infield to him and stood beside him, and he watched me quietly. I put my hand on his shoulder and grabbed his free hand and shook it.

I said, "That was a beautiful play, Mr. Bjorland. I wish you could tell me more about playing short."

They had started across the infield, all of them, and I turned sideways and looked at them; and I think my face showed how I felt. I could fight like hell itself when riled, and my last name was Riley, and they knew me too well. They stopped and looked at us, and then broke up, and the mob became a good baseball crowd.

I dropped my hand from his shoulder, and he said, "Thanks, son."

"No," I said. "Let me thank you."

He bent over and picked up his ragged glove and rubbed his scarred, crooked nose, and then he smiled at me, and I saw the warmth and good feeling in his eyes, where it had been hidden for so long.

He said, "Son, I wouldn't be surprised if you make the big show."

I said, "If I had somebody to tell me how to play this game right, I might make it, Mr. Bjorland."

"Sometimes—" he said thickly, "sometimes I think it'll never get paid for. Maybe it will."

That was long ago, as I said before, that hot afternoon at a county fair. It was just another ball game, you know, with some old duffers playing some kids, and winning because they were smarter. But I never forgot that ball game, and I never forgot Dane Bjorland. And today I know what he meant when he said, "Some things never get paid for." But I think he feels a little different now. If you're ever in town, come out to the stadium. They've got a pretty good shortstop playing for the Red Birds. He shifts on the pitch and plays the slow hoppers and covers the bag without fear, and he hits around .310 every year. His name is Riley, and they all say that he plays short like a ghost. Maybe he does. If that is true, he plays it like the ghost of one of the best who ever made a mistake and spent the rest of his life trying to pay for it.

The Last Pitch

G rover Bell had broken faith with himself in taking the train on this trip, but how else could a man arrive when they expected hired pitchers to travel first-class; and considering the money they were paying him for one game, he had to present a solid front of confidence and prosperity. If they knew how his arm had failed, they might renege at the last moment and leave him two hundred miles from home with the trip expense a total loss. No, a man had a certain amount of unbreakable pride remaining, no matter how deeply the years had cut away within, so that arriving in this way was the only solution.

He came from the train and glanced at Leesville, seeing just another small town of five thousand, and then he saw the local people standing in the depot shade. A stout man with the unmistakable appearance of prosperous merchant broke from this group and approached him, and Grover Bell swallowed a wry laugh. They always met him in this manner, their faces frowning when they saw a skinny, stooped man with bowlegs and gray hair, for even now they could not forget the old stories. They expected a big man with broad shoulders.

Grover Bell said, "Mr. Bailey?"

"Yes," Bailey said. "You're Grover Bell?"

He nodded. "Glad to know you, Mr. Bailey."

"I thought—" Bailey said, and smiled sheepishly.

"I know," Grover Bell said. "How about some coffee? We can talk then."

"By all means," Bailey said. "We've got several things to discuss, Grover. Do you mind if I call you Grover?"

"I like it that way," he said.

Men like Bailey always had innumerable details to hash out, mostly for the pleasure of showing their authority. Bailey would take him to the best cafe and explain how important this big game was and how the town was banking on Grover Bell. Bailey would ask how he felt and would he like to rest before the game. Bailey would bubble over with unimportant questions, the usual routine for a hired pitcher entering any small town across the land.

In the cafe, Bailey sat across the table and said, "Have a good trip up?"

"Fair," he said.

"Sure you aren't hungry?" Bailey asked solicitously.

Grover Bell didn't hesitate. This procedure was always the same; it was civic spirit combined with a mixture of personal pride and small-boy hero worship for Bailey to play host. Maybe there was more to it, he thought bitterly, such as Bailey showing that he had made more of his life than Grover Bell, who had once been famous and now sold his arm for a few dollars to the highest bidder. Whatever it was, he had conquered that piece of pride long ago.

"A little," he said. "What time is it?"

"Eleven-thirty," Bailey said. "You'd better eat now."

"All right," he said. "Order for me. You know the food here."

Bailey swelled visibly and made a small show of ordering steak. The cashier and other people were whispering up front and glancing covertly at him. He smoked a cigarette and then ate slowly, enjoying his first decent meal in two days.

When he finished, Bailey smiled and said, "When did you pitch last, Grover?"

"Five days ago," he lied. "I'm well rested."

"Good," Bailey said. "Did you win?"

"Three-hitter," he said casually. "Six to one. They scored on two errors. You know how local boys blow in the clutch."

"Don't worry about our boys," Bailey said smugly. "Let me tell you—"

Grover Bell listened with false interest as Bailey described the local team and the new ball park. He could not remember how many such teams had been pictured for him, how every boy was an embryonic major-leaguer. Bailey would never understand the difference. He boasted of the local team, but when they made six errors and played their usual game behind someone like Grover Bell, he would say, "I can't understand it. An off day, I tell you." But Grover Bell understood the difference.

"Sounds good," he said. "What about this outfit we're playing?"

Bailey followed the same pattern, running the opposing team into the ground. But Bailey couldn't tell him their weaknesses, how they played, where they hit. Grover Bell had to go out and discover these faults himself, and if he slipped while searching it was never their fault, but his. He could count the few times some man had given him a concise rundown on the other team before the game. Today was not that time; Bailey knew nothing of good baseball.

"How many times you played them this summer?"

"Four."

"Win them?"

"We won one," Bailey said. "But the others were stolen, believe me. Crooked umps. We beat them here, and lost the third game two weeks ago at the county fair by one run."

"Squeeze?" Grover Bell asked, probing for solid facts.

"Squeeze?" Bailey said hesitantly. "Oh . . . yes, it was."

He was tired of this talking. He said, "Will you run me to the park? I'd like to rest a while."

"Good idea," Bailey beamed . . . "Here, here! I'll take that check."

"All right," he said. "Thanks, Mr. Bailey."

When they stopped on the street beside the grandstand, Grover Bell said, "About the money, Mr. Bailey?"

"We agreed on that, didn't we?" Bailey asked quickly.

"Yes," he said. "I meant something else. I know you're in charge, but I've had bad arguments with other people who try to tell a man like you what to do. I pitch good ball and give full value, but sometimes people get mad when I allow a few hits. They try to back water on my pay."

"I'm in charge here," Bailey said stiffly. "Don't worry."

"I'm not worried about you, Mr. Bailey," he said, "but look at my side. Pitching is my business, just as you run your business. Only mine is intangible. Once I've pitched a game, it's over and done. I can't take it back, like a radio or washing machine. That's why I always get at least half my pay in advance as good faith."

"Why didn't you mention this in your letters?" Bailey asked.

"I thought you understood," Grover Bell said mildly.

He knew how Bailey would react. Bailey hadn't hired enough top-flight semipros to learn all the ropes, and Grover Bell was insinuating that Bailey was ignorant of such matters.

"I see your point," Bailey said grudgingly. "I shouldn't do this, but I will."

Bailey counted seventy-five dollars into his hand. Grover Bell said, "Thanks for understanding . . . Say, what's your manager's name?"

"Tom McNulty," Bailey said. "Use his private office, Grover."

"Thanks," Grover Bell said. "I'll see you later."

He entered the dressing room and crossed to the small private office and settled himself on the cracked leather couch. A small, sad part of him was happy in getting half the money from

Bailey before the game, but the other side, almost forgotten, wanted to tell the truth, even to a man like Bailey.

He wanted to say, "Listen, Bailey. Have you ever known how it feels to be on top and slip, and wake up years later, realizing what a fool you were? I made a lot of money and blew it all. I liked a drink and too many other things. I was thirty-six the morning I woke in that second-rate hotel and knew it was too late. Thirty-six in 1936. My arm was gone and I had thirty dollars to my name. I knew one business—baseball. But I couldn't get a scouting or coaching job because they were scared of me. They didn't trust me. They had a dozen reasons for saying no, all of them true. Then came the tough years. I went home and tried to drink myself to death. I couldn't even do that. People forgot me, even in my hometown. I bucked up during the war and saved some money, working in a shipyard, but I was broke six months after it ended. And then, because I loved one thing, I tried to find a little joy where I began. Work had strengthened my arm. I quit drinking. I started throwing. My control was still good. So was my curve. My fast one was gone. And then, because I was beginning to feel my age, I wanted security. And for that, I needed money. I could buy a farm from one of my few remaining old friends for a down payment of two thousand. I had twenty dollars at the time.

"So I began pitching for my hometown team in a pasture league, playing where I first started with another generation of boys. I mowed them down and the word got out. Baseball was booming and prices for good pitchers went up. Remember when I got fifteen thousand a year? Now I got twenty-five a game and was grateful. But soon I could get forty, then fifty, and eventually a hundred.

"I was working in my friend's lumberyard during the off season, so I saved all that money. But I couldn't pitch oftener than once a week, and I wasn't getting any younger. I saved fifteen hundred dollars in the first three years after the war. Now it's the fourth year, and a funny thing has happened. I finally got my two thousand, but I didn't want to quit. It wasn't the money so much; it was something I can't explain. And now my arm is gone. I want to end on a high note, with a good game, but my last six have proved what I hate to admit. I can't last. Nobody will hire me where they know me. But I want to try it again, one last time. I heard about this town and you, Bailey, and sold you a bill of goods. I took a chance you hadn't heard about me. I can use the money, but, somehow, that isn't important. I just want to finish my last game."

Grover Bell was sleeping on the cracked leather couch when a tall, angular man entered the office and smiled faintly. "I'm McNulty."

Grover Bell sat up and shook hands, liking McNulty at once. He said, "Seems like I should know you."

McNulty chuckled. "I was never in your class, Grover. Double A one year, back in thirty-four. I quit two years later. I've been in business here ever since. We played you in Biloxi that spring. You threw me three balls."

He said, "What happened?"

"Strikeout. Well, let's get together, Grover."

He felt much better, meeting this man and knowing the team was competently handled. McNulty brought out several clean uniforms and, while they changed, went over the Backland line-up, Grover Bell learning each hitter's weakness. "They've got a fair-hitting club," McNulty said, "for this kind of ball. We're weak against good pitching."

"I figured that," he said. "Bailey told me you lost three to them."

"Yes," McNulty said, and frowned slightly. "Don't pay Bailey any mind. You know what I mean?"

"I know," he said. "How many runs can you get me?"

"Two, with luck," McNulty said. "How's your arm?"

He wanted to tell McNulty the truth, and then he glanced at the manager's fingers. "Do you still catch?"

"Not much," McNulty said. "My regular boy is a good sticker. Do you want me to?"

"I'd appreciate it," he said. "I've had my bumps with these kids. They mean well, but—"

"All right," McNulty said. "I'll give it a try. Can you go nine?"

He wondered if McNulty had heard things on the grapevine. McNulty would know other old-timers in this territory and hear a lot that men like Bailey never picked up. He said, "If I space it right, Tom. I'll tell you the truth. My fast one is gone. The curve and control are all right. You know these hitters. Give me a good target and I'll do it easy."

"I think you can," McNulty said. "Don't worry about speed. If you can breeze one occasionally, then feed them the change-up, we'll get by fine. What signals do you want?"

Grover Bell breathed freely again, half certain that McNulty hadn't heard about his last six games. He said, "One for the curve, two for the change-up. I'll rub my letters for the fast one, dust rosin for a knuckler. I sneak it once in a while. Do they steal signals from second in this league?"

"This bunch will," McNulty said. "Got a good manager. They're sharp boys."

"Okay," he said. "Rub your leg for the hook if they get on, scoop dirt for the change-up. We can shift if they get wise."

He could hear the young men pouring into the dressing room and changing clothes, talking and laughing, making enough noise for five ball clubs. That never changed, he thought. When McNulty led him into the dressing room, they turned and stared, grinning bashfully while he shook hands around the room. It was a strange, almost sad feeling to read their thoughts.

They were remembering the countless stories about Grover Bell, the farm boy who broke into the big time back in the '20's with the famous buggy-whip arm that mowed down the best of them for twelve short years. They would remember the other stories, too, the clouded side of Grover Bell, who drank and played and squandered his pay checks recklessly. They would recall how he disappeared completely in the mid-'30's and would guess at his age. He would not tell them it was forty-eight. Grover Bell, they were thinking as they shook hands, pennant fights, three World Series, and the one great moment.

He prayed they would not mention that. How could he describe his feeling when they asked admiringly, "How did you do it, Mr. Bell? Coming in cold after winning the day before and striking out the side with the bases full to win the game and the series. How could you after—" And they would pause, embarrassed, not wishing to add the dark side of that great story, how he had got gloriously drunk the night before and dozed happily in the bullpen that afternoon, with no idea he would throw. But that was gone now, and best not remembered.

The shortstop, a lanky boy, grinned timidly and opened his mouth. McNulty said quickly, "All right, time to hit."

He waited until they were through the inner door which led directly into the dugout, and then murmured, "Thanks, Tom."

He tossed twenty warm-up balls with McNulty and then sat in the dugout and watched both clubs hit. This was a nice ball park for a town of five thousand, he thought, with good lights and a well-kept playing field. The grandstand and bleachers filled rapidly and overflowed along restraining fences down the foul lines, a boisterous crowd that yelled and moved and did all the things so familiar to his eyes and ears.

McNulty sat beside him and said dryly, "Over three thousand today. Bailey will be happy in his one touchy spot."

"The pocketbook?" he said.

"No place else. They sank sixty thousand in this park. They won't sleep until the last bond is retired."

Backland was finishing their infield. He said, "I'll warm up now."

He stepped from the dugout into warm sunlight and threw to the young catcher while McNulty took the Leesville infield practice. The stands were close and he heard words, old stories repeated, and felt eyes follow his arm as he threw slowly. They would expect a miracle and he might not reach the commonplace. His arm felt no better or worse than ever. He could snap the curve and push a few high hard ones . . . up to a certain point. Then his shoulder ached and his elbow refused to co-ordinate with his fingers, which, at such a time, grew numb. It was a helpless, completely dead feeling, and had begun only this year.

McNulty came puffing back to put on his equipment while the public-address system announced the batteries, the announcer pausing on his name to bear down hard. He spoke against the applause and mingled boos: "Okay, Tom," and made his walk to the mound.

He threw five pitches to McNulty and waited for the infield to bring him the ball from second. Their faces were tight and grim now, all laughter gone, their voices sharp and tense. He took the ball from the lanky shortstop, smiled at them, and faced the first Backland batter.

He remembered McNulty's rundown of these batters as he took the signal. This one hit an inside wrist ball on the ground. McNulty dabbed his mitt delicately for the spot and talked it up loudly. He wound up and delivered, following through easily as the ball went into the hole beautifully, past the swinging bat for strike one. The home fans yelled happily as he stepped behind the rubber with the return throw and wondered if he could last.

The leadoff man hit another wrist ball to short. The next batter flied out to left field. But the third man was tough. McNulty had cautioned him. This one was a bulky-shouldered boy, eager and strong, unawed by any name on the mound. Grover Bell knew the type too well. They might fan four times and break up the game on the fifth trip. McNulty mixed his signs cleverly and they ran up a two-two count before he broke the curve off the outside corner for the strike-out. Walking to the dugout, he heard the approving shouts and tipped his cap. They expected it; later they might change the tune.

McNulty helped him into his jacket and said, "Nice control. Am I calling them okay?"

"Fine," he said. "Fine, Tom. You're good."

"Good field, no hit," McNulty said, smiling sadly as he turned for the third-base coaching box. "That was me, Grover."

Then the game was moving swiftly. He knew after two innings that Leesville was weak on the stick. The Backland left-hander was a big man with a fast ball and a deceptive slider. He sent the Leesville hitters back, swearing softly and promising more next time. Grover Bell hit in the third inning, taking three called strikes without moving his bat. Hitting meant running, and every extra step destroyed a late-inning pitch.

He held Backland to one single in the first five innings, and in this time began to understand the feeling of these young men behind him. He had vaguely guessed that rivalry was intense, but not until the shortstop and the Backland third baseman exchanged hot words and almost fought in the fourth did he sense how serious the feeling was; then he wished for enough strength to last. They were talking behind him with sharp, nervous intensity, toed up on every pitch; in the dugout they shouted continuously at the Backland pitcher. Backland was equally strident, and Grover Bell was thankful for the neutral umpires, who were excellent.

He weathered the sixth, but it began to go out of him in the seventh, like someone forcing precious fluid from a leaky, patched tube. The first man singled to center and he was forced to field the sacrifice and make the throw to first. The runner danced off second, watching McNulty closely. McNulty switched signals after giving a dozen fakes that left the runner shaking his head helplessly at the batter. Grover Bell glanced at the infield and wanted to say, "Relax, you're tight." But he couldn't, knowing them so briefly. They might not understand. He faked the runner with his eyes and jaw, and delivered.

The ball was hit sharply into the hole between third and short. He saw the lanky shortstop try to watch the runner and make the difficult play to the right. The shortstop kicked the ball while the runner raced from second and slid safely into third. The hitter rounded first, watched the shortstop turn toward third, and streaked for second.

Grover Bell knew how the lanky boy felt in that moment, and called, "No, son!" and stood helplessly as the shortstop threw the ball over the second baseman's desperately reaching finger-tips, deep into right field. One run scored and the hitter squatted on third base, grinning broadly. They brought Grover the ball and he forced a grin.

"I'm sorry," the lanky shortstop said. "I don't know why—"

"Forget it," Grover Bell said. "We'll get 'em, son."

He had to bear down now, with the runner on third and one away. He had dreaded this moment, for it meant spending precious strength needed in the last two innings. He struck the batter out, but McNulty called time and walked to the mound.

He said, "What is it, Tom?"

"You feel okay?" McNulty asked.

Then he was afraid. McNulty knew he was losing everything. No one else would understand, but the catcher always did. Grover Bell wiped his sweaty face and said, "I'm all right, Tom. Tough luck, that's all."

"Sure," McNulty said. "Well, get this guy and we'll sit down."

He got the batter on a fly to center field. Stepping into the dugout, he heard Bailey calling from one of the special boxes just above. He waved, and Bailey called, "Not your fault, Grover! We'll get that run back!"

He forced a smile and said, "Thanks, Mr. Bailey," and ducked into the shelter of the dugout. Sitting heavily, his arm starting to burn in the shoulder, he saw the shortstop fighting hot tears.

He said, "Forget it, son, we all blow 'em."

"If we lose," the shortstop said, "I loused it for you."

"My own fault," he said thickly. "That single and the bunt. I was too slow."

McNulty came from the fountain and said, "We got to get a run. Can you last?"

"When did you know, Tom?" he asked softly.

"Last time," McNulty murmured. "Does it hurt?"

He nodded and watched the side go down without a hit. He stripped off his jacket and shook his head. All he could do now was pray and hope his control lasted. He had nothing else, and the Backland team would know it in a few minutes. He had awed them with his name and a few old, stale memories for seven innings; now they had hit his best pitches and knew the truth. No speed, curve slowing down; nothing but control. They would dig in and swing from the heels on every good pitch.

Grover Bell pushed the cold, heavy thoughts from his mind as he started the eighth inning. The first batter singled, and when the next man drove a sharp single to center, he knew that Backland was scorning a sacrifice and coming at him whole-hog or none. The second baseman made a beautiful trap on a line drive and doubled the runner off third, and the next man backed the left fielder against the fence for the putout. He was lucky and knew it. Coming off the mound, he saw Bailey's worried red face in the box behind the dugout. His arm hung like deadwood and he prayed for a drawn-out inning and a few minutes' rest.

He slumped against the dugout wall and watched the lanky shortstop draw a walk, advance on a bunt and score the tying run on McNulty's double to the left-field corner. McNulty advanced to third on a slow hopper to second, and with two gone, the Backland infield proved itself human. The third baseman kicked a short hopping ball and McNulty crossed the plate. Now he was in the worst possible hole; they had a one-run lead, and the crowd expected only one thing. He had to hold Backland.

McNulty saw the pain in his eyes and said, "Sure you can last, Grover?"

"Yes," he said, and added his inner thoughts unconsciously, "I got to."

They sat alone at the end of the dugout, watching the batter at the plate. Grover Bell said, "I can't lie to you, Tom. I haven't finished my last six games. I was washed up when I made this deal."

"I know," McNulty said gently. "Waddy Malone from Storm Lake still writes to me, Grover. He told me last month."

"And you—" he said. "You didn't tell Bailey?"

McNulty smiled faintly at the distant fence. "Grover, guys like me and Waddy understand. Hell, man, I want you to finish one. And I always wanted to catch you."

The batter fouled off a three-two pitch and McNulty said quietly, "What are you figuring for the future, Grover?"

"Farm," he said. "I'll do all right."

"I wish—" McNulty said, and then was silent, watching the batter.

Grover Bell said, "We all wish for a lot of things, Tom. Most of all, that we could do them over again. The worst wish is trying to stretch something out and make it last forever. That's me, I guess. These kids must feel bad, banking on me and knowing what's coming next inning. I'll never do it again. I'm through."

"Not yet," McNulty said, as the batter struck out. "Come on, Grover. Three outs to go."

His first pitch stripped all remaining strength from his arm and left him standing with a helpless, naked feeling. McNulty called time and hurried to the mound.

"Fiddle with your glove," McNulty said. "Hurry up."

He hadn't employed the old trick for so long that he almost gave it away. He bent on one knee and jerked at the lacing while McNulty asked the base umpire for a knife. The Backland manager came yelling from the third-base coaching box, but McNulty got the knife and then performed a great amount of doing nothing with the glove. He was rested slightly when they stood, but nothing had changed. The batters were waiting; his arm was gone. Behind the plate McNulty talked hoarsely. The infield hadn't understood and he was thankful.

He had no tar or emery on his uniform for a rabbit pitch, but he had never used that sort of crutch and could not begin now. He faced the first batter and almost cried with pain as he delivered. His pitch slipped from the inside corner and split the plate, and the batter smashed this fat cripple for a single to center. Bailey was standing suddenly, a comic jack-in-the-box, watching him with an openmouthed angry look. He thought, *What do you know about it, Bailey?* and toed the rubber. He saw McNulty signal for the regular Leesville pitcher to warm up.

The second batter was anxious. He took McNulty's signal for the change-up and watched the batter check his swing too late, hitting under the floating ball. It went high for an easy pop fly to second base. One gone, and now he faced the bulky boy who had one hit. He wondered if McNulty would gamble on another change-up, and heard the Backland manager shouting from the third-base coaching box, "Easy does it, Jimmy!" and knew they were set for the pitch.

McNulty grinned through his mask bars and called the curve on the outside. Grover Bell's fingers slipped on the seams, numb at their tips, but he gripped the ball fiercely and pitched. It hung and nearly sailed, then ducked across the outside corner. *But not enough*, he thought miserably, *not enough*. The bulky boy hit it solidly over the lanky shortstop's flailing arm, a long drive that bounded off the fence and dropped into the grass. The center fielder made a fine recovery and threw low and fast to the plate. Grover Bell automatically backed up McNulty and watched the runners hold at third and second. When he stopped beside McNulty to take the ball, McNulty shook his head.

"No use, Grover. They're wising up."

It was not the finish he had planned. He wanted to say, "No, let me go on," but held his words. He said, "I know it, Tom. There's nothing left."

"I didn't say that," McNulty murmured. "There's something left, Grover. You never quit in your life. Do you want to finish?"

He said, "What about Bailey and this crowd, Tom?"

"Who cares?" McNulty said. "You want to finish?"

"Yes," Grover Bell said. "I want to finish it, Tom."

"All right then," McNulty said, and smiled. "Let's get at it, Grover."

He was afraid to say another word, and walked to the mound, wondering how many men like McNulty lived in this world. When he glanced at the dugout, Bailey had come down from the box seats and stood beside the bat rack, staring helplessly at McNulty.

McNulty called for a walk to fill the bases. He hated to throw four more balls, but it was the only thing to do. McNulty moved out wide and Grover Bell threw four balls as slowly as he could, while the Backland fans booed and shouted. The batter trotted to first and Grover Bell turned slowly, looking at the outfield and the scoreboard and finally at the three base runners.

He faced the batter, the fifth-place man, and was almost happy; it was better this way. If he had to go down, he wanted the best man to hit the last ball. If he could retire this one, he might come through. He could not remember when he had been so tense, as McNulty called for an inside pitch across the letters. He remembered that the fifth-place man lunged slightly for the ball. He glanced back at the lanky shortstop and saw the boy's face screwed tight in an agony of waiting. Grover Bell prayed that the ball, if hit, would not go there. They were playing back for the possible double play, and the boy might kick it into the stands.

He heard the Backland manager call, "All right, Ed," and made his pitch. He watched the ball go in, and through this split moment, as it left his numb fingers, he knew the final truth. The batter was ready. Grover Bell watched him pull his lead foot into the bucket and wait for the pitch, coming back in perfect position to pull the ball. He closed his eyes when bat and ball met, knowing the sound and hating it with an empty futility that went back thirty years to the first time he threw a cripple.

He felt the rush of air and opened his eyes as the ball, hit squarely, flashed past him, a blur of white, and he turned without thought to follow its low course into center field. He saw the lanky shortstop, running somehow with the pitch, leave both feet in a desperation dive behind second, and thought how the boy, in this last moment, had shown that inner ability really to play the ball. When the ball thudded into the glove, Grover Bell stood in complete disbelief. He saw the lanky shortstop turn a full somersault, come back on his feet and make another dive to second base, doubling the runner off for the third out.

They rushed him then, taking him off his feet, pounding his back and shouting like a bunch of madmen. McNulty was standing beside him, grinning broadly, and the lanky shortstop was holding the ball in his gloved hand so tightly that the veins on his forearm stood out like steel ribbons.

Grover Bell tried to speak and could only say, "Thanks, son," before they turned across the grass toward the dugout. He had won the last one, but not through his own effort. He knew that, and would not forget. When they reached the dugout, he saw Bailey, smiling and waving both arms. Bailey was shouting something, but Grover Bell pushed the man aside and went on to the dressing room.

McNulty said, "Grover, you forgot your glove."

Grover Bell said, "I didn't forget it, Tom," and began undressing. He wondered, with a feeling of deep humility and final satisfaction, who would get the old glove.

Look for the Kid
with the Guts

He called home from Minneapolis that morning and was immensely cheered when the nurse reported a restful night and allowed his wife to talk a few minutes. Bill McGee described the trip thus far and heard her bright, always cheerful voice wishing him good luck, and then said good-by before the continual worry thickened his own words. He met Barney Briggs in the Radisson lobby and did not speak until they cleared the city and drove swiftly north across the rolling hills. He read the town names with interest, Anoka and Elk River, and passing through Princeton he smiled faintly and said, "Williams married a girl from here, didn't he?" and thought how baseball had roots wherever a man might go. They skirted a big lake, Mille Lacs, and entered Brainerd during the noon hour. Gorham was waiting outside the cafe and took them to lunch in the cool, shadowed room. Bill McGee heard the small talk and rattle of dishes, and watched the waitresses hurry skillfully between booths, another scene already repeated countless times in his wandering life.

"Two others here today, Bill," Gorham said.

"What clubs?" he asked.

"Giants and Yankees. Everybody is getting wise to the kid."

He said, "Makes no difference," and ate his lunch with sudden hunger, understanding Gorham's personal worry. Gorham was their bird dog in the lake region, had tipped them about the young pitcher, and now entertained visions of another scout signing the boy and knocking his payoff into a cocked hat. Gorham received the standard hundred dollars for any prospect signed and while the money actually meant nothing to him, Gorham's pride was at stake; for this prospect was the hottest pitcher since Chief Bender and Bullet Joe Bush came out of the jackpines to make history in a bygone day. Bill McGee thought moodily of his wife and pushed that ever-present worry from his mind, concentrating on the pitcher and the game just ahead. How many times, he wondered absently, had he gone through this identical routine in the past thirty years?

Go back to 1920 when Bill McGee bowed out of active play and took his first scouting job with the Yankees. It was different then, train rides on sooty, forgotten lines, miserable buses and model T's in a pinch, and sometimes a horse in the back country. No system, no definite area, go anywhere you heard about a kid, only they weren't kids then, but grown men. South into Florida and the Carolinas, Tennessee and Arkansas, Nebraska, Idaho, anywhere they played ball to watch a pitcher, an outfielder, a strong-armed shortstop with a bonehead, a great pair of hands. Sit on splintery seats in the blistering hot sun, eat greasy food in all the hash joints from Mobile to Terre Haute and back again, sleep in crummy hotels and on the hard yellow benches in railroad stations, on the day cars and the milk trains, watch the kids and measure them against your yardstick and then go down and talk business, use all the patience and cunning and tact learned the hard way over a lifetime of fighting other scouts in close deals. Bet the owner's money against the unpredictable laws of success and failure, and do all this because you loved the game. You had no other life. You did it happily, willingly, because in those early years Ida was with you part of the time, healthy and strong, loving the game with equal intensity. Remember the days you sat together in dingy stands and watched, and went on, and watched again, hoping that among a thousand boys you would find the one who counted, the potential great star in the rough, the pitcher, the natural hitter, the good hands and the speed. And then remember when Ida had her first bad spell, how she made you keep on because she was actually happier, knowing you were scouting the kids, doing the work you both loved. But it was better not to remember any more; this was another time and one more boy to watch, and everything had changed.

"More coffee?" Gorham asked.

"No," he said. "Let's get at it."

"You're tired," Barney Briggs said. "You ought to grab a nap before the game, Bill."

He was dog-tired today after three straight weeks of constant travel, snatching meals and sitting in the ball parks, watching young men play under the blazing sun and the cold white lights. But getting home two days ago, this exhaustion had been forgotten when he saw how weak Ida had become. He had hoped for a few days at home but the call came through that same night, to hurry and watch the kid in Brainerd, and Ida would not hear of him staying. He sat beside the bed that night and told her of the trip just finished, going over every boy he had scouted, all the small pieces of a life they loved together. Leaving the next morning he thought she looked better just from listening to his words. Five years in bed and she still had the same unquenchable spirit and love for the game.

"I'm fine," Bill McGee said. "Let's get out to the park."

They moved slowly across railroad tracks and along tree-shaded streets toward the river where the ball park stood shiny new in the center of a vast fairgrounds, light towers standing high against the blue sky, grandstand painted dark green with white lettering around the fat, curving rear wall. Gorham led them through a side gate into the runway between grandstand and bleachers on the third-base side, and started for the box seats. Bill McGee said, "Not there," and turned into the bleachers behind the dugout. He wondered if Gorham knew the basic principles of scouting, watching a pitcher from the side first off so you could follow the curve and estimate the speed accurately. He settled himself on the worn plank seat and slouched forward, placed a cigarette in the silver holder and forgot everything but the field below and the players now warming up on the grass. Briggs murmured, "Back in a minute," and went away, to return with two fat, red pillows that eased the hardness beneath Bill McGee's thin, bony shanks.

"Thanks," he said. "Where's the boy, Gorham?"

"There," Gorham said. "By the fountain, with the black hair."

He watched Blackie Larsen come across the field from the fountain and began his initial appraisal; over six feet, hundred and eighty pounds, long arms and legs, strong face with a stubborn jaw, thick black hair that made a round half circle on the neck beneath the cap. He watched this boy, object of so much correspondence and travel, and wondered if today was a jackpot. Gorham had written about the boy a year ago and their midwest scout took one quick look and recommended they hold off another year. Now, he'd taken a longer look and passed his approval with the recommendation that Bill McGee come up and look and close the deal. Their midwest scout had made no bones about his own reluctance to talk business with Larsen; the boy was money crazy and wanted a bonus as soon as he knew they were following him. Not only that, Larsen had told Gorham he wanted to start in Class A ball after signing, and left no doubt that he expected a bonus in five figures. *And there was the big trouble*, Bill McGee thought sourly, *all of them had illusions of grandeur these days*. It had started after the war and reached the height of foolish speculation with Pettit; now every kid with a fast ball wanted fifty thousand and a yellow convertible. He had these old, often painful thoughts and watched Larsen slip into a jacket and stand beside the dugout, directly below them. Gorham sighed audibly and said, "He's got it, Bill. Believe me."

"Let's talk to him," Bill McGee said abruptly.

"Now?"

"Why not?" he said. "He knows I'm here, doesn't he?"

"Sure," Gorham said, "but I thought—"

Gorham was thinking that he was going against the rules in

one sense, but actually their midwest scout had sent in an accurate appraisal of Larsen, a report that lacked just one thing. Bill McGee had that God-given talent a man was born with or never had, that of talking with a boy and feeling, somehow, the boy's character and attitude toward the game. He said, "It's all right," and stepped gingerly down the bleacher steps and stood against the fence while Gorham made the introduction.

"Glad to know you," Blackie Larsen said. "Heard you were coming up today."

Too cocky, he thought, *too sure of himself, this big boy in a little league, who had never looked down the alley at Ennis and Musial and Kiner.* He said, "How does this other team stack up?"

"Not bad," Larsen said. "They're in second place behind us. I've beat 'em three times already this year. Listen, what do you want me to throw today, Bill?"

He didn't like the casual use of his first name; most kids called him "mister" until they got acquainted, but the minority, like this boy, had that overdeveloped sense of superiority acquired too young. He said innocently, "You mean you've got a variety?"

Gorham laughed in a strained fashion, understanding the boy's over-familiarity, trying to cover up, but Larsen ignored the warning and said, "Downer, slider, fast hook. You name it, I'll throw it. My changeup's okay, too, and I'll throw some fast ones for you today." Larsen eyed him knowingly. "Couple of other guys here, you know."

"So I hear," he said quietly. "Well, good luck."

He saw Larsen's face stiffen with confused surprise as he turned away and climbed stiffly to his seat. Gorham said something soft, meant for Larsen's ears alone, and then rejoined them. Gorham said, "He's cocky, Bill. He needed that. But he's got it."

"Sure," Bill McGee said drily. "The real McCoy. All bone and a foot thick. He'd better be good."

Yes, he thought, *they've all got it at that age. In the bones and muscles and the arm. The youth and strength and desire to make the grade.*

*If only they had brains, just half of them, the common sense to realize
a Johnson and Feller and Mathewson was born, not made. In the old
days he signed them for coffee and cakes, sent them out to a Class D club
where they got three squares a day, slept in a rented room, stayed a little
hungry and always worried, and worked twice as hard to master
the fundamentals, and when they came up for the big chance they were
ready to go if they had it inside. And today they wanted the money, the
hell with experience and fundamentals. They threw a fast ball and got
the strikeouts and that made them a pitcher. Ida had her idea of this
new business. She called it the greatest pitchout in the history of the
game, and she had been bedfast for five years and still loved the game
so much she made him continue his work because she knew too well
he would die if he ever stopped. And she was dying slowly as the days
and months slipped by, as he sat here, away from her, to watch the old
drama unfold on the grass below.*

Sometime later, during the visiting team's infield workout, he
heard a dry cough and turned to see the other scouts grinning
from their seats on down the line, two friends of many years'
acquaintance. He wondered how far they had gotten in their
preliminary negotiations with Larsen, and then he didn't give a
damn. Ordinarily, he looked forward to these battles of wits
with other scouts, using all the patience and trickery amassed in
a lifetime of baseball; but today he felt dead inside. He had
arrived home from a three-week tour around the farm system,
spent one evening with Ida, and then left the following morning
to travel another thousand hot, lonely miles to watch a boy he
instinctively disliked on first look. He thought of Ida and forced
back worry and anger, thinking how today, this moment, with
time running out for her, he could be home, talking, laughing,
making the hours a little brighter for her; but he had to be here,
watching another boy in the never-ending line. *If only this Larsen
were different,* he thought, *then it would be worth the effort.*

He remembered the time four years ago when Ida was so bad
and the first report came in on the big kid in Carolina, Willie

Smith, and how Ida made him go at once. He watched Smith playing third in a dumpy ball park, back from the coast in one of those dirty, age-old milltowns, and from the first moment everything had been worthwhile because Smith had it all the way. He followed Smith for two months, making absolutely sure, and every moment was joy for Ida when he told her about Smith, one of the finest boys he had ever signed, quiet and decent and filled with a burning desire to play ball. Smith came on to prove himself in three years and Ida never tired of hearing the stories about the boy and following him up the ladder through the farm system; and after Smith's wife had their baby and all three of them came for a visit, Ida had a complete and wonderful picture of Smith, made richer by his soft humor and actions filled with the pure comedy of life well lived. But the Smiths were few and the hundreds in between were enough to keep a man going, and then you got the Larsens who cared nothing about the future, just five figures on a check.

He was smoking chain-fashion now, slouched over with elbows firmly anchored against his knees, a skinny man in his early sixties dressed in a fine gray suit and black socks and narrow, highly polished shoes. His hat, brim down over the sharp eyes and large red nose, was pearl gray and immaculate. He wore these clothes the year around, so that in the profession he was known across the entire country by the silver cigarette holder and the gray hat and the neatly pressed suit. He sat in this way, as he had sat through ten thousand days, watching Larsen warm up beside the dugout. The home team finished infield and the umpires came from the far gate and met both managers at home plate. The stands were filled now with a happy, noisy Sunday crowd that placed a fat blanket of sound about them. Larsen was getting loose, throwing hard and making an act of it, fast balls popping in his catcher's mitt with a loud smack that came sharply against other sounds. The announcer finished his lineups and Larsen glanced toward them as he walked to the mound and took his last pitches. When the umpire called, "Play ball," Bill McGee turned and said, "What's the visiting club?"

"Waniss," Gorham said. "Small resort town north of here. Good ball club, nice bunch of boys."

"Thanks," he said.

And now he watched Larsen in silent, narrow-eyed concentration, thin face growing leaner and almost angry with thought as Larsen made his first pitch, a called strike. He watched, as short feet away the other scouts were watching Larsen's every move, placing the boy against an imaginary pitcher in their minds, against the composite vision of everything the finished pitcher must possess; and watching Larsen fan the leadoff man and the second batter on eight pitches, he already had an accurate picture in his mind. Larsen was fast, very fast, but green as grass. His windup was part waste motion, he came off the rubber crookedly with too little leg action and ended off balance with an inadequate follow-through. His curve ball, used twice on his payoff pitches, was too high, not held low to force the ball into the dirt. Larsen had the power and the speed, that was plain, but he needed four years at a minimum to develop properly.

"Oh, oh," Gorham said suddenly.

The third Waniss batter had run up a two-two count, and now smashed Larsen's high breaking curve ball into right center field for a two-base hit. Bill McGee watched that batter reach second base standing up and thought absently about the smoothness of his stride.

"Good hit," he said.

"That Cookson has always hit him," Gorham said.

Bill McGee said, "Who is he?"

"Their third baseman, a nice boy."

The world was full of nice boys, he thought morosely, and none of them did him any good. He watched Larsen glance back at second base and then fan the cleanup batter on three pitches.

Larsen came off the mound with a smirk, flipped his glove carelessly on the grass, and slipped into the jacket held by the batboy.

"Well," Gorham said. "How does he look, Bill?"

He grunted wordlessly and finally said, "Fast . . . and dumb."

"He's not dumb," Gorham said defensively. "Good student, doesn't smoke or drink, absolutely first-class reputation. Don't be too hard on him, Bill. He's just cocky."

"Sure," Bill McGee said. "Let's watch the game."

He smoked on through the passing innings, crumpling one empty pack and opening the spare he always carried. Larsen was bearing down on every pitch, pacing himself badly, playing to the crowd and the three men who sat anonymously in the bleachers. Brainerd got two runs in the fourth off the Waniss pitcher, an older man who was throwing a cautious, brainy game, and they entered the seventh with this score, as Gorham said, "Want to go behind the plate?"

"No need," he said.

Gorham breathed heavily. "Decided, have you?"

"Let's see it out," Bill McGee said evenly.

Ida always said that, see it out, don't leave too soon, Bill, you might not see what you might miss forever. Watch the boy you came to see but watch all the others because you never know. Half the game can pass and then you might see something that couldn't happen until the right circumstances arose. Keep watching and don't lose patience so you can come home and tell me, because I can't be with you now, or ever again, and you're my eyes and voice and ears, Bill, and without you I'd give up and life would be worth nothing.

Larsen came to bat in the home team's half of the seventh, tipping his cap when the crowd applauded loudly. Larsen swung hard on the two-two pitch, a slow inside curve, and the ball was a white streak down the third-base line, breaking chalk as it flashed across the bag; and then the Waniss third baseman was there, to his right and down with the backhand stab, knocking the ball to earth, pouncing and throwing off balance, a strong-armed peg through the box for the putout. Larsen was caught loafing, beaten by three steps; the crowd sound was suddenly clear and completely sincere. Bill McGee watched the third baseman critically and spoke with deceiving calmness.

"He do that often?"

"He's pretty good," Gorham said, and added apologetically, "in a country sort of way, I mean. That was half luck."

"Not entirely," Bill McGee said. "That boy has done some boxing, hasn't he?"

"Yes," Gorham said. "Best middleweight in the state when he was fighting in the Gloves. How did you know?"

"Reflexes," Bill McGee said. "How old is he?"

"Twenty-one," Gorham said. "Works with his father. Plays ball for fun. That kid really loves it."

When they play it for love, Ida said, they really give it everything in their heart and body. Willie Smith played it for love, and Hammett wouldn't sit out a game unless he broke a leg, and Watkens came back from a gunshot wound to play better than before. All the players he knew who played for love, and the money was theirs because the game came first.

He saw Larsen approach the dugout, face angry and red, and shout something at the Waniss third baseman who smiled faintly and dropped back on the grass, spitting in a worn black glove. Larsen said something more and then the third baseman turned and studied him deliberately, face impassive, saying nothing. Bill McGee knew that look and wondered if Larsen had the guts to back up his hot words. That third baseman, Cookson, was the quiet kind who started nothing and finished everything. He half-hoped that Larsen would be foolish enough to begin a good donnybrook so he could judge the pitcher's courage; and then he was sitting back with bright-eyed approval as the game quickened in these final minutes.

The next batter singled and then the ball was hit into the hole between third and short, a slow dribbler that lost speed on the grass edge. He saw Cookson cross and scoop and throw to first as the runner rounded second safely and made a feint toward third. Cookson was back on the bag, waiting for the return throw, doing the shortstop's coverup job as a matter of course. Bill McGee watched the Waniss pitcher work carefully on the next batter and nodded silent approval. The pitcher was throwing slow inside curves now, making them hit to third base, confident that Cookson would handle the job. The batter smashed a drive down the line, just inside the bag, and Cookson took the ball on a difficult off-hop and made his long, true throw for the third out. Beside him, Gorham said, "Their pitcher is weakening. He always does and then we beat 'em in the last innings."

"A good ball game," Bill McGee said softly. "A damned good game."

Larsen retired the bottom third of the Waniss lineup on strikes and came in to douse his face at the fountain and grin broadly at the stands. The home club filled the bases in this last of the eighth, with nobody away, and the Waniss pitcher brought his infield up close for the play at home plate, then pitched deliberately to the batter. That man, as they all were doing, pulled the tantalizing, slow curve ball down the line. Cookson speared it and made his snap throw to the plate for the forceout. The catcher held the ball, unwilling to chance a throw, and the infield dropped back to play for the double. The first pitch was hard hit to the shortstop who fielded the big hop and threw to Cookson for the force play at third; and Bill McGee found himself standing like any wildeyed fan as Cookson leaped high over the sliding base runner and made the long throw to first while in the air, a snap forearm peg that went straight and true for the double play. He sat heavily then and wiped his face, watching Cookson trot off the field.

"That was a beauty," Gorham said.

"Does Cookson bat this time?" he asked.

"Yes. Their leadoff man comes up. Cookson bats third," Gorham glanced at his score card and chuckled. "Now watch

Blackie bear down. He likes to strike out the side in the ninth. That'll make twenty-one if he does."

"He won't," Bill McGee said evenly.

"He's not tired," Gorham said. "He can go twenty, Bill."

Bill McGee smoked steadily and watched Larsen fan the leadoff man, bearing down all the way, throwing fast balls that were beautifully alive. *Larsen was vain*, he thought, *among other things*. It was foolish to bear down with a two-run lead against this sort of hitting. Larsen was apt to lose his control, of which he had only enough to get by, and walk a man or two. He wanted to smile with satisfaction as Larsen tightened up and walked the second batter on a three-one pitch; and then Cookson stepped up and Bill McGee saw Larsen nod off a signal and completely ignore the runner on first base. Larsen went into his full windup and the runner started, then broke for second and slid in without drawing a throw as Cookson let the ball ride through for a called strike, playing it the smart way.

"See that?" Gorham said. "He's going for the strikeouts."

Bill McGee leaned forward and watched Cookson at the plate. The next pitch was fast in any league and Cookson swung from his heels, breaking his wrists sharply as he rode into the pitch, the sound clear and decisive as the ball began its outward flight over shortstop, gaining speed and arc, going up and over and out of the park at the three hundred-and-fifty-foot sign in deep left center field. Cookson jogged around the bases and Larsen turned off the mound and slammed his glove viciously into the grass and swore in a continuous rage as Cookson crossed home plate with the tying run.

"I—" Gorham said, as the Waniss fans swarmed down from their seats and surrounded the visiting dugout, "that's the first time—"

"He grooved it," Bill McGee said. "He's tired and he lost his hop. Right down the middle, big and fat. He asked for it, he got it."

In the anticlimactic lull that followed, Larsen fanned the next two batters and retired the side. Bill McGee watched the Waniss pitcher warm up and felt a kindred spirit with that older man who was nearly finished, but would pitch with the accumulated cunning of many years spent in this kind of unpredictable ball. The inevitable happened as the first Brainerd batter lived on an error by the second baseman, advanced on the sacrifice, and took a long lead. Cookson raced to the home dugout for a foul fly, but the next batter singled deep into right field for the run and the ball game.

He saw Larsen come from the dugout and yell at Cookson, who trotted across the field without turning his head. Bill McGee waited until the crowd had filed from the stands, watching the Waniss team gather around their pitcher and Cookson, slapping backs and talking it up, gathering bats and equipment in the late afternoon grandstand shadows. The other scouts were down beside the fence, talking and nodding together. One turned away and the other waved to Larsen. *Gentleman's agreement*, Bill McGee thought, *take turns and try to beat one another's best arguments.*

"You want to see him now?" Gorham asked. "Those other fellows are going to do some fast talking. But he'll see you first. He promised me that."

"Tell him to wait," Bill McGee said. "Let him talk with them if he wants to. I'll see him in a few minutes."

He walked quickly to the inside gate and crossed to the Waniss dugout. When Cookson came from the group, loaded down with bat bag and a sack of balls, he said, "Could I talk with you a few minutes, son?"

Cookson smiled and lowered the bat bag to the ground. "Sure. What is it?"

"I'm Bill McGee," he said. "You know me, son?"

"I sure do," Cookson said. "I mean, I've read about you, Mr. McGee. I heard something about you coming up to watch Larsen. I'm glad to know you."

"You had a nice day," Bill McGee said. "That hit was solid."

Cookson grinned. "I waited two months for that one, Mr. McGee. Larsen always pitches fast balls my last time up in a game. Our pitcher—that's Andy—he figured it out for me. Andy said to hit the first pitch because he'd get it in there. But he's good. I won't get another one like that for a long time."

"Look," Bill McGee said. "Have you ever considered pro ball?"

"Me?" Cookson said. "Once in a while, Mr. McGee, but what the heck, I'm too green for that. I play for fun."

"Do you want a chance?" Bill McGee said. "I'm serious, son. Don't answer now. Will you meet me in that cafe beside the newspaper office in half an hour?"

"I don't know," Cookson said. "There's a lot to consider—"

"I know," Bill McGee said. "But come anyway, and let's get acquainted, Dick. That's your first name, isn't it?"

"I will," Cookson said. "I sure will, Mr. McGee."

He felt a warm glow in his chest when he turned away and saw Gorham standing at the gate, holding Larsen's arm and talking rapidly. He joined them and stood in a momentary silence touched faintly by cars pulling away from the parking lot. Larsen was rubbing his arm and smiling confidently.

"How about that?" Larsen said. "One lucky hit—he'll never get a loud foul off me again."

"Finish your other talks?" Bill McGee asked quietly.

"Sure did. I guess we can get down to business, huh? I'm open for bids. How high will you go? And don't give me any of that six-thousand-dollar bonus limit chicken feed."

"You've got the wrong slant on our organization," Bill McGee said gently. "We're all through bidding and coming up with more bonus players, Larsen. You've got a good fast ball, you're young and strong, but if we sign you for a bonus you'll start the worst way a boy can break in."

"I know that line," Larsen said impatiently. "There's ways of fixing it so you can pay me the dough and I won't be a bonus player . . . on the record."

He remembered the year he broke in, before the first big war, playing for one hundred a month, living in a dingy room, eating in side street joints, washing his own socks to save money. The sum total of his five minor league years' pay was little more than the six thousand dollars this boy considered as nothing. It was useless to argue with the Larsens of today. All a man could do was make the long, hot trip and watch them, judge them fairly, and determine their chance of making good; and this boy was dead set to ruin his own future with stubbornness and childish greed and one great intrinsic lack—that of rock bottom courage, real guts in the pinch. A man could spend days talking to no avail.

"We don't do business that way," he said curtly. "Understand that right now. You know our club, our farm system. You'll have every chance to make good if you show the stuff. But not as a bonus player, not when you've got everything to learn before you can pitch winning ball."

He paused and watched angry color stain Larsen's face. He said, "I know what you think. We've followed you for quite a while, we'd like to sign you and bring you along the right way. But there's no use wasting time if your mind is set. I'll give you the limit price but no more, and believe me, it's for your own good."

"Six thousand!" Larson said angrily. "Hell, that's peanuts!"

"Six thousand," Bill McGee said. "A lot of money for any man. That much and the chance to learn and come up the right way. Think it over. Let us know what you decide."

Larsen's answer was plain before the boy spoke. "If those other guys were worth the money, so am I. There's more than one ball club wants me." Larsen laughed and slammed his glove against his leg, and turned away.

"Bill," Gorham said. "You're not going to—"

He was thinking of spring training in that moment, of sitting in the pressbox shade on the green bench, unknown to the fans near by, watching his team take shape and balance for the new year. No one in the stands knew him, but he didn't care. Because the players knew, and they were placed on the field by himself, by Johnny Nee and Heine Groh, by Chuck Ward and Eddie Krajnik, by all the others who traveled across the country a thousand times. The integrity of baseball was invested in the players, and before them came himself and all the scouts who had picked those players, taking only the best, refusing so many like Larsen; and it always gave him a feeling of humble satisfaction to sit in the pressbox shade and watch his team and know they were the best, the kids with the guts.

"Forget him," Bill McGee said. "I know a thousand like him. Believe me, he'll never make the grade. Don't blame yourself. Sometimes we never know what a boy has inside, really inside, until we see him with the chips down. Don't worry, you'll be repaid for the loss. Let's get back to the cafe. We're talking with Cookson in half an hour."

Gorham said, "Cookson?" and stared in openmouthed wonder.

"I'd like to find one like him just twice a year," Bill McGee said. "Watch the Larsens close, but look sharp for the other kind, the Cooksons. They're hard to see if you don't know how to look. Look for the kid with the guts, the kid who has it in a tight spot. That's what Ida always says." Bill McGee smiled then, at some secret, inner thought. "You don't know Ida, but she'll thank you for giving us a great deal today, Stan. Now let's grab that coffee."

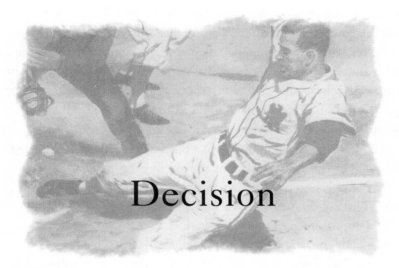

Decision

Whenever I think of Jim Messenger I see a chunky man with clear gray eyes and expressive hands standing in lonely, harsh silhouette against the background of Westport's grandstand and spike-torn infield, facing a gesturing, swearing group of angry ball players with the fans straining behind the wire, waving bottles and fists; and behind all this, unseen but impossible to forget, the small towns and rickety ball parks and partisan fans; the man-killing overnight jumps in buses and milk trains; the second-rate hotels and cheap cafés and twenty-four hour laundries and cracked, polished shoes; and most of all, for it will never change while we play the game, the man in blue standing immovable against everyone. When I see Jim Messenger now, and those times are too few because of distance and life, I can never forget that night last year. That was the night I finally realized what it meant to be an umpire.

I waited for him that evening in the hotel coffee shop, holding the last booth against assorted traveling men and irate customers, wondering for the hundredth time why he kept umpiring in a Class C league with so little chance to advance. I had known him since childhood in our hometown and now, with my business in Westport, one of the towns in the Westline

League, it was possible to see him every time he came around the circuit. He couldn't talk and eat and be seen with just anyone, but I was classed as acceptable, no doubt, by those men who framed the excellent rules of deportment for all umpires in organized baseball. My construction company was growing yearly and I had long been known as an ardent baseball fan, plus owning stock in our Westport franchise.

He came from the lobby with a taller young man his own age, stopped at the cashier's booth for an evening paper, and joined me. I shook hands with Pete Jones, his partner on this circuit, and signaled the waitress for our dinners.

"How are both of you?" I asked.

"Tired," he said shortly. "In the legs."

Pete Jones grinned wryly. "I don't mind nine innings, Mr. Chambers, but thirteen gets a man down."

"Getting fed up?" I said.

"Remember the schoolteacher's song," Pete Jones said. "Another day, another dollar. Wish I'd live a million days."

"That's what I want to talk about," I said. "Remember the proposition I offered both of you last month?"

"Yes," Messenger said. "Did you mean it, John?"

"I don't talk for fun," I said stiffly. "Given it some serious thought?"

"You know we have," he said.

I smiled at them. "Reached a decision?"

"Not yet," Messenger said slowly. "I can't explain how I feel, John. It's just one of those things. Pete feels the same way. Maybe it goes under the head of wishful thinking—"

"Or damn foolishness," Pete Jones said. "Let's eat, then we'll talk."

We ate and Messenger scanned the sports page, reading the account of last night's game. I had read the story and knew why he flushed with anger. The Westport sports writer had patted the local club and given reluctant credit to the visiting losers and finished with a childish castigation of the umpires for their decision at third base in the eighth inning. The sports writer was a callow young man and according to his viewpoint, Messenger had been late covering third while Jones should have come down from the plate and helped. The sports writer, of course, could see much better from his press box above the grandstand.

"Bother you?" I asked.

"Not now," he said. "A year ago this stuff burned me up. Now I get riled but no more."

"We're the umps," Pete Jones said gently." You know, the forgotten men."

I wondered then, as I had so often, if the fans ever thought about an umpire. They saw him behind the plate, on the baselines, making a dozen split-second decisions every game. They booed him, which was perfectly all right, but too often they tried to brain him. A man had to be something of a fatalist wearing the blue. He had to place himself in the fans' shoes and remember when he felt the same way. He had to understand that strange feeling a fan got when his team lost and the umpire seemed entirely to blame. The feeling that caused law-abiding, mild men to grab bottles and attempt murder. He had to understand, and even though he eventually did if he stayed in the game, it was never easy to take. The fans knew very little about men like Jim Messenger and Pete Jones, or anyone else wearing blue in our league.

We finished dessert and I said, "The offer still stands."

Pete Jones glanced at Messenger and frowned. He said, "You're thinking again, Jim. Trying to figure out why we stay in this game when Mr. Chambers offers us good jobs with a future?"

"Maybe," Messenger said, "I can't get the values straight."

"Values," Pete Jones snorted. "You mean the gamble. I've estimated our chances of making triple A or the big show. They give better odds in a crooked dice game."

"Then quit," Messenger said softly.

"So I'm crazy," Pete Jones said, and turned red. "I like it. Or do I. I wish I knew."

They seemed to move away from me when they talked like this, but I understood. They had been together for two years and were as close as two men can ever be. They ate and slept and traveled together, sent their laundry to the same place, ate the same meals, umpired the games and fought off the players and fans. They moved alone in the surrounding world, staying in different hotels than the teams, taking other buses and trains if at all feasible. They began in May and ended this monastic life in September. They were in their second year of umpiring and no longer surprised at anything under the sun. For these reasons, when they talked together, they innocently excluded anyone else from their conversation; and even though I understood them better than most people, a small part was never opened to me.

The waitress said, "More coffee, Mr. Chambers?"

"Please," I said. "All around."

She went away and Pete Jones cleared his throat softly. "I think we ought to give you a definite answer, Mr. Chambers. After all, this is August. I don't suppose you can keep those jobs open forever."

"No," I said. "That's true, Pete. I hoped you would know this time so I could make final plans."

"Well—" Messenger said. "Look, John. There's no use putting it off any longer. I'll give you my answer after the game. How's that?"

"Good enough," I said." I'll be there and drive you to the train. Let me know then."

"I think I know my answer now," Pete Jones said.

He was ready to quit and work with me, I knew, but Messenger was still confused and uncertain. I wondered then if the game that night might not be placed in his mind as a final measuring stick of decision. I hoped, when we parted at the lobby door, that things would go badly for them. I was being selfish but I knew too well what stretched before them in the future, just as I knew their past. They were both twenty-seven years old and before the war had played in fast semi-pro baseball.

They were signed to a pro contract but the war cut that short and they subsequently served four years. They did not know each other then; and oddly enough both suffered the same physical disability, partially frozen feet, which destroyed any chance of a major league career.

But they loved the game and both of them, a thousand miles apart, arrived at the same conclusion. They wanted to stay in baseball and the only opening seemed to be umpiring. The minor leagues were springing up again following the war and crying for competent officials but not so badly, as Jones remarked sourly many times, as to make the salaries really worthwhile. Not even that old gag about the hours being so good made enough difference. Even so, they both decided to give it a try.

They met in a Florida umpire school that winter. They studied hard, showed intelligence and aptitude, and with their backgrounds met the necessary qualifications. Their instructor recommended both of them highly and got them jobs in a Class D league for the summer of 1946. Messenger told me he would never forget that first season. They made the usual mistakes, dodged the bottles, closed their ears to the abuse, and forced themselves to be firm with managers and players. Because I knew Messenger from younger days, I hired them both that winter to work on a construction job; and using all the pull I could muster, knowing they were to be advanced to Class C, got them appointed to the Westline for 1947.

They had discussed their chances countless times. Somebody had to notice them to get the big break, but if that happened their first summer, they didn't know. Other umpires were good, perhaps better than any of them, and chance for real advancement seemed remote. During the winter I discussed the problem with them often, and my arguments were neither for nor against, but a simple statement of the facts as viewed by a businessman. Umpiring was seasonal work; in the minors it meant about five months in most leagues and six in Triple and Double A. During the winter a man had to eat, had to consider the future, and find a decent job. As they grew older, if they continued to umpire, and did not make the big show, that off-season job would become increasingly hard to get. And the pay for a minor league season was far from being adequate for a year's living; and if they considered marriage it was only a drop in the bucket. I told them the cold facts and offered them permanent jobs in my company with chance for advancement limited only by their own efforts and ability. They were intelligent men, quick to grasp things, and I never had enough like them in my crews. I wasn't doing them a favor; I was offering them good money because they would give me full value.

That was the situation when they arrived in Westport for our series with Lake City. The season had only a month to run and they had received no indication from the officials as to their possible advancement. They were good umpires, no question of that, but other umpires in our league were good and on up the ladder, in B and A and Double A, were plenty of other good umpires, all waiting for a chance to go up. I could not hold the jobs open forever. I wrote them a week before they arrived and explained the situation and asked them to make a decision one way or another. And now, two hours before game time, Messenger was wrestling with the problem, and Pete Jones had undoubtedly decided to quit and work for me. But I wanted Messenger, too. Ham is flat without good eggs.

I drove home and called my wife, and the children, who were spending the hot days at our lake home.

I showered and changed into slacks and a loose shirt, and drove slowly across our town to the ball park. Westport had grown during the war and was touching twenty thousand, and we had gotten together in 1946, raised more money, and renovated the park. I always got a thrill, coming down North Fourth and seeing the big grandstand, freshly painted, and then walking to my box seat on the first base line behind our dugout and seeing the newly sodded infield and smooth, thickly grassed outfield.

The fences were high and new, and the scoreboard in dead center field was easily readable from any seat. The park held four thousand people; that night we had a nice crowd just a few hundred short of capacity. Our fans were a tough bunch, rabid and loud, inclined to take matters in their own hands when the team was losing. They disliked all umpires and after last night, were certain to be cocked and primed for Messenger and Jones.

I got settled in my box and watched the pregame infield workouts and the meeting between managers and umpires at home plate. Our manager was a cocky little Irishman named Hennessy, one of those red-haired runty men who always make up their size deficiency in voice and temper. Jones was taking the plate and Messenger was on the baselines, and the batteries were announced as they took their respective positions to begin play.

Westport was two games behind the visiting Lake City club and needed a win badly to stay in the fight for first place which Lake City had held since the opening day. Hennessy started his ace right-hander and Lake City countered with their best. I settled down for an enjoyable evening. Nothing is finer than watching two teams of young men, all of them hoping for a chance at the big show. There is something about their youth and vitality that discounts all the errors they make, and with baseball only two years on the recovery side after the war, errors in our league were more numerous than in pre-war years.

The game began smoothly and moved immediately into a tight pitching duel. Five innings and no score, only three hits for each club, and I wondered if they might not reach eight or nine before something broke. Jones and Messenger were covering the plays with fine precision and I felt good, just watching them be at the right places every time. Jones called strikes and balls fast and loud, raising his right arm and pushing it belligerently toward first for each strike. Messenger believed in coming on top of each base play, and used a right uppercut to signify the outs. Their decisions were given rapidly, without that telltale pause you see in amateur umpiring, and I could not help but think that their work was worthy of advancement. But then, I was prejudiced.

Lake City scored in the first of the ninth on a single, a sacrifice, and another looping single to right-center, the base runner sliding under a high hopping peg from our center fielder. Jones called the man safe, as he was without doubt, but the crowd roared protest and I felt them stir and murmur around me. They cut off the Lake City rally with a fast double play and came in to hit. I looked around and noticed that a good many fans were holding their pop bottles and cushions tightly while the murmur grew into a low roar and their feet started pounding the boards in that old speechless sound that signified the desire for a rally, a big inning, the ball game.

The first man flied to left field. The second batter struck out. The third batter singled to left and the crowd moved with fresh hope. Messenger trotted over behind the pitching mound to cover the logical play at second, but took his position on the first base side because a ground ball with two out would be played toward first in most cases. Hennessy sent a pinch hitter in for our eighth place batter and Jones announced his name to the official scorer while Lake City motioned two pitchers awake in their bullpen. And then it happened.

It was one of those nasty decisions that occur too fast. The pinch hitter singled to left on the first pitch and the runner rounded second and moved toward third. Messenger whirled and followed the play closely, moving with the runner as he always did, so that he was on the third base side of second when the left fielder made a beautiful stop and whipped his throw to third. The shortstop saw the runner halt, and cut the throw off. The runner reversed and slid back to second, he and the ball arriving together in a cloud of silty grey dust. Messenger had turned and sprinted for the bag but was five feet short of being on top of the play. He saw the second baseman take the knee-high throw and make his quick tag at the runner's right foot hooking into the bag. I knew how Messenger was thinking in this moment. He knew that the bag had been kicked when the runner came around, pushing the third base corner off center a few inches; and he knew, too, with his memory of player habits in this league, that the Lake City second baseman was a quick tagger. He knew that the runner was not an exceptional slider and had a tendency to miss the bag with his right foot on a hook slide and hit it with his ankle as the fulcrum when he swerved around. Messenger thought of these things automatically as the play formed and happened in one brief moment, and without hesitation hooked his hand and forearm up in the age-old gesture and called clearly, "You're out!"

And then they were on him from all sides. Hennessy led the rush. I jumped to my feet and looked around at the crowd. They were standing as one man, roaring their anger and watching Hennessy gesticulate and scream in Messenger's face. This was the usual routine and Hennessy was known for his red-faced bellows and protests; and had nothing happened, Hennessy would have yelled and waved his arms and finally turned away growling the time-tested protests against the blindness of all umpires. But someone behind me let out a yell and threw the first bottle, and then it started. I couldn't stop them and the police detail assigned to home games wasn't enough. Fans leaped the box seat railing along both sidelines and headed for Messenger. Jones rushed out and stood beside him while the four policemen ran to join them.

I saw it happen and tried to stop them; it was impossible. I was knocked down and pushed against the front of my box. I got up in time to see the bottles flying and watch Messenger go down as one struck his head. Then Hennessy and both teams closed around them and began a dogged advance toward the Westport dressing room. One policeman ran to phone for help. I fought through people and reached the dressing room door in our dugout and grabbed a bat and swung it with all my strength, driving them back. And then the players pushed through and I was unable to stand aside. We all rolled and slid into the dressing-room and Hennessy slammed the door, locked it, and began pushing benches across the bottom half. One of the players locked the street side door.

They were outside, three thousand strong, no longer ball fans but a mob. Hennessy wiped blood from his face and said "They'll try to bust in, Mr. Chambers."

"I know it," I said. "Put the boys on top."

Hennessy grinned. "Good. I never thought of that. All right, you guys. Come on. Hurry up."

"No," Jones said stubbornly. "I'm no damned sneak. Where's the police?"

"Jones," Hennessy said sharply. "They can't stop these crazy fools. Listen to them. Come on, for my sake."

Messenger shook his head and said unsteadily: "We'd better hurry, Pete. What about an all clear, John. We've got to catch that train."

"Everybody leave," I said quickly. "All lights out, unlock the doors. That way they believe we sneaked you away. Wait until everything is quiet and then come out. Cross the field to the scoreboard and use the little door. Give him the key, Mike. I'll be across the street in my car. Got it?"

"Got it," Messenger said thickly. "Come on, Pete."

Hennessy ran into his cubbyhole office and leaped on the desk and pushed the small trapdoor up. Jones helped Messenger up and through, into the darkness above. They replaced the trap door and we went out of the office and shut the door. I heard later from Messenger about that wait. They lay beside each other and smelled the dust of many years on the rafters and girders and bracing running all around the grandstand. They were between the roof of the dressing room and the slanting floor of the grand-stand, in a dark, sealed place formed when the park was built. Above them was the roar of the crowd; and around them, in the street and parking lots, rose the same angry sound.

"Damn them!" Jones whispered. "Why do we stand for this, Jim?"

"Relax," Messenger said. "We're alive. Let's get a little rest."

He pillowed his head on crossed arms and tried to find comfort on the rough board roof of the clubhouse. Jones swallowed and coughed softly and finally relaxed beside him. They listened to the crowd mill around the clubhouse street door, heard the players leave in twos and threes, talk to the crowd, and go away. Finally Hennessy stepped outside and the questions came loud and angry. Hennessy called, "They're gone, folks. I know it was a bum decision but I'll protest. Let's call it a night and go home."

A few of them agreed loudly and escorted Hennessy to his car. They lay in the dust and stale air, hearing the crowd mill and mutter, and finally begin to drift away. Messenger turned on his stomach and held his watch before his eyes and watched the minute hand tick off an hour and five minutes before everything was still. Jones did not speak in this time.

"Okay," Messenger whispered. "It's all right now, Pete."

"I'm full of dust," Jones said bitterly, "and my own blood."

They lifted the trapdoor and dropped into the darkened office. Messenger stepped to the door and looked across the locker room, seeing nothing but shadows and the white outline of towels drying on the hooks against the far wall. They crossed to the field door and moved slowly up the ramp to the home dugout and stood motionless, peering around the grandstand and field.

"We've got thirty minutes to catch our train," Messenger said. "John's waiting."

"I'd like to—" Jones said, and then swallowed the bitter words and stepped onto the field.

I watched them come toward me across the field in the silence that covered everything, the grandstand and bleachers, the infield grass wet with night dew, the outfield, the narrow path of black cinders at the base of the fence. Behind them lay the litter of the game, on the sidewalks outside the park, in the aisles and between the grandstand seats, around the dugouts and water fountains where the crowd, milling over the field, drank and spat in the dust. Above me the scoreboard was dark against the sky, the numbers still in place, telling the story of innings that passed so swiftly: just the black scoreboard with the hooks in orderly rows, holding the numbers and zeros, waiting for tomorrow night and a reshuffle of their digits which spelled victory or defeat. They saw me and I opened the small door and led them through to the street; and standing together in the stillness, I thought of the game and the people thrown together for two hours and what the feeling meant to someone when you really understood.

It is a strange feeling and it says wordlessly that baseball offers something good to everyone. And something bad, in the sense that all good has a flavor and taste of happiness, and all happiness must end sooner or later in sadness. I remembered the night beginning for them, eating in the café and talking of the game, pro and con, among other subjects, going through the arguments we loved not so much for their value but for the joy of talking baseball. Then riding to the ball park in a taxi, crossing to the private office which served as a headquarters for all umpires, sitting there and hearing people like myself come into the grandstand and move to our box seats. They were in the office and I was in my box seat, but they knew and felt and heard the same things, as though they were beside me. Watching the teams warm up slowly, then taking hitting practice in the cage as the sun dropped low and shadows crept over the grass. Hearing the squeak of the batting cage wheels as the groundkeepers pushed it away, and then the infield workouts, the ground balls and lazy flies to the outfield, the final swift and somehow more alert pegs to the plate; and then they came out exactly on time for the meeting at home plate with both managers. And behind all this was the grandstand and bleachers, crowd noise overlaying all sound but the vendors selling pop and peanuts and beer. And finally the home team trotting out in position and the visiting leadoff man stepping to the plate. Somehow, in the first moment of any game, in the silence that falls as the first batter faces the pitcher, there is a feeling of drama I have never experienced elsewhere. It is a feeling as old as baseball, will never change, and has been repeated countless times, but it remains fresh and new and filled with throat-tightening drama. You sit tightly and watch the pitcher's windup and throw, hear the silence plainly rather than hear nothing, and when the arm comes down and the ball flashes toward the plate, it seems as though someone pulls a long, taut wire from your stomach. If my backbone is ever jerked out instantly, I will know how it feels beforehand. No other sport gives me that feeling. Bullfighting most nearly approaches it; football cannot; boxing lacks the inherent honesty; for nothing can change the ball's flight, the batter's answer with movement, the hit or miss, the drawn out feeling on a hot night before the first pitch.

They were feeling all this when we stood together on the sidewalk. I knew because years ago a young man named Chambers tried umpiring in the old Westline and never got over the empty spot in his heart when he failed to advance and was forced to go into business; and they knew this and understood my silence. This was their moment of final decision in which they weighed all chances, remembered all the bruises and curses, the low pay, the gamble against an uncertain future, having only those thoughts we both understood and the feeling in their hearts.

"Jim," I said gently. "Pete. Made your decision?"

Messenger wiped his swollen face and said, "I guess I'm crazy, John, but I'm sticking. They can't make me back down."

"I'm sticking," Jones said. "Me, I don't know why but Jim's right. You can't quit."

"I knew it," I said. "Let's get you two crooks to that train."

Messenger lit a cigarette and stared at me oddly above the red match flare. He said, "I thought you knew, John. Don't be mad, will you?"

"Don't be a damned fool," I said. "Good luck and I'll look for both of you in October. The winter jobs are still open if you want them."

I got them to the train and watched it move north into darkness before I drove away. The night was clear and still for someone wanting to explain a difficult thought, but all the words in the world could not explain what they felt and why they wouldn't quit. You had to understand and that is why I wait eagerly to see them whenever I can, especially Messenger. For they both went up to Class A this year and who knows how their luck will turn. Maybe it is because I see in them the determination and guts to make the top that I lacked twenty years ago. Whatever it is, whatever it takes to be a fine umpire, belongs to them. I only wish more people understood.

The Magic Circle

A ll night Taft Easterling had slept badly, fearing the rain that might wash out this last game; now, breakfast eaten and the sun bright, he paused at the door and turned his face for his wife's good-luck kiss. He held her with awkward tenderness while she smiled and said, "Well . . . good luck, Taft."

"Last day," he said. "Sad?"

"Yes," she said quietly, "and proud, too. You'll make it, Taft."

"Sure," he said. "Got to, Mary. See you at the park."

Driving from the garage, Taft Easterling decided that everyone in town shared his worry. He ran a gauntlet of waving neighbors; the boulevard cop held up traffic and passed him with a shouted, "Get those hits, Taft." In the parking lot, the attendants trailed him to the sidewalk with their good wishes. He crossed the street and signed a dozen books for the kids, and ducked through the players' entrance and down the corridor to the dressing room. He was early today but the fear was early, too, creeping higher in his chest. Doc Malone peered from the trainer's room and called, "Let's get that rub, Taft, before the mob arrives."

"Right with you, Doc," he called. "Heat the snake oil."

He undressed quickly and walked to the big white-walled

room. Doc Malone said, "On the belly," and when he was flat, chin pillowed on his hands, Malone poured the oil over his back and began rubbing softly, powerful fingers kneading and loosening the muscles. Taft Easterling tried to doze; but the past was catching up today. "Too hard?" Doc Malone asked.

"Fine," he said. "Just fine, Doc."

Today's game meant nothing, the season final between his fifth place club and the Quakers who had cinched the pennant a week ago. Today was a chance to relax, do a little friendly razzing, play nine innings and go home. But today the stands were nearly sold out and four, perhaps five times, during this game all pleasure would cease. For Taft Easterling was playing his last game in the majors; and today, ending fifteen years of distinguished service, he needed two base hits to join the magic circle. One thousand nine hundred and ninety-eight hits to his credit; and next year he'd be on the coaching lines by strict, unchangeable doctor's orders.

"Over, Taft."

He turned and smiled up lazily at Doc Malone, brown eyes soft above the high, slanting cheekbones with their trace of Santee blood. Doc's fingers moved gently over his thick, wrinkled neck and heavy shoulder muscles. He lay solid and thick on the rubbing table, forty years old this summer, the oldest active player in the league. "If," he said absently. "That's the word, Doc."

"If what, Taft?"

"If I hadn't sprained the ankle in '37," Taft Easterling said. "Missed ten games because of that spiking in '40. If the war hadn't come along. If all the lost games could be played again, Doc. Know what I mean?"

"We can't turn back time," Doc Malone said gently. "Stop worrying, Taft. You'll get two hits today. Hell, you'll get four. Nobody around here is worried. Relax."

Taft Easterling closed his eyes and felt the strong fingers on his body; and remembered the beginning of that time he could never bring back. He'd come up in '34, a kid of twenty-three, and stuck as a utility outfielder because baseball was depression-saddled and he was cheap. He filled in for the old-timers and batted a respectable .285 in fifty-four games. The next season he held down left field and took his place as a regular. That was lucky for the Easterlings, married three years and needing more money. He'd been afraid of his chances but Mary never doubted them, even forced him to hold out and drag an extra thousand from the owner.

In those years before the war, he hadn't thought about setting records or becoming an old-timer. He played steady baseball and batted in the second slot after his second year. When he enlisted in 1942, after the season, he left an eight-year batting average of .303 and a hole the team could not fill until he returned in '46 for another try. He didn't think he'd stick. He was thirty-five then, at the age all men lost the big step and felt the muscle strain of age; but Taft Easterling misjudged his own toughness and continued to play the same steady, unspectacular baseball. He took his rests then, letting the rookies spell him, but everyone understood that he was simply too valuable for the junkyard and already slated for a coaching job on the club.

The doctors checked him twice a year and gave him a clear bill of health. Malone said it was his lack of excess weight, his muscle looseness that forestalled the charley horses and groin injuries. Mary said he could go on playing until the doctors called a halt, not a game longer, for they had half their lives to live and she wanted him healthy. So he played through the post-war years and finally, last year, his age began to tell. He filled in during the tough games, spelled the youngsters, and did his usual fine job of pinch-hitting for Wally. He really hadn't intended to play this season, but during the winter he made a belated discovery of one fact.

The local writers added up his record book totals and discovered Taft Easterling had amassed one thousand nine hundred and forty-eight base hits. Once they began running their feature stories, he admitted to the secret, long-cherished desire. He wanted two thousand hits more than anything in the world, for it would put him in the magic circle. Him, old dry-as-dust Taft Easterling could join that small group of players whose names were forever in the game's history: Cobb and Speaker, Ruth and Gehrig, Hornsby, Heilmann, Gehringer, all of them who were, in Taft Easterling's mind, so much better than he'd ever been that reaching two-thousand-hit goal seemed presumptuous. But if he made it honestly, the right was his.

He discussed it with Mary before spring training; and agreed to abide by the doctor's decision. He suffered through a tough physical, all the probing and checking, x-rays and blood tests, electrocardiograms, everything they seemed to do from sheer spite. Dr. Allen gave him the verdict just before spring training: "I realize what this means to you, Taft, but your health comes first. You can play sixty games, pinch hit in others, but no fast starts, no extended running. You'll slow down terribly this year, as you'll discover. I'm going to check you in mid-summer, again in September, just to be sure. But one fact is definite. This is your last year. No more active playing, not one inning."

He said, "Sixty games is plenty, doctor.

"I hope so," Allen smiled. "Taft, can you get fifty-two hits in sixty games?"

"I've got to," he said simply.

But Taft Easterling realized during spring training that sixty games would tax his aging body to the very limit. He trained slowly under Malone's strict supervision and pinch hit sparingly during exhibition games, saving his strength for the regular season. His legs hardened acceptably but his arm lost the snap necessary for a long throw from left field. He worried about being a drag on the team, but Wally McGoveran told him, "We'll get fourth or fifth, Taft, no higher. That means you can play without hurting our chances. We'll pick spots, give you plenty of in-between rest."

He started the season in left field and played ten games, making exactly ten hits, muffing other chances because his timing was rusty and he no longer beat out that occasional slow hopper. He rested then, pinch hitting against right-handed pitchers, settling into a regular pattern. He played three games and sat out a like number; at mid-season after thirty full games and twelve pinch-hit trips he had made twenty-seven hits. He knew then, during the All-Star break, that he should come through with a comfortable margin; but there was no denying the steady weakening of his body, the loss of precious reserve strength built up during spring training.

Starting the last half of the season, he enjoyed two successive days of good luck, collecting five solid hits, and continuing this mild streak with five more hits on the western swing. That raised his total to thirty-seven, with twenty-one to go and fifty-six games remaining on the schedule. Through the early part of August he pinch hit safely three times and gathered six more hits in five full games; now he was just twelve hits shy and the papers began a daily box score of his progress. He was tiring quickly by then and Wally suggested benching him after six or seven innings if he hit safely; but playing against the Giants on August 20th, he hit safely his first two trips and insisted on staying in despite Doc Malone's protest. He was going so good that day, so near the finish, he could not bear to stop.

He went for the foul line fly in the eighth inning and felt his legs buckle; then he was rolling on the grass and his right ankle flamed with pain. They carried him to the dressing room where Malone applied ice to check the swelling; but he knew what this meant: benched indefinitely with ten hits to go and one month of play remaining. He cursed himself bitterly, knowing the very real agony of fear for the first time in his life.

The weeks passed in an agony of treatment, as the games were played and disappeared forever. The swelling reduced but his ankle was still weak beneath full weight pressure. He wanted to make the final western trip but Dr. Allen refused bluntly. "You're dog-tired, Taft, inside and out. Resistance low, muscles lax. Make this road trip, pinch hit as I know damned well you will, you'll reinjure the ankle and never get back in the lineup."

"Doctor," he said. "I've got to. There's no time."

"There is," Allen said firmly. "When the team comes home, we have ten games to play. Stay here during the road trip, rest yourself, get that ankle in shape. Then we'll keep it wrapped and you finish the season. If you can't make ten lousy hits in ten games, then I'm crazy."

"I don't know," he said wearily. "I don't know about that."

"You don't!" Allen said sharply. "Quitting on us, Taft?"

He looked up, some of the old fire in his eyes. "I don't quit. I'll get the hits."

So Taft Easterling stayed home and rested, until rest became punishment. He took private batting practice the day before the team came home, felt the ankle sustain his weight, and sprayed base hits to all fields. After the train arrived that night, Wally McGoveran drove over and Taft Easterling said. "I'm ready. Do I finish?"

"Every game," Wally said. "Taft, we've been friends for twenty years. I'm giving you a direct order now, as your manager. No chasing fly balls, no fielding hits in a hurry. Let the kid come over from center. You stand out there and take it easy. Understand?"

"All right," he said, "but I won't cripple the team."

Then the pressure descended, the race against time, with the odds clear in his mind: forty-some times at bat in ten games to make ten hits; and it dared not rain. He singled in the first game, went hitless the second, and got two singles in the third. All interest was centered on his race against the clock; when he came to bat the fans applauded loudly, cheering him on. Opposing pitchers bore down, as always happened in such cases, and that was fine with him. Taft Easterling had pride running deep and strong in his heart, proud faith in his own ability, pride that made it impossible to accept pity, such as cheap base hits on deliberately pitched straight balls. He had this pride as strong in him as that first day he came to bat, long years ago, and faced a forgotten pitcher on a hot May afternoon.

He went hitless in the fourth game, failed again in the fifth. He was starting to press, go after bad balls, and he sensed the helpless pity on the bench each time he moved into the on-deck circle. Mary talked with him a long time that night, trying to ease his tension. He singled the next day, but that was only four hits, with four games to go. He needed six more hits. The Giants moved in for two games and he doubled in the opener, but could do no more. Wally had moved him to lead-off, hoping he'd get that extra time at bat, but even this failed. He slept badly that night and heard the rain before sunrise. It rained all morning and into afternoon; and the umpires regretfully called the game. It was cancelled, for there was no time to make it up. The Giants had two games at home, and the Quakers moved in tomorrow for the closing two games.

That morning Mary kissed him good-by and said, "Are you giving up?"

"No," he said. "Think I was?"

"You, Taft? You never quit."

Taft Easterling went out that afternoon and doubled in the first inning, singled in the fifth, and doubled again in the seventh. He was back in the fight, one game to play and two hits to go. They gave him a standing ovation that afternoon, and the team almost smothered him in the dressing room. Just before he reached the showers, Wally came from the corridor and said, "I just saw Billy Lawson, Taft. He's starting Robbins tomorrow, Simon the middle three, and Russ Beyer finishes. He wants you to know he's got to loosen them for the series or he'd give you a right-hander all the way."

"No difference," he said. "I hit or I don't."

"You'll hit," Wally said. "Take a good shower."

"Wake up, Taft," Doc Malone said gently. "Batting practice in ten minutes."

Taft Easterling sat up and rubbed his eyes. He'd slept a little and now the dressing room was filled, others waiting their turn on the table, watching him with grave patience. He said, "Sorry, guys," and walked to his locker. Wally came from the office and said, "Come on, sleepyhead," and then he was going through the pre-game routine, hitting in the cage, playing catch with the outfielders, resting in the dugout during the plate meeting. Wally came from the plate and said, "Give 'em hell," and Taft Easterling trotted slowly across this dearly familiar ground for the last afternoon.

When he reached left field the bleachers exploded with sound, voices blending in a happy cacophony of good luck. He tipped his cap and then the game was started, the Quakers hitting two fly balls and a grounder, going down in a hurry. He came in and swung his bats carefully, tired muscles stretching with reluctant lubrication; and took his position at the plate as Semick pegged to second base and Robbins toed the rubber. He nodded at Semick and the big catcher said, "Good luck, Taft."

Taft Easterling crouched in a deep box stance against Robbins, respecting the big man's speed and snapping curve. He took a ball and an outside corner strike, waiting patiently, thinking now, *Got to hit the first time, got to, wait for the inside curve.* Robbins wound and the ball streaked down the middle, dipped sharply, and broke beneath his wrists. He stepped away and dropped his swing, praying for good wood as he chased the curve ball; and felt the wonderful, solid contact as he followed through and broke for first. He saw the ball line cleanly over Cannady's head at second base, a single in the books for any man.

Watkens stepped around him to cover the bag and said, "Good hit, Taft, good hit." They were all for him, he thought, teammates and Quakers. He mumbled, "Thanks, Eddie," and took a spare two-step lead, relaxing on his heels, conserving his strength. He glanced at the third box left of their dugout, saw Mary, and closed his right fist in their secret signal; and watched her hands answer with the fighter's clasp on the box rail. He felt the dream coming true now, with eight full innings to go.

He died on first base as Robbins pitched excellent control ball; and the game moved scoreless into the third inning before the Quakers took a one-run lead on Willie Smith's homer. He was in the hole their half of the third; and watched their catcher strike out, and the pitcher go down swinging. Taft Easterling dug in solidly at the plate, faced Robbins, and then the pressure was cloud thick: one hit, one little hit. Robbins gave him a full windup and a slow curve ball; and Taft Easterling went after that changeup in his eagerness and popped a fly to Hammett on the grass edge. Eddie Watkens said, "Sorry, Taft," and gave him an arm slap as they passed.

He would face Simon his next trip, the finest left-hander in the majors, coming off a twenty-three game season; and then Russ Beyer in the final third of the game. He had two more times at bat against the toughest pitchers in the league. The afternoon was bright, and sun-hot, but he shivered with nervous tension, kicking at the grass as he moved out to left field. He had never hit Simon, and Russ Beyer had crossed him a dozen times this year.

They retired the Quakers in order, and Simon began his three-inning stint to a round of angry protest from the crowd. Simon was loose and fast, a square-jawed Dutchman who pitched just one way, with blinding speed and a wealth of natural stuff. Simon set them down in order, and the Quakers scored their second run in the fifth when Smith smashed another homer. And then play was racing by and Taft Easterling waited on deck in the sixth, watching their pitcher fan for the second out.

He took an open stance at the plate and Semick said, "Dig in,

Taft," and began talking to Simon. The left-hander came over with that whip-lash arm and he took the called strike, unable to follow the ball. Again the pitch caught the outside corner, with no more than Simon's natural hop on the ball. Semick said pleadingly, "Come on, Taft," and the pitch was across, a straight ball over the middle, and he was swinging and turning away, choking back the sob of futile anger. *One more time*, he thought. *Only one more chance.*

He stood flat-footed in the outfield while the Quakers were retired; and coming in for their half of the seventh, Doc Malone fussed over him, giving him a whiff of salts and massaging his shoulders. Dr. Allen examined his ankle wraps and said, "Rest your eyes, Taft. Plenty of time yet."

"Sure," Taft Easterling said wearily. "Plenty of time."

Russ Beyer was hotter than Simon. They failed in the seventh, and the eighth, and Taft Easterling led off in the last of the ninth, his last trip for sure, trailing the Quakers two big runs. He stepped in and Semick said soothingly, "This time, Taft. Come on, old-timer."

He grunted deep in his chest and faced Beyer; and the rangy right-hander came around with that high, overhand wrist snap, the ball out of the glove and across the plate, belt high and down the middle. Taft Easterling could not pass such a pitch. He swung, feeling pain in his chest, and topped the ball past Beyer on line with second base. Running, he knew he had failed on a cripple pitch, given to him by Semick and Beyer. Ten steps down the line he saw Hammett race from shortstop for the scoop and throw; and suddenly Hammett tripped and sprawled, and the ball dribbled over the bag toward center field.

Something broke in him then, something that brought hurt, angry tears to his eyes. Cannady had crossed over and was fielding the ball, but any man could beat it out before the throw. Taft Easterling started his sprint and then the pride jerked him deliberately to a painful trot. Cannady made the peg, face angry, and Dascoli had to call him out by the full step as he limped across the bag. And then Wally was taking his arm as he turned off the line, shaking him angrily and saying, "What's the matter, Taft? You had it, man, you had it!"

"No," he said. "I won't take it that way."

"It was fair," Wally said. "Hammett slipped."

"He tripped himself," Taft Easterling said coldly. "I won't have pity, Wally. You hear me. If I make it, I make it square."

Wally McGoveran led him toward the dugout, holding his arm, and finally Wally said, "You're crazy, Taft. But I wish we were all your kind." Then McGoveran was in the dugout, his deep voice lashing out savagely, "I want two runs! Hit or I'll break every neck here!"

Taft Easterling slumped against the backboard and closed his eyes, letting Malone wipe his face and rub his ankle. He'd never make it now, he thought, but that was all right. If he couldn't do it the square way, he didn't want the honor. He heard the crowd roar and looked up as the single bulleted into center field; and another base hit was down the left field line, putting men on first and third. Russ Beyer hitched up his pants, spit in the dirt, and glared at their next hitter, young McCommiss. The kid waited and the first pitch was a rifle shot over Hammett into the deep hole, between Sipler and Ashton, rolling to the wall. Taft Easterling saw one run score, then another that tied the game, and McCommiss slide into third base with a triple. He called automatically, "Tied now, keep hitting," and then remembered. He sat forward, ashamed of his thoughts, the wish for no more runs and another chance. Beyer fanned their next man; and then Beyer unaccountably lost his control and walked a man, and as quickly retired the side on a weak grounder to second base. Taft Easterling did not move until Wally pushed him and said, "Get out there, Taft. You got another chance!"

He was happy, and he was furious, for he knew what Beyer had done. They'd walked one man on purpose, and after that Beyer could have tossed the ball and retired the side. Beyer had worked through the order until Taft Easterling was third man to bat in the last of the tenth. He crouched painfully in the field, trying to rationalize these confused thoughts, and watched the Quakers push home one run to go ahead. When he came in for the last of the tenth, the entire park was standing and Wally McGoveran was selecting a pinch hitter for their pitcher.

Taft Easterling took a drink and waited at the fountain while their catcher flied out; the pinch hitter was announced and the batboy pushed the bats between his trembling fingers and stepped away, young face tight and very near to tears. He stood in the on-deck circle and the pinch hitter grounded to third base; and then the clapping started, a low crescendo of sound that roared louder as he walked to the plate. Semick looked up at him pleadingly through the stained mask bars and said, "Taft, come on!"

"Look," Taft Easterling said hoarsely. "Andy . . . don't give me—"

Russ Beyer came off the mound in that funny, broken-ankled stride, arms swinging as he came down the alley and stood before the plate, glaring past him at Semick and Lou Jorda, but talking directly to him. Taft Easterling said, "Look, Russ—"

"You old goat!" Russ Beyer said scornfully. "How many lousy cripples do we have to give you? You couldn't hit me with a plank. I'm a generous man but, by God, there's a limit to this stuff. Stand up there and watch 'em go by, take your medicine. I'm through fiddling around!"

He stared at Beyer in astonishment that turned suddenly to rage. Beyer wheeled and almost ran back to the mound, called over to third base, "Relax, Willie, we're goin' home," and then turned, foot on the rubber, waiting for Semick's signal. Taft Easterling found himself crouching in the box, bat up and hands gripping the handle so tightly the white knuckle bones shone through the dirty brown skin.

"You—!" he said. "You big-mouth, you red-nosed reindeer! Come on, damn you, come on!"

Beyer nodded curtly and went into the windup, going far

back and deliberately showing all fingers, held for the fast ball. Taft Easterling could think of nothing in this moment but his vicious desire to even the score, show them all. No one had ever spoken to him like that in all his years.

Beyer came down and the ball was off the mound, white and fast, but not too fast, at belt height and without hop, the fattest, straightest pitch Taft Easterling had ever followed in his life; and behind it, dropping in the follow-through, was Beyer's face, daring him to hit the ball. He did not think now but swung from the heels and felt a solid, meaty contact. He dropped the bat and ran with all his failing strength; and saw the ball bouncing on the grass in right center field. Taft Easterling rounded first base and dug for second; and went in standing up as the long throw hit Hammett's glove. And then he saw their faces.

They were running in from the outfield, closing from the bases, and Hammett was walking over, holding out the ball; and Dascoli was calling time. All of them were smiling, broadly and with absolute joy; and Taft Easterling saw his own team rushing from the dugout, followed by the photographers. Then Russ Beyer was pushing through the crowd and grabbing his hand, pumping it up and down, yelling for a pen, grinning at him widely.

"You stubborn old fool," Beyer said. "We couldn't do it any other way, Taft. Had to get you riled up. The hit's in the book now, so what are you gonna do . . . turn it down?"

He saw their faces and felt Wally's arm slip around his shoulders; and he remembered then all the times he had drawn errors on infield smashes when the scorekeeper could have given him a hit; and all the times he had gotten the benefit of that doubt, so that refusing this last hit was a foolish and stubbornly senseless gesture. He hadn't really made it today; all the fifteen years had given him the magic circle, fairly and with full honor. He looked around while the flashbulbs popped, and then managed his old, slow smile and said, "I'll take it, Russ. Where's that pen?"

The Impossible Play

His wife called softly from the hall, "Time for breafast, Billy."
"All right," Billy Lawson said. "Be right down, Molly."

"It's a beautiful day," Molly said, "for a ball game."

Billy Lawson washed and dressed slowly in a freshly pressed tweed suit. He had slept fitfully during the night, but now, facing the day that meant more to him than any in his past, the worries and hopes and plans flooded into his mind and short, thick body so strongly that the pressure was nearly visible.

He adjusted his tie and walked downstairs with ramrod straightness, ate his usual ten-o'clock breakfast with a deliberate slowness, and rose to take his wife's arm and move through their house to the garage door. His wife was outwardly calm, but her fingers, touching his arm, trembled perceptibly when he opened the garage door and turned to kiss her good-by.

"See you at the stadium," Billy Lawson said.

"Yes," his wife said. "Madge is coming by in fifteen minutes. We'll be there early. Good luck, darling."

"Thanks," Billy Lawson said. "We'll need it."

He drove along the quiet street and as he stopped at the boulevard intersection, a neighbor boy called, "Good luck, Billy."

He waved and saw the boy's face, young and earnest, framed for a moment in his window, and then he was moving swiftly across the city, through familiar streets and old, time-grayed squares, moving even as time was passing forever. He waved to a policeman, an old friend of five years, and it seemed to him as if the city were buzzing with expectancy today. He remembered twenty years ago, in his own playing days, when they held up traffic for the parades, and all the people knew and waved at him and the other members of the team; he could remember one small boy who always greeted them at the stadium. It was a funny thing to remember after twenty years—a pennant race of long ago.

He made the last turn and saw the stadium ahead, light towers lifting high against the sky, pennants floating in the wind, and a great throng of people massed around the gates. He parked in the private section, and two policemen waved the people back, forming a tunnel from his car to the side entrance. He smiled at them and heard the cries of encouragement, all of them wishing him good luck. And then he was within the stadium, walking along the shadowed corridor toward something the writers liked to term a date with destiny.

He chuckled softly to himself, thinking that perhaps they were right, and came to the dressing-room door, hearing the voices inside. Like himself, the players had followed the old routine, getting up around ten and eating their light breakfast and reporting to the park by eleven for the afternoon game. He thought, *Here I go*, and entered the dressing room and watched them turn as one man.

He said, "Good morning," and walked halfway down the aisle and stood within their forming circle, sniffing the odors of all dressing rooms, unconsciously rubbing one shoe against the rubber-matted floor. It was time to go out and warm up, and they stood with him now, thirty men, awaiting his final words.

This was the moment he had dreaded since yesterday afternoon. Whatever he said—and he was at a loss for words—would mean a great deal to them. And yet, thinking back, what could he say? This was their day, and his, and talking could not change what they had done together throughout this season and what they would do on the field within two hours' time.

"We don't have to talk now," he said clearly. "I know you'll play your best. Take plenty of time warming up. Our lineup will be the same. Hanson will pitch." And then he paused, for to say more was to betray his feeling in the words trembling on his tongue. He smiled and said, "It's time," and watched them file out silently, spikes scratching dully as they crossed the corridor and went up the tunnel to their dugout. Only then, standing alone in the dressing room, did he allow himself to think of the past and what this day meant.

Above him, through the concrete-and-steel tiers of the stadium, the cheering was a dulled, happy roar. He was forty-eight years old this late September and that sound was still a fresh and wonderful thing to hear. He had played ball and heard that sound, before many of the people above him were born, and yet it remained the same through two wars and changing generations, a true essence and trademark of the game. All the years, he thought, all the games, all the players and people he had known through those years; many were gone, but he was here, one middle-aged man with his job hanging by a thread, with a dream in his heart and the decision a short two hours away. He had wanted this pennant for so long that even now, tied for the lead with the Redskins on the final day, with their one remaining game representing the payoff, it was difficult to realize that at last his dream was in sight.

He went into his small private office and began changing into his uniform and thought about himself and his team. He had ended his active playing days ten years ago and gone out to the minors as manager with one dream in his heart—that of returning to the big show and managing the Eagles to their first pennant in thirty years. Countless stories had been written about Billy Lawson playing twenty years on a second-division club, wasting his talent and career through a lifetime, never reaching that goal of all players—a pennant and the series.

He had stayed five years in the minors, winning four pennants in that time, and five years ago the new owner of the Eagles had called him back by popular demand. Hathaway wanted a pennant, was willing to build toward it, and assured Billy Lawson he would co-operate to the fullest extent. But Hathaway had never opened his bottomless purse, and other clubs siphoned away the prize rookies, and Billy Lawson had struggled against this handicap from the beginning. In the spring of this, Lawson's fifth year, Hathaway had laid down an ultimatum: Win or get out.

On paper they had no business in the first division, let alone being tied for the lead on the final day. The writers had been unanimous in their predictions when the season began—his Eagles would finish no higher than fifth, with fourth an outside chance—but all of them, heartily disliking Hathaway and respecting Billy Lawson, had expressed the hope he would win, would get that first pennant, the one he had wanted for thirty years.

Well, he had fooled them all up to this afternoon. His team was a strange mixture of youth and maturity; from the opening day in April he had nursed a secret hope they might play as a unit, catch fire, that pitchers would go the distance, infielders move swiftly, hitters would come through in the clutch. But most of all, knowing too well how shallow he was in depth, he prayed that injuries would skip them this one year. He had eight good men built around Rube Briggs and Sam Kennedy, with young Randy Miller the untried quality; injury to any one of those men might throw the entire team off balance.

Even with this behind them, and the future looking bright, Hathaway had called him in yesterday and said, "Win or I find another manager." Billy Lawson had swallowed the desire to smash Hathaway's face and quit on the spot. He could not give up now.

This pennant meant as much to Rube Briggs as it did to him.

For ten years that colorless but great, unsung player had given his best to the Eagles. A dozen times other clubs had offered Hathaway topnotch men and much cash for Rube Briggs; each time Hathaway wanted to sell, thinking of the money involved, and each time Rube Briggs refused to report if sold, especially after Billy Lawson took over as manager. Finally, two years ago, Rube Briggs had told Hathaway, "This is my team. I was a punk kid in my first year when Billy was finishing up. He's my friend. If we can't win a pennant together, then we'll go down trying." After that, as the word got around, the offers stopped.

And now Billy Lawson had Randy Miller, twenty-two years old and the fastest man in the league. Randy was green and, like many boys before him, hesitant about taking chances. Billy Lawson's biggest trouble with Randy was persuading the boy to cut loose, think on his own, do the things he was capable of accomplishing without signals from the manager. Randy would blossom in another year or two—Billy Lawson knew that—but until the moment came, the boy would not realize his full potential to the team. Randy had hit a solid .283 for the season, stolen twenty-eight bases, and improved each day in center field, with Rube Briggs and Sam Kennedy flanking him with advice and support. But today, when Billy Lawson needed the best from every man, he had to be doubly cautious with Randy. The boy had stood up magnificently under the pressure, but today was something different, a pressure worse than any other. No one could foretell how Randy might react. With the boy running those bases ahead of Rube Briggs and Sam Kennedy, using his own judgment instead of being overly cautious in following signals, nothing could stop them. All he could do was hope and wait, and take every break as it came.

Billy Lawson walked slowly through the tunnel and stood in the dugout's protective shade, rubbing his jaw and watching his men and the Redskins move on the field. And now his mind was fully concerned with the game. He saw the Redskin manager and waved his greeting, wondering how that young man felt today. They had entered this final three-game series tied for the lead, split the first two games, and in splitting had exhausted their already weary pitching strength. But the Redskins had big Rousch, who could throw with one day of rest, while he had no one but young Hanson. Hanson was twenty-four, still wild at times and apt to tighten under pressure. Hanson had three days' rest, however, and his other pitchers were dog-tired. He had decided yesterday; it would be Hanson.

When Hubbard signaled to play ball, Lawson smiled at his men and said, "Give your best," and sat erect and sober-faced in the dugout. In this moment he thought of the Redskins and how their owner, the past winter, had told the world that winning was everything, sportsmanship meant nothing; he had never believed in that philosophy, no matter the stake. Today would prove who was the better man.

He knew it would be close after Hanson's first pitch. His lanky boy had it today. They retired the Redskins in order and when they ran in to bat, he patted Randy Miller on the back and said, "Hit away, Randy," and walked to his coaching position at third base, waiting anxiously to see if Rousch was as right as Hanson.

Rousch was fast, with perfect control; more than that, Rousch was the meanest pitcher in the league to bunt when right. This would hurt them today. Rube Briggs batted in the second slot and had no peer in the league as a bunter and place hitter behind the runner, but against Rousch's fast-breaking inside hooks and hopping fast ball, delivered just under the letters, it was almost impossible for any man, even Rube, to lay the ball down decently.

Randy Miller worked up a three-two count, fouled off two pitches and drew a walk. Billy Lawson had to determine Rousch's effectiveness, and signaled for the sacrifice. Rube Briggs took the first pitch, a ball, swung viciously on the next delivery, and gave his own signal for the lay down. The ball hooked sharply and Rube could not hold it fair on the field.

Billy Lawson knew that Rousch was in deadly form. He signaled to hit away and waited.

Rube Briggs flied to left field and Sam Kennedy hit a long ball to deep center. Hank Cummings, the cleanup man, struck out. And then the innings were marching past, the Redskins scoring in the fourth, the Eagles tying it in the sixth.

Hanson was pitching his heart out, giving Billy Lawson the finest game of his youthful career, but the Redskins knew he was not overly strong. Billy Lawson had every man in his bullpen warming up when the seventh inning started; the Redskins were waiting Hanson out to the last possible pitch, knowing how much precious strength those few extra throws wasted.

They got through the eighth somehow—he wasn't sure— after the Redskins filled the bases with one away. Sam Kennedy raced in to snare a blooper fly in short left field and hold the runners with a bullet peg to the plate. Rube Briggs went against the wall and pulled down what seemed to be a sure hit for the third out, leaping and stabbing the line drive with his gloved hand.

Billy Lawson sat back weakly after that play, wondering if they could score and break the tie. But the middle part of his batting order went down on a strikeout and two easy ground balls.

Rube Briggs paused beside him and said, "We've got to do it next time, Billy."

"Yes," he said. "Next time, Rube."

He thought it was gone in the first of the ninth. The Redskin lead-off man singled sharply to center field, advanced to second on a beautiful sacrifice bunt by the manager, a deadly competitor in a tight spot, and went to third as Cummings threw the next batter out on a slow bounding ball along the third-base line. Billy Lawson could do several things now: walk one man and play for a force at two bases, or pitch to the batter. Hanson stepped behind the rubber and dusted his fingers on the rosin bag, waiting for Billy Lawson's command. Billy Lawson gave them the signal—pitch to the batter—and then, his sharp gray eyes moving ceaselessly over the field, caught the signal given by the Redskin third-base coach to the batter.

That coach had found some clue to Hanson's pitches, perhaps had saved this knowledge all season for such a critical moment. Billy Lawson knew his catcher would call for pitches on the outside corner against this Redskin batter, a consistent left-field pull hitter who occasionally bit on a fast outside pitch and popped it up. But the Redskin coach caught the delivery and gave his batter an oral command to step into the pitch.

Billy Lawson acted without thought, jumping to his feet and signaling to Rube Briggs far out in right field. Rube was playing the batter from long experience, but, wonderful team man that he was, he glanced automatically toward the dugout. He caught Billy Lawson's urgent signal and understood immediately.

He called sharply to Randy Miller, who had shifted toward left center, "This way fast on the pitch, Randy," and began his own movement as Hanson delivered the ball.

Billy Lawson held his breath and watched the batter step far into the outside pitch and drive the ball toward deep right center field. Randy Miller raced from center, getting that two-step break, and made the catch look easy, while Rube Briggs, cutting around to back up, turned without breaking stride and trotted in with Randy, tossing his glove in its usual spot behind first base and just outside the line. Billy Lawson found himself standing on the dugout rail while all around them, lifting in a great, happy flood of sound, the crowd released pent-up fear, then began pounding the boards in rhythm and changing the feeling of their roar, calling now for that last rally, that one run and the pennant.

Billy Lawson watched Rube Briggs cross the infield and thought, *They noticed nothing unusual about Rube's play. They'll never know what he's done for this team, for me, in this and a thousand other games.* No, he was old Rube Briggs, who, in the crowd's collective eye, ambled out and caught a couple of flies every game in the easiest position on the field, and protected his job by hitting all those bunts and singles and a few doubles every year for an unexciting .300 average. Ten years in right field, Billy Lawson thought, and no one would ever understand.

Rube sat beside him and said, "You called that one on the nose, Billy."

"You played it beautifully, Rube," Billy Lawson said.

Rube Briggs glanced at Hanson, now buttoning his jacket and rinsing his mouth at the fountain. Rube Briggs murmured, "He's done, Billy."

"I know," Billy Lawson said. "We've got to get it this time, Rube."

He started toward third base, and Rube Briggs said quietly, "We will. Pull all the stops this time, Billy. Everything goes."

Billy Lawson had been waiting for this moment so long that his body felt odd and far away. He considered the countless possibilities they faced when the final chips came down, with everything depending on him. He would give the signals and by those commands, right or wrong, they would win or lose. He knew, as Rube Briggs knew, as everyone in this stadium must understand, that Hanson had pitched his heart out and was finished. Billy Lawson had no pitcher capable of stopping the Redskins in extra innings; it was this time, this moment, the space between three outs. Actually, he thought sadly, his last chance, the moments between his first pennant and oblivion.

"Yes," he said, in the complete loneliness that surrounded him on the third base line. "Everything goes, Rube."

His lead-off man was the eighth-place batter, his catcher, followed by Hanson; and already the crowd was watching, waiting to see who would bat for Hanson. Billy Lawson had to make that decision now, weighing the Redskin pitcher, remembering batting averages and how his utility men had hit against Rousch. In the brief interval before his catcher stepped up, he turned toward the dugout and called, "Casper, hit for Hanson!"

Now the crowd would roar its instant disapproval, and Hathaway, in the owner's box directly behind the dugout, would become apoplectic. He knew what they were thinking: "Lawson's gone batty in the clutch." Sending a first-year rookie up at a time like this, with two experienced utility men on the bench. They would think that way, forgetting, as so many did under pressure, how young Casper had hit Rousch five times during the season, while the other utility men had failed against the same pitcher. He might be wrong or right, but that was the chance, the weighing of the odds.

His catcher worked a two-two count and hit the ball squarely; for a moment Billy Lawson's heart beat faster, before the ball thudded directly into the leaping glove of the Redskin manager at short for an unassisted out. And then young Casper stepped into the box, face working nervously, hands sliding up and down his bat handle. Billy Lawson gave the signal to hit away. Casper bit his lower lip and faced Rousch. Billy Lawson wanted to look and could not; he closed his eyes with the pitch, heard bat meet ball and forced himself to look.

Casper had topped a little dribbler to the mound and was thrown out by ten steps. Billy Lawson rubbed one hand across his eyes and turned from the coaching box, walking toward the on-deck circle where Randy Miller and Rube Briggs stood watching him anxiously. Billy Lawson raised his hand and called for time, and Hubbard stopped play.

"You all right?" Rube Briggs asked.

"Yes," he said. He looked at Randy Miller, and his mind refused to function, then seemed to trickle slowly over the past into bygone days, as if searching for the solution. He said, "Act like I'm giving you a pep talk. Randy, if you get on, steal second whenever you wish."

Randy Miller said grimly, "Maybe I'll be on second without stealing, Billy."

"Either way," Billy Lawson said softly. "Listen to me. When you are on second, Rube will bunt—"

"With two away?" Randy Miller said sharply.

"Rube will bunt," Billy Lawson murmured, and now his mind was fresh and clear and eager. "You hear me, Randy. When Rube bunts, you come all the way!"

Randy Miller said, "But—" and then stopped talking, his eyes suddenly shining with some new strength and feeling. He said, "Yes, sir. I'll come. Don't worry, Billy. I'll come all the way."

Billy Lawson watched the boy half run toward the plate and turned a last moment to Rube Briggs, who was watching him curiously. He said, "Did you hear me, Rube?"

Rube Briggs nodded. "It hasn't been tried for years, Billy. I'll lay that ball down if I have to use my teeth."

Billy Lawson said, "Pick your pitch, Rube, if Randy makes second. It's in your hands."

He returned to the third-base box and waited silently while Randy Miller smashed a two-two pitch down the third-base line, a grass cutter that skittered fair by inches inside the bag and bounced against the new box seats in left field. Randy rounded first and went on and came into second standing up; and then the crowd was deafening and Billy Lawson was watching Rube Briggs and thinking, *I'm a fool. If it doesn't work, we're beat, and I'm to blame.* But Rube Briggs smiled once, facing the pitcher, and, without speaking, seemed to say, "Don't worry. This one is for you."

Billy Lawson had guessed the Redskin strategy correctly. With a fast runner on second and two away, they would not walk Rube Briggs, setting up the force, because Rube had not hit Rousch all day; and behind him was Sam Kennedy, who might break up the ball game. They were playing the right odds in pitching to Rube. Billy Lawson knew he would play it that way himself. He saw the Redskin infielders move back deeply on the grass and the outfielders come in a few steps. They had not thought of a bunt, Billy Lawson saw with almost savage intensity.

Rube Briggs gave no signal, stepping into the box. Randy Miller

danced off second, shouting encouragement, watching the Redskin manager closely for their famous pickoff play. Rube Briggs
took the first pitch, a ball; took a strike, another ball and
another strike; and then stepped back to dust both hands and
give his bunt signal to Randy Miller before he moved again into
position. The loudest sound at this moment, Billy Lawson
noted, was the slap of the infielders' fists against their gloves;
the crowd was standing, one vast and silent entity waiting for
the pitch.

Rousch took his signal and delivered, giving everything he
had on this ball. Rube Briggs waited until the last possible
moment before swinging into the bunt; and even then, following the ball as it came in chest high on his short body and
dipped sharply, the worst kind of hooking, spinning ball for a
squatty man to bunt, did not come completely around. He
pushed the bat down along his shoulder and met the ball, in this
moment of sudden bedlam an artist poised against the eternal
background of his life work.

Running as he bunted, Rube Briggs felt the slashing spin of the
ball against his bat and wondered if it would hold and drop fair, if
he had enough wood on the ball; and then he had no time to
think, for the ball was gone forever on its way, and he was running
for first base, seeing Randy Miller already breaking for third.

Billy Lawson stood motionless, the hope and dream of twenty
years coming up thick and strong and living in his throat, his old
legs racing every step with Randy Miller as the boy rounded
third and went for the plate. It had been almost thirty years, Billy
Lawson thought strangely, since he watched Cobb make this
impossible play. He was a fool, he was losing his mind and his job
and a pennant, but his legs moved and his eyes saw everything on
the field. It was not to be, a feeling seemed to be crying aloud in
his chest, but somehow it had to be.

Billy Lawson saw the first and third basemen, caught far back,
charging belatedly from their deep positions; saw Rousch
almost on his knees from that last vicious, all-out follow-

through that came with his hoped-for last pitch, scrambling toward the rolling ball, half on his feet, knees and hands scraping the grass. He saw the Redskin catcher, as if in slow motion, begin his charge from behind the plate, hold up suddenly as realization struck him, then cover the plate and, voice completely lost in the crowd's roar, shout desperately for the ball. He saw Rube Briggs round first base safely as the Redskin third baseman reached the ball, now dead on the line halfway between home and third base. He saw the third baseman make a desperation one-handed stab and magnificent underhand toss to the plate, going head over heels with the force of his movement and landing sprawled out on the base line as ball and runner came together.

He saw Randy Miller, running faster than a man had a right to move under any condition, go headlong to the right of the plate, diving in a streak of twisted, blurred features and dust and spikes gleaming in the slanting sun, left hand darting out and slapping the white rubber as the Redskin catcher caught the chest high throw and lunged for him with the ball. He saw Hubbard standing over the play, huge and hunched low, arms at a strained, tight angle along his thighs; and then Randy Miller and the Redskin catcher were rolling together in a mad ball of arms, legs and faces, covered with the swirling dust as Hubbard was sheered from his own feet and rolled with them, all three stopping and lying completely still for one last, breathless moment.

Billy Lawson thought, *If it is my time to die, let if be now*, and waited.

Hubbard got to his knees, and then on his feet, and then extended his arms in the old, old gesture, palms down and fingers stretched tautly, while his deep voice, hoarse and trembling in the utter silence, called, "Safe!"

Billy Lawson could not remember the moments immediately following, but eventually he was sitting in the dressing room on a traveling trunk, shirt unbuttoned and torn half apart, his hands shaking as he shook, one after the other, the dirty, sweating hands of his men; and then, as bedlam increased and everyone seemed to be yelling and slapping backs and crying openly, the writers fought their way into the dressing room, with Hathaway and the photographers crowding behind. Rube Briggs had taken his shower and now sat beside Billy Lawson on the trunk, wrapped in a wet towel, his wide, usually placid face proudly red-eyed and wet with emotion.

The oldest writer, a friend of many years, motioned as many players into the group as possible, so that Randy Miller sat on his left with Rube on his right, while they snapped the pictures. As the flashbulbs popped and the big room quieted a few degrees, Billy Lawson could hear the crowd above and in the corridor outside, shouting as he could never recall a crowd going so happily crazy in the past.

The writer was grinning, and kneeling on one knee, oblivious of the water-soaked floor, and saying, "It's wonderful, Billy! How the devil can we write this? When did you decide to try that play?"

"When I saw we had to take the chance," Billy Lawson said.

"I hadn't seen it since Cobb retired," the writer said. "You played it all or nothing, didn't you?"

"Yes," Billy Lawson said humbly. "Hanson was finished. They had us licked if it went extra innings. We had to do it."

Hathaway had finally broken through and stood beside them, smiling broadly. The writer glanced up, and then said, "I know how you feel, Billy. I won't ask a lot of questions today. But I'd like to ask one that everybody in this city is waiting to hear. You've won your first pennant, Billy, the first for Rube Briggs, the first for this team in thirty years. What we want to know is," and the writer's voice turned sharply ironic, "now that you've won a pennant with such a strong team, if you should happen to lose the World Series next week, will you lose your job?"

In the silence that followed, a harsh and grimly angry silence, Hathaway turned white and then said, in a meek and surprisingly warm voice, filled with some new understanding, "He will not lose his job. You may quote me as saying I will offer Billy Lawson a contract for three years just as quickly as my lawyers can draw it up. Does that answer your question, Lance?"

The writer smiled and said softly, "It certainly does."

Billy Lawson patted Rube Briggs on one bare knee and got to his feet and stood short and poker-straight on the wet floor, pulling at his torn shirt and feeling for lost buttons. He smiled then and bent his head, and walked toward the door of his small private office.

The
Heavenly
World Series

J ohn McGraw came politely into the Lord's presence and
explained his problem with forceful eloquence. When John
finished, the Lord smiled thoughtfully. "And this argument
cannot be settled in another fashion, John?"

"We've tried," John said. "Lord, we've tried." Thereupon,
John talked for forty-two minutes, telling the Lord exactly what
he thought of those American League upstarts who, for so many
years, had been touting the superiority of their league.
Following a heated discussion that very nearly ended in a dis-
graceful fight, all parties agreed there was only one manner of
settling the argument forever: hold an All-Star World Series
between picked teams from the two leagues.

"Can this be done?" the Lord asked.

"Yes, sir," John said. "Judge Landis approves. The National
League has chosen me to manage. The American picked
Huggins. We'll select our teams and submit rosters to the
Judge; he'll bring them to you for final approval. After that it's
up to you, Lord."

"How so?"

"You select the starting date," John said. "Honor us with your
presence in the dugout box and throw out the first ball. You can

sit with us one game, then with the Americans, and so on. We'll play five out of nine for the championship, and it oughta be a sellout."

"That it should," the Lord agreed. "Have you picked a squad, John?"

"Not complete," John said. "So far I'm sure of Christy and Pete and Three-Finger on the mound. Bresnahan will catch. We'll have Wee Willie and Big Jim Delahanty in the outfield. At short, second, and first we naturally will start with Tinker, Evers, and Chance."

"Naturally," the Lord said. "And has Huggins picked his men?"

"The Big Train for starting pitcher," John said, frowning at the thought. "Rube Waddell, Eddie Plank, and some other bushers. They'll have the Babe of course, Lou on first, Eddie Collins at second, with Lazzeri backing up. When can we start, Lord?"

"Patience," the Lord said. "There are several details to iron out. For instance, umpires."

"Well, we've got Bill Klem behind the plate, but there's the catch. We can't locate another umpire in heaven. I guess—"

"I know," the Lord said sadly, "I know, John. Perhaps we can arrange a short option deal and bring up three more."

"Five," John said. "New rules for a series. Got to have them on the foul lines."

"I'll see," the Lord said. "I know Bill will do an excellent job. He always said he never called a wrong decision in his heart."

"Humph," John said. "Well, Lord. Can we play the series?"

The Lord pressed a button and waited until a new group of visitors were shown inside. John McGraw turned and saw the Judge, Miller Huggins, Ban Johnson, Abner Doubleday, and a dozen-odd other old-timers. The Lord smiled upon them all, and said, "I took the liberty of inviting the interested parties to join us, John. Judge, you and everyone here are familiar with the subject at hand. I wish clarification of certain points before you take the field. The type of ball, the rules to follow, uniform, rosters, pass lists, the segregation of players' wives in the dugout boxes. Can these things be worked out?"

"They are," Judge Landis said proudly, and placed a thick sheaf of papers on the Lord's desk. "We began yesterday, ironing out the details. Everything has been settled satisfactorily—" the Judge coughed humbly and added, "I made the final decision on certain small points, of course. Everyone agreed. If you will give us the go-sign, I'll handle everything."

"Well—" the Lord said.

"Think of it, Lord," John McGraw said eagerly. "To see them all again on the same field!'

"You are persuasive, John," the Lord said. "Tinker to Evers to Chance," he murmured. "Ruth and Gehrig. What a sight to see. Gentlemen, I bow to your sincerity. We shall have our series. For the duration all players will once again play in an atmosphere of time, corresponding to their very best seasons on earth. Thus, each man will be at his top."

"When do we start?" John McGraw said happily.

"One week from today," the Lord said. "We'll use the new stadium. I regret that it seats only two hundred thousand but we'll heavenize all the games so that every fan can watch if they do not secure a ticket. I was thinking of Graham McNamee doing the commentary."

"The only one," Judge Landis said. "Sid Mercer and Hype Igoe will be official scorers. Damon in charge of the press box. Now, Lord, if there's nothing else—?"

"Not now. Gentlemen, you have a week to practice and make ready. I will see you all at the first game." As they filed away, the Lord added softly, "With misgivings."

When the news spread, excitement bubbled up in every corner of heaven. Heated arguments over eligible players occupied the time of countless fans; these, and other points of question, were settled with the appearance of rosters and all rules covering the series. At the same time, messages went out to players selected by the respective leagues; by nightfall the two squads had gathered in their special quarters near the stadium. The National League was assigned the stadium for morning workouts, the American League taking over in the afternoons, with six days of practice before the first game. The Babe reported two hours late and listened meekly while Huggins dressed him down, and thereupon ordered two dozen hotdogs and wandered off to join a group of selected friends in a quiet all-night card game.

While the daily workouts continued, the fans were informed of the seating arrangements for the series. Ticket holders to be chosen by lot from all districts of heaven. National League fans would occupy that half of the stadium behind their team's third base dugout, American League fans behind first base. One section in the centerfield bleachers, directly under the flagpole, was reserved for Brooklyn fans, this deemed a wise spot by the Lord, knowing the volatile temperament of those enthusiasts. Players' wives were in their respective boxes, carefully sorted out so that wives of two shortstops were not seated together, and so on through the rosters. The new ball would be used but pitchers might employ any special methods used during their careers on earth. Concessions were in charge of Mr. Stevens and medical aid on the grounds was assigned to Doctors Lister and Hyland, assisted by Florence Nightingale. Five bands under Sousa's baton would play. Game time was two o'clock and the lights would be turned on if necessary to complete any extra-inning game.

The stadium was packed at noon on opening day. When John McGraw appeared before the Nationals' dugout and Miller Huggins popped up behind first base in the Americans' dugout, a great roar of applause filled the air. The Nationals, by right of seniority, took batting practice first; and Cy Blanton went to the mound, with Ned Hanlon standing behind him, tossing out the balls and watching the hitters step up and swing. Uncle Wilbert Robinson, resplendent in a tan gabardine suit, plumped down on the Nationals' bench, took a generous chew, and made mysterious notes on a large pad. Along the first base side, the American Leaguers warmed up leisurely while Huggins and Fielder Jones held sober counsel in the dugout shade. When the Babe and Gehrig came on the field, the cheer was loud and long. The Babe turned, face split in that broad, red grin, and lifted his cap in answer. Writers and photographers crowded up behind the batting cage; high above in the press box, the old-timers were batting out a few lead paragraphs of local color. Irvin S. Cobb arrived and sat carefully in a special, reinforced chair. Damon Runyon and Sid Mercer ate a lunch of cheesecake and hamburgers, while Hype Igoe prepared the official scorebooks. And down on the green field, the Nationals moved in and out of the batting cage. . . .

First came Bresnahan, then Kling, and McGuire, Jim Wilson and Ivy Wingo and Chief Zimmer; then Frank Chance and Cap Anson and Kitty Bransfield, Jake Daubert and Konetchy, Foghorn Tucker and Eagle Eye Beckley; then Evers and Kid Gleason, Joe Tinker and Art Fletcher and Herman Long, Mike Mowrey, and Harry Steinfeldt; then the outfielders moved in and the fans were cheering as the balls sailed far against the distant walls, four hundred feet down each foul line, five hundred and fifty to dead center—Delahanty and Keeler and Joe Kelly, Bill Hamilton and Sherry Magee and Bill Lange, Jim O'Rourke and Frank Schulte, Joe Schultz and Jimmy Sheckard and Ross Young, Kiki Cuyler and finally Hack Wilson who drove five into the distant stands.

The gong sounded and the Nationals trotted off. Urban Schocker and Matt Kilroy came out to pitch the Americans' batting practice, with Hugh Jennings carrying the ball bag and releasing a loud, happy, "Eee-yah!" as he took station behind the mound. Then the Americans took their turns in the cage—Gabby Street and Les Nunamaker, Pinky Hargrave and Ossee Schreckengost. A fan yelled, "Nailed any steaks to the wall lately, Ossee?" and Schreckengost grinned broadly as he finished hitting and trotted off to the bullpen. Then came Gehrig and Eddie Collins and Lazzeri, Ducky Holmes and Ray Chapman, Kid Elberfeld and Eric McNair; and Kid Foster, Dots Miller, Harry Lord, fewer infielders than the Nationals boasted, but good men all. Then Chick Fewster stepped in, followed by Fielder Jones, Germany Schaefer and Bob Veach; then came Harry Heilmann who drew a tremendous roar of applause; and finally the Babe stepped in, chewing a hotdog and waving his big bat. The stands roared, "Over the wall!" and the Babe began driving them far, far out over the grass, the white balls bouncing in the upper deck of the right center stands. Charley Comiskey sat in the Americans' dugout, counting those balls, adding up the total, and frowning over the cost. Matt Kilroy made his final pitch, the gong rang, and the groundkeepers came out to remove the cage and screens. John McGraw shouted from the dugout and Ned Hanlon walked out to hit the Nationals' infield workout.

On this first day the Nationals were the home team, taking their outs; thereafter last bats would alternate each day. While infield practice moved along, John McGraw gathered his coaching staff for the last minute strategy, and Christy Mathewson moved up to begin his warm-up pitches to Chief Zimmer. Miller Huggins and his coaches were talking in the tunnel behind their dugout, and Walter Johnson stepped from the shadows with Gabby Street and began throwing easily from the first-base rubber. Infield practice was almost through, then finished, and it was five minutes until game time. Judge Landis came down the aisle with the Lord to the box behind the Nationals' dugout; the stadium rose and applauded them, and Judge Landis gave them all a handwave and flirt of his long white hair. The Judge waved McGraw and Huggins over for the box picture, and cleverly stole the scene from the Lord with his chin-on-hands pose against the rail. Then Bill Klem came from the tunnel with his umpires for the plate meeting, and the P.A. system called out the starting lineups, and as the names rolled across the clear blue sky, the crowd fell silent in this great moment.

"Starting for the National League," the huge speakers blared, "leading off and playing second base, Johnny Evers; centerfield, Wee Willie Keeler; left field, Jim Delahanty; right field, Hack Wilson; first base, Frank Chance; third base, Harry Steinfeldt; catching, Roger Bresnahan; shortstop, Joe Tinker . . . and pitching, Christy Mathewson!"

The applause rose and died away expectantly, and the announcer spoke again: "For the American League: at second base, Eddie Collins; centerfield, Bob Veach; right field, Babe Ruth; first base, Lou Gehrig; left field, Harry Heilmann; short-stop, Ray Chapman; third base, Kid Foster; catching, Gabby Street . . . and pitching, Walter Johnson!"

The Lord turned to Judge Landis. "It seems the Americans have a preponderance of hitting power."

"Maybe a little," Judge Landis said cautiously, "but don't value that too much. This will be speed against power."

"And I see we are commencing much as I suspected," the Lord said drily, glancing toward home plate, where McGraw and Huggins were arguing heatedly. Bill Klem allowed them a minute, then cut off further talk with a sharp word. McGraw turned away wrathfully and Bill Klem approached the Lord's box with a shining white ball. The Lord stood and made a perfect throw to home plate, where a scramble ensued and Pongo Joe Cantillon emerged triumphant with the prize. Bill Klem dusted off the plate, moved behind Bresnahan, and called,

"Play ball!"

Eddie Collins stepped to the plate, and Mathewson took his sign, went up and came down in that beautiful sweeping motion; the ball was a white streak across the inside corner for the called strike. Collins grounded out to third and entered the Americans' dugout, shaking his head, for Christy was fast today. Veach fanned on three pitches and Ruth stepped in, worked up a two-two count, and swung mightily on a curve ball that broke beneath his flashing bat. John McGraw barked at his men as they came off the field, his face red with pride in their beginning. And on the mound, throwing easily, Johnson waited for the first National batter.

"Christy looks sharp today," the Lord said.

"Never better," Judge Landis agreed. "Now watch the Big Train."

Johnny Evers stepped to the plate and the National League fans greeted him with a tremendous roar of applause. Johnson came down with his first pitch, a blazing fast strike that left the bat helpless in mid-air.

Evers fanned and Wee Willie Keeler waggled his short bat, crouched low in the box, looking for that hole to send his famous push shot. Johnson gave him a curve, then the fast one on the outside and Keeler grounded to second base, an easy hop and throw. Big Jim Delahanty stepped in, took a ball, and connected with the next pitch. The crowd yelled, then sighed, as Veach gathered it in centerfield for the third out.

And then the game was moving through the early innings with gathering intensity. McGraw exhorted his men and Huggins spoke quietly, and the coaches barked on the baselines as the batters came and went. Up came the great hitters, and down they fell as Christy and Walter dueled through the second and third without a hit, then the fourth, and into the fifth and sixth; and still it was a hitless game.

The seventh passed, and the eighth; the press-box was silent with wonder and expectation. Runyon wrote a lead and ripped the page from his typewriter as the eighth inning destroyed its meaning. In the dugouts, players studiously avoided any mention of innings as Christy and Walter toweled their faces and sipped water. Mathewson began the ninth by fanning Kid Foster, got Street on three pitches, and mowed Johnson down in the same way. John McGraw turned along the dugout line and sent Van Haltern up to hit for Bresnahan in the Nationals' half of the ninth.

Van Haltern flied out to left field, Joe Tinker fanned, and Bill Hamilton went in to hit for Christy. Johnson took a hitch in his pants, fingered the ball carefully, and set Hamilton down with three fast balls that looked small and fleeting in the bright sunlight. McGraw turned to Ned Hanlon and said, "Send Brown in," and watched the American bench closely. When Johnson slipped into his jacket and disappeared down the tunnel, McGraw grinned and rubbed his stubby hands together. "We'll get 'em now," he chortled. "We'll get 'em, boys!"

And across the field, Miller Huggins got the nod from Fielder Jones that Eddie Plank was warm and ready to go. Huggins said, "Plank goes," and turned to call encouragement as Eddie Collins stepped to the plate. Three Finger Brown began his chore on the mound; and it might have been the crowd, or Hugh Jennings snarling at him from the third base coaching box, for he walked Collins and faced Veach as the signs went on. McGraw was signaling his bullpen and waving his centerfielder over; and the crowd was humming with expectation.

"What do you think, Judge?" the Lord asked.

"I don't know," the Judge said. "I've just witnessed a great sight—two perfect nine inning pitching jobs. What else can happen?"

"Whatever it is," the Lord said, glancing at John McGraw, "it will."

Veach hit the first pitch into left center for two bases, Collins pulling up at third as Keeler made a fine cutoff and throw. And then the Babe was striding in, McGraw was signaling the intentional pass, and the crowd was booing mightily—from the Americans' side—as the Babe took four balls and trotted down to first. Gehrig came up for his fourth trip and no one thought he could be held longer. But as Lou smashed a terrific liner down the first base line, Chance was over and making the stab and doubling Ruth off first, all in one beautiful motion, then making the long throw across to third, barely missing a triple play. McGraw was talking to himself in the Nationals' dugout, face red with excitement. When Heilmann flied deep to Keeler in center, ending the inning, Uncle Wilbert Robinson came off the bench and welcomed his boys with great backslaps and much expectoration.

McGraw was shouting, calling for that run, but Eddie Plank stepped to the rubber and mowed the Nationals down. Evers grounded to second, Keeler poked a single between short and third, but this was a short-lived hope as Delahanty hit into a fast double play, Chapman to Collins to Gehrig: and the tenth was over. And the eleventh went in the same fashion, as Brown grew stronger and Plank, after allowing hits by Chance and Wilson, retired the side without further trouble. The Lord said, "Judge, this surely can't go on," and Judge Landis answered, "You never know, Lord."

Plank fanned to start the twelfth but Eddie Collins got his first hit, a line single to center, and Huggins played against the percentages, having Veach lay it down. Brown threw Veach out at first, but Collins danced off second and the Babe was up. McGraw again signaled the walk, and again the American fans roared their protest. The Babe trotted to first and Gehrig stepped in, took a strike, and then the ball was going deep down the line in right, bouncing against the wall and coming back. Collins scored and Wilson made a wonderful throw to the infield that held Ruth on third. Heilmann was walked purposely and Chapman did his best, but the sinking liner was gobbled up by Keeler in short center. The Americans had one run, and McGraw was on the dugout as his team came in, ruddy-faced once more, tongue working overtime.

Evers worked Plank to a three-two count, then grounded to short as the National fans groaned. Keeler got a walk and McGraw sent Big Jim Delahanty up to hit away. Everyone knew that when Big Jim missed a first strike, and then the Nationals were yelling madly as the ball was smashed into left center, a long rolling drive that caromed off the fence for three bases, scoring Keeler with the tying run. Hack Wilson stepped in and Miller Huggins gave the order to pitch to him. Plank spat morosely on the grass and threw a fine breaking curve. The ball was a flash down the third base line, then into Foster's glove, and Delahanty was doubled off in the next split second, ending the inning.

The thirteenth inning was scoreless, and the fourteenth found Ruth leading off. The Babe growled, "Now walk me, you bushers," and smashed Brown's first pitch high and far toward the right field wall. The ball went up and over, into the upper deck, and the Babe cavorted around the bases, tipping his cap. He shook Gehrig's hand, and ambled into the Americans' dugout, while McGraw glared in helpless rage. When Gehrig singled sharply to center, McGraw called time and had a conference at the mound. Brown scowled and finally McGraw left him in. Heilmann came up and the strategy paid off in a fast double play, Tinker to Evers to Chance. Chapman singled to left field and McGraw shouted angrily at Brown, but Foster grounded to third to end the inning.

"Well," the Lord said. "This will surely do it."

"Evers is leading off," Judge Landis said. "Don't be too sure, Lord."

Evers singled to center and Keeler sacrificed perfectly. Delahanty took two balls and singled to right center, bringing Evers home with the tying run. Huggins went out for a conference and McGraw shouted at Klem to make the Americans stop stalling. Hack Wilson popped to second and Chance stepped in, took a strike, and singled to left field, a great throw by Heilmann holding Delahanty at second. Steinfeldt flied to center and the National fans sighed with chagrin as the inning ended and the game remained all square.

The Americans went down in order, in their half of the fifteenth, and Huggins sent Waddell in to pitch against the

Nationals. The Rube toed the rubber with great confidence, facing Jim Wilson, and Wilson promptly singled to center. Joe Tinker laid down the sacrifice and Wilson stood on second base, shouting insults at the Rube. McGraw glanced along the bench and sent Cap Anson up to hit for Brown; and Anson, working the Rube slowly, fouled off three pitches on the full count and drew a walk. Johnny Evers flied deep to left field and the Americans breathed more easily; and then Keeler slashed a looping single into center.

"It's over," the Lord said.

"Not yet," Judge Landis shouted. "Look at that throw!"

For Veach was racing in, taking the ball with a scoop, making the low, hard throw to the plate where Gabby Street took the one hop and applied the ball vigorously to the sliding Wilson. Klem bellowed, "Out!" and the Nationals erupted from their dugout, milled around home plate, and were sent flying by Klem's angry stare and curt word.

Jeff Tesreau came out to pitch for the Nationals, and Veach grounded out to short, opening the sixteenth. Ruth drew his third walk and Gehrig, ordered to hit away, singled to left field with the Babe pulling up at second. Heilmann fouled a long ball into the left field stands and hit into a fast double play, Tinker to Evers to Chance, their second of the game, the Babe advancing to third. Chapman worked Tesreau for another walk, but Foster fanned to finish that threat; and the Nationals came in, talking it up, only to go down in order before the Rube's flashing speed and great curve.

"Rube looks good," the Lord said.

"True," Judge Landis said, "but Huggins wants that run."

Pinky Hargrave came up to hit for Gabby Street and relieve him of a long catching chore. Pinky singled to right field and Huggins sent Kid Elberfeld up to hit for Waddell. The Rube promptly tore up a jacket and stormed into the tunnel, yelling back at Huggins as he left the field. Elberfeld laid down a sacrifice, advancing Hargrave to second, but the strategy went for naught as Collins and Veach ground in succession to Evers, and again the game went on. Addie Joss came out to pitch for the Americans and retired the Nationals in perfect order in their half of the seventeenth.

"What is the record, Judge?" the Lord asked. "For a game?"

"Twenty-six innings," the Judge said. "And I certainly hope this doesn't go that long."

"Or longer," the Lord mused, half to himself.

The Babe was leading off and taking a ball. Then he drove one deep into right center, nearly five hundred feet to the wall where Keeler gathered it in. Gehrig walked but the Nationals were talking it up, confident now, just before lightning struck. Heilmann, hitless all day, goat of two double plays, drove a liner between left and center, good for three bases and the run as Gehrig crossed the plate. Tesreau shook off McGraw's bellow of rage, walked Chapman, and made Foster hit into a double play started by Evers. But the damage was done, and the crowd was sullen on the Nationals' side as their men came in to hit.

Eagle Eye Beckley came on to hit for Tesreau and singled to right field. Johnny Evers sacrificed and Keeler popped another looping single into centerfield, scoring Beckley and tying up the game. When Delahanty doubled on the first pitch, sending Keeler around to third, the Nationals came up from their dugout and shouted hoarsely for that one big run. Hack Wilson stepped in and Huggins, knowing how far Wilson might hit a ball in the air, gave the order to walk the batter. Then Chance drove a fly into left field and the crowd came up, sensing the finish as Heilmann judged the drop and came on the run and Keeler crouched at third. The ball was caught and the runner was streaking for home, and the throw came in, a perfect strike that nailed Keeler by five feet for the third out.

"I don't know," Judge Landis said weakly. "Now I sure don't know how long we'll be here."

"Oddly enough," the Lord said, "I feel the same way, Judge."

Amos Rusie came out to pitch for the Nationals in the nine-teenth, and retired the side, with one single by Collins the only damage. Addie Joss treated the Nationals in identical fashion, and the game was in the twentieth inning. Rusie again set the Americans down, getting through the murderous trio of Ruth, Gehrig, and Heilmann; but Joss had plenty of trouble in the Nationals' half. Tinker grounded to third and Rusie fanned, but Johnny Evers singled and Keeler sent him to third with a bloop double down the right field line. Huggins called the walk to Delahanty, filling the bases, and brought in Coveleskie to pitch against Hack Wilson. The switch worked as Wilson fanned on Coveleskie's flashing two-two count curve ball.

And up came Eric McNair to hit for Chapman and play shortstop. McNair drew a walk, and Huggins sent up Ducky Holmes to bat for Kid Foster. Rusie pitched carefully, expecting the sacrifice, but Holmes faked a first pitch bunt and drove a single into left field. McNair stopped at second and Hargrave sacrificed both runners along. Fielder Jones came in to bat for Coveleskie and McGraw ordered the walk to fill the bases. Jones trotted down to first and Eddie Collins passed two strikes, took a close ball, and lined the next pitch into center. McNair and Holmes, running like the wind, were in to score as Chance cut off the late throw and held Collins at first. McGraw retired to the deep center of the dugout, and the Lord heard sounds of futile rage as Veach hit into a double play and ended the inning.

Big Ed Walsh came in to pitch for the Americans, and McGraw sent Ross Young up to bat for Hack Wilson and play right field. Young singled to left and Frank Chance, ever dangerous in the clutch, smashed a ringing double into right-center and pushed Young to third base. Up came Steinfeldt, and in from the Americans' bullpen came Jake Chesbro to relieve Walsh who apparently didn't have it today. Huggins talked with Big Jake, who nodded and shifted his plug, and made his warmup throws. Steinfeldt was passed purposely, filling the bases. Ivy Wingo batted for Jim Wilson and struck out. Joe

Tinker, riding a miserable batting slump, fanned on three pitched balls; and McGraw sent Jake Daubert up to bat for Rusie.

"Chesbro looks very capable," the Lord said hopefully.

"Ever check Daubert's record?" Judge Landis asked, "Don't anticipate, Lord."

The words were scarcely spoken when Daubert's bat flashed, the ball was over shortstop in the hole, and two runs were scoring to tie the game again and send the Nationals' fans into wonderful spasms of joy. Daubert was on second, Steinfeldt on third, and Evers coming up. Chesbro spat eloquently on the grass and walked Evers then got Keeler on a weak grounder to second base. The inning was over, but again the game was tied.

"Five to five," the Lord said. "This simply can't go on much longer."

Vic Willis was now pitching for the Nationals and getting into trouble at once. Ruth singled, Gehrig singled with the Babe taking second base. Heilmann lashed a terrific hit to right field and Jennings, yelling like a pirate, sent the Babe for the plate. Young's throw came in low and true, and Ivy Wingo tagged Ruth three feet up the line, but Gehrig had raced to third and Heilmann reached second on the throw. McGraw called the walk, and McNair was passed to first: and now Dots Miller, playing third base, stepped up for his first time at bat. The infield played back for two and Miller lofted a fly to left field on the second pitch.

"Here's a run," the Lord said.

"And here's a throw," Judge Landis said.

For Delahanty made the catch and again Jennings sent the runner in, trying to make a break. Gehrig and the ball arrived together, but Wingo's quick tag was seen by many as Klem raised his right arm in the out sign. With Heilmann on third and McNair on second, Willis shook his head stubbornly at McGraw's signal, and fanned Hargrave for the third out.

Chesbro mowed the Nationals down in their half of the

twenty-second inning; and the twenty-third went by without a threat by either team. Ruth opened the twenty-fourth by flying deep to centerfield, and Gehrig hit to the same spot. The Lord said, "Two away, no danger now," and shook his head in complete surprise as Harry Heilmann drove a home run into the far reaches of left field. McNair grounded out to short, but again the Americans had their lead; and the way Chesbro was pitching it looked dark for the Nationals.

Keeler popped to second base, leading off and Delahanty immediately doubled to left field. Ross Young was walked, Chance laid a surprise bunt down the first base line and beat it out, to fill the bases. Steinfeldt fouled off two pitches. and hit a long fly ball to dead centerfield, four hundred feet out. Delahanty scored from third and it was tied again.

Wingo grounded to third, ending the inning, and the Americans ran in to start the twenty-fifth. Willis set them down in order, and Chesbro did the same to the Nationals, getting Foghorn Tucker, the one pinch-hitter, when he batted for Willis. Red Donahue came on to pitch for the Nationals as the twenty-sixth inning started, and Judge Landis said, "This ties the record, Lord."

"I trust it won't be broken," the Lord said wearily.

Eddie Collins was an easy out to second base, but Veach singled sharply to left field and the Babe, taking one menacing swing at the ball, played it cunning and dumped another single into left field, pushing Veach to second. Lou Gehrig ran up a two-two count and drilled one into centerfield, scoring Veach and sending Ruth to second. McGraw called time and stalked to the mound, while Joe McGinnity came from the bullpen to relieve Donahue.

McGinnity took his warm-up pitches, shifted his chew to the left cheek, and delivered one ball to Heilmann. That was hit like a bullet past the mound, and then the crowd was up and roaring as Tinker made a diving catch, kicked second base to double the Babe, and flipped over to first, doubling Gehrig and completing a triple play to end the inning. The Nationals rushed in while the crowd went wild, and the Lord said, "I am immune to anything else, Judge."

Judge Landis wiped his glistening forehead with a fine lawn handkerchief and said weakly, "Me, too."

Big Delahanty singled and Ross Young slashed another hit into right center that carried Delahanty to third. Huggins was up on the dugout step as Chesbro pitched to Chance. Chance dropped a bunt along the third base line and beat it out as Delahanty scored and Young held up at second.

Huggins called time and Pennock came on from the Americans' bullpen. "Was saving him for tomorrow," the Judge explained. "Huggins is getting desperate."

Pennock finished his throws and faced Steinfeldt. The third baseman took a ball, a strike, swung hard on the next pitch. The Lord saw a flash of white toward shortstop, then the American fans were going wild as McNair collared the line drive, raced over and tagged second, and threw to Gehrig for another triple play. McGraw was close to a conniption fit as the Americans ran off the field to bat in their half of the twenty-seventh; and Judge Landis simply murmured, "It's a new record now."

The triple play seemed to shake McGinnity. McNair walked and Dots Miller laced a double down the left field line, sending McNair to third base. McGraw ordered the intentional pass to Hargrave; and while McGinnity pitched wide to Wingo, John looked down the line toward his bullpen. On the Americans' side, Miller Huggins turned from the dugout step and motioned to someone; and as that pinch batter came to the bat rack and moved toward the circle, the P.A. system announced, "Tony Lazzeri batting for Pennock."

"Takes me back a good many years," Judge Landis said absently. "I remember that day in 1926 when . . . Lord, look!"

Lazzeri was in the box and McGraw was calling time; and from the shadows down the left field line, a bent-shouldered man was making the long walk to the mound. McGraw was coming out to join him, and the P.A. system blared again, "Coming in to pitch for the Nationals . . . Grover Alexander!"

Old Pete came on and took the ball from McGraw, and made eight leisurely throws to the plate, took a hitch in his baggy pants, and faced Lazzeri with the bases full and none out. And the stadium was silent in this moment, sitting back and watching, unable to find more shouts or claps after so much drama, now faced with a scene once played and being repeated before their awed gaze. Both teams were up as one man, lining their dugout rails, and the press-box was a sea of faces pressed against the wire high above the field.

"I wonder—" Judge Landis murmured. "I just wonder if it will happen again."

Alexander delivered and the ball was a streak, white and fast, on the inside corner and dipping across the plate; and Lazzeri swung and the sound was sharp and decisive in the stillness. The ball was over third and winging deep down the line toward the left field stands, going, going, and gone into a waving ocean of outstretched hands; and then the foul line umpire far down the left line was signaling foul, and the third base umpire was signaling fair, and Bill Klem was throwing his mask to the ground and glaring toward them in helpless, confused rage.

"Fair," Judge Landis said.

"Foul," murmured the Lord.

"FAIR!" Huggins was shouting, racing toward the plate and from the Nationals' dugout, screaming, "FOUL . . . FOUL!" came John McGraw. Instantly home plate was a mass of red faces and waving arms as McGraw and Clarke and Stallings swarmed around Klem; and Huggins danced up and down with furious rage, abetted ably by Hughie Jennings and Cantillon and Charley Comiskey, all shrieking, "Fair!" at the top of their lungs. Now the players were joining the argument, and McGraw had his nose against Klem's, and the other umpires were running in, waving their arms. McGraw roared something and Lazzeri gave him a shove; and then it started.

"I knew it!" the Lord said.

"STOP!" Judge Landis bellowed. "STOP, I SAY!"

"Such language," someone said, behind the Lord. The Lord turned and saw Ban Johnson grinning at him from the next box. The Lord found time to smile in return, an understanding grin at Ban Johnson who had suspected all along what might happen.

The Lord turned and called, "All right, boys!" and as suddenly as the fight began, it ceased and they all faced the Lord with sheepish eyes downcast. The Lord said, "All of you come over here. . . . Now listen to me . . . Bill, was it fair or foul?"

"Lord," Klem said, "I've got good umps. One said fair, the other foul. What can I say?"

"Exactly," the Lord said gently. "And what about the argument . . . which league is the best. One says the American, another the National. And you have played twenty-six innings of wonderful baseball, and no one has won the first game. Even when I brought back time, gave each of you to this series as you were in your top year on earth. You promised there would be no arguments; no strong words exchanged, no hot tempers, but you see—" the Lord smiled—"it is impossible to play the game without a good rhubarb now and then, and heaven is no place for that. Gentlemen, you can never settle the argument for one simple reason: neither league is better than the other. You are both the best in baseball, you will always be so. Should we continue, nothing would be proved. I doubt if we could ever finish the series. So I am calling it off as of now. There'll be no more of this in heaven . . . I couldn't stand it."

As the announcement went out to the crowd and the Lord departed from the stadium with Judge Landis and Ban Johnson, John McGraw slumped disconsolately beside Uncle Wilbert in the dugout shade and was heard to murmur, "I still say we can beat the ears of them bushers—"

Nothing New

W hen you think of the game and how it has been played all
these years, it seems as if nothing new can happen now;
and this in the technical sense of the word is true. All the plays
under the hot sun or boldly silhouetted light towers have been
made by great men in the past years; and the young men, blazing
now like the lights, and making those magnificent plays, are
simply the flesh and blood reincarnation of the old-timers long
gone from the field. The decisions and rulings and arguments
have all been seen and heard before, so that today we really hear
them as echoes from the past. Even the fans shouting hoarsely
from the stands, using the current slang of the present, are no
more than the sons of their fathers expressing the rougher and
perhaps finer language of the past in a sharp and biting modern
idiom. But new things still happen, and I will never forget the
day we sat high above the screen and forgot our typewriters for
two hours, watching Elbertson make plays that, in the truest and
greatest sense of the word, had never been made before.

I had talked with him that morning, just a few minutes in his
hotel room, and he was nervous on the eve of his first game in the
majors. He wouldn't have talked, even to me, if it had not been
my good luck to know him for several years; and on that day I
didn't blame him. I knew how he felt, or thought I did. I had gone

through the same feeling years ago, and when my legs gave out and I discovered a rusty talent for putting words together, I continued to watch and see the players come and go, and write about them. But even so, with the weight of years and past experience, I felt somehow that I did not know everything in his mind.

I had met him just before the war in a small town west of Omaha. It was one of those fair games and he was playing short for a traveling team. I had stopped in Omaha, enroute to the west coast, and someone mentioned that his team had been mopping up the local semi-pros in a series of games played throughout the state. I asked if they had an outstanding man and the man told me yes, they had a shortstop who played the game beautifully and hit with regularity. I had five hours between trains. We drove west over the river hills and into a long valley and came to the town holding the fair. I do not remember the town or the people or the fairgrounds; for once the game began and I saw him take the first smoking ground ball from a rough, pebble-speckled infield and make his long throw from the right, I saw no one but Elbertson.

He was all over the field that hot afternoon, playing a spirited game at short and getting four for four against better than average semi-pro pitching. I shoved through the crowd after the game and managed to catch him at their bus. I introduced myself and he waited for me to extend my hand, and then shook it warmly and firmly, smiling at me shyly. I told him how much I enjoyed his playing and hitting, and he thanked me. The others were piling equipment aboard the old bus and the manager, a small gnome of a man, was shouting, "Hurry up, hurry up. We got two hundred miles to drive tonight."

I said, "You're ready for triple A right now, you know that?"

"Thank you," he said softly. "I think I could hold my own, Mr. Thatcher."

"Have you been with this outfit long?" I asked.

"Just during the summer," he said seriously. "I'm in college on the west coast. I got to be back the middle of September."

"How many years left?" I asked.

"Two," he smiled. "If I'm lucky. This is school money I'm making in the summer time."

And then we had no more to say, for they were waiting for him. I called, "Good luck, Elbertson. I'll see you again. And I'll tell a couple of men about you."

His face broke into a smile, white teeth shining, and he waved from the dirty window as they lumbered across the race track and out the main gate onto the highway. I watched him go and thought of the great shortstops I had known, and felt that I had seen another. And then the war came and in the rush of things, I lost track of him. I did not hear of him again until the summer of 1946.

We were in St. Louis and it was August, and no one hated that river weather as I did in late summer. I had played there too many times, and now sat in the pressbox, my shirt wringing wet, trying to get excited about the ball game which, in all honesty, was just one in a never-ending string of hot weather games between two clubs out of the race. We were talking about this and that, remembering the old days when two hundred people made a record-breaking crowd at these games; and someone said, "Tomorrow's our day of rest. Let's go down river a ways and see a ball game."

"Postman's day off," I said sourly. 'I'm sticking in the hotel."

"Look," he said. "This is between a couple of good ball clubs. I saw them play two weeks ago and they've got a shortstop on that one club like you never saw before."

"Name?" I asked automatically.

"Elbertson," he said. "Reason I know it, I talked with him a few minutes. He's a fine young man."

I said, "I know him. Count me in."

So it was five years later that I saw him again, this time on a bad diamond in a small town south of St. Louis, playing short and hitting like a fool, but with a difference. I sat in the bleachers under that blazing, melting sun and did not feel the heat or the sweat dribbling down my sunburned neck. I saw him stripped of the roughness, the tiny uncertainty, the pieces of playing a man has to lose along the way if he expects to be great. Elbertson had overcome most of the faults, and it should be understood that in the beginning they were only minor, and had gained twenty pounds or so, and stood tall and just beyond ungainliness on that field. I saw him hit good pitching, and it was good, for two doubles and a rocketing triple as hard as Hornsby ever blasted one to the center field wall. He went naturally to his left, and ranged beautifully to his right, and threw from any position. I watched him and thought of what he might have been but for the war, not blaming the war in any actual sense, and could not wait for the game to end.

I caught him beside another bus, newer and painted a rich blue. It seemed as if we were always meeting beside a bus. I came around the hood and said, "Elbertson," and he turned from the bat bag, holding his own bats—I knew that from the way he handled them—and saw me and hesitated a moment, trying to place my face. Then he grinned, that same fine smile and said, "Why, Mr. Thatcher. How are you?"

"Older," I said. "Fatter. You looked great out there."

We shook hands again, the second time in five years, and the other players watched me furtively and began climbing into the bus. He said, "It's been five years, hasn't it?"

"That's right," I said. "What happened to you?"

"I graduated," he said proudly. "I'm married now, got a little girl."

"Good," I said. "That's wonderful. How long were you in service?"

"From '42 to '45," he said. "I got out in the fall and worked in Los Angeles. I played around there during the winter. I've been with this team since spring."

"Look," I said. "This is a good ball club but you're ready for better stuff. Don't you know that?"

He grinned, that same shy smile, and said, "I think so, Mr.

Thatcher. I've got a chance to go with Kansas City next week. Do you think I ought to?"

"Yes," I said. "By all means, Elbertson."

And again a little man was calling, and he was shaking hands and waving to me from a window that was slightly cleaner, and I watched him go and turned to my friend and said, "Jones, let's get back to town. I've got a letter to write."

He looked at me and said, "Sure, Thatch. Let's go," and led the way to his car. All the way north to St. Louis, I thought of Elbertson and it was like remembering music set to movement, with the action predominating to such an extent that in the final summation movement became music in his arms and legs and body. He was potentially the greatest ball player I had seen in ten years; I could not take a back seat and watch him waste time playing out all that talent on the small diamonds and little towns. It was a shame and I knew it; and I wrote a letter to Richards that night.

Richards talked with me on the eastern swing and told me I was probably letting my imagination run away with me, but if the boy was a tenth as good as I painted him, it was worth a look. So Richards took his look, a personal one, in Memphis a month later; and the next time I saw him, he took me into his private office. He closed the door and put one hand on my shoulder and stared at me from those big, innocent blue eyes that had no innocence behind them, and then he said, "Thatch, I apologize. Elbertson is everything you said, and more. I watched him three times. I've had him scouted thoroughly ever since. He doesn't know it. Nobody knows it, thank God, or I might have unexpected competition. Can I depend on you to keep quiet and wait?"

"For what?" I asked.

"What?" Richards said. "Listen, he's going to play short for the Eagles next year, that's what."

I hadn't expected anything that sudden and for a moment my misgivings frightened me. It is always that way when you have praised a young man to the sky and then, without warning, seeing him about to get his big chance. I was frightened for him. I said, "Now wait, Jim. Don't you think a year in triple A is best?"

"Thatch," Richards said. "Now you tell me. Just what do you honestly think?"

I couldn't lie to him. I had known him too long. I said, "Go to it. He's ready."

"That's all I wanted to hear," Richards said. "I'll give you the word."

And now it was afternoon and the first game of the season, with the big crowd and the bands and all the tenseness and smiles and expectation of opening day. I had talked with him a few minutes, for the third time, and it was about to begin. I had watched so many rookies play their first game that it no longer made me feel one way or another. Until this game. I had the jitters and frankly admitted it; and the men around me knew why and were waiting eagerly to see what my prize prospect would do. I tried to remember what we had talked about that morning, if I had said the right things, if he had felt better from the talk. I remembered that saying goodby and good luck at the door, he had shaken hands and said, "I know who gave me this chance. I won't let him down, Mr. Thatcher."

"I know you won't," I said. "I'll be up there with a shotgun, just in case you blow one and try to crawl in a hole."

That was about all. It was a clear day, with a bright April sun, and the band played the national anthem and they raised the pennant and the flag, and the umpires met at the plate with the managers, and we all breathed deeply, perhaps from habit but I doubted it for once, and tried to sit back in our chairs. Sixty thousand people had watched him take his hitting and infield; and I remembered how sharp and clear he stood out against them all. But that, again, was undoubtedly my own imagination.

The Eagles took the field and the first Red Wing hitter

stepped into the box. I found myself saying, "Don't hit it to him, not the first one," and the pitch came in, hard and high-hopping. The hitter swung and the ball went to him at deep short, a nasty, twisting smash into the hole between him and third. I saw him move to the right and then something snapped in my chest and I said, "Watch the throw," and felt the tension leave my body. For he was on the ball, smothering it on the off-hop, never an easy play, straightening and making his long throw that came across like a buggy whip uncoiling and smacked, against the dead silence, into the first baseman's big trap mitt with all the authority in the world. He threw the runner out by three steps, and I knew he was in, that much in, with so much more to come.

The game moved then, a succession of the usual hits and runs and plays, with Elbertson swinging in the sixth hole at the plate. He flied to center field his first trip, grounded to third his second, and walked his third time. It was three to three in the seventh, a good game, played rapidly; and it was all Elbertson in the greatest sense of the word. He moved around that shortstop hole with more grace and feeling and ability than any man the Eagles had been able to put on that field since the twenties. My inner pride made me state that to myself, with slight misgivings. After all, a man named Thatcher had played that spot for fifteen years. But not like Elbertson. I had to admit, not caring, and I looked around at the crowd and wondered how they liked him and how they really felt.

They came into the ninth all tied, and the Red Wings scored two runs on a single and a couple of doubles; and the Eagles came in to hit. Elbertson was due fifth, if he had a chance to hit. We leaned against the shelf and watched them get the first two men on, a couple of clean singles to center, work the sacrifice. The next man flied to left field. Two away and Elbertson stepped into the box; and now the mutter grew around the field. I watched the Red Wing pitcher and their infield. I said, "Duster," and it was, a high one at the cap, sending Elbertson into the dust on his back, falling away from the pitch. He got up and dusted himself off and stepped back in, and the Red Wing catcher spoke to him, something I could not hear, of course, but guessed very closely. Elbertson did not turn his head, or answer, but waited for the next pitch.

They dusted him again, whether intentional or not, but they did. I found myself standing and roaring with the crowd; and the sound was about equally divided, half in favor of and half in protest. Elbertson got up and dusted himself again and settled into the box. He had it all the way, I knew then, for he stepped into a curve ball and singled cleanly into to right field to tie up the game. He rounded the bag and came back on the fast throw into second, and took his customary long lead which looked foolish unless you knew his speed.

I remembered the plays just finished in that game, how he had covered the bag on two double plays, leaping high and making his throws over the flashing, high spikes coming in. I remembered his quietness and once, in a sudden calm, his deep, warm voice talking it up, saying, "Now we go, now we go," and nothing more, as if he had been afraid of saying too much to any of them. I looked down at Duggan, coaching third, and wished I had the signs. And then I didn't need them for Elbertson went down on the first pitch.

Flew is the word for him. He was away with the arm and moving away with a blur of legs and white uniform, coming in from the outside and hooking the bag below the knee-high throw, swinging around and behind the bag in a cloud of dust. And he had not come in spikes high, as they had initiated him. He was safe a foot and stood slowly, dusting himself with those big hands, peering at Duggan on third. He was the winning run, with two away, and he danced off second for the pitch.

Duggan sent a pinch hitter in, old Malloy who could hit but no longer field, and Malloy worked a three-two count and hit the ball. It went sharply over second into center field and

Elbertson was running with the bat crack. And then it happened, just a little thing, nothing that had not occurred before, but somehow completely different. I said that Elbertson made plays in this game that, in the truest sense of the word, had never been made before. He rounded third at an impossible running slant, hitting the bag with a flying spike and going for home. They couldn't get him, we all knew that, watching the throw come in from center field. No center fielder could get that man with a breakaway start.

The Red Wing pitcher, and this happened in the seconds it took to hit and run, came off the mound automatically, crossing between third and home to back up either play. He was a big man and no longer young, and he turned an ankle and fell full length on the base path, completely accidental, rolling face up as Elbertson rounded third and was upon him instantly. Eight out of ten men I know, despite their agility and the reflexes necessary for major league baseball, would have struck the pitcher, possibly cut him, and gone down in a pile of arms and legs. Elbertson had one step and in this moment, the pitcher's face rolled and turned upward, twisted with the sudden pain, Elbertson turned in unbelievably, just a few inches, threw himself sideways and rolled in a long, smooth tumbler's dive toward the mound. He rolled and came up, still running, and angled back for the plate; and as the ball hopped, a perfect throw, Elbertson seemed to move away from the ball and make his slide. He hooked across the plate and beat the throw by inches, that catch and quick stab by the catcher already blocking with all his body. He was safe and the ball game was won; but the game was incidental.

He came to his feet as they surrounded him and stood there in the sunlight, his sweaty black face still moving with the force of his run, his dark hands quivering below the stained white sweatshirt and jersey, his eyes smiling at them quietly; and I looked at my typewriter and the clean sheet of white paper, untouched throughout the game. And I thought that new things can still happen in the game, and some of them coming late are the best of all. Elbertson was in, and I waved at him, and caught his return wave and broad smile, still a little shy, and sat at my typewriter to put the black words on the clean white sheet.

One More Inning

He was up hours too early and already felt the practical urge to fall back and sleep until ten, but the sun smiled on any city and made it look different to him. He padded heavily to the windows and stared across the endless rows and tiers of the city, looking automatically toward the stadium. He could not see the gray walls or the light towers, but they were out in the smoke-dimmed distance, just as they had stood ten years ago in the same smoke and soot and sunlight.

This city had changed since the thirties, he thought, had grown immeasurably and become choked with people and business. He was probably cockeyed in his feeling, but walking downtown the night before, after his arrival, it seemed as if the old warmth and spirit of camaraderie had disappeared. He remembered in the old days during the stretch drives for the pennant, how he could not walk ten feet from the hotel before fifty people recognized him and clustered around, grinning and shaking his hands and shouting above one another's likewise loud voices, "How do you feel, Farmer? Will you take 'em tomorrow? How's the old soup-bone?" But last night he had walked ten blocks and no one had known his face.

He could not sleep now, remembering the past and getting

fresh sunlight in his eyes. He took a warm shower and shaved carefully, and returned to the bedroom and dried himself with the big towel, rubbing his heavy shoulders and thick neck, moving carefully over his right arm, across the stomach, now padded with some fat, over the thighs and knotty lower legs, touching the spike marks and the misshapen toe. His feet somehow were the only unchanging parts of his body; they remained flat and long and wide, giving rise to the sportswriters' dream of the perfect farmer coming up from the cornfields. Size thirteen—and how they had loved to dwell on that—with big toes and no arch, and strength enough to kick the side out of a barn. And now he was thirty-eight and growing fat, not loose and sloppy weight, but the kind any man put on when he reached the end of an active career. He grinned crookedly at his feet and turned for his clothing as the phone rang.

He reached for shorts and socks and said, "Yes?"

"Farmer?" the voice said. "I knew you'd be up. The sun is shining."

He smiled with old memory and said, "This wouldn't be Salsbury, would it, the demon baseball reporter?"

"How are you, Farmer?" Salsbury said. "I wanted to meet your train, but the kid was sick."

Time had passed, he thought, if Salsbury was married and had children and did not meet an incoming train. He said, "How old is the kid?"

"Six," Salsbury said. "I've been married eight years, Farmer. I thought you knew?"

"You don't hear much," he said gently, "out in the sticks."

Salsbury coughed and said, "Farmer, I'd give a lot to do some things over. You know what I mean?"

"Yes," he said quietly, "but we'd just do them the same way, regardless. What do you want?" He spoke shortly and knew that Salsbury felt the change.

Salsbury said, "I'm doing a column on you, Farmer. I just wondered if you wanted to say anything. You know, coming up again after ten years and playing against your old team. What about it?"

"Well, I'll tell you," he said flatly. "It's a nice day and I hope my corn is growing good out home."

He slapped the phone down hard and turned away to the window, no longer feeling sun warmth, thinking of the old days and how Salsbury and the other writers had made life unbearable for him with a few cruel words. He hoped Salsbury remembered about the corn. He just hoped he could stuff those words down their throats. Ten years was a long time to pay for someone else's laughter.

It was a bright day in '37, and the sun was warming his back and dribbling good sweat down his arm; it was a wonderful day and he was twenty-eight years old and newly married and going on a radio program right after the game. They needed one to cinch the pennant and he wanted one for his twenty-fifth win; and then he would sit in the studio with Salsbury and the other reporters and talk about how they would whip the Cards in the series. He felt so good it almost hurt when he took the mound and threw his first pitch; he felt better when he made the last one and walked off with a two-hitter and the pennant cinched.

That night he sat in the studio and watched them prepare the script and knew what they were thinking: here was a big farmer with no brains and a strong right arm, winning a pennant and cutting in for the big money while here they sat with all the brains and a few pennies.

They went on the air and he answered their questions, and halfway through the program Salsbury, then just starting his career, asked, "How does your wife feel about all this?" and he grinned, thinking of her back home waiting for the baby, and answered, "She feels fine." And then he had to do it, national hookup or not, and said with all the joy bubbling over in his throat, "How'm I doin', Maggie?"

The moment the words were gone, thrown out and across the

country, he knew his mistake. The reporters held their mouths and struggled for soberness, and Salsbury swallowed laughter and concluded the program. The next day the wolves were in full swing, even the home-town writers. He was so sick of "How'm I doin', Maggie?" by the next night that he was afraid to call home.

But he had to; and when he did, his wife said: "John, why did you say such a foolish thing? You know what they'll do with it?"

He knew. He knew the first game of the series. He'd taken bench riding before, but never like this, and for the first time in his career it got under his skin. They got a hitter on in the third and lined the dugout steps, all of them singing and calling those words, and it threw him off. He felt the curve slide out and go up fat and big, and Manske leaned and came into it with all his great power; and after that he didn't have a chance. He came off the mound, heading for their dugout, and it took all the cops and umpires and sane players to get him off the field and into their dressing room. Mahoney went in and finished, and they were beaten badly. No one spoke to him after the game; they were furious and he deserved all their anger.

Two days later he went in again and lasted five innings and they finally got under his skin. He allowed four straight hits, good for two runs, and that was the ball game. His manager blew up that night.

"You're a man," O'Keefe said bitterly. "You've played ball six years up here. Are you turning rabbit ears on me? I'm telling you now, you'll throw tomorrow and if you blow, one of us leaves this club. And that's flat."

He threw the next day. They weren't likely to forget it, ever, for he shut his ears and pitched as only he could when his arm and body and mind worked together. In the fourth he was working on a one-hitter and they were riding him viciously. He threw an inside ball and the hitter smashed it back, low and fast into the box. He felt the ball hit his foot and knew something had snapped, and the third baseman took the carom and made a beautiful peg for the out. He was white-faced and bending over his foot, fumbling for the shoelace, when O'Keefe came out and said hoarsely, "Don't give me that, Johnson. You're not hurt. Stay in and pitch."

He knew what they thought: the riding was getting him and he wanted the easy way out. He had never been a mild-tempered man and in this moment, with everything at stake, he lost his temper and said, "All right, damn you! I'll pitch. Just play some ball behind me."

He pitched that game on the foot that swelled and pained until he no longer felt the pain, it was so terrible. He allowed four hits and refused to limp off the mound when it ended. He passed through everyone and went to the dressing room, and when O'Keefe and the owner came from the inside office he had removed the shoe and sock.

It seemed as if everyone in the room turned and looked at the foot; and the owner gasped and said, "Don't tell me you—" and had to look away.

He said, "Happy now, O'Keefe?" and looked around for the trainer.

O'Keefe said, "Why didn't you tell me, Farmer?"

"Why—" he said, and closed his mouth. They knew why. He turned his head and spoke to no one while the trainer and doctors came, and they took him to the hospital. The big toe was broken and the foot itself had been twisted and torn until everything was out of line.

He never forgot that winter; it was the worst of his life, limping around the farm, waiting for the baby, trying to keep Margaret happy. He was limping only a little when John was born, but the first day of spring training he felt the pressure and knew he was done. He couldn't bring all his weight around in the swing and follow-through; and not to do so ruined his entire delivery.

They called him in, a month after the season began, a month after he had been knocked out six straight times, and used the time-rusted words and condolences. O'Keefe wouldn't look at him and the owner fumbled around with platitudes and he boiled over and said, "Cut the foolishness. Pay me off, get waivers. Is that what you want to say?"

"Now, Farmer," the owner said awkwardly, "don't be too hasty. You'll be all right. Just a little rest. However—"

However meant a lot of things but mostly it meant they knew the truth. It meant selling him before the truth got out, a hundred thousand dollars' worth of sale, and him unable to offer a dollar's worth of value. He went to the Grays and lasted another month, and they knew it then, but too late. No one took the waivers and they called him and shook hands and the business manager said, "Farmer, it wasn't your fault. I'm going to do the best thing possible. As of now you're a free agent. Go home and get that foot in shape. When you feel it coming back, call me. And here's a year's pay, in full."

"No," he said. "I didn't earn it. You don't have to—"

"You didn't earn it?" the business manager asked softly. "When you went out for us five times and tried where most people would have tossed in the towel before they started. Listen, Farmer, we don't do it that way, you hear. You take the money. And remember—when it feels good, call me."

He said, "All right, and thanks. Thanks for a lot more than the money."

He remembered the years after the war, three of them, while he pitched for the town team in the Sunday league. He could get by on his head alone, he knew that, and during the long evenings he worked on the fast hook and the slow change-of-pace hook that followed it. He did not use it until '46, and when he threw at the hitters in the league, they told him in all honesty that it was like batting birdshot. And most of all, the foot was coming back, not halfway, but almost the same as in the long-forgotten past. He could rear back and come down with the new side-arm delivery, lay his full weight on the foot, and follow through until his fingers scraped the ground.

And the memories came back in the deep night and he thought of them all through the winter and into the following spring and summer. And remembering, he watched the standings. The Eagles were in first and riding high. The Grays were three games back on the Fourth, and it looked as if the Eagles, still under O'Keefe, were going for their first pennant in ten years. Ten years, he thought, since O'Keefe had come through. The writers made no bones about it; O'Keefe won, or lost his job.

He had to discover something before he reached for a phone. He drove fifty miles to a small but red-hot baseball town across the state line. An old friend was managing that team and he sat in the office and made Thomas promise secrecy and then asked for help. Thomas' team was the best in the state, equivalent to a fast Class B club. It was the best he could do, and Thomas promised to co-operate. The next week his name for two hours was Jones and he came into the town and pitched for another semipro outfit against Thomas' club. He had to see what he could do against fair hitting and starting, he felt no confidence. Two hours later he drank a beer with Thomas and grinned as they went over the charts kept by Thomas' wife in the far upper corner of the stands.

Three hits, one hundred and forty pitches, fifteen strike-outs. Thomas slapped the charts and said quietly, "Farmer, these boys of mine are good. You've got it yet. Not so much speed, sure, we know. But savvy now, and that change-up is tops." Thomas smiled wickedly. "Farmer, go back and do it to them good. They play the Grays four games the middle of September, four more the last series. That'll decide it."

"You really think so?" he asked.

"You know me," Thomas said. "I say yes. Hell, man, we know the truth, a lot of us old fogies. And after you do it, tell O'Keefe I've got just the job for him out here. Cutting my outfield grass at fifty a month."

He went home and waited until the middle of August, and then it got him. He called the Grays, and the business manager, the same fine man, answered the phone and listened and said, "We're five back, Farmer, and we can't make it unless we get help. You say the foot's okay?"

"It's all right," he said quietly. "Can I do you any good?"

"Get here soon as you can," the business manager said. "What about the contract?"

He laughed softly. "We'll talk it over later. I still owe you some money. Remember?"

He reported on the first of September and the Grays kept it quiet until the contract was signed. Everyone agreed on one thing: the Grays were complete fools to sign a pitcher with a bad foot ten years out of the major leagues. Salsbury wrote a short paragraph about the Eagles waiting for the Grays with great eagerness, so the young men on the team could learn about first-class bench jockeying on the prime target of all time, old "How'm I doin', Maggie?" Farmer Johnson.

They started him against the Red Sox and he threw four innings, allowed eight hits and five runs, and went out, losing the game. But in losing he felt wonderful. And the Grays' manager, as old and wise as he was himself, knew also. He hadn't put on the pressure, and he didn't use the new change-off hooks. He pitched in relief four straight days, winning one in eleven innings and saving the three others. And now the papers were taking notice. They caught the new side-arm curve, and one of them, a reporter from the old days, wrote about his new delivery and the effectiveness of the curves in the pinch. He smiled, reading that, and found it difficult waiting for the series with the Eagles in mid-September.

Hanson said, "We're only four games off, Farmer. Now look, you'll work only relief against them this time, if we win the first two games and get a cinch split. I think we can do it. That way, we save you for the last four with them. We both know that series will decide the pennant."

Hanson was right. The two young right-handers beat the Eagles while he sat deep in the dugout and watched O'Keefe and the few old members of the team still on the squad. They did not look at him. They lost the third game, and then Hanson pushed in a young lefty and came up with a lucky win to cut the Eagles' lead to two games. He was satisfied then; it would come to the finish and he would be fresh.

It happened in a much better way than he had hoped for. The Grays came to life while the Eagles suddenly blew, in one of those inexplicable slumps that affect a really good team; and today, standing in his hotel room, the Eagles were three games behind the Grays and to lose one meant losing the pennant. And he was going out to the Eagles' park, ten years late, ten years older, and pitch a ball game. The suit would be different, the dugout on the first-base side, the crowd no longer shouting his name but the game hadn't changed and he was pitching a ball game. He was pitching just one more ball game, no more, and then he would go home.

He saw the gray walls of the stadium, cleanly washed and shining brightly against the grimy surroundings, and then moved across the sidewalk into the tunnel and to the dressing rooms. He sat quietly on a bench in a far corner, changing into his uniform, watching the young, vital men of the Grays talking and laughing and changing rapidly for the game. They had disappeared up the ramp onto the field ten minutes before he followed them, coming alone onto the playing field.

Time had changed it very little; and yet, looking about deliberately, it was all strange to him. He saw more booths added to the second-deck railing behind the plate, the television booths, and more for other reasons; and out in center field, above the wedge-shaped bleacher section, a new scoreboard had taken the old one's place. He smelled the air, and was awed by the immense towers of the lighting system, and caught the first whiff of popcorn and hot dogs, and remembered with childish nostalgia that day the Babe passed him, chewing with gargantuan bites on a dog, holding

three others, walking as only the Babe dared. Too many memories, he thought, and then saw O'Keefe in the Eagles' dugout, and
lost the sadness.

He warmed up carefully, slowly, moving his arm and body
from coldness to warmth and easy heat, and finally, as the P.A.
system gave the line-ups, to a pleasant heat beneath his sweat
shirt and uniform. When his name was announced, a small
murmur hung and grew and then died away. He continued to
warm up until the first Gray stepped to the plate, before slipping into his heavy jacket and sitting beside Hanson.

He watched Ashton, the young Gray center fielder, a grey-
hound on the bases, and without doubt the rookie of the year.
It made him feel warm, watching Ashton move and hit and run.
Ashton singled to center and rounded first on the dead run,
forced a fast throw, and returned to the bag with a broad grin.
Still kid enough to show it, he thought, but a fighter all the
way. He hoped for a quick run, but the big Eagle right-hander,
a man named Kennedy, was ahead of the next three hitters,
getting them on a short fly to left, a force at second, and a
strike-out; and then he was taking the short walk and his
warm-up throws, and the first Eagle hitter was waiting.

Duggen called him halfway to the plate and they stood close,
breathing easily, and Duggen said, "Take it easy, Farmer. We got
all day."

Duggen called for control only, on the inside and low, then
outside for the waster, then inside, and he hit the hole with excellent control. They had two and two on the first hitter, and
Duggen called for outside and low, and the hitter came up and
swung on the bad ball, chopping it into right for a clean hit. The
Eagle dugout roared up loud and the old refrain began again,
and it sounded almost like a welcoming band and the key to the
city. He wasn't bothered, he thought with wonder.

He was sick, moments later. Duggen wanted control and he
couldn't argue with the catcher. They hit him like cousins, three
straight singles, a double, and a base-cleaning triple by the big

Eagle catcher, for four runs that could win a ball game. Duggen squatted implacably behind the plate, calling the signals, talking it up hoarsely. No one warmed up in the bullpen. He knew that, for he turned to the rosin bag and stared quickly across center field at the well-remembered gate; and in the Eagle dugout, someone called, "Better radio for Maggie, has-been. You're all washed up."

The next man popped to short and he got the second out on a topped ball to Holt at third, Holt making his throw after holding the runner on. The third out was a handle hop to second. He came in slowly, shaking in the body, his face wet, and Hanson smiled and said, "Never mind, we'll get this baby."

He prayed that Hanson was right; and the game moved swiftly then. Duggen called for the control and suddenly he had it razor-sharp, just that difference from the first inning which spelled pop-ups and ground balls instead of hits. It was coming home again, stepping back ten years, feeling the control and knowing then that Duggen was saving the curves for the clutch. He knew how O'Keefe was thinking in the Eagle dugout: *Nothing left but control and he'll slip again. Just a has-been, trying to get in my hair, and all he'll make is a fool of himself.*

He came in from the fourth, holding them to that four-run lead; and Hanson squinted at the big Eagle right-hander and said loudly, "Now let's rattle the boards," and he felt the coldness run fast along his back, watching these young men come off the bench and line the dugout steps, getting onto the right-hander, beginning the chant, moving toward the bats; it had the old feeling of the inning, the big inning, and it was good to experience again. Duggen, hitting eighth, worked a long count and fouled three and drew a walk.

Farmer turned to Hanson questioningly and Hanson said, "Go up there, Farmer. We don't need pinch hitters today."

He stood loose and watched the Eagle third and first sackers edge in, and the first ball was wide and low as they made their rush. He dumped it carefully before the plate. He did not run fast and was thrown out twenty steps early while Duggen went into second standing up. When he reached the dugout, Hanson grinned and said, "Now we go."

He turned and watched it start, and gather momentum, and he knew when Ashton dropped one short and beat it out by three steps that here was the big inning. He could feel it in his chest. With Duggen on third and Ashton dancing maddeningly off first, McCall waited on the count and hit a low ball to left field. It dropped and bounced, and Duggen came across as Ashton rounded second, running like a deer, judged his space and came into third on his stomach, sliding twenty feet in a curving hook that carried his body inside, one hand catching and holding a bag corner. It was foolhardy and daring, and Ashton was safe and McCall slid into second on the throw.

Beside him Hanson said, "Nobody like that kid, nobody!" and grunted deep in his thick chest. And then Evans doubled for two and Blankship, the other rookie up from Class A, chewing a wad of tobacco bigger than an apple, looked at two and swung. Farmer said, half to himself, "That's it," and watched the ball disappear in the reaching hands of the left field lower deck. Five to four.

"Go on," Hanson was shouting. "Keep it rolling. Keep it hot. Don't stop now."

He wondered if they could; one run wasn't a safe lead, the way he felt, suddenly old and finished compared to these boys who were giving him the lead. He watched the shortstop single and the first baseman double; and an outfield fly brought in the sixth run, and O'Keefe called time, too late, he thought silently, and changed pitchers. A left-hander came in, O'Keefe's ace coming in early when he should have rested for the next day. The left-hander got them, but Farmer had two runs to the good, and five innings to go.

He came through the fifth, and the sixth, and in the seventh lost the edge of his control. Two men singled and Duggen called time and walked to the mound. Farmer wiped sweat from his forehead and said, "I lost it, Joe."

"Sure," Duggen said calmly. "Now we give 'em the hooks, Farmer. How's your arm?"

"Good," he said truthfully, "Feels good, Joe."

Duggen chuckled softly. "Let's win us a ball game, Farmer. I'm getting tired."

He thought, *Now, O'Keefe. Now we'll know*, and toed the rubber.

Duggen called for the fast hook on the inside and he came down in the peculiar side-arm whip and felt the ball leave his open, splaying fingers, sign of strength to spare, and watched it cross-fire in, duck and catch the corner for the strike. O'Keefe was shouting from third base now, where he had moved an inning before; and he knew they were crossed up and working hard to catch on to him before it was too late.

He checked his runners, on second and first, and threw the same hook on the outside. The hitter came over, too anxious, and popped to second; and then he felt it inside and knew it was coming strong and good. They got the next man on four pitches, his first strike-out, and the third hitter flied to Ashton in center field.

O'Keefe was red-faced when they passed on the line, and he stared at the ground and walked slowly into the dugout. Beside him, Hanson said, "Well, well!" and went for a drink.

The left-hander was fast and good, and they did not score. He went out in the eighth to face the lead-off man; and now Duggen was mixing them up cannily. He struck the lead-off man out on four balls, got the second hitter on a ground ball to short, and faced the big gun, McAllister, who could hit anything and would not be fooled by change of pace. Duggen knew this and moved to the left and they walked McAllister on purpose while the Eagles and the crowd roared their protest.

He was thinking of many things now, of the past and the way

you threw to certain men, and how all the knowledge of years never really went away but only lay dormant until a man needed it most. This clean-up hitter was a long-ball man, not a clothesline batter, and Duggen called for the slow hook. He pulled McAllister back to the bag with a toss-off and then made his delivery; and the clean-up hitter swung and fell facedown with the force of his swing, missing the slow hook by inches.

He was frightened but strong, and he threw the fast one to the outside corner for a ball, and came back with the slow hook, which the hitter ignored for strike two. O'Keefe was shouting from third and he knew they had orders to wait the string out. Duggen called for the fast hook and he bent it in on a fine edge, too fine. The hitter caught it squarely and rode it into deep center. He turned and then ran to back up third, and Ashton raced to the flagpole and made a beautiful throw in while the run scored and the clean-up hitter held at second. *Five to six*, he thought, *and they're getting to me.*

They got the next hitter on a ground ball to second, and passing O'Keefe, not looking, he heard O'Keefe say, "Next time, has-been, next time we get you good."

He did not answer, and sitting in the dugout beside Hanson, he thought with wonder that he no longer hated O'Keefe. It was strange, and when he had changed he did not remember, but now he hated no one and saw O'Keefe as the man was within himself, slipping and hating the world, desperate for this ball game, for all the games he needed to keep his job.

They went out in order and when he removed the heavy jacket, Hanson took it carefully and said, "One more inning, Farmer."

He said, "I'll try, Bill," and walked to the mound.

O'Keefe was on him from the third-base coaching box, growing louder even above the crowd sound, and the first pinch hitter, a left-hander, came in. They would put pinch hitters against him now; this one; not the next hitter though, who was a lefty; and then for the catcher, and for sure the pitcher. O'Keefe had the old-timers for that, and one of them he knew. Bradford, who had been with him in those past years, now playing out his final year on the bench. He pitched to the hitter and behind him the Grays shouted their fight and dug in.

The left-hander flied to center field, Ashton taking it against the wall on the dead run, spinning and falling, rolling, and getting up still running with the ball. That one had almost slipped, he knew, and only Ashton had saved him. He turned and grinned at center field, and the kid's strong voice floated in, "Do it again, Farmer. We're still kicking, boy."

Duggen called for the slow hook, and this time it slipped an inch and the hitter singled to center. And Bradford stepped to the plate and rapped dirt from his spikes and settled his chunky body carefully in the deep corner. Bradford watched him calmly, bat back and held still. He tried to remember what Bradford hit best while Duggen pounded his mitt and signaled for the fast curve. He checked the runner and made hs delivery; and Bradford moved into the curve, catching it on the break, smashing it low and straight into the box. He thought, "No, no," as the ball hit his foot and bounded high into left field; and then he was on his side, the foot burning, his eyes searching for the ball and seeing only sky.

He came to his knees, biting away the pain, and was on his feet when they surrounded him, their faces tight with understanding worry and sympathy. Duggen ran from the plate, calling "Time, time!" and Hanson took his arm and looked at his foot and made a swift arm signal for the trainer. He looked around at the runners on first and third, and said, "I'm okay. Let me stay in."

"Your foot," Hanson said. "Farmer, your foot is hurt. Let's take a look."

"No," he said huskily. "It's okay. Let me stay in."

He heard the voice and did not believe his ears were faithful to his heart. O'Keefe was charging in from the third-base coaching box, pushing players away with his thick arms, his red face choleric with rage and determination and something foreign to the man's stubborn, never-yielding way. O'Keefe came into their tight circle and took his arm and pushed his face, sweating and white now beneath the red flush, against Hanson's.

"No," O'Keefe said thickly. "Listen, you dumb Swede, listen to me. That toe is busted. I know it is. He knows it is, but he won't tell you. He stays in here, he'll ruin it for keeps, and his arm with it. Take him out, Hanson. He's good for five years if he doesn't aggravate it."

Johnson said, "What for, O'Keefe? What for?"

O'Keefe turned and stared at him and shook his head, his eyes dropping away and looking miserably at the ground. O'Keefe said, "I don't know, Farmer. I just know it's right. Please go out."

Hanson said, "He's right, Farmer. You can't go on. Let Shane finish. We'll pull it out for you."

The plate umpire said, "Time's up, Hanson. What do you say?"

He looked at O'Keefe and wondered how much courage it took in a man's heart to do a final, decent thing; and he took Hanson's stubby arm and grinned weakly at the players and said, "All right. Let's go in."

They helped him to the dugout and he sat on the bench while the trainer stripped away sock and shoe, and the doctor began working on the foot. Shane made the long walk from center field and took his warm-up throws, and he watched O'Keefe shouting from the coaching line, sending in another pinch hitter. He wanted to say, "Take me downstairs," and then he gripped the bench tightly and had to watch.

Shane ran the count to three and two, and threw himself nearly flat with the pay-off pitch. It was hit and he wanted to cry, seeing the ball rise and sail toward the right center wall. It was gone, in one hit, and he could not feel anger. He saw

Ashton run back, still back, reach the wall base and push against it with his bare hand and leap high and take the ball as he smashed against the wall. Ashton dropped and rolled over, flipped the ball to Wheeler running from right. Wheeler turned and made his throw, and he saw the base runners, already far gone and racing for home, stop and turn in desperation. Wheeler's throw was long and accurate, into short center. The second baseman took it and whipped it across the diamond to first, doubling Bradford by fifteen feet. And then Hanson was beside him, pounding his back, shouting words he could not hear below the heavy roar of the crowd. The doctor said, "Cut it out, Swede," and Hanson pounded him harder.

They came in around him and patted his back, rubbed his cheeks with their dirty, sweaty hands; and Ashton came last, yelling like a wild Indian. Johnson held out one hand and rubbed the boy's bloody chin, filled with dirt and paint from the wall, the same gesture he used on his own children.

He saw O'Keefe moving slowly across the field toward the Eagle dugout; shoulders down, hearing nothing, eyes on the ground. O'Keefe was taking the long walk, through the dugout and dressing rooms, into the street and on to nowhere; and he sat, unable to help the man. And seeing Salsbury fighting through the crowd, he knew O'Keefe wanted no help from anyone, for O'Keefe lived one way and could not change.

Salsbury said, "How's the foot, Farmer?"

"Good," the doctor answered for him. "Not broken."

"Go away," Ashton said curtly. "Go away, pencil pusher."

"Will you say something for the press?" Salsbury asked.

He stared at all of them and he smiled. He said, "Write about O'Keefe. He needs a lift, Salsbury. Write about him."

"He's done for," Salsbury said. "You're the hot news, Farmer. Please say something."

"All right," he said quietly. "I'm going to call my wife in a minute, Salsbury. You won't be listening, but I'll tell you what I'm going to say."

"Good," Salsbury said. "Then I can quote you?"

"Yes," he said. "Just quote me as saying, 'How'm I doin', Maggie?'"

Salsbury flushed and turned away, lost immediately in the crowd, and Farmer Johnson walked down the ramp holding young Ashton by one arm and Duggen by the other.

The Greatest Victory

I 've watched a lot of them come and go these twenty years, each man possessing his own individual talent or mark of greatness: Old Diz going out that last afternoon against the Yankees with nothing on the ball but hope and heart; the Babe calling his shot in Chicago and the ball going, going into the stands while the crowd was silent and then roaring out in sincere tribute; and Gehrig moving slowly across the half-shadowed, sun-softened grass of Yankee Stadium, the tears tracking down his brown cheeks, the silent thousands watching him go, every one of them with a lump in his throat, for there was a great man who didn't know what the word "quit" meant. But there was another who walked with them through the years and will not be remembered; yet in some way he was perhaps the greatest of them all. Each time I see a skinny little guy trudge in from the bullpen, hitch up his pants and start his windup, I think of Lefty Smith.

Most of us didn't know his first name; and the way I found it was rooting back in the record books and running down the pages until it popped up among the so-so boys: John A. Smith. Lefty was a small man with sloping, stooped shoulders and a head such as you see on a thousand other men, squarely common and strong-jawed, with steady blue eyes and a thinning shock of black hair, rubbing bald from twenty years under a sweaty cap and too many showers in cold, stuffy locker rooms. Just a little guy with a battered black glove and a chew of tobacco in his cheek, seen mostly for scattered, brief moments in the sun, making that long walk from the bullpen to the mound, with runners squatting on first and third and the infield waiting to give him a pat and then play ball.

I thought about Lefty as we neared St. Louis last fall. The series was a natural, a streetcar series they called it, with the Red Wings and Grays set and waiting. Lefty was number eight on the Gray pitching staff that year; he went in when the regulars were frazzled or took a turn when someone turned up with a sore arm and threw their rotation out of kilter. The boys call a guy like that "insurance," a sort of slack-taker-upper. That was how Lefty rated when the series began.

Because I'm from the Middle West myself, Nebraska, I still have a small spot in my heart for any guy who comes up to the big show from that neck of the woods; and I knew Lefty came from a little town near mine and I got to thinking about him—you know, where he started and how old he was and all those things a writer worries about. I questioned the other boys about him and got the grand total I already knew—relief pitcher for the Grays and not so hot. That was all they knew, or cared to know.

I got to thinking hard about him the day before the series opened and I went down to the Sporting News and dug up the old record books; and that was when I first felt the little jerk you get around your heart when you suddenly realize you are reading the story of a fine man, a tough story and not very pretty. It went back twenty years to that Nebraska town, to a kid with bright blue eyes and a thick black thatch of hair, dreaming big hopeful dreams about the future.

I read this dope on Lefty and then, because everything that meant something was missing, I grabbed my hat and went after him. I found him at the park with the Grays, taking their final workout before the opener. He was shagging flies in center field and I recognized him at once because he was smaller than the others and seemed to fit and blend into the background of the ballpark, as though all those years had given him a sort of natural coloring. I introduced myself and explained we were from the same county back home, and when practice broke up we walked across the infield and sat in a first-base box. I offered him a cigarette and he accepted gravely and we lit up; his face above the match was a study in age and knowledge and a generous share of understanding and pain.

I asked him about his boyhood and how he got started in baseball, and he warmed up slow, but eventually got to talking, not like so many players I've interviewed who use "I" once a sentence, but soft and pleasant, rubbing his forehead and squinting a little into the slanting sunlight as he talked. I could see a farm kid of eighteen pitching a two-bit baseball against the barn door every night and working from dawn to dark in the fields. He pitched for the town team and one day that summer they played a fast semi-pro outfit at a county fair and he was right, setting them down with three hits and fanning fifteen. The manager of the North Fork State League club was in the stands, and the next week he went up for a tryout. He was scared and plenty excited, but he turned in a nice job, nothing spectacular but steady, and the manager signed him on the spot. He pitched ten games that summer, winning eight and losing two.

It was a long road for any man to travel from that day, for baseball was in his blood and even when the breaks were bad he couldn't quit. He played with a dozen clubs, maybe more: Joplin, Moline, Houston, Kansas City, Atlanta, and in his seventh year he came up to the Blue Sox for his first shot at the big time. A guy named Clary was the Blue Sox manager. He shoved Lefty into the game the next day, without rest or a decent workout, against the Yankees. He didn't have a chance, but he pitched because he had never learned any other way; and they belted him out of the park in two innings and Clary shipped him back that night and told him he was lousy. So he went back to the minors and stayed there, pitching his heart out from coast to coast, never making headlines because he had no color, but turning in good dependable jobs. He was just the ninth guy in the batting lineup and when he won a ball game the writers would say that Smith pitched nicely and won with excellent support, and then rave on about the hitters.

When the war came he was thirty-eight and too old to volunteer, so he quit baseball and went back to his farm to grow crops for victory. He was married, he told me, to his childhood sweetheart; and he showed me a picture of her and their two boys, ages eighteen and fifteen. She was a sweet-faced little woman and the boys were stocky and had curly hair and big ears, just like his. He told me the older boy was in the Navy and the other one a senior in high school. He had this farm back in the hills, a good quarter section bought the hard way, with money saved through those long years of pitching his arm off in a bunch of whistle stops for peanut money. He didn't say that, of course, but you could tell he was proud of his family and that farm. I know—my father was a farmer and I know how a man feels about his own land. Anyway, he had been out three years when Gerrity, the Gray's new manager, made a personal trip out and asked him to sign with the Grays as relief pitcher and general adviser for the young kids on the club. Lefty wrote his older boy, the one in the Navy, and asked what he thought; and the boy wrote him to go ahead, that he'd be proud to tell all the guys on his cruiser about his father helping to keep the game they all loved going strong until they came home. So he signed with the Grays; he was forty-one years old, just my age.

I said, "How do you feel about being in a World Series, Lefty?"

He grinned shyly. "Kinda funny," he said quietly. "I never thought I'd make it. I wouldn't of, you understand, if it wasn't for the war."

"But you're here," I said, "and that counts. Do you think you'll get a chance on the mound?"

He shook his head slowly. "I doubt it. I'm the last man Mike would use. You understand that, don't you? I'd like nothing better, but Mike don't think I can last." He paused and then said softly, "Clary is managing the Red Wings, you know."

"Sure," I said. "Clary manages the Red Wings. What about it, Lefty?"

Then I remembered and I could feel that little quiver in his voice, that feeling of intense longing built up over the years, when he thought about taking his turn in the Series and at last knowing how a man felt when he stepped on the rubber in the biggest game a man can pitch. "Yes," he said calmly, "it sure would be something for the kids to remember."

We talked a little more and he thanked me for saying hello and invited me out to the farm when I got home for a visit; and I said I'd be glad to and we shook hands and he walked across the infield to the locker room, a little guy in a big ball park. I watched him and somehow or other I felt something tugging around inside like the day I saw Gehrig take that same walk; and it came to me then that Lefty had the same love for the game in his bones that Lou had. And Lou will never be forgotten and nobody will remember this little guy. I felt bad, I don't know why, riding uptown to the hotel.

The Series got under way and in the excitement and pressure of writing up games, I forgot about Lefty Smith. You remember how it went; good baseball for wartime and plenty close. They came down the line together and suddenly we were in the seventh day, all squared off at three games apiece, with the sun shining down on Memorial Park and thirty-eight thousand fans packed together like sardines, waiting for the National Anthem and that first ball. Lefty hadn't been in the first six games, but I saw him warming up in the bullpen every day, and then someone else would get the call and he would sit down and wipe the sweat from his face and wait and watch.

But today we were sitting in the press-box and the talk was

centered on just one question: who in Hades was Mike Gerrity going to pitch. He had used five of them the day before in a desperate try for No. 4, but the Red Wings blew them down and won going away; and today, with the chips down, he didn't have a man left. Clary, the Red Wing manager, was pitching Morton O'Conner for the third time. We all knew the big boy would go the route because he had strength and plenty of heart.

But the Grays? The starting pitcher hadn't been announced and it was fifteen minutes before game time. We reviewed the list for the tenth time and made our guesses. My good friend Jim Becker, of the Express, was thinking out loud: "Galvin, no soap. Jackson, can't hold them. King, with a sore arm. Potts, too tired from yesterday. Malone, tried yesterday," and so on down the line.

"What about Lefty Smith?" I asked.

"Smith?" Jim said. "Who the devil is Smith? Oh, that old guy. He's just window dressing. Too old, too stiff, no stuff."

"Ever watch him work?" I asked.

"No," Jim said, "but the record shows, doesn't it? He's relief pitcher and he couldn't last nine. They only used him eight times this year."

"Maybe," I said, thinking about a boy throwing a two-bit baseball against a barn door. "Who, then?"

"I don't know," Jim said. "Probably he'll start Potts and hope for the best."

That was how it shaped up. Gerrity started Potts and we stood up for The Star-Spangled Banner, with the service men and women saluting our flag proudly and everyone quiet and sober-faced, for in this moment we thought of the war and all those guys, our friends, listening to this game from every part of the world; and then the umps called, "Play ball!" and Morton O'Conner took the sign from his brother behind the plate, nodded, and served the first one up to Grady and we were away. It took just one inning to see how this would go.

Morton O'Conner set the Grays down in order and Potts took the mound and got ready for Littleton. The Orangetown boy singled to right, Hopper laid down a drag bunt and beat it out, and Music tripled to the right-field wall before our seats were warm. And there it was, a first-inning break and the Red Wings running wild with no one warmed up in the Gray bullpen. Gerrity called time and they gathered around Potts and I wondered who he would call in, for it was a cinch Potts was off today. Then I looked toward the right-field bullpen and saw a small figure pick up a black glove and start the long walk to the mound.

"Who the heck?" Jim asked, shading his eyes.

"Smith," I said. "Lefty Smith."

And then I thought about his wife and those two fine boys listening in and I didn't feel very good. What a break for a guy, coming in with two runs across, a man on third and nobody out, and no time for a warm-up. Twenty years to reach this moment and it might end before he had a chance really to taste its sweetness. For I knew, and Jim knew, what Gerrity was thinking. He didn't have time to warm anyone else up, so he took the long chance and called on Lefty, hoping the little guy could pitch all out for a few minutes until King or Malone got loose.

"Lord!" Jim said. "This thing is going to be terrible. The lamb to the slaughter. Look at the little guy. They'll murder him."

He did look small, coming across the infield, that big black glove hanging down and his shoulders stooped inside the loose shirt. Gerrity said something to him and they all patted him on the back, and you could see that those Grays really liked him. He took his five warm-up tosses and stepped behind the mound for the signal. He picked up the rosin bag and dried his fingers, dropped it, got the sign from Haywood, and rubbed his nose. Walker O'Conner was waiting, his big bat poised, and no one was deadlier than the Red Wing catcher with ducks on the pond. I wondered if Lefty was nervous out there, and then

I knew he was the calmest man in the ball park. I held my thumbs and said a short, silent prayer for him. I was almost afraid to look. I'd never watched him pitch and I didn't know what to expect.

He stretched and glanced over toward Music and threw; it was quick and effortless and he followed through beautifully. And I knew I was seeing the result of twenty years' experience, probably the only man who appreciated the beauty of his style. The ball moved toward Walker O'Conner and dipped suddenly, taking an inside corner with the sweetest hook I'd seen in years. Walker O'Conner watched it for a called strike and rubbed dirt on his hands. He stepped in again, but this time you could tell he had more respect for the little guy on the mound. And then I had that funny feeling. I swear I looked down on Lefty Smith and felt that something great was going to happen. I remembered what he had said about wanting to win, that day before the series in the first-base box.

He struck Walker O'Conner out on four pitched balls, and Kubisky, always tough, broke his back on a slow curve and popped to Johnson at short; and then Martin, riding a terrific hitting streak, went down swinging and the crowd woke up. I looked at Jim and said, "Never heard of Smith, huh?"

"Take it easy," Jim said, but I saw the light in his eyes. "The little guy can't last. Look, Malone is warming up."

Maybe he couldn't last, but the innings began marching past and he stayed in there, trudging out to that mound, hitching up those saggy pants, and throwing with all his skill and cunning; and the Red Wings popped out and hit weak rollers and went away from the plate cussing and banging their bats on the ground. And then we were in the seventh and the score was still two to nothing, and I tried to keep my voice steady when I said, "Jim?"

Jim said, "Yeah?"

"Six complete innings," I said. "Without a hit. He can't keep it up, huh?"

"I know it," Jim said, his eyes shining. "The wonderful little guy." He pounded my arm. "Listen, he can't stand this, I tell you. You know it, I know it. He's too old. He'll ruin his arm. He ought to ease up."

The Grays were up in the first of the seventh. Mullins worked Morton O'Conner for a walk. Johnson singled to center and Mullins pulled up at second. Liebert came up and the crowd roared. The big boy swung viciously on the first pitch and then dropped a surprise bunt. Walker O'Conner got him at first but the runners moved up. Then McKay, who was hitting hard, looked at two strikes and drove a clean hit to left center that scored both runners and knotted it up tight. Morton O'Conner blew his nose on his sleeve and retired the side, and we faced the last of the seventh with the score tied.

Lefty was working a little harder now. I could tell that by his shoulders and his breathing. But he was still pouring them through and the Red Wings were still breaking their bats trying for a solid blow. He got them in the seventh and in the eighth and in the ninth and then Jim was pounding my arm and yelling. "A no-hitter for him, a no-hitter," and I realized it was actually true. The little guy had pitched a no-hitter because he came in with no one out in the first inning, and this was the first of the tenth and the Red Wings hadn't touched him. It was wonderful and beautiful and impossible, but there it was. And then I thought about that boy of his, that sailor on his cruiser in the Pacific, and how he must be feeling and how those buddies of his would be slapping his back and cheering his old man on. I wondered if he could last, if only those Grays would get him another run. Just one run, and soon.

The tenth went by, and the eleventh, and now the crowd was standing up solidly, tier after tier, and they weren't yelling now, they couldn't, and the tension was building up to fever pitch; and all over the world the wires were pounding out the story and the announcers up on the roof were hoarse and excited, maybe worse than most of us. And little Lefty was walking out there for the last of the twelfth, his back wet and dark where the sweat had soaked through, his cap pulled down over those blue eyes, walking slowly to the mound and only throwing three warm-up pitches to Haywood and then stepping back to take the sign. I guess I was staring at him, I don't know, my hands putting a piece of paper into my portable, tearing it out, crumpling it up, doing the same thing over and over again. I had a feeling that he couldn't go on much longer, and if he didn't win this game I would be sick for a month. I wanted him to win so bad I could taste it myself. But not because I was a Gray fan; it wasn't that. It had nothing to do with the Grays or the Red Wings or the money or anything like that. It was just that I wanted him to win that ball game as I wanted our boys to win this war, and that was with all my heart.

You could almost feel the pressure build up in this inning. And Hopper was up, one Nebraskan facing another. Hopper took two, fouled one off, and then caught one of those sneaking curves, stepping back and chopping with a choked bat, riding it over first base for a Texas Leaguer to right field. The first hit off Lefty in eleven innings! Hopper was on first and Music came up and he was anxious, you could see it, and long overdue. He looked at four pitches, two strikes and two balls, and I knew the Red Wings had orders to wait him out as long as they could, making him tire that arm to the very limit. Music took a third ball and a long sigh ran around the park. Music leaned back and then in, and little Lefty stretched, looked at Hopper, and threw it down the alley. Music swung and you heard the crack, and the ball was a streak over second base and Hopper was running like the wind, around second and into third standing up.

Walker O'Conner came up and I looked down at the Gray dugout. Gerrity was not coming out. Malone and King were warming up. I thought, *Leave him there, Gerrity, leave him in there. Let him play the string out, let him have it one way or the other.* And I guess Gerrity must have been thinking my way, for he didn't make a move. Lefty took the sign and stepped on the mound. He walked Walker O'Conner purposely and the bags were full. The Gray infield drew in close and you could hear their voices, husky now but strong, encouraging Lefty, helping him all they could. Kubisky was up.

Lefty struck him out. It was beautiful. On three balls. Three vicious screw balls, such as Hubbell used to throw when the chips were down, coming in and fading away like a bullet. You couldn't hear yourself talk; no one was sitting now. They were up on the seats. Martin stepped in.

Lefty struck him out. On five balls. Slower now, bent over. Three more screw balls and two blinding fast ones pulled from only God knows where. I heard a crash beside me. Jim had smashed his folding chair with his feet and didn't know it. He was holding his portable and looking down at Lefty, and he was yelling with the rest of us.

Sanderson stepped in and the Gray infield moved back and the outfield went deep and the pitchers stopped warming up in the bullpen to watch with everyone else. It was on the little man now, on him and the big boy at the plate; and I don't think that anyone in the park wished for a hit, not even the Red Wings themselves, deep down inside.

For Lefty was tired, so tired you could see it from where we stood. He was rubbing his fingers on the rosin bag and his steps were painfully slow. He took off his glove and rubbed the ball and took the sign. I knew there wasn't a thing left in his arm. There couldn't be. Not after those long innings; not after twenty years. Maybe a couple of throws, no more. I hoped he had something, just three more good ones. He didn't look at the runners; he stepped on the rubber and wound up slowly and the arm came down and the ball went in.

There was a moment then while the ball was in flight to the plate and Sanderson was crouched, the bat poised, motionless, and Haywood was waiting, his big mitt stuck up like a black box, and the crowd silent, not a cry, not a word, and the outfielders and infielders waiting, hands on knees, a moment when everything stood still or seemed to, and you could almost feel the hope in everyone as they wished that pitch past Sanderson. And then the bat swung and the sound was clear and final.

The ball went over Lefty's head and he threw up one arm in a desperate stab; his fingers touched the ball and you could hear the "flup" and then it was going into center field and dropping, and Hopper was streaking across the plate; and I saw Lefty standing there, the glove on the ground behind him where the drive had knocked it off his hand. He was rubbing his numbed fingers and you could see the smile on his face. That was the greatness in him, the greatness that had been there all the time, all through those long years; he was smiling and the game was over and the silence still hung for a moment.

And then Sanderson was running from first base and shaking his hand and the Grays and the Red Wings were pouring out on the field around that little man and all of them were shaking his hand and trying to pat his back, and I knew that Sanderson was saying he was sorry, you could tell by his face, and the little man was smiling still and finally he came through the players, heading for the locker room; and then, all at once, you could hear the roar start and gather force, the way it did the day Babe hit that one in Chicago, and then it rolled up and out of the park and I think they heard it in Kansas City and over in Illinois, and he took off his cap, and walked into the locker room and out of sight.

There isn't much more to tell. I saw him that night at the station when he called and asked me to see him off. He had gotten away from the autograph hounds and the others and he stood in the station, smoking a cigarette and licking his lips. He was small when I stood beside him, smaller than I had realized. He looked like a farmer or a bank clerk in a little town. He wasn't using his left arm much and I knew it was sore as a boil. We talked about this and that, and then the announcer bawled the Kansas City train and we shook hands.

"Good luck," I said. Then I grinned. "You don't need it now, Lefty. You can write your own ticket next spring."

"No, Sam," he said mildly. "I'm through. I lost the game, but it was a good one and a fine way to bow out. Maybe a lot of folks wouldn't see it that way, but I feel like I won that game, no matter what the score was." He grinned faintly. "I sort of got even with Clary, didn't I?"

I said, "More than even, Lefty. You'll read it in my column tomorrow. Clary is always bragging how he never misses real talent. I'm going to tell the world how he shipped you back to the minors without a fair chance fifteen years ago, and what you did to him today. And listen, I still think you ought to come back next year. Your arm will be all right with a winter's rest."

He grinned and shook his head. "Something snapped in my arm when I threw that last ball to Music. I didn't have a thing on it but a prayer. The arm is done for keeps, Sam."

Then I knew he was right. I said, "Lefty, don't come back."

"How about getting out for some hunting next week?" he said. "I got some nice fat pheasants on the farm."

"You got a customer," I said.

And then he shook my hand again and was gone, walking down the ramp in the crowd and moving out of sight. I bought a cigar at the newsstand and went out to catch a taxi. I don't know what made me think of it, but standing there, waiting for a taxi to pass, I thought about courage and twenty years of work to make the grade finally; and then I grinned, thinking of those two boys and that little woman, and the night was very bright.

The Last Time Around

H e came from the office and sat on the spike-chewed bench before his locker, staring vaguely at clothing and extra shoes and undershirts. Ashton clattered across the cement veranda and dug for a Coke in the box, and the lunchman brought the big trays of sandwiches and bottled milk to the equipment trunks outside. Earling was lecturing the rookie pitchers in the bullpen just beyond the trainer's open window, and Wecheck was working on Nickols' sore thigh muscles, kneading the leg with strong fingers, laughing at something spoken between them. A faucet dripped unevenly in the shower room, and the smell of rubbing fluid and sweat laid a thin, familiar perfume throughout the clubhouse. Training was in the last days and the team was taking shape under Lawson's calm hand, but Kit Morgan did not hear the outside sounds or smell the perfume that had become an inseparable part of his life for sixteen years. He looked down upon the traitors who were taking him away, his scarred, thick legs, and shook his head with a small private gesture of acceptance. The end had to come, everyone knew that, but it was a difficult task to admit the truth.

He had gone through the past season with a decent record,

playing sixty games at second base and filling in later when the younger men needed rest, and that season in no way abused his long record of consistent play. He was thirty-three then and his legs felt strong and his reflexes were still the catlike movements fans would remember years after he was gone, and with this feeling of confidence in his body, with ten years behind him, he had spent the winter in their Florida east coast home playing golf and running on the beach, keeping himself in top physical trim. Thinking back now, he knew that Flora had suspected the beginning of the end, but she was too wise to speak her doubt. Even the girls had known, but they believed in him.

He knew the truth now; it was the culmination of many symptoms amassed over the past five years, waiting until the alchemy of his body faltered briefly, then driving straight into that chink. He had been a trifle slow to his right last summer, nothing to worry about, but this spring in the first infield workout he was a full step slow, admitted it inwardly, and hated the knowledge. He worked doubly hard then, pushed himself to the limit, took off five pounds, ran extra laps, hit every possible chance in the cage, and today, in the yannigan infield workout with the other utility men, he faced the truth.

Dusty Baker was batting infield, and Dusty hit them just one way, hard and fast, the only way an infield could profit. He was on second, with Cannady at short, Glenn at first, and young Carloski at third. Baker fed them hot, handle-high hoppers the initial round and they threw the ball around fast, talked it up, and felt good under the sun; and then Baker aimed for the holes, down the lines, extending them, making them move and stretch for every ball. On the first double play round he went over in the hole for a grass-skimmer and found himself bending, making the squeeze, and watching the ball skate on past into right field. He lifted his head and laughed, as he always did when he booted one, and trotted back for his second try; but he knew then, and so did Dusty, for the next grounder was handmade, to his right on the big hop, an easy scoop and underhanded flip to Cannady coming over the bag. They all knew it, had to, and some of the day's brightness was gone forever.

He finished infield and came off with Cannady, licking salt from his lips and squinting at the early customers filing into the grandstand for today's grapefruit game with the Red Sox. Cannady veered off to talk with Ashton and Hammett, the young and truly fine shortstop, met him under the press-box and said, "Hot as hell, Kit," and went on by with a warm and kind smile that hurt him worse than harsh words. If only, he thought, Hammett was cruel and cocky taking his job, it would have been much easier. But Hammett was kind and could never hold malice toward him, for he had helped Hammett the last two seasons, revealing all the tricks and secrets, wanting Hammett to make good.

He saw Lawson within the office, a little distance from the open door in inner shadow, and when Lawson waved him in, he knew it was the time. He turned off the grass and entered the small room, and Lawson closed the door. The manager was sweating beneath a red nylon warm-up jacket, bald head gleaming with tiny beads of moisture. Lawson offered a cigar from the community box and said, "Well, Kit. I guess there's no use making a speech."

"Don't try to," he said. "Just give it to me straight, Billy."

Lawson sat heavily on a folding chair, crossed one leg, and rubbed the foot slowly. "I want you to know we tried everything. I thought the Reds or Cards might go for a sale, nothing came up. I think it was the salary most of all. We asked waivers, nobody offered. The only thing to do is make you a free agent, give you the outright release. Maybe you can make a deal for yourself. Is that all right?"

"It has to be," he said. "I knew it two weeks ago, Billy. I'm that big step slow. It was bound to come." He looked at the cigar smoking between his fingers, in the hands that were big and fast, best in the league for ten long years and now betrayed by time. "Funny thing, Billy. You never think it'll happen to you. Is that strange?"

"We're all like that," Lawson said. "A man feels he can go on forever, and one day time catches up. If there was any way we could keep you, I'd do it. But we can't. The young ones are too good. That's where sentiment and business go down different streets."

"Well—" he said. "That's it, Billy. Thanks . . . thanks for everything. Do you mind if I hang around and try to make a deal?"

"Anything you want, Kit," Lawson said. "I'll have the release for you at the hotel."

He said, "Okay, Billy," and went through the inside door to the clubhouse, to his locker; and now he sat before that open wire cage and tried to rationalize and found it impossible. He untied his shoes and kicked them off, slipped out of pants and socks, and pulled shirt and undershirt from his wide, thick body. He lifted the cigar gently from the bench and drew a deep puff; and behind the expelled smoke, fought for and found the old grin that had been his trademark for eleven years. In the trainer's room Nickols was sitting up, stretching the leg cautiously, talking to Wecheck.

Kit Morgan dropped his wet undershirt and went to the smaller room and boosted himself on the side table. Nickols chewed his dead cigar and glanced at him carefully.

"How's the leg?" he asked.

"Sore," Nickols said. "Always sore in the spring, Kit. Why can't I get in shape easy."

Nickols was talking to fill silence between them, for Nickols was thirty-four this spring, veteran of eleven years, and also felt the leg aches and body warnings of the last time around. Kit Morgan drew on his cigar and said, "Well, I'm on my way."

Wecheck turned from the medicine shelf and pushed at his glasses. Nickols ashed his cigar on the floor and stared mildly at the white wall; in this moment there was an old, set routine to follow, known to them all, in which the man going down had to maintain his sense of humor while his teammates accepted the fact with a minimum of outward sympathy. For sympathy had no legal place in their life, and he would be hurt far deeper by kind words. Nickols nodded and said, "Anybody take waivers?"

"No," he said. "They all passed."

"I thought the Reds might," Wecheck said. "Here, put this on that lip."

He took the jar of white ointment and rubbed a fingerfull over his sunburned lower lip. He said, "Thanks, Frank. Damned thing always gets sunburned. No, they didn't bite."

"Done any phoning?" Nickols asked.

"Not yet," he said.

Semick came padding from the clubhouse and stood beside the whirlpool machine, pulling at the towel around his middle. The big catcher knew, his rough, dark face impassive, only his thick fingers picking at the towel betraying his feeling. Blix Donald hurried in and jumped on the table, stripped off rubber jacket and shirt, and extended his arm to Wecheck for a pre-game rub. Semick spoke, as if he had listened from the start:

"You tried the coast league?"

"No," he said. "Don't know much about it."

Wecheck said, "Loosen up, Blix," and began stretching Donald's right shoulder. The smell of rubbing oil was sharp against the sweat odor. Kit Morgan leaned back on the side table and rested his shoulders against the wall.

"Watch that money arm, Frank," he said. "Old Blixer may not last the month of May."

Blix grinned. "I'll get by, fathead."

"I was talkin' with Candeny," Semick said. "He says they pay good on the coast."

"They do," Blix said suddenly. "I was out there in '42. "

"You won twenty-six that year, didn't you?" Kit Morgan said.

"By grace and God," Blix smiled. "The coast club paid us one check, the front office another. Some of the guys were making twelve hundred a month. That's pretty good, Kit."

"I'll give it a try," he said. "You catching today, Andy?"

"Stash starts," Semick said. "I think Ken'll work the last three. Where you want to eat tonight?"

"I'll see you at the hotel," he said.

No one spoke for a moment. They sat awkwardly, searching for words, wanting to break the feeling they all held close in their minds and bodies. Outside, the noise increased as the team came in for water and a breather while the Red Sox started batting practice. The clubhouse silence was broken and they heard Silvestri kidding a Boston player near the front door. Pesky and Doerr entered the room and Nickols said, "Hello, strangers," and Pesky shook hands all around, looked critically at Nickols and said, "You're fat as a hog." Semick turned on the whirlpool and steam rose in thin streamers from the aluminum tank. Doerr said, "Got a piece of tape, Doc?" and smiled at Kit Morgan. "How's the boy, Kit?"

"Good," he said. "Good, Bobby."

And then he had to get away because they all knew, and it was too much to bear any longer. He said, "Well, the old man can take a rest while you kids fight it out." He walked from the room to his locker, got his soaptin, and almost ran for the shelter of the showers. Behind him, faintly heard in the trainer's room, someone said, "Yeah? . . . damn, I hate to hear that."

He soaped and washed down, stayed under the shower until they were gone, with only a few rookies arguing along the front locker line facing the door, and then he hurried to his locker and dressed. When he stepped from the clubhouse into veranda shadow, the game was just underway and Bill Stewart was raising one stubby arm to call a strike on Pesky as Robbins delivered to the plate. The wives were sitting on their chairs between the press-box and veranda, Babe Allen was talking with a group of writers, rookies were playing pepper farther down the left field line in foul country. He heard the typewriter clatter in the press-box, the sound of the teletype, the voice of the broadcaster filtering through game and crowd sound in disconnected word bursts, talking to the unseen audience a thousand miles north in Quaker City. Kids were perched on the outfield fences and the spring crowd filled grandstand and bleachers with a vivid patchwork of sport shirts and bright dresses. He saw and heard and smelled it all, and walked quickly behind the wives and coaches, through the bullpen to the side exit, away from the park. He had to get his personal equipment, but not now, he couldn't carry that past them all in full view.

The crowd shouted as he walked south; someone had made a good play, gotten a base hit, the game was running its course for two hours and a few odd minutes, as a thousand forgotten spring games had been played here in the past. Semick was back there on the bench, talking it up, watching the game, thinking of him, and Nickols was there, and Blix Donald, feeling the same way. A good many of them would be feeling his sadness, and the young men would be playing entirely with mind and body, with no thought of him now, for that was how a man felt in his early years. A boy had to think of himself, every minute, if he wanted to stick, and no one could blame a boy for forgetting the last workout of another old-timer going down.

He walked fast, holding himself erect against any pity, any kind word; entering the hotel, he glanced at his box for mail and went upstairs to the room he shared with Semick. And there, the door locked, only the window showing outside sky and clouds, he lay on the bed and stared wide-eyed at his clasped hands. He had to call Flora now; she was across the state with the children, waiting for this call. He could see her plainly, as though she sat beside him in the hotel room, smiling and brave. She had been his greatest bulwark from the very beginning, up the hard, tough road from the minors, through the early years when the competition was rough and unbending. And the girls, they had to know, they were old enough. He sat up and looked at the phone, and knew it was cowardly to wait any longer.

He placed calls to Seattle and San Francisco, accepted the notice of delay, and hung up. He lit a cigar, kicked off his beach shoes, and sat on the bed, waiting, rubbing one foot against the other. The calls came through and he spoke with men he didn't know, who knew him intimately by means of the baseball network that extended across the country. They asked the routine questions: are you in shape? would you come out for a look? how much do you figure in salary roughly? A thirty-day trial? all right, we'll talk it over and call you back. Yes, within twenty-four hours, Kit. Glad you called. Good-bye.

He had done all he could; this was the start of something he faced for two or three years if he wanted to play ball. Triple A this year, maybe next, then a drop to Double A. He would never play lower, he knew that, but two or three years meant money they might need later on. He stood in the window a minute and watched the elderly guests play shuffleboard beneath the palm trees on the bright green lawn, and placed his last call. He heard the connection go through, across the narrow width of state, until Flora's voice came clear and warm, "Is that you, Kit? How are you, dear?"

"Fine," he said. "How are you and the kids?"

"Right beside me," Flora said. "Begging to say hello. All right, take your turns."

He grinned when Mary said, "Hello, Dad," and then Betsy wrestled the phone away and half shouted, "Hello, Daddy, how are you?"

"Fine," he said. "Both of you been good gals?"

"Awful good," Betsy said. "Gee, we'll be starting north pretty quick, won't we, Daddy?"

"Yes, baby," he said. "Let me talk to mother."

Starting north, he thought. His children had lived all of their years in this double-home life, going north in April, coming back in October, attending two schools, living in two homes, knowing the life that so many children envied with a naturalness that was innocent of normal living. And all that would change, for them, in a short time.

"Yes, Kit?" Flora said.

He had been afraid to tell her, and suddenly realized that she was one person in the world he could tell. He said, "It happened, Flora, an hour ago. Nobody took the waivers. I guess that's it."

"Oh, Kit," Flora said softly. "Well, it was bound to come. Don't feel too bad, Kit. I know you got a fair deal."

"No question there," he said. "I lost the big step."

"What will we do now?" Flora asked calmly.

"I called the coast," he said. "Won't hear until tomorrow. If I make a deal, I can go home for a couple of days before I fly out."

"That's wonderful," Flora said. She turned from the phone and Kit heard her say, "What . . . yes, Mary." The phone changed hands and Mary said, "Dad, did it happen?"

"Today, honey," he said. "But don't worry, everything is still fine."

"I'm not worried," Mary said. "Are we going to the coast league?"

"I think so," he said. "We'll know tomorrow."

"Dad," Mary said, "they don't pay as much, do they?"

"I'm afraid not," he said.

"Well, don't you worry, Dad," Mary said. "We'll just have to economize, won't we? You can cut my allowance if you want."

He said, "That's not necessary, honey. Now put your mother on." He held the phone and wondered how lucky a man could be, with a pair of daughters who understood well enough to give him courage when courage was supposed to come from him. He said, "Flora, I'll call you soon as I get word. I'd better hang up now." He chuckled. "This is costing us money, you know."

"We're starving to death," Flora laughed. "I'll be ready to pack, dear. Good-bye."

He turned from the phone and began packing his bags.

Tonight and tomorrow would be as bad as any time he might ever live through, but he had to keep grinning and wait the long hours out. He put on a clean shirt and tie and went downstairs to the hotel garden. He stayed there on a marble bench, reading the morning paper, until five-thirty was announced by the first faint call for dinner and players appeared on the porch, talking and smiling to guests they had met during March.

People were moving slowly from the garden. He couldn't sit out here forever and look at the grass, and read yesterday's box scores. He followed a couple up the steps and got inside the doors before anyone saw him, but he couldn't dodge them in the lobby. They were all around him, in groups and little knots, and he knew how the talk was going, just as it always ran on all nights during spring training and on the road. They were re-playing the game, talking of other players, recounting this hit and that play, moving hands and arms to illustrate—for ballplayers without gestures were speechless—certain chances and pitches. Cy Perry was telling the rookies of someone from the past who played with the A's, and Benny Benson was beside the desk, laughing, shaking his shining bald head, making one of his numberless friends feel better just to be near him, and George Earling was deep in a serious pitching problem with the youngsters in the far corner; and Lawson, with the considerate, deeply understanding kindness that was inherent in the man, had already entered the dining room early for one reason: so he and Kit Morgan might not be forced to speak together before the team. Blix Donald came from the elevators, wearing another new bow tie, and touched his arm.

"Want to eat?" Blix said.

"Thanks," he said. "I'm waiting for Andy, Blix."

"Okay," Blix said. "Be good, Kit."

Blix passed and he felt the pitcher's hand on his arm, pressing down hard and tight, and then Blix was away and he was alone again. He passed through the lobby, speaking to them all, keeping the smile on his face until he reached the elevator alcove; the last set of doors opened and Semick stepped out, saw him, and nodded toward the north side entrance steps.

"Where do we eat?" Semick asked.

"Any place," he said. "You want to eat here, Andy?"

"Cut it out," Semick said gruffly. "You want to, Kit?"

"I'm not running from anybody," he said stiffly.

"Who says you are," Semick said. "Hell, let's go somewhere and talk."

For a moment he wanted to change his mind and eat in the dining room, for tonight would be the last time he was a part of that scene; after tonight the feeling would be different. He could always come back and eat with old friends, here in Clearwater, around the circuit in the Chase and Edgewater Beach and Commodore, but the feeling would never be the same. He was afraid, thinking of others he had known, how he had felt when they came back to say hello.

"What about the Beachcomber?" he said.

"Okay," Semick said. "I could go for some fried chicken."

They moved from the elevators toward the north lobby stairs. Ashton came trotting from the desk, grinned at them, and jumped into the elevator. They heard him saying, "Open it up, Joe," and he knew that Ashton had forgotten something in his room and was hurrying to get it and return for dinner, young and happy, without a worry in the world.

"Heard from anybody?" Semick asked.

"Probably tomorrow," he said. "About noon."

"You'll get a deal," Semick said. "Don't let them beat you down."

"Andy," he said, "I'll be pretty easy to beat down."

Semick stopped and grasped his arm. "Don't ever talk like that, damn it!"

"Only to you," he said. "To Flora. I never thought it would be like this. Eleven years of it, until a man gets to thinking it can last eleven more."

They stood together in the back lobby gloom and Semick's

hand was tight and warm on his arm, and as they turned silently to the stairs, the bell captain came from the desk and called, "Mr. Morgan, phone call for you. Will you take it here?"

He wondered who could be calling so quickly, and decided the coast league must be desperate for players if they were responding that fast. Must be O'Doul, he thought, old green suit. He said, "I'll take it here," and followed the bell captain to the ledge phone near the desk.

"Morgan," he said. "Who is it?"

He recognized the voice immediately, the manager of the club training in the adjoining town. "You're a free agent now, Kit?"

"Yes," he said. "As of today, Eddie."

"Made any deal?"

"Not yet," he said.

"Listen," the manager said. "Can you go two weeks if necessary."

"Sure," he said. "Longer than that."

"Want to come over tomorrow for a look?"

He did not trust his own voice now; and with this sudden, unexpected change, did not trust his own judgment. He said cautiously, "I guess so."

"Hell," the manager laughed. "We're acting like a couple of rookies. Look, Kit. What are you getting this year?"

"Fifteen," he said.

"Pretty steep, Kit. Would you take a twenty-five percent cut if we sign you?"

Semick was beside him, squeezing his arm, shaking his head. He said, "No, Eddie. No soap."

"Twenty?"

"I'll split," he said. "No more."

"You got a deal," the manager said. "If you can show the stuff. Be here at noon."

"I'll be there," he said. "And thanks, Eddie."

"Don't thank me," the manager said. "You're still the same old Kit. See you at noon."

He placed the phone carefully on the hook and looked at Semick; and then he had to grin, like a kid signing his first Class D contract for a fifty-buck bonus. He said, "You hear it?"

"Sure," Semick said. "You'll get a deal, Kit. They need utility bad."

He looked around at the lobby where the last players were going up the steps to the dining room. He said, "We'll eat here. You go on in, Andy. I've got to call Flora right away."

"Give her my best," Semick said. "You lucky Dutchman."

He walked swiftly to the elevator and pressed the button, and riding upstairs, he could see Semick taking their regular table and leaning over casually to tell the nearest player that Kit Morgan had just caught on with the Red Wings as utility. And when he came down and sat with Semick, they would look at him and wink, and grin, and show plainly their feeling, a feeling of relief and joy for him, for staying with them in the same league another year. But even with this happy knowledge, fumbling nervously for his room key in the dark hall, he thought of next spring and knew that he had only delayed time a few short months. He hadn't said good-bye just yet, but this was the last year, and he must watch it, remember every day and game and word, for it would never come again.

One Ounce of Common Sense

S keeter Logan took the low whip peg from the plate and made his little dance up and over the bag, dabbed the runner's hooking foot three inches before contact, leaped clear above the other high-flying spike and flipped the ball to Maloney coming from the backup on the grass. The crowd roared approval as they trotted into the dugout and the Giants took the field, another potential rally cut off by fine infield play, guarding their narrow one-run lead as they moved into the last of the eighth. Logan had made that play with a left-handed hitter pulling his second baseman over, crossed from deep short for the rifle shot throw and completed the tag, another in a series of plays that went far back through past years and forgotten games. It was a strong and good feeling for any man, but today the elation was dead in his chest.

Randall stood on the dugout step, clapped his hands once and passed them by with a curt, "We need another run," going to the third-base coaching box. Skeeter Logan bent over the fountain and rinsed his mouth, took the weighted bat and his own from the boy, and stood in the circle, watching Elliot lead off. Maglie was growing stronger as the innings passed, allowing them two runs in the third, then closing the door as the Giants pecked away with continual threat. Randall talked it up from third and Maglie took his signal, went into that jerky, off-balance windup and slipped the curve over the inside corner for strike one. Skeeter Logan dusted his hands on the rosin bag and swung the bats easily. Elliot hit the next pitch to Maglie's left, a grasscutter that topped off his stabbing glove and dribbled across second base for a scratch single.

Skeeter Logan dropped the weighted bat and moved toward the plate, saw the first base coach give him the bunt sign on the relay from Randall, and tugged his cap in acceptance. Durocher was prowling the Giants' dugout, glaring at Maglie, talking to the bench, and Skeeter Logan watched the first outside pitch slip by for a ball. He gave a half dozen take-off signals, slipped the next pitch for another ball, and again refused, putting Maglie in a deep three-nothing hole count as they tried to force him into bunting the bad pitch for a pop-up. He put on the signal and waited patiently, saw the fast ball come off Maglie's fingers and dart inside, and dragged it down the third base line as Elliot broke fast. Thomson made the play and throw to Stanky, catching him by three steps, but Elliot was safe at second and the run was in scoring position. Skeeter Logan trotted around to the dugout and someone said, "Good going, Skeeter," and began shouting for the base hit.

He sat in the dugout shade and watched a pop-up to the infield and a lazy fly to Mays in center and their half of the inning, and running out, passing Randall, knew exactly what would happen after the game. He shouted encouragement to young Macey, and hoped they could get by this last time, but Stanky worked the walk, Dark faked a bunt and pushed a single to right field on the ground as Stanky broke with the pitch and slid safely into third. Mueller hit a long fly ball to center, scoring Stanky after the catch, and Irvin tripled down the line to put the Giants ahead. Skeeter Logan made a diving catch of Thomson's liner and flipped to Comas at third for the double off to end the inning, but the damage was done. He came in and watched Randall juggle pinch hitters and call hoarsely for a run, but Maglie set them down and walked away with the win. Skeeter Logan went down the tunnel to the dressing room, wondering if the blow would fall today.

Randall passed through the big room, head down, and vanished into his office. He looked out a minute later and waved, and Skeeter Logan walked to the office and stood just inside the door, waiting for Randall to speak. Randall had stripped down to pants and socks, and sat wearily at the desk, smoking a cigar and rubbing his fat stomach in a circular motion.

"Wish you hadn't bunted that three-nothing pitch," Randall said. "You could of got the walk, made a lot of difference."

"You put it on," Skeeter Logan said tonelessly. "You never took it off at the three-nothing count. I looked. No take off, that means bunt in my league."

"You always got an answer," Randall said, "haven't you?"

"To a simple question," Skeeter Logan said.

"And all the others, too," Randall said bluntly.

Randall was working around to the crux of everything that lay between them since spring, needling him, hoping he would blow up and give them the excuse they wanted. Skeeter Logan fought down anger and nodded curtly. "You think that way, all right. Anything else?"

"Not now," Randall said. "One thing, you're not hitting paper weight these days. We'll have batting practice at nine-thirty. Be here."

He said, "Nine-thirty," and went from the office, down the carpeted aisle to his locker; and there, with his face hidden inside, swore softly and ripped at his shirt and pants. He heard Grogan's heavy barefoot steps behind him, and then Grogan was patting his shoulder and saying, "Nice pickup on that throw, Skeeter. I got it a little low."

"Good throw, Mike," he said. "Nothing wrong with it."

He turned and found a smile for Grogan's benefit, and gave the big man a gentle push in the ribs. Going into August, facing the third western swing after tomorrow's game with the Giants, he worried about Grogan's condition. The catcher was working too much during these damp, hot afternoons and entering September would lack the five extra pounds of hard weight needed for the stretch drive. That was more of Randall's work, catching Grogan in forty-six consecutive games, refusing rest to the big man because Grogan was too fine a team player to object. Skeeter Logan said, "See you at the car," and went to the showers, whistling stridently as he elbowed into the long tiled room and appropriated the corner shower for his own. He had pushed that cocky mask against all the world for ten long years in the big show, and it was too late to change, no matter how he felt inside. They expected nothing softer from him, and would not have understood him if he changed.

He washed and toweled off, dressed quickly, and got out of the dressing room before the rush started. He crossed the street to the parking lot and sat in his car until Grogan walked slowly from the players entrance; and drove west through the city, halfway home, before Grogan spoke what was lying thick and distastefully in their minds.

"He's trying to get you," Grogan said. "You know that, Skeeter?"

"Tell me something new," he said. "That's just an everyday routine for him, Mike, like eating and breathing."

"No," Grogan said slowly, thinking out each word carefully. "It's not funny any more, Skeeter. And not only him—" Grogan hooked one crooked thumb upward toward the sky, making their sign for the owner.

"Aw, forget it," he said. "I can take care of myself, Mike."

"Damn it," Grogan said, "I keep thinking if you hadn't helped me in the spring, they wouldn't be down on you. What you gonna do if they pull an undercover deal?"

"I'll get by," he said. "Stop worrying about me, Mike. You stick to that catching," and then, knowing that he was speaking too many words again, went on angrily, "and you listen, Mike.

Tomorrow you tell Randall you got to have rest pretty soon. My God, he never gives you a blow."

"I'm okay," Grogan said. "We got to keep winning, Skeeter."

"And ruin you for next year," he said sharply. "You haven't got the weight, the extra strength, Mike. Work yourself to death this season, it cuts a year off your stay up here. Get tough with them, will you? How many times do I have to tell you?"

"All right, Skeeter," Grogan said meekly. "I'll tell him tomorrow."

He turned on the quiet side street and stopped while Grogan got out and said, "Good night, Skeeter," and then drove on, deeper into the suburban district, to his own house on the very edge of the city. He parked on the driveway apron and entered the kitchen, whistling loudly and calling for Louise. She came from the living room, gave him a kiss, and smiled when he shook his head happily, and said, "Just like a bride, baby. Did I do okay today?"

"Fine," Louise said. "Was that throw in the eighth a little low?"

Skeeter Logan winked. "Half a foot but don't tell anybody. Mike's overworked now, Louise."

"And did you tell Mike that?"

"Sure," he said. "The poor dope won't talk for himself."

"Oh, Skeeter," she said. "Why don't you stop it? You know Mike will go straight to Randall tomorrow, and Randall will know why and who sent him. Skeeter, I'm worried. Randall is completely down on you, and we don't know how Mr. Big feels after this spring."

"Baby," he said gently, "do you want a man or a mouse?"

"A man," she said thinly, "but that's not being a mouse, Skeeter, keeping your mouth shut. Honey, you've only got two years left at most. We'll need that money, and if we win this year, the series share will help so much."

"I can't change overnight," he said, "but I'll try. I'll not say a word to anybody from now on out."

"I hope you keep that promise," Louise said. "Did Randall say anything today?"

"Indeed he did," Skeeter Logan lied cheerfully. "Told me I was probably the best shortstop since old Honus."

"Ah," she said, "don't, Skeeter. You're not telling me everything."

He took her arms and turned her toward the stove, and said, "What I don't tell you, baby, isn't worth repeating. What's for dinner? I'm starved."

He ate heartily that night and read a book until eleven, and then dozed off before Louise came to bed; but sometime in the night he woke and lay in the darkness, feeling her hair against his crooked arm, remembering the past spring and the way things had built up until he no longer could hold his silence. They had enjoyed a good season the year before, climbing to third place and showing plainly that the Grays would be fighting for the next pennant all the way. Grogan had caught one hundred and forty-one games, hit a respectable .272, and batted in seventy-eight runs; and all this, as Skeeter Logan knew, for a paycheck of eleven thousand dollars.

When they arrived at the Florida spring training camp, Grogan and Skeeter Logan settled into their hotel room comfortably, knowing one another like brothers after three years of rooming together on the road and in Florida. Everyone knew Grogan was holding out for a split with the owner, but not seriously, for Grogan was always too eager to play ball. Grogan went down to the owner's suite after dinner that night, and returned an hour later with a puzzled look. Skeeter Logan glanced up from his book and said, "What happened?"

"Doggone it," Grogan said. "I figure I ought to get at least fourteen this year."

"So—?"

"Well, we talked a while, and he offered me thirteen."

"Thirteen!" Skeeter Logan said sharply. "You didn't sign?"

"I want fourteen," Grogan said stubbornly. "I'm worth it."

Skeeter Logan swung around and sat up. "Mike, you listen to me. There's humpty-dumpties in both leagues drawing down twenty grand for doing half your job. You ask for twenty, and settle for two less. Nothing lower."

"Golly," Grogan said, "he won't pay that, Skeeter. And practice starts tomorrow. I got to get in shape, and you know the law. I can't start till I sign."

"Sign?" Skeeter Logan said impatiently. "Sign my foot! You good-natured fool, don't you see you've got them over a barrel? Who's behind you? Two kids that can't hold up the job yet. Berra's getting twice what you ought to ask, and he can't hold your mitt behind the plate, and won't until Dickey works with him another three years. Get some guts, Mike. When did you promise to see him again?"

"At breakfast.'

"All right," Skeeter Logan said. "You ask for twenty, settle for eighteen."

"That would be swell," Grogan said, "but what if he won't come across?"

"Take it easy," Skeeter Logan said. "Go swimming, fish off the causeway, see a movie."

"All right," Grogan said. "I'll try it, Skeeter."

Skeeter Logan came down late to breakfast, as was his custom, and found Grogan waiting in the lobby. Grogan looked woebegone and confused, and Skeeter Logan said, "What luck?" half-guessing before the catcher spoke.

"He just laughed at me," Grogan said miserably. "Told me catchers were easy to get. He offered fourteen and said if I didn't take that, I could go home and stay there."

Skeeter Logan felt the old unreasoning, wild rage against the system he had bucked, and half-defeated, over ten long years. He spoke harshly and rapidly: "All right, Mike, you go home."

"Go home!" Grogan said. "And miss practice?"

"Believe me," Skeeter Logan said, "they need you. What the hell are you, Grogan, man or mouse? Call their bluff. Go home and sit until they call. Not you! Make them call."

"But, Skeeter," Grogan almost wailed, "what if they don't call?"

"They will," he said grimly. "If they don't call, I'll turn over my year's pay to you."

Grogan said, "I don't—" and Skeeter Logan turned away with a grunt and said, "All right, let them bounce your bonehead on the pavement. I'm going to the park." He walked away, down the front steps, up the street alone. Grogan did not follow and he thought that finally he had instilled a little fight in the big man, that Grogan had gone back upstairs to talk with the owner again. He did not know until late afternoon, coming from practice, that Grogan had taken the noon plane home. That was the beginning of the rough time.

Randall stopped beside his table at dinner and said, "Your roomie went home, Skeeter. You know that?"

"Yes," he said. "Can't he get what he's worth?"

The other players looked at him sharply, those quick little stares of disapproval. Randall chewed his cigar and said, "Seems to me that concerns Grogan, not you, Skeeter."

"Well, let him settle it then," Skeeter Logan said curtly. "He's of age."

"Funny thing," Randall said. "Grogan never acted this way before."

Randall walked away and Skeeter Logan knew, too well, that the owner and Randall were clearly aware of the influence behind Grogan's decision. He worked through the next week of practice while the writers sent reams of copy north about Grogan's holdout, guessing at the price and who would give in first, and mentioning in their doubletalk that sounded authentic and meant less than nothing, that the owner was setting up two trades for two good catchers from other clubs. The owner passed him one afternoon in front of the clubhouse, gave him a casual nod, and went on to call cheerily at a group of younger players. Skeeter Logan smiled faintly and hoped Grogan would keep holding out.

The owner called Grogan that night and made a deal. Skeeter Logan read it in the morning paper, the usual jacked-up price to make things look fine and dandy, and wondered what Grogan had finally taken. The next morning, taking his laps, going through infield, he did not see Grogan come from the side gate and enter the clubhouse. The squad was spread across the field, working at increased pace, and Skeeter Logan trotted from infield workout to wipe his face and get a drink. The clubhouse was empty and silent when he bent over the fountain, and went to his locker for a towel. He heard the voices from the trainer's room, Grogan and the club's director of publicity, Hank Arnow.

"I wish you hadn't gone home," Arnow said.

"Doggone it," Grogan said heavily, "he never made no move for a week. Why didn't he call? He knew I was willing to split the difference. Skeeter told me I was a damned fool, letting you people give me the runaround. You need me and you know it. If he didn't want me, all right, going home was my privilege. Talk contract, sell me, or trade me. I've got feelings just like anybody else. I'm no slave. Didn't I give you a good year last time? If some of these humpty-dumpties can draw down that big dough, then I got a right to my share."

"Did you figure all this out by yourself?" Arnow asked quietly.

"Sure," Grogan said. "Why not?"

"Come on, Mike," Arnow said pleasantly. "I know you better than that. Was it Skeeter?"

"We talked about it," Grogan said cautiously. "You know Skeeter is smart about them things."

"So he recommended you go home and let the front office call first?" Arnow said, deceptively calm.

"What if he did?" Grogan said. "It worked out okay. Made folks know I got some rights. And you know the writers lied about the pay, too. I asked for twenty, he offered fifteen, we split at seventeen and a thousand bonus if attendance goes over one and a half. I'm worth that much, ain't I?"

"Of course you are," Arnow said gently. "But I wish you hadn't gone home."

"Why not?" Grogan said. "I'm in good shape. Nothing's lost."

"I suppose not," Arnow said. "Whatever happens, it was certain to come anyway. Well, start working that blubber off, Mike."

Arnow came from the trainer's room and was almost to the door when he saw Skeeter Logan. Arnow flushed and then he said casually, "Hot today, Skeet," and went on through the door to the field. Skeeter Logan wiped his face with the rough-grained towel and wanted to wrap a bat around Grogan's trusting, kind head. *My big mouth*, he thought, *my big fat mouth always saying too much*. The owner knew, Randall knew, everybody would know, and God help Skeeter Logan if he didn't play the best shortstop in the league from now on out, until he lost the big step and went down for good.

He did not mention this to Grogan as training ended, the trip north ran its tiresome course, and the season began. Louise came from their winter home and opened the house in the city, and knew everything within a month, picking up the story in little dribbles and dabs. Skeeter Logan laughed her out of worry in May, kept her happy in June, but in July a batting slump hung on for two weeks and his average dropped to .252, twenty points below his lifetime mark. Then the catty remarks came out in the open, and Louise stopped going to the games, as she had so many times, in the past years when Skeeter Logan's sharp, free tongue pushed them recklessly into one hotbox after another with writers and owners and managers. They were fighting for the pennant all the way, in a tight four-cornered race with the Giants, Phillies, and Dodgers, never more than five games out, and now, in mid-August, had fought into a second place tie with the Giants, two games behind the twin leaders. The third western road trip would tell the story; and Skeeter Logan, despite his usual excellent game afield, was hitting a light .264. During the long home stand he felt the difference in Randall, evinced in the little movements and casual words and fleeting glances. And Skeeter Logan, playing on a possible pennant winner for the first time in ten years and four different clubs, knowing as did the league that nothing could stop the Grays next year and the next, felt at last the strong, almost frightening desire to win and remain with this fine team.

And tonight, while he lay open-eyed in bed, it might be ending for him. He had always believed strongly in premonitions, and the feeling in his chest was tight and bitter. He would survive, he always would, but in doing so someone else was always hurt; and the nearest one was Louise. Skeeter Logan turned in bed, bit savagely on the pillow, and rubbed callused fingers against his tired eyes.

He dressed slowly for the final game of the home stand, took batting and infield, and went downstairs again for the brief pre-game meeting. Randall went over the Giants carefully, rechecked on Hearn who was going today, and said finally, "We need this one, no use telling you all that. Win it, we go west no less than two games behind, with all the chance in the world. Lose and we'll have to fight to make up that game. Let's work today. Okay, go out."

Skeeter Logan followed the others through the door and met Randall's eye for one short moment. Randall looked away and frowned at the wall. And then they were going again, under a hot sun before a fine mid-week crowd of almost thirty thousand faithful fans, holding the Giants and being held themselves in the first inning, as Hearn and old Purcell started with strength and good control, in a game that was certain to be decided by the one break when it came. Skeeter Logan talked it up in his harsh, high voice, sparking the infield as he had for years, roughing Purcell with his tongue when the pitcher needed that astringent prod, and playing today with

the feeling of five years past as heat and sun loosened his legs
and his arm felt like a rookie firing the rifle to first base. He
moved into the hole on a smash by Thomson in the third, for
a backhanded pickup and long throw that cut off the potential
rally, and again in the fifth, with Irvin on first base and one
away, went behind second for a diving stab and flip throw to
Maloney, forcing Irvin and getting Mays at first for the double
play on Maloney's leaping pivot and snap relay. He grounded
out in the second and flied to center field in the fifth, as the
game wore on in a scoreless duel.

Grogan was handling Purcell just right, using Purcell's good
control to nip the corners and hold the ball low between knees
and belt, forcing the Giants to hit into the ground. And Hearn
was equally sharp, his curve breaking off the table, his inside
pitches keeping them off balance as young Westrum caught a
fine game. Skeeter Logan handled eight chances through the
sixth; in the seventh Westrum singled through the hole, a rifle
shot that neither Skeeter Logan nor their third baseman could
reach, both diving and touching the ball, but no more. The
bunt went down automatically and Westrum raced to second
as Purcell made the play to first for the out. Grogan was
shouting now, shaking one dirty fist, calling them up and ready.
Stanky bounced and wiggled, leered and moved in the box,
worked up a three-two count and hit the pitch into center field
to score Westrum with the game's first run. Lockman drove a
sizzling hopper at Maloney's ankles and Skeeter Logan, racing
for the bag, cursed aloud as Maloney juggled the ball, then
recovered and made a snap, high throw. Skeeter Logan leaped
and made the catch, could not drag a foot or stab the bag in
his dash, and threw to first for the second out, and Maloney
came over, face twisted in anger, and said, "My fault, Skeeter,
all my fault."

Skeeter Logan said, "Forget it, kid. Come on, Purc, let's get
out and in!"

Grogan roared, "Come on, come on!" and crouched behind

the plate as Mueller stepped in, and Skeeter Logan caught Grogan's signal for the pickoff as Stanky led and cupped his hands, shouting at Mueller, trying to rattle Purcell. Skeeter Logan watched Purcell toe the rubber and make his stretch, shouted, "Work hard, Purc," and began his silent count. He hit three and broke for second as Purcell swung inside and whipped the ball at the bag. Stanky poised an instant on his toes, whirling and diving, and Skeeter Logan took the ball at his shoetop and slapped the rigid extended fingers and leaped on across the bag as Dascoli hooked the thumb for the out and Durocher came raging from the Giants dugout. Skeeter Logan flipped his glove to the grass and saw Stanky chasing Dascoli and Durocher closing in, and ran off beside Maloney, talking it up now, slapping backs and hearing the loud, happy crowd sound well above them.

Randall was calling, "This time, now we go," then talking quickly to Maloney who was leading off in their half of the seventh. Maloney fouled off four pitches and singled to left field, and Randall gave a dozen take-offs and allowed Johnson to hit away. Hearn pitched outside and Johnson faked the bunt, then caught a curve ball on the handle and dribbled it past Lockman toward second base, a fluke bleeder that Stanky could not reverse and take, as both runners were safe. Skeeter Logan stepped into the circle and thought, "If Elliot bunts, I'll go out for a pinch hitter," and wished now, as he had in bygone years, to stay in and hit, to help win this game they needed so badly. Elliot took the sign as Randall turned toward the dugout and glanced along the bench, picking his man, and then Hearn's inside pitch sailed at the last split-second and caught Elliot in the shoulder before the big man could drop away. Elliot rubbed his arm and lumbered down to first, and turned, hands cupped, shouting, "Now get that hit, Skeeterboy, get that hit!"

Skeeter Logan looked at Randall and wanted to say, "You can't jerk me now. There's no percentage. You got to leave me in," and Randall nodded him in, and sent young Charles out to run for Elliot, lessening the double play chance. Skeeter Logan stepped in and rocked, felt his right heel set firmly, came through twice and set himself, watching Hearn's arm and chest, thinking only of the game, with everything else forgotten in the moment of pressure. Hearn rocked and the ball was a streak of white, bobbing grayly as it flashed within the lengthening stand shadows, cutting under his elbows for strike one. He relaxed and set himself again, and felt good inside, for he had followed that one all the way and it hadn't hopped as Hearn's fast ball was jumping on them before. *Now*, he thought, *now throw the curve and if that edge is gone, we'll get a piece of cake.*

Hearn took the signal and nodded sourly, checked the runners and went into a full windup, long arm dropping back behind the shoulder, leg coming up, and the ball out of the bleacher's white shirts, at the shoulder and slicing down, and Skeeter Logan followed the break and swung viciously, catching the curve and feeling the solid shock in his hands and forearms as the ball was going and he broke from the box. Randall was waving the runners on and Skeeter Logan rounded first, saw Mays chasing far in right-center field, and dug for second base, leaning in and going on for third, catching Randall's signal and sliding inside and around the bag, under the relay from Dark, with a base-cleaning triple. He bounced up then, dusted his pants, and yelled, "All right, Purc! Get your hit and we'll keep it riding!"

Randall was talking to Purcell, encouraging the pitcher, speaking no words to Skeeter Logan. He led off the bag and played it close while Purcell struck out, and then scored the fourth run after a long fly ball. He sat on the bench and they slapped his back and laughed and the good talk ran thick and strong around him. They ran out for the eighth and Skeeter Logan knew the game was theirs, one of those feelings he had mastered long ago, and foretold perfectly to his senses as Purcell bore down hard and retired the side in the eighth, and then, in the ninth, allowed two doubles for one run and retired Lockman on a grounder to Skeeter Logan for the final out.

He heard the people in the box seats calling, "Nice going, Skeeter," as he ducked into the tunnel; and only when he reached the dressing room and took the bottle of cold beer from Grogan, and drank it slowly while Grogan ruffled his hair, only then he remembered and wondered if today would make a difference.

"Just like a kid," Grogan laughed. "You get younger every year, Skeeter. Old clutch Logan, that's our boy."

He saw Randall signal from the office door, and said, "Better take your shower fast. Mike. You might tighten up."

"Sure, sure," Grogan grinned and ambled away, snapping a towel at the batboy's legs. Skeeter Logan undressed and finished the beer, wrapped a towel around his hips, and walked to the office. Randall said, "Close the door," and when they faced one another, alone in the small room, Randall said, "Nice going. We needed that game."

He felt a small warm hope in his chest. "We can take it now."

"I think we can," Randall said flatly. "What I wanted to tell you is, the trade went through this afternoon."

Skeeter Logan said, "What trade?"

"The front office," Randall said evenly. "You're traded to the Browns. Report as soon as possible."

Skeeter Logan snapped without hesitation, "I won't report. I'm a ten-year man. I demand the right to make any deal I can." And saying the words that meant nothing in this situation, for it meant the league had waived him through; and more, that other clubs had allowed the Grays' owner to run this deal in return for future favors, he thought of the game just finished and the pennant that could and should be won, and the series he had never played in, and never would, in the short future remaining at his age. Randall hadn't forgotten; nobody had or ever would forget Skeeter Logan thought of the words spoken in anger, the clubhouse lawyering that had always seemed honest and right, all the harsh, abrupt, unthinking words of ten past years; and nodded silently and walked from the office.

He would never give Randall the satisfaction of cutting him down, making him beg; he would never do that, but this had been coming for years, he had known the risk and accepted it, and now he had no words of answer. He walked to the trainer's room and rubbed salve on his scraped knee and sat on the side table for a moment. The big pitcher, McCally, stood on the scale and scowled at the bar and grunted in disgust. "Damn it," McCally said. "I wish I could get that ten pounds off."

Skeeter Logan looked at McCally for a long, silent moment while the others watched him covertly, understanding already with their sixth sense of feeling trouble, and then slid off the table and moved slowly to the door. He paused a moment, his face working with some thought held secret inside him, and finally said, "I'd trade ten pounds for just one ounce of common sense."

He was gone then, through the door and down the aisle into the dressing room, while they stared dumbly at the floor, all of them, and wished they could do something, anything, to help Skeeter Logan go back and change the past and make life move along the way it should with all of them. But it was too late now; and time never stopped.

The
Terrible-Tempered Rube

R ube got the "red-nosed reindeer" name during the first exhibition game that spring. We'd been working out two weeks
and Rube looked mighty good, but the front office had snatched
him from the Cards in that winter trade and we knew he was a
slow starter. When Skip named our three regulars to pitch the
game against the Tigers, Rube took it as a personal insult.

"Skip," he said, "how come I don't work today?"

"Too early for you," Skip said.

"I ain't no rookie," Rube protested. "I been up three years."

"Yea," Skip said, "and how many have you won during April
and May?"

"That ain't my fault," Rube said. "Them Cards never give me
a fair chance. They knew if I worked in turn I'd win twenty and
be in line for a big raise."

"See the owner about a raise," Skip said. "Meanwhile, you go
shag some flies and work off that pot."

Rube wandered off, growling to himself. Castleton pitched
three innings, Brush took the middle workout and Rube came
sidling into the dugout.

"Skip," he said. "Just two innings, huh?"

"Not today," Skip said.

"One inning, then," Rube begged.

Rube hung around, giving Skip seventeen different reasons why he should pitch one inning.

Finally, during the fifth, Skip said, "So you're ready, eh?"

"Skip," Rube said, "they won't touch me!"

"All right," Skip said. "Warm up."

We had a two-run lead when Rube came strutting out to start the seventh. He walked like a sailor on turned ankles, his elbows were a pair of battering rams, his jaw always led his Adam's apple by six inches. He had the confidence of Johnson and Newsom and Grove all rolled into one and displayed by the way his jaws chomped up and down on five sticks of gum. He was all set to push those Tiger bats right down their windpipes. He walked the first man on four pitched balls.

" Well," Skip said, "our twenty-game winner!"

Rube filled the bases on twelve pitches. He got madder and madder, knowing then he wasn't ready, and he sneaked an imploring look toward Skip.

"Better jerk him," Benny said.

"No," Skip said. "I'll teach him a lesson if he stays out there till midnight."

Benny nudged me. "Si, come on."

We hurried down the left-field line to the clubhouse and helped the trainer stow all loose objects in a safe place. By that time Rube had walked two runs home and was removing himself from the game. He'd walked six men on twenty-four pitches, and he headed for the clubhouse with steam rising from his ears. He passed us like a pay car does a tramp and began wrecking operations.

"He do this often?" I asked.

"You won't grow a beard waitin' for next time," Benny said. "Just let him alone."

Rube kicked the lockers over, busted three windows and upset the benches. When he quieted down and we peeked inside, he was hitting himself in the head with one fist.

"Well," Benny said, "he sure told the truth. They didn't even touch him."

"Can the Eagles afford this damage?" I said.

"Rube," Benny said thoughtfully, "Rube, the red-nosed reindeer."

"The Cards warned us," I said. "Now we've got the proof."

"Lefty was worse," Benny said, "and he won three hundred games. You've got to admire a man who wants to win that bad."

"Sure," I said, "but who goes crazy first, him or Skip?"

Well, Rube got in shape and pitched his spring turns and did fine. When we finished the northern swing and faced opening day, Rube was No. 4 in our rotation. He was his own worst enemy, but he could pitch.

"Rube," Skip told him that day, "you'll take your turn. Just don't bite any umpires."

"Listen," Rube said. "You ever had to see them faces behind your catcher for nine innings?"

"No," Skip said. "Among us managers, Durocher's the authority on close-ups."

"Someday," Rube said, "I'm gonna sneak a fast one in there and bounce that Dascoli clear to the screen."

"What for?" Skip said.

Rube snorted. "Because I hate umpires!"

Skip went to home plate with his line-up card and Rube squatted beside us on the bench. The boys were all calling him Reindeer on the sly, but nobody called him anything but Rube to his face. And even being called Rube bothered him, because, all at once, he turned to Benny and said, "Listen here, I'm no rube."

"Where you from?" Benny asked.

Rube said, "Peruque."

"Is that a stomach medicine," Benny said, "or a name?"

Rube said, "Peruque, Illinois."

"What's the population?" Benny asked.

"Eighty-seven when I'm home," Rube said. "And I'm proud of my home-town and maybe you want to argue about it?"

"Simmer down," Benny said. "If you pitch like you boost your home-town, I'll come out in October and ride raw down Main Street for you."

"That ain't allowed," Rube said seriously.

"Never mind," Benny said. "You just throw that ball, Rube."

One day in May, Rube started against Jansen in the Polo Grounds. He retired two men and walked Thompson. The Giants began razzing him, and Rube hit Irvin in the short ribs with a fast ball. Durocher stood up and tickled Rube's sensitive eardrums, and Rube did just like Leo wanted.

He came off the mound, yelling, "Get a bat and come to the plate and say that!"

Durocher grinned and sat down. Rube walked the bases full and Thomson hit one into the left-field stands for four runs. When Rube got the third out and came to the dugout, he was purple-red and breathing fire.

"That lucky bum," he said. "Had no business swinging at the pitch."

Skip said, "He thought it looked pretty good."

"Oh, it was," Rube said, "but on a two-two count he should've been expecting the curve ball."

"Never mind second-guessing," Skip said. "You pitch where Rocky says."

"I did," Rube said. "Why don't he call my best pitch in the clutch?"

"Was that a good pitch?"Skip said.

"No," Rube said. "It was six inches inside."

"That's funny," Skip said. "He hit it like it was good."

"He closed his eyes," Rube said. "He didn't even know it was curving."

We went scoreless and next inning Rube fanned Westrum and made Jansen pop up on a nice change curve. He was talking before he got his jacket on, glaring at Rocky, saying, "And that there was a mistake too."

"It worked good," Skip said.

"Should 'a' been a fast one," Rube said.

"Rocky gives the signals," Skip said. "You just throw them."

In the sixth we got three runs back. Rube was mowing the Giants down and we kept our fingers crossed because he hadn't disagreed with Stewart's calls as yet. Irvin came up with two on and two out, and the Giants gave Rube the double-barreled razz-ma-tazz. Rube worked a two-two count and Irvin lined to center field. Rube grinned all the way to the dugout.

"What was that?" Skip said.

Rube said, "My fast ball."

"Thought your curve was your best pitch," Skip said.

"It is," Rube said.

"How come you didn't shake Rocky off, then?" Skip asked.

Rube said, "I thought he called for a curve."

"But you threw a fast ball," Skip said.

"Sure," Rube said. "It slipped."

We tied the game in the seventh and Rube staggered through the Giants' half. We went one ahead in the ninth, and Rube strutted out like a fighting rooster and sneered over at Durocher. Nobody could sneer like Rube when he was ahead and feeling good. He retired two men and Lockman came up. Rube built up a two-two count, shook off Rocky's signal, and shook off the next one. He shook off a third signal, wound up and let one go. Lockman busted it just fair down the right-field foul line, into the stands for a tie game. Rube watched that dinky homer, glared at Lockman and slammed his glove on the rubber.

"All right," Stewart called. "Watch that, Rube."

Rube threw the rosin bag at third base. Stewart gave him the thumb right there. Rube went off the mound and pushed his jaw against Stewart's and spoke a few choice words.

Stewart said, "That'll cost you a hundred, Rube."

We got him off the field before he did anything real foolish.

Our fireman came in from the bullpen while Skip cornered Rube and said, "What was that last pitch?"

"My fast ball," Rube said.

"Did Rocky call for a curve?" Skip said.

"He did once," Rube said.

"Then why the blazing, burning hell," Skip said, "did you shake him off three times?"

Rube said, "I was foolin' Lockman."

"You were?" Skip said. "In what way?"

"Why," Rube said, "Lockman was looking for my curve ball, so I kept shaking off so's he'd figure I was finally coming in with it."

"He hit it just the same," Skip said.

"I slipped," Rube said.

"You slipped!"

"Sure," Rube said. "I was goin' to throw the curve and the doggone ball slipped."

"Stewart slipped you a hundred," Skip said softly, "and I'm adding another hundred to that. Try slipping out of those curves."

The Giants beat us in the tenth. The club paid Rube's fine to the commissioner's office, but Skip made him fork over the other hundred.

Going home from that Eastern swing, Benny cornered Rube in the diner and said, "Tell me, just what is your best pitch?"

"My fast ball," Rube said, "and I ain't dumb."

"Then you're a good actor," Benny said.

Rube winked at me. "That's what they always said back home."

"They did?" Benny said.

"Sure," Rube said. "They told me a fella had to blow his own horn."

Rube was fined twice and booted out three times by the middle of July. We were trailing the Grays just three games, and if Rube had held his temper and gone the distance in those three games, we'd have been tied for the lead. The front office was taking a roasting for making the trade, when Rube caught fire in the stretch. He won eight in a row and was willing to pitch with two days' rest. We cinched the pennant five games before the finish, and Skip put Rube in the last game to limber up his arm for two innings, and Rube came out with a sore shoulder.

You know how the series ended; the Yanks beat us four straight and Rube didn't get in until the ninth inning of the last game. He relieved Brush with one away and our second baseman missed two chances that went for hits and should have been outs. Then the Yanks hit Rube with everything but the clubhouse attendant's sandwiches.

That didn't bother Rube. He went home to Peruque and held out. He returned three contracts and came down to spring training and hung around the hotel, telling everybody exactly where our owner, Mr. Hockenschmidt, could go with those contracts. The day before training officially started, he ran into me and Benny in the hotel garden.

He came through the side-street gate with a big package under his arm, and Kenny said, "Slow down. Been shopping?"

"You bet," Rube said. "I got some sport shirts."

Benny poked me and grinned. Rube was the flashiest dresser on the club. He had enough suits, sport coats, and ties to outfit a Vero Beach tryout camp. The only drawback was, Rube seemed to be color-blind. He wore pink slacks with blue coats and green ties, and he owned six pairs of those two-toned wing-tipped shoes. And he was always looking for bargains.

Benny said, "Where'd you get em?

"The Beach Shop," Rube said. "They was on sale. I got six for eighteen bucks."

"What color?" Kenny asked.

"What do you mean, color?" Rube said. "They're all colors. You don't think I buy them solid-colored shirts. That's how them big manufacturers make so much money. It don't cost near as much for just one color."

"You must feel confident," Benny said, "spending all that money before you get it."

"I deserve a raise," Rube said. "I told Hockenschmidt I'd

win eight in a row to start off this season, and that's worth a good raise."

"What you holding out for?" Benny asked.

"It ain't your business," Rube said, " but I'm asking twenty."

Rube had come from the Cards with a hold-over contract for nine thousand. He'd won seventeen and lost nine, so he did merit a raise, but he'd never get twenty.

Benny said, "Why don't you compromise, Rube?"

"Not a penny," Rube said. "I know my rights."

"Maybe you've got a case," Benny said. "You need the extra dough to pay your fines."

" I won't get fined once," Rube said. "I'm reformed."

"Since when?" Benny said.

"Since last month," Rube said. "I'm gonna be married."

"The heck you are," Benny said. "Hometown girl?"

Rube said, " We grew up together."

"And she still said yes?" Benny said. "When does it happen?"

"When I get my raise," Rube said.

"I hope she's young," Benny said.

We hung around the lobby that night until Rube finished his conference with Hockenschmidt and Skip. When Skip came down for a goodnight beer, he told us Rube had finally signed for sixteen-five.

"And lucky," Skip said. "Hockenschmidt don't like him at all."

"Hockenschmidt isn't alone," Benny said. "But likes or dislikes won't matter if Rube pitches ball."

"Hocky told him," Skip said, "that he better stay out of trouble or get sold to Albuquerque."

"You think he will?" Benny asked.

"I don't know," Skip said. "He told us he was getting married and his wife would calm him down. Rocky asked him why he always fought umpires and Rube said that wasn't true, he never fought with Klem."

"But Bill's gone," Benny said.

"Sure," Skip said. "That's the way Rube put it."

Well, Rube lost his first game that season. We went into a tailspin and he lost eight in a row, got fined twice, and kicked out of two games. He finally staggered through his ninth start against Boston, just before we went on our second Western trip, and everybody knew it was make or break for the Eagles in those games.

Skip started Rube in the last game of the Pittsburgh series. Everything went fine until the sixth, then Dascoli called a ball on a corner pitch and Rube came off the mound like the bull of Bashan.

He glared at Dascoli and then he surprised us. He turned around and went back to the rubber. He threw another pitch, that was called a ball, and Rube blew up. He whacked his glove on the ground, rared back and gave the rubber a terrific kick. Next thing, he was rolling on the mound, holding his right toe.

When the trainer removed his shoe, his big toe was swollen up like a tennis ball. They rushed him to a doctor and took x-rays, and the report came in that Rube had sustained a hairline fracture of his right big toe. He was waiting at the hotel, his foot in a cast, when we got back from losing the game.

"Skip," Rube said, "don't worry. I can pitch in a couple days."

"On what?" Skip said. "Your head?"

"My feet," Rube said. "Look, I can walk."

He limped around the sofa and did a little jog to prove his point.

Skip said, "You take the train home."

"Skip," Rube said, "the team needs me."

"The team needs a lot of things," Skip said. "Are you under the impression we're playing football?"

"Skip, I'm sorry," Rube said. "I tell you my toe ain't bad. I ought to—"

"Take the train," Skip said, real cold. "See our doc when you get home."

Rube went home and we kept on going. We started that road

trip in fifth place and we came home in sixth. Rube was in the dressing room next day, the cast off his foot, jumping like an acrobat to prove he was all right.

"I told you," he said. "I can pitch any time you say, Skip."

Skip said, "Can you come off the rubber?"

"Look here," Rube said.

He planted one foot against a foot bath, took a windup, and lunged forward and almost stuck his right fist into Skip's mouth. He didn't flinch and he followed through all the way.

Skip said, "It's against medical science."

"I can't help that," Rube said. "Castleton's got a sore arm and you worked Brush four times. When do I start? "

"Tomorrow," Skip said.

"You can pitch me every three days," Rube said earnestly. "I won't let you down, Skip."

Now, Rube knew he had to win some games or face a full cut next year. Then we heard his folks had come back for a visit and brought his girl. He beat the Giants next day 3-0 on a two-hitter, and he didn't start one argument. His toe didn't bother him either.

It shouldn't have. That night our team doc told us about his big toe. When they took x-rays in Pittsburgh, the hairline break that plate showed was an old one. Rube had broken that same toe three years ago in St. Louis, when he fell over a water fountain trying to brain a box-seat heckler. The hairline break was there, but it was three years healed.

"I knew he was hardheaded," Skip said. "I never figured he was bone all over."

"You see his girl?" Benny asked.

"I sure did," Skip said. "I wonder how much she'd take to hang around all year."

"Don't tell Rube that," Benny said. "He'll make her hold out."

"If she helps him," Skip said, "I don't care what she wants."

She was a mighty pretty girl and she always sat in the rail

box, and Rube spent the next afternoon hanging over the rail, holding her hand, saying whatever he might say in that situation. The words would be different from the average fellow, Benny said, because Rube wasn't average. He was probably reminding her how much it cost him to pay for box seats. She might not know that he got passes.

Anyway, Rube's folks and his girl stayed ten days. Rube won two more games, and Hockenschmidt, who was a great believer in married ballplayers, sneaked down from his rooftop penthouse and took a look at the girl. He sure picked the right time.

It was her last day there. Rube was holding her hand when Hocky reached the aisle. Rube said something and she answered, and they both stood up, jaw to jaw, and she outtalked Rube. They staged the best premarriage battle we ever saw. She got red as fire and shook her fist in Rube's face. He shook both fists, they took time off to draw breath, and she yanked off a shoe and smacked him between the eyes. Rube was just starting a roundhouse swing when Benny grabbed him.

Now, Rube's old man was a carbon copy of Rube. He'd spent ten days telling the Eagles what was wrong with their team, and you could hear him a mile against the wind.

He growled, "Leave him go."

Benny said, "All right," and let loose. Rube just wound up again and made for her, and his old man hit him in the face with a seat cushion—they're not so soft—and yelled, "Reuben, you apologize right now!"

Hocky had seen enough. He went back upstairs and sent a message to Skip to bring the staff in for a meeting after the game. We got Rube calmed down, and Benny said, "What was the trouble?"

"Nothin'," Rube said. "Just a little family argument."

"Let me know when you have a big one," Benny said. "I want front-row tickets."

"Nellie's like that," Rube said. "She's got an awful temper. I keep telling her not to be that way."

"Do tell," Benny said. "I suppose this was her fault."

"It sure was," Rube said. "She wants the wedding in October."

"I heard that was the woman's privilege," Benny said.

"We agreed on September and sent out the cards," Rube said. "She can come over to St. Louis when we make the last road trip, just like we planned."

Benny said, "Don't you want to get married in Peruque?"

"And stand all that expense?" Rube said. "Nothin' doing."

"Then why send announcements?" Benny asked.

"I thought you knew better," Rube said scornfully. "That's etiquette."

"Oh," Benny said, "I get it. If the guests want to attend, they can drive to St. Louis."

"Sure," Rube said. "I ain't begging nobody."

Hockenschmidt laid down the law that night. He could stand one like Rube, but two—never! And he meant Nellie. If Rube lost his temper just once more, he was going down the river. Skip passed the good news, but he didn't mention Nellie.

"I'll try," Rube said. "But pitch me every three days, Skip."

"Maybe," Skip said. "I make no promises."

But we were down to bedrock with starting pitchers, and Skip had to give Rube the chance. Rube won four in a row and brought his record up to eight-nine. By the time we left on the final road trip, Rube had smoothed out his family troubles via three-cent stamp, and we were all cordially invited to the wedding—in St. Louis.

It came off fine. Rube was a perfect gentleman and Nellie looked sweet enough to butter up anybody.

"Good luck," Skip said. "Rube's going tonight. I hope he gives you a wedding present, Mrs. Jones."

"He better," Nellie said. "That'll bring him up to a five-hundred average."

"I'll tend to the pitching," Rube said. "You just handle the pots and pans."

"Excuse me," Skip said. "We'll see you tonight."

In the taxi, Skip sighed. "Married five minutes and fighting already."

That night was one for the book. Rube started like a ball of fire. He had a one-run lead when we batted in the sixth, we got two on with two out, and Rube stepped to the plate. Like all pitchers, he figured himself a DiMaggio. He usually got three hits a season. He topped a dinky roller down the third-base line, our man scored from third, and Rube crossed first base a hand width after Bilko took the peg.

Rube ran down the line, chest out, feeling that he'd got a hit and batted in a run. When he turned and saw the Cards trotting off the field, he started for Pinelli. His jaw was going eighty miles an hour and the words were spitting out like bullets. Pinelli folded his arms and turned away. Rube kept after him. He told Pinelli all about ancestors from the eighteenth century down to the present moment, and then he started over.

Pinelli was reasonable to the extreme. He waited the full minute before he gave Rube the thumb. Rube was so mad he didn't stop, and Pinelli looked around for help. We dragged him into the dugout and Pinelli fined him a hundred and mentioned a five-day suspension.

Even then, Rube wouldn't calm down. We pushed him into the tunnel and he got down on his knees and stuck his head between Benny's legs and got in the last word. Pinelli wasn't far off, behind first base, and Rube kept butting against Benny's legs and shouting, until Skip said, "Rube, take your shower."

"I was safe!" Rube yelled. "He's a blind—"

Benny squatted down and shut off what could have been five hundred dollars and a month's suspension.

When Rube went up the tunnel, Benny wiped his face and said, "That does it."

And it did. Hockenschmidt heard the story and told Skip that Rube was going far and fast. We finished out the season and Rube won his last game and finished with a nine-nine record.

When we said good-by for the winter, he told Skip, "Don't worry about me next year."

"We won't," Skip said. "Because you won't be here."

"Don't kid me," Rube said. "The Eagles ain't trading a twenty-game winner."

"No," Skip said. "They're trading a temper."

Rube said, "You serious, Skip?"

"I warned you," Skip said. "Hockenschmidt means business."

"Listen," Rube said soberly. "He don't understand. I'll be all right next year. Nellie's a cinch to calm me down."

"Nellie!" Skip said.

"Sure," Rube said. "She knows how to handle me."

"How?" Skip said. "With a bat?"

"She knows," Rube said wisely. "That's our family secret. Listen, Skip. You know I don't lie. I'm telling you the truth. Don't trade me."

"No," Skip said. "It's too late."

"All right," Rube said. "But you tell Hocky for me, if he trades me and I land with the Grays, I'm gonna be the difference between their pennant and your pennant."

You know how the trade came off in December. Hockenschmidt traded Rube to the Pirates for a third baseman because he hit a long ball. The Pirates traded Rube that same day to the Grays for six young ballplayers and a bundle of cash. When interviewed at home, Rube was quoted as saying he was happy to be with the Grays and he'd win the pennant for them. He spent the winter returning their contracts and finally signed in camp. We heard that he took a full 25 percent cut, but the Grays put in a bonus clause of ten thousand if he won twenty games. The day we played the Grays in Miami, Rube came over and shook hands all around.

"Told you I was lucky," Rube said.

"I guess you are," Benny said. "You're still alive."

"I'm on a pennant winner," Rube said. "I'll wave when we pass you in August."

"Going backward," Benny said.

"Listen," Rube said. "You two were my friends, and you still are, but I'll make old Hocky regret the day he traded me for a has-been third baseman."

"Has-been?" Benny said. "He's hit six homers already."

"In grapefruit games," Rube sneered. "Wait till the season starts. He won't hit two-seventy for you."

"How many games you goin' to win? " Benny asked.

"Twenty," Rube said. "Maybe more."

Benny said, "Your wife goin' to stay with you?"

"Sure," Rube said. "She's up there now, finding a place, moving in our clothes."

"That's a big job," Benny said. "Now, I'll just bet the steak dinner you don't win twenty."

"Took," Rube said. "What about you, Si?"

"Same bet," I said. "You're asking for it, Rube."

"Sit tight," Rube said. "I'll show you."

Well, you know how the season came out. The Grays hung right up there with us and the Giants. Rube won games like he'd found the secret. He had fourteen wins and three losses on August fifteenth, and he'd been fined only once for fighting. That was on a road trip, and his three losses had come on road trips, too. Benny and I cornered the Grays' bullpen coach the day we pulled into Gray Park for the big three-game series.

Benny said, "Herman, what's the story on Rube?"

"Good pitcher," Herman said. "Good boy."

"Then what happened to him?" Benny asked.

"He got married," Herman said. "Wonderful little woman. She sure calmed him down."

"Herman," Benny said painfully, "break that down simple for us, please?"

"Simple as A, B, C," Herman said. "Nellie's got a temper just like Rube. They fight all the time when we're at home. Rube comes out to the park so tired from fighting, he don't want to start trouble with nobody, not even with Leo. That lasts him about two hours, which is all we need. He still gets mad on road trips; you know he got fined in Chicago, and he lost three on the road. But we ain't worried. I hear the boss is thinking of taking Nellie along on the road trips next year."

"Oh," Benny said. "I see."

Rube beat our pants off that night for his fifteenth win, and got a hit to boot. He fanned our new third baseman four times and sent his average down to .262, and he let us know about that in the last inning. He tipped his cap to our dugout and made a few choice remarks, and then fanned our third baseman for the last out.

The Grays cinched the pennant on September twenty-sixth in our stadium. Rube shut us out 2-0, and it just happened to be his twentieth win of the year against five defeats. When he retired the last batter, he stepped off the mound and grinned at Skip and looked up at Hockenschmidt's box.

He pulled off his cap and made a big bow and shouted loud enough for everybody to hear "Thank you, Mr. Hockenschmidt! "

And everybody knew exactly what he meant.

Moment of Truth

D uke DiSalvo woke reluctantly that morning, prayed for rain, and opened the drapes to brilliant sunshine that hurt his tired eyes. In the old years, before the war and even two seasons ago, each morning was a fresh challenge that found him restlessly eager for game time, but that was the past when his body was strong and nothing mattered but getting the hits and making the catches.

The knock came on schedule and Duke DiSalvo called, "Come in, Henry," and began dressing while the waiter set breakfast before the windows.

Henry smiled hesitantly and said, "Big one today, Duke," and waited for the tall man to answer.

Duke DiSalvo grunted, "They're all big, Henry," and knotted his tie with an impatient jerk.

He saw Henry's face in the mirror, frowning with concern, and then the door closed quietly. Duke DiSalvo could never be pleasant with people, giving only curt answers and his sober, long-jawed stare, and it was too late for change. He was a legend now, the silent man who rarely spoke to anyone, even his teammates.

He glanced at the morning paper and threw it across the

room; reading the sport pages only irritated him more, with every writer insisting he should have retired last fall. They were enjoying a field day at his expense, now the stretch drive was beginning and he had to play regularly. He must play every day and deliver if the team wanted this pennant, and his ability to play fifty-some games without rest was the major point of the writers' barbed words.

Duke DiSalvo ate methodically, reviewing the past months, cursing the writers with each untasted bite. Let them count him out, he thought; he was still on the field, making the difference between a fair team and a good one. Maybe his legs had slowed up and his plate reflexes betrayed his age, but he still possessed his God-given sixth sense of getting the jump on a fly ball, and he hit in the clutch. Give him an occasional day of rest and he'd finish the schedule.

When the phone rang, Duke DiSalvo smiled and lifted the receiver. "George?"

"Hey, Duke," George Borland said. "Ready to go?"

"See you in five minutes," Duke DiSalvo said. "Much wind today?"

"Little," George said. "How do you feel, Duke? Yesterday was tough on you."

"I'll get by all right," he said. "Be down soon, George."

He finished his coffee and started for the elevator, wondering how George put up with him this summer, the way he'd grouched around. He was lucky to have one real friend in the city, and luckier that the friend was George Borland. The little lawyer had broken through Duke DiSalvo's taciturn reserve many years ago, and since that time George had taken over all his business affairs and become a true friend. George was the only person who seemed to understand why Duke DiSalvo signed for this year. Now George was having doubts.

He crossed the lobby and walked quickly toward George's big convertible, but the kids were waiting, waving notebooks and pencils. He signed every one and smiled wearily, for he couldn't let the kids down, and then he sat beside George in blessed silence, rushing northward through the green park, nearing the gray stadium that appeared on the skyline much too soon these days.

"Lemon today," George said. "Your meat."

"He's tough," Duke DiSalvo said. "We need some pitching ourselves."

"Need?" George said. "Got is the word for today, Duke."

He did not speak for several blocks, thinking of the truth in George's words. Today was the rubber game with Cleveland in their current series; win this one, tied as they were for first place, and that precious one-game lead could be the margin in late September when they played the Indians on the western swing. Today was that game toward which a team unconsciously pointed, the day every man must show a champion's spirit.

"We can do it," he said. "I feel like a couple of base hits, George."

They drove between the grimy buildings, amid the city's incessant sound; the stadium appeared beyond those ragged rooftops, gray and solid against the sky. George Borland shifted his small body behind the wheel and said, "Duke, mind if I say something?"

"You would anyway," Duke DiSalvo said. "So go ahead."

"I want straight answers," George said. "None of that Italian double talk—or no talk."

"Well?" he said.

"How many games have you played in a row?" George asked. "Ten during this home stand. You had a week's rest before that. Yesterday you were barely able to finish."

" I got a hit," Duke DiSalvo said sharply. "Drove in the tying run. How many did I miss in center? We won. What else do you want?"

"I'm not thinking of yesterday," George Borland said. "Not even today, or next week. I'm worrying about next month during the stretch drive. What will you do then, Duke? Play every game, get the hits, make the catches? On what? Your reputation?"

"Cut it out," Duke DiSalvo said thinly. "You're getting like everybody else, George. I'm not dead. I'll play it out."

"Sure you'll play," George said softly. "Because Stinson won't bench you unless you give the word. Nobody can bench you, Duke. You're the team, everything the team has meant for sixteen years. All the pennants, the world championships, the records. Don't you know it has to be you, Duke, giving the word, saying you're done? For the good of the team. And your own good, Duke. Did you read the paper this morning?"

"No," he said sullenly. "Nor any morning."

"Why not?" George asked. "Because you won't accept the truth. I'm your friend, Duke. I don't give a hang that you're bowing out this year. I'm no fair-weather hanger-on. You don't have to do anything more to prove yourself, Duke! You're the Duke, the one and only. But what came first with you from the day you joined the team? Winning the game, always that was first with you. Don't you feel that way now, Duke?"

" What are you trying to say?" Duke DiSalvo asked.

"Quit!" George said bluntly. "Before it's too late. Don't play on borrowed time. You're thirty-seven years old. All right, crawl into that shell. I know what you're thinking, how you feel. You still get the break on those fly balls, you get the base hits; not as many, but enough. That's fine, but don't you realize what'll happen any day? You'll lose everything, all of it, in one moment, one play. And when it goes, the team goes down with you. Tell Stinson to bring young Mahoney back up and put a catcher on the inactive list. Let the kid play, Duke. Help him. Be there to pinch-hit, maybe go in the final games. We can win it again, but not if you wait too long."

"George, that's crazy talk," Duke DiSalvo said coldly. "Nobody loses it all at once. Sure, I'm a step slow. I admit it. But I still get around."

George slowed for the turn and stopped in the reserved

parking space before the players' entrance. He laid a hand on Duke DiSalvo's arm and said, "Mad?"

"We'll get over it," Duke DiSalvo said.

"Good," George said. "One thing more. They've got a saying in Mexico about a certain time in a bullfight. It can apply to almost any man. It comes once in a man's life. They call it the moment of truth. I hope you never feel it, Duke. Good luck today."

Duke DiSalvo said, "Don't get bookish on me, George," and walked swiftly from the car, down the long corridor to the dressing room.

George was getting like everyone else, only more radical. Duke DiSalvo thought briefly about that moment-of-truth business and pushed through the big door into the sound and smell and action of the long room that, for sixteen years, had represented the core of his life. They wondered why he came back this year, played on beyond the average age. He loved this room and all it meant, secretly and jealously, for no man held a permanent place here, and it was hard to say good-by.

The jukebox played softly and players gossiped along the locker line, spikes rasping dully on the carpet strips. The trainer shouted for his next victim and Stinson peered owlishly from the manager's office, calling to a coach. The bat boys hurried past Duke DiSalvo and the clubhouse man stacked his sandwiches and cold milk on the corner bar.

Duke DiSalvo stepped between the walls of his cubicle and began the routine that was more familiar than eating to him: undress and hang his clothes neatly, sit down and draw on the uniform that small boys by the millions dreamed of wearing some glorious day. Adjust the garters, move his shoulders under the clean, smooth-pressed gray flannel, reach up on the shelf for cap and glove. Then sit back and smoke a final cigarette before batting practice. Talk to nobody unless forced, then answer in a curt word or grunt, because long ago he was a scared kid in this awesome room, fighting for a job when the game was rough and tough, and rookies amounted to nothing. He had talked to nobody for so long that after his fright disappeared and he wanted friendship badly, the legend had become reality in his own mind and he could not change.

Duke DiSalvo smoked and fiddled with his glove lacing, thinking of the Cleveland hitters, of Lemon's pitching. But his thoughts wandered into the past today, like the old-timers who appeared during World Series and reminisced of bygone days. He could hear them in the hotel lobbies, behind the cigar smoke, through that high-pitched, excited drone of sound. Remember the '36 Series, Duke, your first? Remember '41, the year you broke all the records? How you sparked the team in '47 and won the flag when nobody gave you higher than third place? Remember a thousand games, the catches and home runs, the hundred-odd records, the way it felt to lead a great ball club through sixteen wonderful years? Remember it all? Duke DiSalvo wondered why the past was so clear today, there must be some reason.

The others were filing past, heading for the tunnel, and the hollow murmur of filling stands filtered down through the stadium walls.

Stinson came from his office and motioned to Duke DiSalvo, then disappeared like an old terrier entering his den. Duke DiSalvo thought *Now what?* and strolled leisurely across the dressing room.

He remembered the first time he came here, that spring of '36, to face the grim, thick-bodied Irishman who had managed the team to two championships already, and would lead them to another six before retiring; a gruff man whose silence nearly equaled young Duke DiSalvo's. That old man had called him into the office and said, "Play ball for me," and sent him out on the field. Duke DiSalvo remembered that day. Now, with sixteen years gone by, he entered the office and faced Stinson in almost surly silence.

"Sit down, Duke," Stinson said.

"I'll stand," he said. "What is it, Buck?"

"You," Stinson said. "I'm going to tell you something, Duke, before it's too late. How we feel about each other isn't important. You're the last of a great tradition and me, I'm the upstart, the funny guy who came along and had good luck with a team that never belonged to me. Forget all that. I'm not concerned with last year, with the years ahead. I've got to win a pennant now, this year, next month. I can't win with you out there."

"Take me out," Duke DiSalvo said flatly. "You're the skipper."

"Take you out!" Stinson said. "Duke, I can't take you out. And nobody knows that better than you. Duke, this team and you are one and the same thing in the eyes of about eighty million people. You're the class, Duke. And not by luck, by ability. You owe those people something now, mostly to have enough guts to bow out when you're through. I can't bench you, Duke. You've got to do that yourself. You can't last through September, playing every day. Now you know what I want to ask, don't you?"

"You want to bring the kid back up," Duke DiSalvo said tonelessly. "All right, bring him up. I've nothing against Mahoney, against any kid. But he's a year away. I can last this year out. I'll play it the way you want. We'll win this one. Sure, I'm tired, dog-tired, but I can last."

"Who you kidding?" Stinson asked mildly. "Not me. I'm telling you for the last time to wake up and be honest. Will you take the bench?"

"No," Duke DiSalvo said.

"All right; you want it that way, you'll have it. But remember this—one of these days you're going to lose it all and the pennant with it, and then you'll know what I mean. You don't believe me, but it's true. We better go up now, before those scandalmongers decide we've had a duel down here. No hard feelings?"

"What for?" Duke DiSalvo said. "I'm too old for that."

He walked through the silent dressing room, hating Stinson for repeating the same words George Borland had spoken minutes ago. They were all against him; no one had any faith. So let them feel that way. He'd push the lie down their throats the only way he could: on the field, at the plate. Duke DiSalvo came up the tunnel and onto the field with a twisted, sullen face, and walked, head down, to the bat rack.

He swung easily in the batting cage, getting good power against the ball, driving several hits into the left-field boxes. When batting was finished, he loped slowly in center field, catching a few lofty fly balls and flipping his easy throws to the fungo man behind first base. Cochran was in left field today, and Johnson in right. Stinson was flanking him with the fastest outfielders on the team, placing Meeker on the bench today. Duke DiSalvo wondered about that selection. Meeker was a left-handed hitter, Cochran batted right, and Meeker always had good luck against Lemon. Meeker was slow, but Duke DiSalvo could always cover any territory beyond Jake's reach. Starting Cochran was an open slap in his face, Duke DiSalvo thought, the only way Stinson could even their score.

They finished infield and the umpires took position, and Ollie Rankin toed the rubber for his first pitch, and Duke DiSalvo forgot everything but the game, slipping into the old familiar pattern of his life. He moved with the batters, playing each man with his wealth of experience, taking the relayed signals and shifting as Rankin's arm went up and over, playing the curve balls and fast ones, feeling loose and warm today despite the ever-present soreness in back and legs.

The sun was always an old friend, keeping him loose and ready. He shifted and talked it up automatically as Rankin got two men on ground balls before Doby smashed a long fly that Cochran took on the left-field line, a doubtful catch until the moment of contact. Rankin had his stuff today, that was plain, and all that remained was testing Lemon before the game's pattern adjusted for the afternoon.

Duke DiSalvo trotted in and took his center dugout seat, and watched Lemon pitch to their lead-off man. Lemon fielded the soft dribbler for the first out, then fanned Cochran on four pitches. Duke DiSalvo moved from the dugout and took the bats, and stood in the on-deck circle while Johnson ran up a two-two count. Johnson popped a lazy single into short center field and Duke DiSalvo walked up to the familiar round of applause.

Desmond shouted from the first-base coaching box, and Stinson gave the hit-away sign. Duke DiSalvo took his wide-spread stance and cocked himself, watched Johnson take a short lead, and accepted Lemon's first pitch on the outside corner for a called strike. He felt good inside and the ball looked big and white today. He stroked the next pitch into right center, a solid single that pushed Johnson around to third and started the roar from the capacity crowd.

Dusting his trousers on first base, Duke DiSalvo glanced toward the dug-out box. George was there, giving their old handshake of congratulations, letting him know they were all pulling for the team. Duke DiSalvo thought, *Moment of truth!* and started with the pitch as Burrows slammed a hot grounder down to short. Coming into second base, Duke DiSalvo saw Boone make the fast scoop and flip to Avila, and stayed on his feet, forced out by fifteen steps. He was relieved at that, hating the slides into bases on his legs, not to blame for the force-out that would have doubled the fastest man in the league. He passed Avila and trotted on to center field, wondering who would get the first break.

Rankin was hot, but Lemon matched the big Cherokee as the innings passed. Duke DiSalvo crouched in center field and played the hitters, made two routine catches and one play on a base hit in the third; and flied to right field his second time at the plate. They moved into the sixth and now the sun was dropping low, suddenly hot against his face. *Four innings to go*, he thought. Something had to break soon.

He moved on the curve ball, and the hit was over third base, a rifle shot that Cochran knocked down near the box seats. Cochran made a fine throw, but Doby slid safely into second base. Duke DiSalvo pounded his glove and moved over as Easter came to bat, and Rankin called time to give his outfield a quick look. Duke DiSalvo wanted to call, "All right, I'm here. Let him hit it!"

Easter hit the second pitch and Duke DiSalvo was running as the bat came around, loping into the big hole between left and center as the ball came out, high and deep. Cochran shouted "Duke, Duke, Duke!" and Duke DiSalvo answered "Got it," and at the last moment was forced to take one quick stride backward as a vagrant air current off the river buoyed the ball's flight. He made the catch over his shoulder, pivoted, and slammed his throw at third base. Doby tagged up and faked the advance, then returned to second as the throw hopped once, true and straight to the bag. Duke DiSalvo thought, *What was wrong with that, George?* and jogged back to position. Rankin got a strike-out and forced the next man to pop weakly, ending the inning.

Doby met him behind second base and said casually, "Awful big field out here," and went on past with a faint smile.

Duke DiSalvo wanted to say something sharp, but held his tongue. When he reached the dugout Stinson was talking it up harshly. "Let's go," Stinson said. "Ollie can't do it himself. Come on, get him a run!"

" We'll get 'em," Cochran said. "Nice catch, Duke."

Duke DiSalvo nodded and took his seat in the dugout's comforting shade. He watched Lemon retire the side in order; and he was under the sun again, moving his shoulders cautiously, flexing his leg muscles, feeling the stiffness creeping upward into the heavy groins, just as it had for the past five days. But it didn't matter; he had three innings left and he'd play those standing on his head. Something was bound to break.

Rankin got the Indians again and they came off for their

half of the seventh, the stadium shouting for a run. Duke DiSalvo waited patiently in the dugout while Lemon fanned two men in a row, and came out to the circle and swung the bats while Johnson took his turn at the plate. The weighted bat moved beneath his fingers and crowd sound grew steadily behind him in the rising stands. Here was the past repeated, repeated countless times during those forgotten seasons. The team came down to the wire, a man got on base, and the Duke was waiting, face expressionless, big bat cocked. How many times had they seen it, he thought. Too many for number; the pitch and the ball going, and the run coming home and another game for the team.

Jolmaon worked up a full count, and Lemon's pay-off pitch missed the outside corner for the walk. The roar swelled when Duke DiSalvo stepped in and spread himself deliberately. Lemon called time and pinched some resin, monkeyed with his cap, and wiped his face. They still respected him, Duke DiSalvo thought grimly, still took that deep breath before the pitch. *Come on*, he thought, *you and me, boy!*

He took a strike, then a ball, and knew the next one would be outside, and remembered how, in past days, he had scorned that hit to right field. But today he found himself guessing, and when the pitch rode across he stepped nearly to the plate edge and met the ball with a soft swing. Some old-timer had said once, "When you start guessing, it's nearly over." But the ball was bounding far down the right-field line and he was running, and Johnson was rounding second, then third, and Desmond was shouting, "Go on, Duke, go on!"

Duke DiSalvo made his turn and dug for second, and saw the long throw come in, not for the plate, but low and hard to second base, where Boone waited, glove outstretched. Duke DiSalvo clenched his teeth at what had to be and threw himself into the hook slide, inside the bag, one leg under, toe catching and holding a bag corner, pivoting his body viciously away from the tag as Boone took the throw and slashed downward with the ball. Big Hubbard was looming above them in the flying dust, arms out and palms down, and Boone stepped away as Duke DiSalvo lay quiescent for a moment on the ground.

"You okay, Duke?" Hubbard asked.

"Sure," he said curtly. "Just catching my breath."

When he rose and slapped the dust from his suit, Desmond was shouting happily at first base, and Johnson was bending over the fountain. They had the big run. He heard the crowd sound vaguely, and felt good inside, but his body was sore and the sweat was sticking icily against his skin. Six more outs, he thought; a few lousy minutes and it would be done.

Burrows fanned, but that didn't matter now; everyone knew that. Duke DiSalvo started his trot to center field and the stiffness came up in waves of pain against his belt, slowing him to a walk as he stooped for his glove. The sun was hotter, it seemed, but his mind was clear and the familiar endearments from the bleachers were sharp and emphatic. Cochran edged over, grinning broadly, and called, "You got 'em that time, Duke."

"Stay awake," Duke DiSalvo said. "Give them nothing."

"Right," Cochran said. "That slide shake you up?"

"No," he said sharply. "Just my wind."

Then Rankin was pitching the same beautiful ball, and Duke DiSalvo hoped the Indians would hit on the ground. Rankin again retired the side in order and as Duke came off, he saw George Borland standing in the dugout box, watching him with sober intentness.

George called softly, "Take a rest, Duke," and motioned toward the bench.

He wanted to go over and say, "Sit out a half inning?" He ducked into the welcome shade and took his drink, and relaxed like a tired old dog.

Stinson came along, studied him gravely, and said, "Want me to send Meeker out for the ninth, Duke?"

"I'll finish it," he said.

"No need," Stinson said. "We got them."

Duke DiSalvo said curtly, "I'd as soon finish!" and heard the movement down the bench, more a feeling than a sound.

Stinson turned away and watched the plate, and Duke DiSalvo thought wearily, *Three more outs.*

They went down in order and now was the ninth for Cleveland. He crouched in center field and felt the pain in his groin, the sun heat and age lying thick on his body. But it didn't matter. He was over the day's big hump, the tough game under the belt, and they would go on from today and hold the lead.

Rankin got two men in a row before Duke DiSalvo fielded Mitchell's single, holding the lead-off man at first base. Avila worked a pass and Doby came to the plate, and Stinson was out of the dugout, signaling the bullpen. " Why worry?" Duke DiSalvo said aloud. "Let him hit in the air." Only one out to go and Rankin was still hot.

Duke DiSalvo felt his legs turn stiffly as he caught the pitch signal from shortstop; a fast ball on the inside corner to loosen Doby up. He shifted as the ball shot from Rankin's wind-milling arm, and it was a bad pitch, not far enough inside. Duke DiSalvo was loafing on the signal and failed to react. He caught himself in that position and wanted to curse for some reason. He saw the bat come around, heard the contact, and he was running with the swing, but that one step ahead was only in his memory.

He was running, turning as the ball came toward dead center field, making his run for that invisible circle of grass within which the ball and his glove would come together as if by magic. He was running with his memory, he had missed the break, and he was behind the ball.

"Deep, Duke!" Cochran's frantic shout came across the grass. "Deeper!"

He knew it then, trying to lengthen his stride, feeling his legs break and give as the pain became sharper; knew it was going from him in one terrible, empty-bodied moment, all the greatness and instinct and beauty that had been second nature, something so natural and precious he had never given it a thought. It was going even as he recovered his broken stride, and it was gone as he ran; ran not for the ball, but for the years that were vanished, for the body that was strong, for the memories and the joys of yesterday. He ran and made his shoulder turn and said to himself, "It drops here," and brought his glove and eyes up to meet the falling ball, and it was over his head, far over, skidding on the grass, bounding viciously off the wall. He saw Cochran coming like a wild man, scooping up the third bounce, wheeling and making a long desperation throw to the infield. He saw all this and stopped, legs trembling, and he heard Cochran's agonized grunt of despair and knew the throw was late. When he faced the plate, Doby was on third base, two runs were across, and the game was lost beyond recall.

"Blamed wind!" Cochran said breathlessly. "Took it over you, Duke."

"Sure," he said. "Sure, the wind."

"We'll get 'em back," Cochran said savagely. "We'll get 'em, Duke!"

But he knew Cochran was merely phrasing overworked words. He went painfully back to position and watched Rankin fan Easter for the last out; and then he was trotting toward the dugout, across the grass, and pulling up in a shuffling walk that carried him past first base into the dugout shade. He saw the faces around him, and suddenly he wanted to duck into the tunnel. Stinson was barking encouragement and the team was on the step, talking it up; but the game was gone.

And not so much this one game, Duke DiSalvo realized, but all the games to come when never again would he feel the same, and they, his teammates, would no longer get the lift they needed so badly, the feeling that Duke DiSalvo in center field meant they were never beaten.

He sat numbly while they went against Lemon, and failed to put a man on base. Lemon fanned the last batter and walked off with a big grin; the Indians were leaving town in first place and Lemon smelled that series money now, thanks to Duke DiSalvo.

He sat motionless while the team ducked into the tunnel. Stinson lingered at the fountain, and George Borland was leaning over the box railing, peering into the dugout, saying nothing, just looking.

Duke DiSalvo looked up as Stinson passed, and realized it took more guts to say the words than it did to go out every day and play. "Buck," Duke DiSalvo said, "you better send for the kid."

Stinson turned and rubbed one hand against his wrinkled jaw. "You mean that, Duke?"

"You heard me," Duke DiSalvo said. "What else do you want me to do—crawl on my belly?"

Then George Borland was beside him, holding his arm, and Stinson was smiling, not a smile of triumph, but a look of deep understanding and compassion.

"We'll get the kid by tomorrow noon, Duke," Stinson said. "And listen, it's not too late. We'll get 'em yet. You want to know why, Duke?"

"Why?" Duke DiSalvo asked wearily.

"Because we've still got you," Stinson said.

Close Play At Home

O ssie," I said, "what are you thinking?"

"I'm a Christian," Ossie said. "It's not for publication."

We had finished the game ten minutes earlier and above us the stands were already silent. In bygone years the dispersing crowd whooped it up for an hour; now the stadium echoed with silence as the Eagles blew another game and settled deeper in eighth place. Today, our first game following the midseason All-Star break, was a loss to the Pirates. When the Pirates licked a team, true bottom was plumbed.

"We've got to do something," I said. "We're tearing the heart out of that old man upstairs."

"Hank," Ossie said, "don't tell me what I know. Tell me what to do."

"Simple," I said bitterly. "Cash in the bank!"

We sat in the coach cubbyhole and watched the Eagles shower. They had no life, no cussing mistakes and swearing to do better, just silence, the growing sullenness of twenty-five men who had accepted defeat. We were twenty-four games behind the Giants, in last place, and that bank in New York was tightening the vise around the Old Man. He needed six hundred thousand paid attendance to break even, amortize his yearly payment and keep up the interest on his two-million-dollar loan. We had thirty-five home games remaining, and the Eagles had drawn a hundred and eighty thousand paid fans. Disaster no longer threatened the Old Man from afar; it strutted boldly along every corridor of the stadium he had built with his life.

"It's not the team or us," Ossie said. "We'll get along. But this could kill him, Hank."

Ossie never gave up if one last chance was available. We'd come together under the Old Man thirty-five years ago and were coaching for him now, and we knew and loved the tradition behind him. He'd played and managed, and scraped together the money to buy the Eagles forty years ago. He'd been up and down before, but baseball was changing now, becoming big business, and you needed a winning team to make the turnstiles click.

I finally spoke the words that had stuck, undigestible, in my craw for weeks, "Ossie, you think he's given up?"

"I can't tell you how to save this club," Ossie said. "But he'll never give up. He'll do something."

"Sure," I said, but my heart lied to my tongue.

We had all given up. Nothing could save us now, no matter what the Old Man tried. We dressed and left the stadium, and were too heartsick to look back at the soot-stained walls. Next morning, arriving for the afternoon game, we were called to the Old Man's offices high on the grandstand roof. When we entered and saw the other man sitting beside the Old Man, we couldn't believe our eyes.

"Hank," the Old Man said, in his reedy voice. "Ossie. I'm sure you both remember Si."

We shook hands with Si Collins, who glowered at us from his bushy, overshot brows and cracked his big-knuckled hands over bony knees.

The Old Man said, "I'm having Charley up in a minute. With you two. Si is taking over the team as of this afternoon."

Ossie said, "Si! "

"Yes," the Old Man said mildly. "I'm sure you'll give him your very best."

"For whatever that's worth," Si Collins growled. "Casper, if these two monkeys don't like my profile, give 'em a vacation."

Si Collins was one of a few baseball men who had earned the privilege of calling the Old Man by his first name. Then we knew this was no joke, and the old legends raced through our minds, bringing back the vanished past.

Si Collins had retired twenty-seven years ago, after twenty-three years in the game as unchallenged champion of the rough, high-spiked days when a man gave everything and didn't quit until he was carried off the field. Si Collins held a hundred records for batting and bunting and stealing, had played and managed his original club for twenty-two years, and played his final season for the Old Man.

His last game was an epic in baseball history. All year Si and the Old Man had argued over strategy and players and how to win; after that final game they staged a knock-down, drag-out battle. No phony swinging, looking frantically for teammates to pull them apart, but a jaw-shattering fight that wrecked the dressing room and sent them both to the hospital for minor repairs. When asked why, Si Collins had given his now-famous reply, "Our business, not yours." No one had heard the true story behind that fight, but their hatred had never diminished.

Si Collins was the last man anyone would pick to manage the Eagles. He'd been out of baseball all those years, and he had more money than most millionaires. He had announced that he was through for keeps, and had kept his promise all these years. The Old Man was seventy-two, Si was pushing seventy; it just didn't make sense.

The Old Man seemed to understand our bewilderment, for he said, "Si is in charge. Whatever he orders, you do it!"

The door opened and our young playing manager, Charley Sterret, entered the big office and nodded glumly to us and stared incuriously at Si. Then he recognized the hawk nose, the thin mouth, the heavy brows.

The Old Man said quietly, "Charley, can you take it?"

"Yes, sir," Charley said. "What is it?"

"Charley," the Old Man said bluntly, "you know my situation; you know the team has got away from you. Don't feel badly. It's not your fault; it just happened. I've waited a month, hoping they'd pull together, start winning. Charley, I'm going to relieve you for the balance of the season. If I'm still owner next year, you come back as manager. That's my promise, before witnesses, and you know I mean it. Si Collins here will take over for the last half. You're listed as a playing manager, Charley. Will you stay on the roster as a player for Si? This is breaking all the rules, but we need you. Will you do it for me, for the team?"

Charley clenched his hands tight, but he looked at Si Collins and said, "I'll play."

"Casper," Si Collins said raspingly, "stop telling me those lies."

The Old Man smiled. " What lies?"

"Saying the ballplayers with guts were gone," Si Collins said. . . . "Sterret, you're on my ball club. Let's go down and take a look at these china dolls."

We followed Si Collins down to the manager's office, and we all felt the first surge of that desperate chance the Old Man had tried. He was on the phone now, and the entire country would be blazing with the story within two hours. The Old Man was attempting an impossible gamble; Si Collins had accepted an impossible challenge. Yes, I thought, but there was a year—1914—and there was another man, named Stallings. It could be done.

While Collins was getting into a uniform, he fired sharp questions at Sterret concerning this man and that, and finally nodded. He looked down owlishly at the huge, onyx-based pen-and-pencil set on the walnut desk.

He said, "What the hell is this?"

"For notes," Sterret said.

"Use your head," Si Collins rasped, and swept the set to the floor. The base broke, ink spilled over the carpet. Si Collins cocked his bald head and listened to the sounds outside the door, marking the arrival of the team. " Work 'em out," he said. "Bring 'em down ten minutes before we start. I'll wait here."

By that time the news had come down from the press box. When Sterret took his swings and worked out with the Yannigan infield, a surprised murmur swept through the stands. We could hear the traffic outside the stadium when we took the team off the field into the tunnel. We might have hoped for, and barely got, a crowd of three thousand for the afternoon game; now the cars were rolling in from all over the city. We followed the last man through the dressing-room door. Then the office door opened and Si Collins faced the Eagles. I knew he'd been studying the roster, and now he gave them a look that held open contempt.

"My name's Collins," he arid. "I'm taking over as of today. Same line-up, Wilson pitching. We'll use three signals. I'll rub one hand over the letters for steal, two for bunt, tip my hat for the hit-and-run."

Zilbrosky spoke up. "You want the sequence change to go on every third inning?"

Si Collins studied Zilbrosky for a moment. "What for?"

"But—" Zilbrosky was thinking, as were all the Eagles, that such signals would be stolen within two innings.

"Three signals are plenty for this team," Si Collins said. "If a man can steal, he steals. If he can bunt, he bunts. Same goes for hit-and-run. You do it right, who gives a hang if the commissioner knows the signals? Now get up there and impersonate a ball club."

He stared them down and sent them through the door, every man boiling with rage. He went forward and touched one man on the arm, held that man back, and I knew he'd been checking the pictures. Fentress was our rookie shortstop, and Fentress met his gaze with white-lipped fury.

Si Collins said, "I hear you can handle your dukes."

Fentress said, "I'm afraid of no man," and snapped his lean jaws shut.

"You want to win ball games?" Si Collins asked.

"I want to win," Fentress said. "Every game!"

"Will you listen to me?"

"Name it!"

"Start a fight today," Si Collins said. "Don't hold back, let it rip. I'll pay your fine, you'll sit about five days out, Sterret can fill in. Will you do it?"

Most men would argue, ask foolish questions. Fentress seemed to understand immediately. "I get you," he said. "You'll have your fight . . . skipper!"

"Show me a good right hook," Si Collins said, with just the trace of a smile, and led us up the tunnel.

When the umpires grouped around home plate, he went up the step and moved across the grass, and eight thousand people stood and began clapping. The photographers were waiting and all the Pirates were watching from their dugout. Si Collins went forward, bowlegs swinging, long jaw pushed out.

He handed his line-up to Bill Stewart and growled, "You got a little fat too! Get on with it!" and shoved his hands into his hip pockets, ignoring the photographers, facing center field while the crowd kept applauding.

This is not about one game, but seventy-six games played through half a bitterly fought season. We came on the field that day with twenty-seven wins and fifty-one losses. The Giants, in first place, had won fifty-one and lost twenty-seven. That gives an idea of how impossible our climbing into the first division was, let alone pennant hopes. The Old Man was above us in his roof-top box, listening to the wonderful sound of people beating down the doors, but knowing that one fair day did not make half a season. Si Collins had come back—enough to fill any ball park for a few games—but, to win, this team must win in September.

We won that first game. Our cleanup man, Tug Zilbrosky, smashed a home run with two aboard in the eighth, but we really won it in the second inning, when Fentress singled and went down on the first pitch. He went in, spikes high, slashing as he drove across the bag and ripped a pair of foot-long slits in the second baseman's pants, and when that innocent protested, Fentress was on him like a tiger.

We all saw the right hook, a vicious blow, then he whirled and met the shortstop with another knockdown punch. When the smoke cleared away, Sterret was playing short and the Pirates were after our blood. Zilbrosky homered, and we came down to the dressing room with everybody talking it up and looking around furtively to see if this was actually true.

The door closed and Si Collins said in a mild voice, "Good one to win."

A few of them grinned. Then he tore into them with more fury than Fentress had unleashed on the Pirates.

"Good one to win!" he said scornfully. "What a ball club! We should have won it in the fifth, in the sixth, even in the seventh!" And then he told them how, and why, and ripped their complacency and their cherished so-called knowledge of the game to ribbons. And finally he turned to Zilbrosky. "Hit a home run, win the game!" Si Collins said. "Get paid twenty thousand a year to hit thirty-some home runs! Do they pay you to watch signals? Yes, you, you bonehead, you missed it in the fifth! You can't bunt, can't hit behind the runner, can't or won't steal! Think because you hit a few cheap ones and bat in a hundred runs, you're the Babe himself! Everybody out here at ten tomorrow morning! I'll try to make ballplayers out of you! I've got my doubts, but I'll try!"

He turned and stalked into the office. He slammed the door so hard a bottle fell off a shelf, and then I knew how it would go. Ossie whistled softly.

"They think he's shot his wad," Ossie said. "They don't know, do they? "

"They don't," I said. "And neither do we."

It was going back thirty years and reliving a life we had believed gone forever. There was no secret about the purpose either. The writers went hogwild over the Old Man's last-ditch gamble and the return of baseball's greatest fighter, and they made a field day of the sentimental attachments and the romantic aspects of the situation. With the Giants and Dodgers in a two-team battle for the pennant, the return of Si Collins was sauce atop dessert.

He dragged them out to long morning practices. He had a sliding pit ready that first morning, and within ten minutes they were bunting and sliding and hitting behind the runner. He sweated them dry in the damp, hot summer air; he walked from sawdust pit to home plate, and back again, his alligator tongue pouring out the vitriol. He was sixty-nine years young; he showed them bunting they couldn't believe; he hit behind the runner; he went into the pit and showed them how to slide. He stood behind the batting cage, and his silence, as they blooped off the bunts and slashed measly grounders toward first base, was more eloquent than the lashing words.

He used Zilbrosky for his shining example. Zilbrosky couldn't slide, or bunt, or hit behind the runner. In one morning Si Collins stripped Zilbrosky of his six-year power-hitting record and, in doing so, showed them all what baseball had come to—no more or no less, just enough. That afternoon he dropped Zilbrosky to eighth in the batting line-up, put Sterret at short and stood at third base giving his signals openly. We lost a 2-1 game to the Dodgers when Zilbrosky was given the squeeze in the last of the ninth with one away and a man on third. Zilbrosky popped into a double play. I knew that Si Collins gave that signal, hoping we'd lose, because he was thinking ahead to what could be if this Eagle team caught fire.

For we had a good team. We were solid, we had good pitching and catching; our big casualty was the Old Man's meal ticket, our left-hander, who hurt his shoulder in June and was trying to get back on the active list. Si Collins watched them all as the days passed and we finished our play in the East and squared off for the Western road trip. We split those games and lost no ground, and it was worth a month's play to see Si Collins come back to the Polo Grounds. Durocher shook hands with evident admiration at home plate—and he was no man to give an opponent an inch—and it felt strange to see the last of the old-timers with the last of a new generation, cut from the same cloth, the same belligerent jaw and roller-bearing eyes.

Si Collins said, "I can stay here until midnight, son. I've got no other place to go." And then matched Durocher at his own drawn-out type of game, and we took two of the three from the Giants. We came home for two games with the Pirates, and the Old Man was up above, counting the packed stands and wondering, as we all were, how long it could last. The novelty was still working, but we were twenty games behind and the Western road trip would tell the story. We beat the Pirates twice and entrained for the West, and Si Collins threw off the wraps, and within two games turned the Eagles into a team that belonged forty years back in time. That road trip was like a giant gone mad and rolling free, with no brakes and a cool-eyed madman at the throttle.

No one will ever know when he caught them, that moment in time when the last man swung over and lost his former identity and became one with Si Collins. Maybe it was the riot in St. Louis, or the brush balls in Milwaukee, or the way he lashed the Cub pitchers from the coaching box in Chicago. He was judging the Eagles in the first days; then he struck quickly into their very insides.

Two men wouldn't change, and they were gone in Chicago, with two youngsters sent up from the farm clubs as replacements—one pitcher and one outfielder. And there was Si

Collins on those hot afternoons and muggy nights, giving his signals, running his team, lashing out with words and looks, playing crazy with the rotation, sending in pitchers on what seemed to be foolish hunches, keeping Zilbrosky in the eighth slot, cowing umpires and managers, cutting a raging path through the West with a team that suddenly came alive and began playing the ball we knew it had deep inside all the time.

We won ten of twelve games on that road trip. How we won is what counts, not scores or base hits or pitching efforts. But the way Si Collins ran the Eagles, he brought back forgotten baseball, the bunt and steal and hit-and-run, the long chance whenever it came, the total disregard for all the so-called natural odds and rules. He ignored all the present-day platitudes about left-handed batters going against right-handed pitchers; he believed in nine tough men who fought to the finish, and pinch-hitters who went up there and hit anything, right or left. I know some say that type of baseball is still played by a few teams, but they lie. It is played in snatches, an inning here and there, one game out of ten, but not every day, every inning, piling up the pressure upon pressure until the spirit becomes a visible quality, a tenth man on the field with the team that goes all the way. No one gave us a chance at the pennant; that was too crazy even to consider. But we came home off that road trip, and the stadium was full when we opened against the Braves, and Si Collins sprang his next surprise.

Our injured left-hander, Krantz, had stayed home and tried to get back in shape. Si Collins talked with him the first morning before the usual bunting and sliding session—oh, yes, they were still doing it, and better every day—and Si said bluntly, "Well, are you ready or not?"

"I can pitch," Krantz said.

"Hard?"

"No," Krantz said. "Then it hurts. But I can pitch."

"Then listen to me," Si Collins said. "You're the difference for us, little man. We know that. You go out there and pitch easy. You've got control. Show these bushers how a man can make 'em hit on the ground and in the air."

"I can do it," Krantz said. "I'll be ready every fifth day."

"Then you go today," Si Collins said abruptly.

Krantz pitched a ten-hitter that afternoon and made me think of Dean against the Yankees so long ago, and I think the Braves had those same thoughts as Krantz scattered the hits and we won it on Fentress' double with the bases full. Fentress had sat out his suspension, drawn another five days for starting the St. Louis riot, and was back in the line-up, hitting like a demon and playing the best shortstop in the league. Zilbrosky was still batting eighth, hating it, but slowly understanding what it meant to play for the team and not just a twenty-thousand-dollar paycheck. We swept the Braves, lost one to the Reds, blanked the Cubs, and went wild against St. Louis.

Zilbrosky wasn't talking to anybody when the Cards arrived. He let his bat do the talking in that three-game series. Si Collins stood at third base and turned his back on the big man, and Zilbrosky went up there muttering some choice Polish words, smashed five home runs and three doubles, and ran the bases like a bull, daring infielders to get in his way. And after the third game, won by Zilbrosky's fifth homer, Si Collins stopped at his locker and said, "You still can't bunt," and walked away.

I don't know where August went; it was one long, crazy flicker of afternoons and nights, with pitchers winning games and batters coming through when you knew, absolutely, all the averages were long-gone and used up. We won twenty-two and lost five in August; we came into September and it was a sudden shock to awake and realize it could happen. We were seven games back when we started the final Western swing; we were four games out of first when we came home. And the Old Man was up there, looking down as the attendance skyrocketed and the writers couldn't stop printing what might be; and then, as it always happens, half a dozen syndicates were formed in the city, every one with the ready cash to help the Old Man if he missed by a hair.

We blazed through the Dodgers and Pirates, as Si Collins gave his signals and used his tongue and let the Eagles run wild. He had got very thin through those hot weeks, his voice was a croak, his bowlegged walk from dugout to third sometimes strayed a little as he hung on doggedly and let no one see how he must feel inside. And then we were into the two final games with the Giants. We had passed the Dodgers, and the Giant lead was whittled to one lone game. We won the first game 4-3 on a squeeze bunt in the last of the ninth. Fentress was on third base with one away and Zilbrosky at the plate. Si Collins walked down the white chalk line under the lights and the dark-blue night sky, and gave the bunt signal as Zilbrosky turned his head, gave it so plainly the batboy knew what was coming.

Si Collins rubbed two hands over his letters and called, "All right, big man! Prove it to me!" Zilbrosky laid that bunt toward first base, a beautiful twister, and ran directly along the inside of his legal path as Lockman came in; and Zilbrosky blocked him just enough with one huge shoulder. Fentress slid under the throw and we knew, watching Zilbrosky cross first base, that Si Collins had made a real ballplayer out of a dime-a-dozen slugger.

They deliberately ignored the fire laws that last afternoon. Forty thousand people crowded a park built for thirty-six, with ten thousand more milling around outside, refusing to go home, carrying portable radios and listening to the shouts that came down from the high gray walls, and nobody cared.

We went out there that last afternoon and Si Collins gave the nod to little Krantz, and Maglie was going for the Giants, and there couldn't have been any business going on in the United States. Si Collins met Durocher at home plate, and after Dascoli said, "Play ball," Durocher stuck out his hand and Si Collins shook it, and for a moment we were in the past. I could see McGraw and a younger Si Collins, and Chance and all those others who had known only one way, and that was go, go until you fell and they carried you away.

That was a game, and I wish it could have ended the way it

did in '14, when Stallings brought the Braves from oblivion and won a pennant in the greatest finish known to baseball. I wish it could have been that way, but it seemed that when the ninth inning came around and Krantz went out to hold a 2-2 score, it couldn't go on. Krantz was pitching on nerve alone; he had just a few pitches left, and they were all slow curves and change-ups and, if he dared, the knuckle ball.

He got two away before Thompson singled and Irvin followed with another broken-bat hit to left field. Zilbrosky's throw held Thompson at second base, and Krantz faced Willie Mays, and I knew it had to break. I looked at Si Collins, but he stayed, unmoving, on the dugout step. Krantz glanced over at him, but Si Collins only smiled and lifted one thumb that said, silently, "You're my man. I go with you."

Krantz hitched his belt and checked the runners and pitched to Mays. The hit was into left center, deep and hard, and Thompson was a cinch to score, and Irvin was rounding second, then third, as Durocher gave him the go-ahead, and Zilbrosky came over into that hole and made a scoop and threw on the run from the wrong angle, and that ball beat Irvin by three steps for the tag and out. The Giants led by one, and Si Collins waited at the dugout step when Krantz came in, crying, and put his hand on Krantz's shoulder and said quietly—the only time he'd spoken quietly in three months—"You won it, little man. Remember that."

Then Maglie was pitching to Fentress, and the ball was into right center, and Fentress was into second base standing up. Maglie got our next man, walked the next, and Grissom came in from the bullpen. Grissom got the second out on a pop-up, and Zilbrosky almost ran to the plate and dusted his hands and looked out at Si Collins. You couldn't hear your own voice, but Zilbrosky looked for the signal just the same, even with two away, and Si Collins came down the line and cupped his hands, and I saw his mouth curve upward as he formed the words, "Hit away, big boy."

And then we waited.

The Giants deserved that pennant. They hadn't slipped. We had just played such great ball that we caught them, but they never gave up. Grissom threw one ball, Durocher called time, and Wilhelm came on the long walk from the bullpen. Everybody was standing now, and the roar seemed to go on up and reach an impossible peak, and then rise higher. Wilhelm worked the count to two-and-two, and came down with everything he had. Zilbrosky hit that pitch over second base and Fentress broke for third, and I watched Si Collins out there as the ball hit the bright green grass and bounded, small and white. Si Collins moved his right hand in one gesture, and Fentress made the turn and lost his cap and seemed to stretch out and become a shadow racing down the line; and it ended as it should have ended for the Giants.

Mays came in and made a barehanded pickup, and threw—a rifle-shot throw they'll remember as long as they remember Si Collins. Westrum and Fentress and the ball came together in duet, under the thunder of the crowd. Dascoli bent over the play, and then his blue arm came up and the thumb hooked and it was over.

Si Collins had walked down the line, following the play, and we all had the same thoughts as he approached Dascoli. He could do anything in that moment, and be forgiven. It was so close only the man in blue could know, and I knew what a hundred others would have done. But Si Collins walked around Dascoli, took Fentress by the arm, and kept going into the dugout, and that was all. He'd brought them here, and everything was within their reach, and then he showed them how to lose. And sometimes that means more than winning, with such a team, and the future stretching out ahead.

He entered the dugout and stood beside me a moment, staring across the field, and then he turned to Sterret and his raspy voice croaked, "You'll go all the way next year! You know that!"

"Yes," Sterret said. "We all know that, Si."

"Keep at that bunting," Si said. "Don't be thinking you're perfect yet."

He turned into the tunnel, heading for a shower and then upstairs, and whatever went on between him and that happy Old Man, nobody would ever know. Not the words, we'd never know that, but we did know the feeling. For we all had the feeling now, and no man on this team would forget.

The Catcher

I watched him step from the taxi and look upward at the stadium's sooty gray wall. He tossed his half-smoked cigar into the gutter with a gesture of unmistakable decision. We had not talked for seven months and, in the future, I might see him twenty-two times each year; but the number of meetings did not matter for I knew him like a brother, and the bond between us could not scuff away in passing time. I knew too much about him and his family and his way of life.

All the little things—trivial in themselves—but massing together and making the whole of any man's life. I knew that his wife had brown hair and soft gray eyes, and her large-boned body was plumped out from having their children. I knew she had tried unsuccessfully to break him of swearing in public, and she bought every hair restorer on the market and massaged those sticky mixtures into his balding scalp. I knew they lived in a small Illinois town with two children and three dogs, and some eighty relatives who placed him one step below the President in importance.

His boy wore blue sport shirts—or did until last fall. His daughter was still too young to show distinct personality but had taken from him a goodly amount of humor and courage. He smoked ten cigars a day and read Western stories on road trips and liked scrambled eggs with sausage for breakfast, even on the hottest August days in St. Louis, and he carried a quiet confidence in himself that lay so deeply in his heart and blood that it had become a creed, a code by which he lived. Somewhere in his early years while fighting his way up, he had learned the great, simple lesson that any man, lacking such a code, lacked the best of life. I considered him one of my few friends and I had waited not just this half hour beside the players' entrance, but seven months, to meet him here.

He was the same sober big man with heavy arms and thick torso, wearing one of his conservative gray tropical suits and that old brown hat set firmly on his balding head. He made me think of a professional man, and he was that, but far divorced from offices and desks. He was a catcher, one of the best, and he was coming home for the first time in the new season to play against his former teammates. He was coming home and, in my opinion, he deserved a band and the mayor and welcoming speeches. But I stood alone there on the dirty sidewalk in the stadium shadow so I did the next best thing and called, "Hello, Bill."

"Stan!"

Bill Malloy turned from paying the taxi driver and came across the sidewalk with his rolling walk.

"Stan, you old bastard! It's good to see you."

I said, "You knew I'd be here."

"I knew it, Stan."

We shook hands and grinned foolishly, and he spent five minutes talking about his family, the trouble he'd had finding a decent house in the new city. He told me about his hunting dogs, and I mentioned the fishing trip I'd taken during spring training and the marlin I'd almost boated. And finally, because we were both delaying the words that must come, I said, "You look good, Bill. Now, speaking for the press, have you got a few minutes?"

"For the press?"

"The Great American Public," I said. "They await your words."

"Anything for them," he said ironically. "Anything at all, Stan."

I had written a hundred-odd stories about him in the past seven years and I held a hundred questions on my tongue, but nothing had the ring of truth, nothing seemed proper tonight. All I could say was, "How does it feel, coming back?"

"Officially?"

"Yes," I said. "For the public."

"Just another ball park now," he said. "You know how it goes, Stan."

I knew. The old feeling of home, of belonging here, would never come to him again; after tonight he'd speak to the Blues for they were still his friends, but the bond was broken. In the way of the league, the impersonal and coldly professional way, the Blues already spoke of Bill Malloy in the past tense. They'd say—and mean it—that he was good, a great guy, and unselfishly recount fine plays he'd made, but they would no longer include him in the present, for he was on another team.

"I know," I said. "Well, your first game against the Blues. Will you win?"

"Try," he said. "Ken's going for us, the kid, for you. Ought to be a battle."

"Think you can hit the kid?" I asked. "You know what I mean, Bill. You caught him five years, taught him all he knows. Will you use that knowledge against your old friend?"

He smiled at some old thought—perhaps shadowed with fear—carried a long time in his heart.

"Think?" he said. "I got to hit him tonight."

"You will," I said, and then I had to ask about the ankle. "How is it, Bill?"

"Good," he said. "Good as new, Stan."

"This is off the record," I said, "this part."

"For the record," he said, "and for you, the ankle is good as new. Follow me?"

"Thanks," I said. "That makes me feel good as new, Bill. Do I see you after the game?"

"Steak?

I said, "My treat."

He looked at me and fumbled without thinking for another cigar, and then pushed it back into his coat.

"That take care of the press?"

"Yes," I said. "Unofficially, how do you feel toward—"

I motioned upward where the unseen press-box perched above the stands and, above the press-box, the owner's private box.

"Not too bad," he said. "Just sorry for the poor bastard, that's all."

"That's all?"

"No, but why go into it, Stan."

"No reason," I said. "Well . . . good luck, Bill."

"Thanks," he said. "Give my best to Jocko."

"I will," I said.

"See you, Stan."

He poked me gently in the ribs and went down the dark corridor toward the visitors' dressing room. I walked around through the pass gate and took the elevator upstairs to my seat in the press box beside Jocko McCune. He was stripped down to shirt and pants, his red hair curling around his ears, his pug-nosed face turning and looking expectantly.

"See him?"

"Yes," I said. "He sends you his best."

"How is he?" Jocko asked.

"Ready," I said. "Ready and able."

While I arranged my scorebook, paper and typewriter, ate a sandwich and drank a beer on the management, and while batting practice began on the field, I thought of Bill Malloy. I didn't see the players below in their gray suits and white home uniforms, smell the popcorn and cigarette smoke, hear the sound of balls hit cleanly from the batting cage. I saw and heard and smelled a fine spring day seven years before in Florida, the day Bill Malloy joined the Blues.

He was down for his first try at the big show, another face to watch and study and judge, another character to write up in the training-camp columns, another man who might turn out good, or bad, while the grapefruit games were played, and we watched from the press box and around the clubhouse and in the hotel. He did not know us—the press—from Adam, but soon we would know him well and be able to answer the questions that come with each new face. Was he a bedroom hound who allowed the Sadies to catch him on road trips? Did he play cards and shoot craps? Did he drink reasonably or go on benders? Could he read a contract and sign his own name? Was he a club-house lawyer? Did his wife do all the thinking and talking? There is no end to the speculation for, in watching a new man, the past certified data was his record. In Bill's case, the record was good.

He was a veteran catcher with six years of minor-league experience. I should amend that to say, with deep admiration for his kind, a veteran of hard knocks and cheap meals and long bus rides and bruised legs and broken fingers and low salaries. Six years in the minors spoke volumes for his tenacity; it took a good man to stick behind the plate and learn his trade and still have love for the tools of ignorance. With the emphasis, and the large bonuses, placed on other positions these days, catching is rapidly becoming a lost art, and this fact apparently is due to life itself today. People are rushing toward their goals, taking all the short cuts, and catching is not an art you acquire overnight.

Catching takes patience and courage and time, and Bill Malloy had these in abundance. He reported in shape and handled himself with complete assurance behind the plate, and even so, he was so broad and thick-chested and short-legged that he appeared clumsy to the amateur eye. I remember the first game he caught that spring, his trouble with the wild kid on the mound, his going hitless in four times at bat—the worst possible start for a rookie who, if he stuck on the roster, must beat out three veterans and three eager kids for his job.

We watched him that afternoon and exchanged our opinions in the press box—all highly expert and technical, you understand, for the Baseball Writers' Association knows and sees all— and agreed that he was the best catcher we'd seen come up in years, in spite of his clumsiness and his failure to hit. Other people did not share our opinion, however, as we learned that afternoon.

Walter Jonas, the Blues' owner, wandered into the press box during the seventh inning and sat beside me and shook his head as one old-timer to another.

"What do you think?" he asked.

"Of what?"

"Him," Jonas said. "Malloy."

"He'll do," I said.

"Too clumsy," Jonas said. "And too old. Our kids are better."

That was one of Jonas's more endearing traits—his frank and honest and expert judgment of his players; that wisdom was from a man then two years in the game. And two million dollars in, at the time, to give him his honest due.

"Don't sell Malloy short," I said. "He's got it."

"Not him," Jonas said. "He won't stick."

I said, "On what say-so?"

"Why," Jonas said quickly, "the coaching staff's. Who else?"

"Mere curiosity," I said. "I was trying to remember where you acquired your experience behind the plate."

Jonas lost his good-natured smile and gave me that stare which, in baseball, meant he would cheerfully throw my ass from the ball park and get my job tomorrow. But only for a moment. We have unions now, and our newspapers are large concerns; and most of all, having learned the value of free advertising, Jonas knew that his Blues lived or died on the sport pages of the papers in his city. Jonas recovered his smile and searched through the compartment of his mind labeled "Humor" and cerebrated vigorously to discover and appreciate the joke.

"Now, Stan," he said, "you know what I mean."

"I know," I said. "But you watch him, Walter. He'll do this club a lot of good."

Jonas became serious, the executive striving always to strengthen his team through the expert advice of well-meaning friends.

"But, Stan," he said, "let's face the facts. We've got Watson and Chambers, and Piggy for the bullpen, and I'm not mentioning our kids and they certainly deserve a fair chance. Where can Malloy hang on, whose place can he take?"

Jocko McCune had sat beside me silently, listening to Jonas, building up a fine head of steam. He turned from his typewriter, adjusted his glasses on his red nose and said politely, "The roster allows you twenty-five men, Walter. Do you want a cripple holding down one of those all-important spots?"

"What cripple?" Jonas said. "They're all in top shape, Jocko."

"Please, Walter," Jocko said. "We're home folks. Don't give us that publicity shit. Watson can't go a hundred games through any given season. Chambers is a nice guy, a pretty fair receiver, but he's over the hump, and he can't hit his hat. As for Piggy, you are absolutely right. A good bullpen catcher if you don't let him think. And your kids are two, three years away. I suggest we watch Malloy and hope—even pray—for the best."

"All right, Jocko," Jonas laughed. "But *you* watch."

We watched, and I got to know Bill Malloy that spring. He was good copy, coming from a small town in the southern Illinois coal country, and he frankly admitted that he took up baseball as his only means of escape from the mines. He explained that, without emotion, when I interviewed him, just a simple statement of fact, but only a blind man could miss the implications and fail to read, in his record, of the fight he'd made to get this far.

He was the oldest of seven children, his father was dead, and for six years his minor-league pay had helped support his mother and the younger children. He was married now, to his high-school sweetheart, and they had a two-year-old boy and another baby on the way. He was the living answer to the question: Why do so many of our best fighters, football and baseball players, come from the steel and coal country, bringing those jawbreaker names and that tight-lipped, deadly ambition which shows so vividly in their eyes? Sociologists have made quite an issue of that question, offering many learned reasons, but there is no great secret explanation. It comes under the heading of survival. Ask Dempsey, ask Louis. Ask a thousand others. They know why, and Bill knew. He had to make good. All around him was the horn of plenty, and he wanted his share.

He made a liar of Walter Jonas that spring. He stuck as third-string catcher, assigned to the bullpen, and he did not realize that he had joined the Blues in a strange time.

The old, broken-down club, the league doormat, was under new ownership. Gone were the days when players scarcely had time to meet their teammates because the turnover was so rapid; when the payroll was met by squeezing pennies—not nickels— and often was augmented only through league help. Gone were the last-place days. The dirty suits and scuffed balls, the managers coming with hopeful smiles and departing with addled brains. And the war years—the unforgettable seasons—when fielding a team of nine men offered the same thrill you might get spinning a roulette wheel. When, for instance, the Blues needed a shortstop to play in the next day's game in Chicago, a nattily dressed gentleman of uncertain years and red eyeballs was tucked on the westbound limited by the front office the night before, and removed the following morning in Chicago with an empty fifth in his berth and a glazed smile of anticipation on his innocent face as he shouted, "Where's my suit, where's the women?" But we didn't talk about those days any more, those days and many other things, for the Blues were under new management.

Walter Jonas was the wealthiest man ever to enter baseball, and to give credit where it is due, he poured out money with a lavish hand. From this regeneration came a fairly intelligent front office, good publicity, a growing farm system, better scouts, and youngsters by the dozen signed and started on those farm clubs. At our initial press conference Jonas made it clear that he wanted no part of Tom Yawkey's well-meant failure. The Blues were building their own team, based on youth, and there was no room in the organization for old-timers. That is why Bill Malloy came to the Blues at a strange time.

Bill wasn't old in years, but very old in experience, practically ancient when compared with the Blues' kids. At twenty-six Bill was growing bald and wore a tight cap that never flew off when he ripped his mask and chased a foul, and this habit which everyone quite naturally saw as Bill's attempt to conceal his bald head—and the association of age that goes with lack of hair— led to a good deal of joshing from fans and players alike. Bill took it in good stride and refused to lose his temper.

"Why should I?" he told me. "I can't help losing my hair."

"But why wear that tight cap?" I said. "That's why the boys are writing you up."

"I wear it," he said, "because it's sort of a reminder never to lose my head."

"That's a deep thought," I said. "Where'd you read it, Bill?"

"In a book," he said curtly. "Do I look like a dumb bastard or something. I went through high school. I can count to ten and spell my name."

"I'm sorry," I said. "And I won't write that, Bill. Remember, if you don't want me to quote you, tell me so. This is a cutthroat business—you know it by now—but a man has to keep some honor."

"I know about you," he said. "Old Joe Devers told me when he came down to our club last year."

Joe Devers had played fourteen years in the league and was one of my old friends. I knew Joe the way a writer gets to know just a few ball players. If Joe Devers had liked Bill Malloy, there was no need to doubt Bill's ability or common sense.

"What else did Joe tell you?" I asked.

He grinned at me. "That you'd been writing baseball twenty-seven years, you were getting soft-hearted but you knew a little about the game, and your only trouble was, you had a hard head and a soft heart."

"That all?" I said.

"No, but the rest won't please the ladies."

I said, "Did Joe say you'd stick here?"

"Yes," he said. "Joe told me I'd stick."

"Know what you've got to buck?" I said. "If you don't, start looking around, Bill."

He grinned and massaged the pocket of his mitt. "I know, Stan. Nothing comes easy."

Bill made the understatement of the year. He rode the bullpen bench until late June when Watson pulled a muscle and Chambers, taking over, couldn't hit his hat size. Bill had been catching the second games of doubleheaders and the last innings of games already lost, and when Watson went out indefinitely Bill caught every third day, relieving Chambers, and suddenly he was handling the full load.

The moment he took charge we could feel and see the difference. He caught the veterans and the wild kids with quiet, steady assurance, giving them the confidence all pitchers need. He kept the team awake, made them feel his spirit, and literally pulled them together. His batting was lousy off the average—never above .225—but he hit in the clutch and he stroked a long ball. He had that dead-game dangerousness that made him far more valuable than a banjo hitter who batted .300 and did nothing in the clutch. The Blues finished sixth and Bill, by season's end, had caught ninety-two games. He had proven his worth and we knew he would improve steadily, and yet, the next spring in Florida, we saw the pattern form.

Walter Jonas had clung stubbornly to his original prejudice, and it seemed the coaching staff also lacked confidence in Bill. They brought three youngsters into camp, plus Watson and Chambers, and it was plain that Bill Malloy was fighting all over again for his job; nor did their announcement that every position on the team was open make good sense. There are different schools of thought concerning that little trick, foremost being that it makes all players get in shape fast and work harder; but another thought is that veterans are more apt to get in better shape when they are given time and placed under less pressure. I wrote a column reviewing Bill's value to the team, and Jonas came to the press box that afternoon with the expected protest.

"You came out fairly strong for Malloy," he said. "How do you think that makes our kids feel?"

"My opinion," I said. "Not official, Walter."

"Damn it, Stan," Jonas said. "One year doesn't make a catcher."

"Seven does," I said. "He's got seven years behind him."

"But he's slow," Jonas said. "Look at his batting average."

"Averages lie," I said. "And he isn't slow."

"A case of Scotch," Jonas said, "against one box of cigars that young Samuels beats him out for the third spot."

"Pardon me," Jocko McCune said, "but are you, by chance, rating Watson and Chambers above Malloy?"

"Certainly," Jonas said. "They're veterans; we know what they can do."

"We certainly do," Jocko said, "And I'll take that same bet."

"Taken," Jonas said. "And good cigars, no ropes."

Jonas wandered away toward the clubhouse and Jocko McCune leaned over his typewriter and scowled at the distant right-field fence.

"God protect us," he said. "We are overwhelmed with the voice of experience. Watson is thirty-five, Chambers is thirty-four on the books and thirty-seven back home. Samuels is twenty with two seasons of ball under his belt. I have a nephew at home, age ten, who is catching this season. Perhaps I should tip off Jonas and offer Malloy more competition. Do you think we made a wise bet?"

"Yes," I said. "Nothing ever came easy for Bill. He likes it better when he has to fight."

"He must," Jocko said. "He's a tough man with a dollar."

"Contract, you mean?"

"Just going to tell you when Jonas arrived," Jocko said. "Bill got his price. He told Hawkins, and Hawkins told me last night. That's part of Jonas's reason for feeling indisposed toward Bill. Jonas believes in paying a man well, but not too well, shall we say."

"So Bill got eight," I said.

"Every last dollar," Jocko said. "And he deserves it."

Bill had received five thousand his first season, the customary minimum salary for rookies signing a try-out contract, and had deserved a bonus for his fine work and got nothing, and we knew he was holding out for eight thousand this second year and hadn't signed until the night before training started, and then only after a two-hour session in Jonas's suite. Bill hadn't told me how he came out—for it was none of my business—but Hawkins was his room-mate and Jocko had known Hawkins six years, so I knew it was true. Eight thousand was a bargain but, knowing owners and players, I could visualize that two-hour session in the big hotel suite. The picture of those owner-player talks is that of friendly, calm deliberation in pleasant surroundings, with good cigars and perhaps a drink or two. That may be true when the player is easily influenced, or a big star, but in Bill's case, knowing his stubbornness and Jonas's ability to beat down a price, such a meeting goes more in this fashion:

"Now goddamnit, Bill!" the owner will say, "we're being more than reasonable. We're willing to make it six with a bonus if you do good work, but you've only got one year behind you, and you know goddamned well one year doesn't prove a man in this league. Now, does it?"

"Eight," Bill would say. "I earned part of it last year, and you offered no bonus—"

"All right, so we slipped up, but .225 is no batting average for a bonus, and you've got to admit that."

"I batted in fifty-two runs," Bill would say doggedly. "In ninety-two games."

And so on in this way for perhaps an hour while the owner tries to explain—in simple words, of course, for he knows the player cannot possibly assimilate higher finance—that costs have gone up, the club lost money last year, the players have got to co-operate if the club is to stay in business; and the player, if he is Bill, sits adamantly and sticks to his eight thousand until, finally, the owner becomes less pleasant and raises his voice for the last round, knowing that he must either browbeat the player with the old familiar threats or, at the last possible moment, give in and pay off.

"All right," the owner says, "I've tried to be reasonable, Bill. We've been talking damn near two hours and you won't listen to reason. I'll give six and that's my final offer."

"Eight," Bill says, and now his voice is a little tighter and his temper is frayed as he tries to picture the owner's wealth in terms of tens of millions of dollars, as stacked against the few thousand he demands to feed his family and save for his old age.

"Eight," Bill says again, "and not one goddamned cent less, and that's MY last offer."

"It is!" the owner comes back. "All right, you know where that leaves us, Bill!"

At this point Bill is expected to think belatedly of the owner's power over him, in the form of the contract Bill signed when he joined the club, giving them absolute power to trade, sell, or option Bill wherever the club may wish. The owner is now preparing—Bill is expected to know this—to tell Bill he can go home and sit on his ass all year at no pay, or the owner may call the front office and give orders to option Bill back to the minors or sell him to another club if anybody wants him. Bill should break at this point and give in, but if he stands fast the owner must come to a decision within seconds. And Bill stands fast.

"All right," Bill says. "That's it. No use taking up your valuable time. Let me know when I leave."

Bill gets up and starts for the door, and the owner either lets him go or calls, "For Christ sake! Of all the stubborn bastards. Sit down, Bill. For the last time, be reasonable. I'm willing to meet you halfway. How about six-five?"

"Eight," Bill says, being Bill.

Someone else might at this point take six thousand five hundred and feel morally victorious, but not Bill.

"Eight," he says, "and I am a stubborn bastard, in fact, I'm about seven kinds of a stubborn sonofabitch and that's the way it lays"—Bill is getting mad now, really red-faced, coal-country mad—"but I get eight or you can do what you damn well please. If I'm not worth eight lousy thousand to this ball club, then you don't need me and that's the size of it and you can shove it up your ass."

Bill turns the door knob and the owner says, "All right, I'm not going to waste my time arguing. Eight thousand, and no bonuses, and that's my last word!"

The owner puts it this way so that he will be persuading himself that, by giving his last word, he has actually won the argument. So the meeting ends on a note of trust and warm feelings of mutual understanding. Bill signs his contract for eight thousand and the owner cannot sleep that night, wishing—even praying—for another catcher who could fill Bill's shoes. But the manager and the coaches have instructed the owner that they must have Bill. The kids are too green, the old-timers are about to lose it—so argue to the bitter end but give in if need be.

So once again Bill began the season on the bench; again the veterans failed to carry the load, and the rookies stuck until the last deadline and went down for more experience. Bill stepped into the breach and pulled the team together and caught the games. He improved steadily and proved once more how past experience could help when a man applied all his wits and strength and courage to his job. Bill lived catching during the season; nothing else counted. He finished his second year with one hundred and twenty games and a batting average of .256. There were better catchers in the league, but Bill was only reaching toward his potential. I wrote another column at season's end and predicted Bill would rank with the best in two years; and Jocko McCune and I collected our bet on the day the column appeared.

"You win," Jonas said reluctantly. "He did fairly well."

"Fairly well?" Jocko asked.

"Well . . . good then."

"He's your spark plug," Jocko said. "Even we poor, illiterate baseball writers can see that. But it seems other people can't appreciate the fact."

"Oh, come off it," Jonas said. "That's too thick, Jocko. Malloy's not that good."

"No," I said. "Not this year, or next, but from then on, Walter. And he's good for seven more years."

"You may be right," Jonas said. "But I doubt it."

He continued to doubt Bill's ability during the winter, and the Blues signed half a dozen young catchers fresh from high school and legion ball, giving one a twenty-thousand-dollar bonus. Now there is nothing that pleases a veteran more than opening the morning paper and reading that news. Eight years behind him, six in the minors, facing another contract battle before spring; and then he reads about the eighteen-year-old boy getting twenty thousand just for signing his name. He feels no personal animosity for the boy—that has nothing to do with it, for the kids are only the symbols—but it makes him feel that his club thinks less than nothing of his ability. So he stays in shape and builds a few pieces of furniture or goes hunting, and another spring rolls around.

Another spring—Bill's third—and the rookies were down in force, touted as the budding Dickeys and Cochranes, and Bill Malloy had to fight for his job. It went that way for five long years; each spring the veterans could take it easy, condition

themselves slowly, save that precious energy for the last month
of the season.

Not Bill.

He had to go all out from the first day of training, and we
never ceased to wonder how he kept fighting that prejudice—
that fixation—or whatever mental quirk caused owners and
managers to doubt the ability of a proven ball player. Battling
for salary increases that finally brought him fifteen thousand in
his seventh year, fighting off the challenge of the rookies—we
wondered where he got the strength, both physical and moral,
but he was always fresh and ready, in May, in August, through
the final day of September.

And through those years the Blues were slowly building their
fine young team. Each season found another boy coming up,
proving himself, taking his rightful place on the field. Hitting
improved and the infield acquired the polish of experience, and
the young pitchers were coming along. Much credit was due the
manager and the coaches for the steady improvement in
pitching—the backbone of any championship club—but we knew
who worked with the young pitchers during spring training
behind the clubhouse, through the summer, talking with them
and teaching them the little tricks and giving them confidence.

Bill worked with them all and, more than the others, with one
kid named Skimanski, a wild left-hander who had signed for
fifty thousand dollars at the age of eighteen. Skimanski couldn't
hit a blanket at sixty feet and his curve ball was a minus quality,
and many of my friends wrote him off as a bad investment. He
stayed in the minors the one year allowed bonus rookies, then
he had to come up and ride the bench, deadweight, or be lost in
the draft.

Skimanski had earned more money just signing a contract
than Bill had saved in all his years of baseball; yet, having every
right to dislike Skimanski, Bill worked quietly with the kid for
three years. An hour here, a few minutes another day, through
the spring-training months, through the seasons, teaching the

kid all he knew, trying to give the kid a philosophy of pitching that, in turn, would give him confidence. Like one day during spring training, the kid's second year with the club, on the grass along the left-field line behind the clubhouse out of sight and sound of everyone late in the afternoon—Jocko McCune was taking a nap in the small back room, not feeling too well that day, and heard them talking, sitting in the grass beside the sliding pit, the kid ready to give up, having tried for control and a curve ball, and feeling he was getting nowhere.

He was saying as Jocko woke, "What's the use, Bill? I can't get it in there."

"You just did," Bill said. . . . He had just finished catching the kid for half an hour.

"Sure," the kid said. "Back here. Then I go out and look at a hitter, and I can't do nothing."

"You scared?" Bill asked gently.

"Of what?"

"The hitters?"

"No," the kid said. "But Jesus, Bill, you know I can throw hard, but I tighten up and the ball goes all over the place."

"Look," Bill said. "You're learning, kid, but I think you're a little mixed up. What are you looking at when you pitch?"

"Your mitt," the kid said.

"Sure," Bill said. "At the mitt, but you got to see the batter, too. What you think he's doing up there, kid? Picking his nose? You've got to pitch to the mitt, sure we know that, but you're pitching to that hitter, too, and you know what he thinks of you? He's up there to knock that goddamned ball down your throat. Know what Russ"—Russ Jones was one of the older pitchers on the Blues—"thinks about hitters?"

"I guess so," the kid said.

"Guess so?" Bill said sharply. "That's not enough. Russ goes out there, and he hates every bastard that steps to the plate. They're trying to get his bread and butter away from him, kid, and all he's got is his arm and his head, and while he's on that mound and those bastards are coming up, he hates every stinking bone in their bodies. He hates them, kid, and he pitches to set them down, to shove those bats right up their rectum to the trademark and make 'em like it. Look, kid. This is no parlor game. You either got it or you go down, and that's up to you. I'll tell you everything I know, but you've got to do it in the end."

Bill kept on that way with the kid, through the seasons, and things happened in the spring of 'fifty-one. The Blues were assigned fifth place by all my forecasting associates. I had a feeling during spring training, but I was hesitant to go out on a limb and voice my thoughts. And yet . . . the infield was set, the outfield was strong, Bill was one of three top catchers in the league, the pitching was potentially great. Still, they were young, nobody gave them a chance for another year or two. When we finished the trip north and prepared for opening day, Bill was riding the bench as usual while a young catcher had the starting assignment. While the pre-game ceremonies were going on, I caught him alone in the tunnel behind the dugout, enjoying a last-minute cigar.

"Well," he said, "here we go again. What do you think, Stan?"

"About you?" I said. "Same old story. You'll be catching in a few days."

We both smiled; then he said, "I didn't mean that, Stan. What about our chances this year?"

"Sometimes I think. . . ." I said ". . . but hell, I've been around too long to think. You tell me."

"I'll go out on a limb," he said. "If the kid finds himself, we'll take it. And I say he'll find himself about the middle of June."

"Can I quote you?" I said.

"Off the record," he said. "Between us. Story like that might hurt the kid."

"But you feel it?" I said.

"I feel it," he said. "I've been around a long time; you know how guys like me dream of playing in the series. I've got no illusions, Stan, but I sure feel it this year."

"If you do," I said, "I'm with you. I'll go out on that limb. I'll predict we take the pennant. That okay with you?"

"Yes," he said thoughtfully. "That kind of story won't hurt the kid, or the team. But how about you?"

"What can I lose?" I said.

"Hell, man. Your reputation."

"Lost it long ago," I said. "Now you show me, friend, or your name is mud."

I went upstairs and during the game wrote my prediction, and the next afternoon Walter Jonas came to the press box and patted my shoulder and said, with heavy sympathy and a big grin, "Poor old Stan, we hoped you'd be around another twenty years. Now we don't know. I think it's getting you down."

"Just foolhardiness," I said. "Confidence in our brave lads. Don't you have confidence, Walter?"

"You know I have," he said soberly, "but not quite yet, Stan. You know our timetable, the way we figure it. Maybe next year, 'fifty-three for sure."

"This year," I said. "And I'll take another bet like our last one."

"Taken," Jonas said. "And believe me Stan, that's a bet I'd love to pay off."

Jonas wandered away and Jocko McCune regarded me solemnly. "Stan, you really feel it?"

"Yes," I said. "I've got that hunch, Jocko."

"We lost yesterday," Jocko said. "We're losing today. It smells like a lousy start, Stan."

And it was. Skimanski was on the pan in this, his fourth season, and they were starting him in regular turn, knowing that only the steady work and the pressure could make or break him. He lasted an average of four innings in each of his initial five starts, and with the entire team playing spotty ball only the general sloppiness of the league kept us out of the basement during April and May. Bill took over as usual and began his duty which, for the past five seasons had meant some hundred and twenty games per year. And a few days after Bill stepped behind the plate, something happened to the Blues.

When you live with a team eight months of the year, season after season, its thoughts and responses and spirits become your own. I never felt it stronger than the week Bill took charge behind the plate. Not that it happened overnight. The making of a team never does. It creeps up on players and writers and fans alike, until one day you look down on the field and the feeling chokes you because, building up in everyone, unseen and unknown, it finally becomes so strong you blink your eyes, just once, and it is all there. We saw it in the press box, that way, the second week in June.

Skimanski was making his sixth start, and from the opening pitch it appeared he would maintain his perfect record of getting blasted, hot and fast, before he worked up a good sweat.

He walked two men, allowed a single that drove home one run, and staggered out of further trouble by the grace of some benevolent god and a fast double play. He was a wild, discouraged kid in that first inning; the next, ten minutes later, he began to pitch. He fanned two men on eight pitches, the fastest we'd seen in years, smoking fast balls that suddenly hopped, and curves that broke like buggy whips. When Skimanski threw his pay-off pitch and retired the second batter, Bill called time and walked out to the mound.

We saw him put one arm on the kid's shoulder and speak a few words. The kid stiffened and glanced quickly at Bill, and then we saw his shy, boyish grin. Bill told me about it that night; he had gone out there and said, "Well, kid. Are you ready?"

Because Bill knew, even before the kid understood the truth, or realized what had occurred in a matter of minutes on that hot June afternoon.

It was the accumulation of four years' work, the sum total of all advice and practice, of taking the written abuse and the hard knocks, the covert looks and the wanting to quit fifty times and somehow hanging on. But mostly, it was Bill Malloy catching, lifting that big mitt and talking to a wild, uncertain kid, never giving up hope. The kid could feel Bill's steady confidence and many times, ready to give up, only Bill's faith and a few rough words kept him going. If your catcher believes in you, if he never gives up, and you—the kid, any kid—have got it inside, the guts and the savvy and the intangible greatness, it will come through in time. And it came that afternoon when Bill walked out and said, "Well, kid. Are you ready?"

The kid stood there, holding the ball so tightly his knuckles faded dirty white before he turned his hand palm up and stared at the ball's stitched cover as though he'd just discovered what a baseball was for. Then he looked up and grinned shyly and said, "Yeah . . . yeah, I'm ready, Bill!"

"Well then," Bill said. "Let's set these bastards down and start for that series gravy."

The kid pulled at his cap brim and squinted past Bill at the next batter waiting in the box, and lifted the ball and looked at it for a moment and then said, "Yeah, Bill. Tell that sonofabitch to stay loose or I'll blow his head off!"

That was why Bill had a broad grin on his face when he turned and walked back to the plate. For the kid was no longer a boy; he was a pro, all the way, and he had begun feeling it, like Russ Jones and every pitcher worth his salt.

Skimanski won that game, the first time he'd gone the route in four years. He won with blazing speed and a curve ball that did tricks; and suddenly, within the week, the Blues had pitching, timely hitting, and rising spirit. They began winning the one-run games, the tough games that counted when you went for the flag, and they drove into first place on the twenty-eighth of July. They held first place straight through the year until the final week of play, and in that last week came Bill Malloy's finest time.

I've watched ballplayers who gave everything for their team, men who went out on the field with injuries an ordinary man could not bear. They played ball in that way long ago, but it doesn't happen often today. Di Maggio had it, and a few others, but today they scratch a finger on the beer-bottle opener and yell for the trainer and a doctor. That is why I say Bill Malloy had his finest moment in the last week of the season when he won the pennant for the Blues.

They had a five-game lead with five games to go; win one, just one game, and they were in. The tickets were printed, the programs ready, the stadium washed and decorated with gay bunting; everything was set and waiting for the gala event. Walter Jonas had a victory party scheduled and those plain white envelopes with bonus checks all signed. The Blues were conceded the flag, and then they got it in the neck.

They had played all summer without serious injury, and this was the finest sort of luck considering how thin the bench sat behind the regulars. Pitchers had gone out in regular turn week after week, suffering nothing more serious than sore leg muscles. Then, at the beginning of the final week, Russ Jones developed a sore arm; and it was so sore he couldn't lift it above his shoulder and couldn't take his regular turn on the mound. The team was tired, nobody really knew how tired. Still, we felt that Skimanski and his running mate, Traynor, would surely win one of the last five games and cinch the flag. On the night before we began that last week, Skimanski caught his hand in his hotel room door and bruised the fingers until he could not close them or hold a ball. He was out for the remainder of the season, one of those foolish little accidents that come like lightning and cut the very heart from a team.

That left Traynor, overworked and arm-weary, to face the Dodgers at Ebbets Field. The Dodgers murdered him and the pressure came down. The next day in the make-up doubleheader, Bill prepared to catch both games. The Blues were starting second-string pitchers; even they were tired and nervous, and no one else could handle them with Bill's steady confidence. We lost the opener and began the nightcap, and then bad luck came down and roosted on the Blues like a buzzard.

In the fifth inning with the score tied, the Dodgers sent a runner home from second base on a looping single into left field. Hawkins made a fine pickup and peg, and Bill took it the only way he dared under the circumstances, standing up and reaching for the high hop while blocking the plate with his right leg. We all saw the slide and Bill's late tag, and then Bill was writhing on the ground. The runner's spikes had smashed into and around Bill's ankle, twisted it while knocking Bill off his feet and sprawling him in the dirt.

I say "somehow" the runner's spikes, when the truth was, as we all knew, the runner had waited a month for one clear shot at Bill. Don't misunderstand; that is the way tough men still play ball, no holds barred and all out to win, and Bill is the first man to absolve others from blame in the moral sense. A month before Bill had rammed into third base against the Dodgers and blasted their third baseman halfway into the box seats with a vicious blocking slide. Bill had been the winning run that day and the peg was coming in and he knew unless he made third base safely, the rally was done and possibly the game. So he had come in full blast, put the Dodger third baseman on the bench for four days with body bruises. The runner who hit Bill was the third baseman's close friend, and when you play the game for blood, you don't forget. It was one of those things, and it came at the worst moment.

They carried Bill from the field and word soon came up to us that Bill had a bad sprain, the ankle was swollen, he could not catch the final two games against the Giants. And then the Dodgers went on to score five times and whip us thoroughly; and it was not the score, or the fact the Blues had frittered away a safe lead, but the feeling we saw on their faces during the final innings of that game. When it ended I rushed downstairs to the dressing room and pushed through the mob to the trainer's room. They had Bill all fixed up, everything that could possibly be done. He was lying, white-faced, on the rubbing table, talking with our trainer.

"Well?" I said.

He smiled faintly. "I'll live, Stan. No obits today."

"Broken?" I asked the trainer.

"No," he said, "but a bad sprain, Stan."

"Damn the luck!" I said. "Goddamn the miserable luck to hell. Bill, don't worry. The boys will do it."

"We'll do it," Bill said. "I'll catch."

Walter Jonas came through the mob and stood beside me, wiping one hand across his red face, looking numbly at Bill. He was thinking—had to think that way—of seven years spent building toward his first pennant, of the pride and the honor and the personal glory he'd been savoring for a month, and it was turning to ashes in his mouth because of one high peg, one slide, one ankle no stronger than other flesh and bone.

"Of all the—!" Jonas said bitterly.

"I'll catch," Bill said.

Jonas glanced at the trainer, then at Bill. "But the ankle?"

Bill looked up at the trainer. "Fly that specialist of ours over here right now. I'm catching those games."

I thought Jonas was going to bend over and kiss him. I couldn't say a word about the ankle; it wasn't my affair, it was team business and Walter Jonas owned the team. If he and the others wanted to back something like that, all right; certainly they understood and appreciated the risk Bill was taking.

I said, "See you tonight, Bill," and turned away, out of the room. Passing between the lockers, seeing the players faces and hearing their words, I knew the Blues were frantic. The Giants had hung on, were two games behind, and if the Blues lost those final games and allowed the Giants to tie for the lead, we'd never win the play-off. And with Bill out, our chances were less than nothing.

I went to his room late that night and found him sitting up in bed, his leg wrapped from knee to toes. The specialist and the trainer had just gone down for coffee. They'd be out of the way for half an hour, and I almost smiled with relief for I wanted a few minutes with Bill.

"Are you serious?" I asked.

He nodded. "Got to catch, Stan."

"Have you phoned your wife?" I said. "You've got to consider her, Bill, knowing what this might do to that ankle."

"I called her," Bill said. "She told me to catch if I wanted it that way."

"And you want it that way?" I said.

"Hell, Stan," he said gently, "this is the year. We got to win. These kids have worked their ass off, seven years of it, putting together this team. Skimanski's earned it, Traynor's earned it, Russ Jones and Hawkins, everybody. If I can help a little, being out there, then I catch."

"Help a little," I said sarcastically. "Sure, you can help. But please be careful. Don't strain it, don't twist it."

"Doc knows his stuff," Bill said. "There's no danger. When they get done taping it up, I won't feel a thing."

"Just tape?" I asked.

"Sure," he said. "That's all it needs, Stan."

"You're a damned liar," I said.

"Now, Stan," he said. "It's late and I need my beauty sleep. See you tomorrow."

"You're a beauty," I said. "You sure are, Bill. All right, tomorrow."

There was more to say and I knew, if I insisted, he'd tell me other things but we didn't need words. I knew him too well. I punched him lightly on the arm and went down to my room and turned on my reading lamp. I didn't sleep much that night. Sleep was something you used when things were smooth and clean and neat. At breakfast I saw other faces that matched my own, red-eyed and tight-drawn. Jocko McCune joined me at the table and said, "You see him last night?"

"Yes."

"He catching today?"

"He goes," I said. "Ankle and all."

"My friend," Jocko said quietly, "do you suppose his owner appreciates this effort?"

"I don't know," I said. "If he doesn't, then he can't really understand the game."

"My sentiments," Jocko said, and turned to the waiter. "Coffee and toast . . . somehow I can't find my appetite today."

"The same," I said. "And that's too much."

We rode to the Polo Grounds and took our accustomed seats in the press box, and waited for the lineups. Bill caught against the Giants. You remember that. What you may not know is how he caught, what he went through to play. The specialist stayed with him all night and just before game time in the trainer's room they shot his ankle full of novocaine and wrapped it so tightly the skin turned pasty white. Bill limped out on an ankle he couldn't feel—he hadn't lied to me about that—a deadweight below the calf of his leg, and caught the game.

The Blues lost by three runs . . . but the next afternoon, with Traynor pitching and Bill again behind the plate, the Blues won their first pennant in thirty years.

It was one of those great games in the history of baseball, filled with impossible plays and fine pitching, but there was just one player in my eyes that Sunday afternoon. Bill couldn't hit but he did, getting a single and drawing one walk. He couldn't run, but somehow he managed to run. He crouched behind the plate and brought Traynor home, and the Blues won it in the twelfth with a dramatic three-run homer by Hawkins. There wasn't a dry suit, shirt, or eye in the press box when Traynor got the last man on a pop fly, and the Blues exploded from the dugout and ran, with their teammates on the field, across the Polo Grounds toward the center-field steps and the dressing room . . . and the flag.

The dressing room was sheer bedlam after the game. Flashbulbs ground under spikes and bare feet, photographers all over the place, wires and mikes and sweating sport announcers bellowing at this and that player for a few words. Beer spurting from opened cans and bottles, a fifth of Jack Daniels being upended as fast as it could change hands. Players crying and laughing and swearing a blue streak so that it must have been genius alone that kept those words off the air. I worked through the howling mob, shaking hands and taking the drinks offered, and found Bill sitting on the rubbing table in the trainer's little room.

He was smoking a cigar, watching the trainer and the specialist unbandage his ankle. I saw the skin puff as the wraps came off and the short, shaved hairs tear away on the tape. Bill's hands were steady—he held a can of beer in his left—and he grinned at me happily.

"Well, Stan . . . we did it, huh?"

"Yes," I said. "*We* did it, Bill. You damned fool!"

"I'm all right," he said quickly. "Couldn't feel a thing, Stan."

No, he couldn't feel a thing! I knew the novocaine had begun wearing off in the ninth inning, and I saw the tightness of his face as he leaned back on the rubbing table. His cheeks were bloodless and despite his steel-nerved self-control, I saw the absolute, bitter agony in his eyes. It takes raw guts to smile when your leg feels no worse, perhaps, than a red-hot poker.

"You don't need to catch the series now," I said. "We won the flag. That's all that counts."

"I'll catch," Bill said. "Give me these three days' rest and I'll be fine."

I looked at the trainer, then the specialist. "What about it?"

"It's up to Bill," the specialist said.

Jocko McCune touched my back and coughed gently behind me. "You are saying, Doctor, that you recommend Bill catch the series?"

The specialist said, "He can catch, Jocko. It's up to him."

"And he will suffer no after effects?" Jocko said. "No delayed repercussions, say, a year or two from now?"

"You never know those things," the specialist said. "Too much may happen between now and then."

"I see," Jocko said softly. "Stan, my boy, shall we go and get drunk?"

I patted Bill's good leg and said, "See you at home," and went away with Jocko McCunes, and spent three days, doing all the routine work that comes at series time; and finding no thrill in the fact that we had the series at home, in our own stadium, for the first time in so many years. I waited for that opening game and went through the motions of work, and when the lineups came and we saw Bill's name, I looked at Jocko McCune and couldn't find a decent word to say.

Bill caught the Series. With his ankle bandaged, with novocaine freezing his leg from the calf down. We lost the Series but that was no surprise, with a physically and mentally exhausted team that played fine ball despite weary pitching and nervous players and a catcher who couldn't hit or run or play at his peak, who didn't sleep one of those nights for the pain in his leg.

But he caught, and for me there was no other man on the field. They give medals for bravery in battle, to men who deserve those medals richly, but bravery in battle is a spontaneous thing as any man who knows will freely admit. Bill Malloy had a kind of courage that transcended words and medals. He was hurt, he knew that playing those final games of the season, and then the Series, might easily cut his career short. But he played, because he loved his team, he loved the game, and he would not accept defeat. When a man is under that deadly pressure, knowing how it could end even before he willed himself to play, he goes far beyond common courage.

We all rode home together after the fourth and last game, on a special train that had all the enthusiasm of a morgue. Bill was quiet and I knew he wanted to pack up and head for home within hours. His wife didn't speak and the boy slept peacefully while we smoked and tried to make small talk. Finally, when his wife went for a drink of water, Bill said, "I got to admit, it sure as hell is sore."

"Good for you," I said. "Nothing like admitting the truth . . . a week late."

"I'm okay," he said. "Be good as new next spring, Stan."

"I know it will," I said. "But be careful, will you. Not so much hunting."

"All right," he smiled. "Anything you say, Stan."

Two weeks later the news came. Bill had broken one of those small bones in his ankle, had caught the final games on a bone that shifted and ground into the flesh. The ankle had not responded properly to treatment after Bill went home, and his local doctor took the x-rays that showed the break. With his ankle in a cast and treatments scheduled daily, Bill was under strict orders to do no walking until given permission. As to the ankle healing and once more returning to full strength—well, nobody seemed to have that answer.

I placed a call and talked with him an hour after we heard the news. He said, "It's one of those little bones, Stan. You know, underneath the big ankle bone on the outside of the foot. About the size of a toothpick."

"Will it heal?" I asked.

"Sure," he said. "Why not? Bone that size won't take very long."

"Can you use a cane?" I said.

"Not yet," he said. "Doc wants me to give it plenty of rest."

"You listen to him," I said sternly. "No cheating."

"No cheating," he laughed.

Then I tried to ask more questions, but Bill at home, among his own people, was a different man. He seemed to put on a reticence that held his tongue, and I had to settle for the apparent facts.

"All right," I said. "Sign my name on the cast and have a good winter."

"I will," he said. "See you in the spring."

I wanted to call him every day and report his progress, but that was foolish, so I did the next best thing and wrote a column and retold how he had caught the series on a broken ankle. They ran the column on a back page of the sport section because football season was in full swing and the fans wanted a rest from baseball . . . at least, that is what I was told by the powers above when I protested. . . . I couldn't get it out of my mind and two weeks later, attending a banquet of some sort—after so many years on the peas-and-chicken-a-la-king circuit that you can't remember which banquet is which—with Jocko McCune, we met the specialist at the punch bowl.

"Doctor," Jocko said. "Nice seeing you."

"Nice seeing you boys," the specialist said. "Seems our paths never cross during the off season."

He chatted a few minutes and excused himself, but Jocko said, "Doctor, do you have a moment?"

"Of course," he said, but I saw the flash of annoyance in his eyes. "What is it, Jocko?"

"Well," Jocko said innocently, "I've been thinking of Bill Malloy and his ankle, and a question keeps recurring in my mind. Perhaps you can answer it, Doctor?"

"I'll try," he said.

"A simple question," Jocko said. "I can't understand why x-rays were not taken of Malloy's ankle immediately after the accident occurred that afternoon at Ebbets Field. Wouldn't x-rays in Brooklyn show the bone as plainly as x-rays did in Malloy's home town?"

"Certainly," the specialist said. "x-rays are the same, Jocko, if the equipment is good and the technician knows his job."

"Then why weren't x-rays taken that same afternoon?" Jocko asked.

The specialist looked at us and filled his glass from the punch bowl, and said with great reluctance,

"Apparently it was only a bad sprain. Malloy didn't want x-rays taken. He said the ankle was okay, just a bad sprain, he wanted it fixed so he could play and never mind the crapping around . . . his exact words as I remember them. Please understand, I only assisted in bandaging his ankle and"—he coughed gently—"in doing what I could to alleviate his pain while he caught. Taking x-rays was a decision vested in the team proper."

"I see," Jocko said. "And apparently no one deemed the sprain serious enough to warrant taking x-rays at that time?"

"Apparently," the specialist said. "Now, if you'll excuse me. . . ."

He faded away into the crowd and Jocko McCune dipped punch into our glasses and set his glass carefully on the heavy linen tablecloth. We turned away without speaking and entered a side room—we were in the hotel grand ballroom—and stood in one of the old-fashioned grilled windows, looking down across the city.

"That's what I like about our profession," Jocko said. "The spirit of co-operation and trust, the deep sportsmanship, the concern for our fellow man. Sometimes I wonder how poor bastards like you and me manage to survive in the midst of all this sweetness and light."

"It isn't easy," I said. "Or even very much fun."

"What a story!" Jocko said softly. "What a column for the Sunday sheet! Call Malloy and ask him if he wanted x-rays that afternoon—see what he says, and I know what he'll say before he answers, and if you could ask him fast he might slip that cautious tongue of his. What a story! Think we could do it justice?"

"We could try," I said.

"No use," Jocko said. "Do you think they'd run it like that, like you and I can write it now?"

"No," I said. "No chance, Jocko."

"How do you feel, Stan?" he asked harshly. "Clean . . . neat . . . at peace with your soul? The Blues win a pennant and Malloy sits at home with a broken ankle, and does he know if it'll respond next spring? He can't know that, and he's thirty-two years old and bones don't knit so fast once you pass the thirty mark. How about that thought for a nice clean taste in your mouth? Malloy lies there on the rubbing table and they look down at him and he says, 'Sure, I'll catch,' and they say fine and does anybody think of x-rays right at that moment? Why, no. Nobody happened to think of taking an x-ray of a sprained ankle, twisted so badly it looked like a pony keg of beer half an hour after it occurred. Nobody happened to think of x-rays so Malloy, being the man he is, went out and caught and won a pennant, and for good measure, caught the Series too. Jesus Christ, if a man tears a hangnail during the season they take x-rays and use penicillin and smother him with attention. But not at that particular moment. Not with a pennant and tickets printed and programs ready and all the glory waiting and—shall we say the nasty word—money hanging on who won a final game. All I can say is, I hope some people think of Malloy now and remember him next year, and the next, if his ankle doesn't respond. There's no sentiment in baseball, Stan, and we know it better than anyone in the world, but in this case sentiment is a poor bedraggled bitch of a word to use for Malloy. I'm going to worry about him all winter, and next spring I'm going to watch him like a hawk. Aren't you?"

"Yes," I said. "You've said it all, Jocko, and I double it in spades. I'll probably worry a little myself."

I worried all winter and went to spring training with doubt in my stomach the size of a baseball. And that spring, for the first time in six years, the Blues front office announced that Bill Malloy was the first-string catcher.

Think of that!

It was, we all decided, a kind and considerate gesture; more so, when they added that his catching depended, of course, upon recovery of his broken ankle. It was something like taking a man's leg to improve your business, then begrudging him the use of the stump to make a living. It was telling the child, "Go swimming, kid, but don't get wet."

It was wanting a pennant so desperately that x-rays happened to be overlooked, and knowledge of a man's courage and love for his team was turned upon the man himself to assure the sale of tickets and bring home the bacon. It was . . . but why go on that way? You never bring things back as they were before, and the truth is, they were never that way in the first place. All we could do was watch Bill, and hope for the best.

We watched, and Bill had a miserable season. His ankle responded slowly to treatment—and believe me, when he reached spring training he got nothing but the best, which brings to mind the open barn door and the horse that stole itself—and just when he began finding himself in June, he was beaned. He rode the bench three weeks with headaches and double vision. Then his stomach grew upset—a by-product of the beaning and the secret worry—and he went on a diet of food lists and pills. By that time we were moving into July and the Blues were hopelessly out of the race. Picked to repeat, or at least finish second, the Blues fell apart from the very beginning of the season. Jocko summed up their ailment briefly: "Swellhead."

Nothing went right, nothing seemed to bring them together and give them the cohesive quality that makes a team. The truth was—and we hated to see it and write it—they had developed a fatal case of overconfidence.

They finished a very sorry sixth, and Bill caught just sixty-two games, and fell off in his batting to .247. Even so, considering the ankle and his beaning and his stomach, it was nothing to be ashamed of, to worry over. Many good men can look back on long major-league careers and remember that one bad season, that nightmare time six months long, in which everything went wrong and no explanation or remedy could solve the problem. But no more than one bad season, for a good man who proves his worth over five or more years, and has a bad season, is different from the rookie who fails once and never comes back. Bad luck doesn't strike more than once. Bill was thirty-two, but he had four good years left, and if ever a team needed one man in years to come, the Blues needed Bill Malloy. True, they were weak in other spots, but behind the plate, where your team lives or dies, they had Bill.

That fall Bill fought against a salary cut with the front office. The winter before, after the pennant win and during Jonas's burst of happiness, Bill had asked for, and gotten (and richly deserved) a pay raise to twenty thousand dollars, the first time he'd made good money. But now, after the Blues' collapse and Bill's terrible season, Jonas wanted him to take a full twenty-five percent cut.

Bill expected a cut—only two men on the team deserved a raise following that miserable year—but not the full amount. Bill returned the first contract—they sent it to him in November—and wrote that he deserved a cut but not five thousand. He wrote, too, that his ankle was almost well, his headaches were gone, he'd be in top shape by spring. Bill didn't lie. He couldn't, being the man he was. He wrote that he was willing to take a three thousand cut. Jonas remained adamant and, as we followed the exchange of letters, it developed into the usual waiting game until the middle of December. At that time the Blues front office announced the trade.

One of their key men, following a great pennant year, had flopped miserably during the previous season. He was gone, sold, and his position created a hole the size of a truck when the front office took inventory and began planning for the next year. They burned the midnight oil and polished up the old prejudices and weighed the values of crippled players, and made the trade.

They traded Bill for the Eagles' third baseman, throwing in another player from the club and one of the promising rookies in Triple A. The Eagles threw in two other players to even the deal. The Blues' front office issued a statement to the effect they hated to see Malloy go, but third base was wide open, they had no replacements available in the farm system, but they did have young catchers almost ready, so there was no choice; they must consider the fans and field the finest possible team the next year.

The other players didn't matter. They were throw-ins. Bill and the Eagles' third baseman were the key men.

I'll always remember going to the Blues' offices with Jocko McCune the day they released the story. We sat around with a drink and smoked their expensive cigars and listened to the same old manure about Bill's ankle not responding and how they hated to see him go, but you know how it is, men, you can't let sentiment override logic, and the players understand, they know that front offices must think ahead, not just one year, but two and three and five . . . a tremendous patting of their own back, for there has yet to appear the front office that can think ahead more than three months . . . and all through that time of much talk—two hours—I tried to justify the trade in my mind.

So have you. How many times have you tried to figure the latest trade? You know a little, but you don't know the rest.

Trades are so common these days that just keeping the players straight is a full-time job and like so many writers, I have felt for years that wholesale trading is not the answer to the building of a winning team. Many trades are justified by grim necessity; others are made by shrewd general managers who spend a year making the proper moves to get one man; player sales by poorer clubs must also be, for the sake of economics. But too many trades are the result of premature fright, of panic, of prejudice on the part of men who should think, and know better, for they are the men who run a ball club.

You cannot build a solid team spirit with a transient organization, when players are coming and going like streetcars. A player has got to feel he belongs to a club, that he is valued and respected, listed on the roster as an asset of flesh and blood and brain, and not a block of muscle to be sold, traded, or moved around at the whim of the front office. For that reason—and baseball can only blame itself—many players have lost all semblance of real team spirit.

They reach that point where playing is just a day's work, two or three hours of controlled effort by a skilled craftsman, for which they receive pay in ratio to that skill. The time comes when the player takes stock and says to himself, "Why put out that last ditch effort for this club? They won't remember next year, maybe not next week, and I may be on a train tomorrow night. So take it easy, play good, but don't risk your body and your future."

Bill Malloy was not that kind. He was a throwback to the forgotten generation of ball players—and Ty Cobb could have told you what I mean. Bill played to win every game, he played all out every minute, and he expected nothing less from his teammates. He was the *one* player a club should never trade, no matter the circumstances, the personalities involved, the old grudges that so often get the better of clear thinking. There are too few like Bill in baseball today and I thought in that way while we smoked the cigars and drank the good whisky. And Jocko McCune, never one to hold his brash and eloquent tongue, gave voice to our unspoken thoughts just before the meeting broke up.

"A fine story," Jocko said, "for a dull time of year."

"Yes," the Blues general manager beamed. "Milk it out, Jocko. Should be good for a week or two."

"Yes," Jocko said. "Let me get the values straight. The trade is three for three; but Bill and the Eagle third baseman are the key players. Now let me see, Ace McBride"—Ace was the Eagle in question—"has been up six years. His batting average for that time is around .252. He's a good journeyman third sacker, he's thirty-one years old, he has spirit, he'll help the Blues a great deal—"

"That's the way we feel," Walter Jonas said. "Ace is a good man."

"Yes," Jocko said. "Now, it seems to me the Blues have a dozen young infielders, four in Triple A last year, who must go somewhere very shortly. Right?'

"Well, say a year or two," Jonas said.

"And of course you've got young Stevens," Jocko said. "As fine a utility-man as there is around, on the bench these last four years. I know what the talk is—Stevens can't hit—but it's hard to make a flat statement when the boy hasn't played ten full games a year. His fielding is excellent, his spirit good, and I just wonder if he might not outhit McBride, given the chance?"

"He might," the general manager said quickly. "But he's young, and McBride is an old pro."

Jocko smiled, that innocent little grin. "So we have that situation, and then we consider Malloy's batting average and runs batted in, and his age, which oddly enough is only a year older than McBride, and the fact that his ankle will be well next year—"

"How do we know?" Jonas asked curtly.

"Why," Jocko said, "he told you that, Walter."

"Promises!" Jonas said. "You know ball players and their promises."

"I know," Jocko said. "I know about all the promises in baseball. And I know. . . ."

He stopped and looked down at the rug, and I could guess the words coming up in his throat, the way he wanted to mention x-rays and all the other parts of a stinking, dirty deal; and could not say the words because that was going too far, even for us, and all it would get us was trouble. There had been times in the past when we sat on big stories, and held our tongues, and that is a shame all of us bear continually. There is no way to rationalize the feeling, no way to defend ourselves, other than saying honestly a man must eat, and support his family, and a man can go just so far. Jocko came to the edge of the wall that afternoon, the nearest he'd ever been, and held his tongue.

"Hell," he said. "Forget it, gentlemen. Thanks for the lovely time."

We shook hands and parted company, and as we walked to the elevators, not quite able then to face each other, Jocko said softly, "Ah, yes! Forget it, gentlemen. Thanks for the lovely screwing. I shall go home and write an essay on the philosophy of prostitution."

"Forget it," I said sharply. "Write one on how the Eagles feel. Nobody brought that up, if you remember."

"No need," Jocko said. "We all know how they feel."

We all knew. The Eagles felt great. They needed Bill Malloy and were willing to gamble his ankle was healed. They were even willing to shift their regular shortstop to third base and bring up an untried rookie from their Triple A club and give him ample chance to make good at short. They welcomed Bill with open arms, signed him a week later, and did not haggle over money. They gave him eighteen thousand, a cut of two from his last contract with the Blues. I know that, for I called him a week later and got a statement from him, and after he told me about signing the new contract and we beat around the bush a little more, I said, "You know how I feel about this?"

"Yes," he said.

"How about you?" I asked.

"For the press?"

"For me," I said.

"All in the game," he said. "I'll play wherever I am. The Eagles have been fine so far. I've got no kicks."

That was Bill. He wouldn't speak openly, no matter how bitterly he resented the trade, and the slur that went with it. Knowing him so well, knowing how much he had given the Blues, my own bitterness—and Jocko's—toward the front office was difficult to conceal. And tonight—for we are back again in the press box and batting practice is finished and they have started infield—looking down on the field, there were other values at stake in this first game of the season between the Eagles and the Blues.

The Blues were still a disorganized team. With the best pitching in the league, with McBride filling out a strong infield, with the odds in their favor, they had gotten off to a miserable start. Skimanski had lasted twice in four starts—and he was much better than that—and Traynor seemed to have lost his fine control edge for the present, and the Blues were in seventh place. This was, on the surface, a small worry with only twenty games played, but people could not understand how we felt upstairs in the press box.

Skimanski was starting tonight and this game was one of those times, a single game in which an entire season's success might ride on the result. This was the final series of the Blues' first homestand, and the other Western clubs preceding the Eagles had mopped them up. The Blues needed a win tonight, for the team, for Skimanski. They needed it desperately, to recover their courage, their confidence, their will to win.

And tonight, needing that win, Bill Malloy was down below in the visitors' dressing room, preparing for a game he wanted to win. I could picture him coming through the tunnel to the dugout, slightly bowlegged, big shoulders and arms swinging loosely, chewing one last puff from his cigar, smiling with his eyes even before his mouth lifted and his white teeth laughed at something spoken by a new teammate.

Bill Malloy was back, and expected in the tradition of all traded players, to beat the ears off his old team. But he was coming back in another way that few people can understand. Not so much to hit the kid and beat the Blues and make Jonas look like the perfect ass, but to prove his own worth again, prove to himself that he was still good, in the heart and the body, still as good as before, and good for a long time to come, capable of taking charge and playing the game.

You see, you think all this while you look down on the field and watch the players, and so many people will laugh at these thoughts because they can say, "What's so important about a man's feeling for a game? It's just a game, after all . . . and don't tell me a man thinks that deeply about it."

Well, what is the difference in men and the depth of their love for the one thing they can do better than most? Is the depth of feeling any deeper, and more sincere, for the scientist, the lawyer, the butcher, the carpenter, any man doing a job? Do those men love their work more than the ballplayer, more than Bill, and does the nature of their work—not a game, but something more applicable to life—make their love finer and deeper?

You hear that sort of argument many times, often in condescending tones as if the argument itself is beneath real dignity, from people who maintain there are varying depths of feeling in different professions. These people argue that a doctor's feeling—and I only use a doctor for example with no slur intended—for his work is much deeper than Bill's. Yet both are specialists.

And remember . . . while the doctor studied hard to learn his trade, Bill went to a school that lasted just as long and gave him a continuous test that ran for years. Yes, they say, but take him out of baseball and what can he do? The easy reply is to say, "Take the doctor away from medicine and what can he do?" but that isn't fair. Jocko McCune has the best answer; and while it is entirely prejudiced on our part, still it makes a point. Jocko says, "Let's swap them around, picking them the same age. Let's see the doctor become a major-league ball player. And while he's trying let's send Bill to school and let him study medicine. Bill would come out a pretty good doctor, but let's see the doctor make the big league?"

I thought of the words I couldn't write, and leaned forward on the press-box ledge, waiting for game time, wondering how Bill would play. Tonight was one of those games for me. I'd watched something like twenty-five hundred ball games in the past years, and just a few stood out in memory because of great plays, of magnificent efforts by certain players, of displays of team spirit that refused defeat. Tonight, with the feeling growing in my chest, and in the others beside me, I knew that anything could happen.

I nfield practice had run its course, the warning gong had sounded, and the groundkeepers were out, smoothing the basepaths and laying the white lines. The sky was darkening above the light towers and the lights seemed brighter against the blackness. In the press box the scorebooks were open and the lineups written, the typewriters and phones and wires were ready; the radio and TV crews were fidgeting nearby, waiting for the game time signal and the air. The Blues took the field, and Skimanski walked out to the mound and began his warm-up pitches, and the umpires settled themselves in the familiar spots, and it was time.

You could feel—almost touch—the tension when Skimanski took his signal for the first pitch. The Blues were talking behind him, letting their voices come—sharp and husky and hoarse as each man added his to the blend—out against last year's failure, this spring's indifferent start, against their own failure as individuals to make good the great promise they contained. There are times when the chatter cannot be heard against the crowd sound, but tonight, waiting, the big crowd was almost silent, and the voices rose from the infield and drifted into the press box, giving us a share of their tightness and anger.

For they were all men now, their kid years no longer counted, and they knew at last just how dead that season's pennant really was. They had learned it the hard way, through a year and a half of time, through a pay cut and the secret struggle each man had fought to face the truth and call himself a bastard who had let his team down. They felt all that, and knew what tonight meant, but part of their feeling certainly was due to Bill's presence. It was akin to the moment when the bell rang for a championship fight, and the two fighters touched gloves in the center of the ring.

The Blues had to prove themselves a team without Bill Malloy's steadying influence behind the plate, while Bill Malloy was making them feel his own desire to win. And the Blues' front office—the powers that be—what were they thinking, ten feet above us in the private box? Did they understand what could happen tonight, that defeat might easily cause them to build all over again, start another team, because this team had been down, all the way down, and was just fighting back, and if it went down once more nothing in God's world would save it. Did they think deeply enough to realize that should the Blues lose, one man was in the position of the keystone, that block which supported the whole and if removed had been known to bring down an empire in ruins? I don't know if they were thinking above us, but we were, and we leaned forward and forgot our cynical masks as Skimanski made his first pitch.

Skimanski and the Eagle veteran, Ken Rafferty, wasted no time in locking horns. The kid was fast, his control seemed better tonight. Not pinpoint, for a left-hander never threaded the needle if he had a world of natural stuff. But the kid was pitching fast, his ball was alive, and his curve was dropping off the table. He retired the Eagles in order and Rafferty ambled out on the mound and returned the compliment, serving up his slow, deceptive assortment of junk. Rafferty was a cagey old-timer with a dozen pitches to compensate for the loss of his fast ball. Rafferty was pitching beautifully, and behind the plate was the big reason. Bill crouched low and gave Rafferty his target, talking it up in his deep voice, handling Rafferty with the cunning of fifteen years spent behind those white rubber plates. We leaned forward, all of us, and watched him closely, for tonight was our first chance to judge his physical condition, and we had the questions on our tongues.

Could he move as fast, we were thinking, handle the low pitches, get those tough foul balls? Was his ankle strong and his vision normal? Was his stomach acting up or once more cast-iron as we remembered him from many meals together? And most of all, was he thinking as he had in past seasons, his eyes and his mind and his body working as one instrument?

Rafferty got the Blues lead-off man on a pop fly, retired number two on an easy grounder to second base. Bill was mixing up the pitches, using Rafferty's bewildering assortment of curves, change-ups and sliders, working on the Blues with the stored knowledge of seven years, knowing exactly what every man in that lineup could hit. The third batter fouled one high and far back near the screen below us. Bill whirled from his crouch with that catcher's instinct for the direction from the sound of the foul, flipped his mask, and raced for the screen. He looked up once, judged the spinning ball, bounced off the screen and moved a step to his left, and gathered it in. When he flipped the ball to the plate umpire and trotted over into the Eagles' dugout, I heard the grunts of approval on both sides.

"Well!" Jocko McCune said. "Bad ankle, eh?"

"Bad vision," I said. "No speed."

"I shall make a note," Jocko said.

I made a note, too, that Bill Malloy was back in form, good as ever, with the same judgment of fouls and plenty of speed. And I remembered him writing Walter Jonas that his ankle was all right, his vision perfect, that he'd be good as new this year. I made a few more notes, but they didn't mean anything, and Jocko called the press-box boy and ordered two Cokes, and we sat back as the Eagles came to bat in the second inning.

Bill was batting sixth for the Eagles, his usual spot with the Blues in past years. Skimanski got two quick outs, and Bill came from the on deck circle into the box, and our partisan home crowd stood up—actually stood up—and gave him a prolonged cheer. Bill knelt down on his right knee and dusted his hands, and then looked around and tipped his cap, showing his bald head for a moment, gleaming under the lights. That was something we'd never seen before, Bill Malloy showing that bald head to the crowd. I knew why he did it. Above us in the private box, Walter Jonas was watching, hearing that applause, and squirming on the hot seat. Bill held no animosity for the Blues, but his contempt for the front office—and Jonas—was rising clear and hard past our press box into the box above.

"Wonder how he feels?" Jocko said. "Batting against the kid."

"No different," I said. "Bill's an old pro."

"Sure, but he liked the kid."

"And he'll hit him," I said, "if he can."

Bill squared off, legs spread wide in that odd half-open stance, and cocked the bat high behind his right shoulder. On the mound, Skimanski fiddled with the ball, reached down and pinched the resin bag, rubbed his pitching hand against his shirt front, and finally went into his windup. The first pitch was inside, whistling fast, above the letters and taken for a ball.

"The kid remembers," Jocko said.

Yes, I thought, the kid was remembering Bill's instruction. Bill had lectured many an hour on batting weaknesses, making the kid memorize the weak spots of every hitter in the league, and in doing so had explained his own weakness which was common knowledge. If a pitcher could hold the ball inside above the wrists until he got ahead on the count, Bill was in the hole. Bill's stance made him resemble a straight pull hitter who would pull an inside pitch down the left field line, but Bill actually took a step with his left leg that crowded the ball as he started his swing. Bill was good for twenty home runs a year, but he hit them to right center and right field on outside corner pitches and curve balls because of that odd stance and follow through. And here was the kid, pitching against Bill, using all the knowledge Bill had given him so freely. And rightfully so, for that was the kid's privilege, and Bill would be happy inside to see how his pupil remembered.

Bill ran up a two-two count, the kid tempted him with a

change-up curve that dropped off low inside for the third ball, and then the kid came in with everything in his body, a blazing fast ball that cut just above Bill's wrists on the inside corner for a called third strike. Bill followed the pitch as he stepped in, his head snapping around and looking down, for one moment, into the catcher's mitt before he turned away toward the Eagle dugout. The kid looked great, and Bill was apparently nailed to the mast, handcuffed for the evening. The Blues ran in to bat, talking it up, slapping the kid's back, and Bill walked slowly away, into the dugout, then back on the steps as he got into his gear.

"The kid's got him," Jocko said. "If he can hold it in there, Bill won't touch him."

"Looks bad," I said. "But don't sell him short."

"I'm not," Jocko said, "but right at this moment I'd say Bill is worried."

Then we were sitting forward, watching a beautiful ball game. Rafferty matched the kid through six scoreless innings; and during that time Bill batted again in the fourth and grounded out, a weak dribbler on one of those fast inside pitches that caught him stepping into the pitch and leaving him helpless, looking worse than the veriest rookie. And in the last of the sixth the Blues finally touched Rafferty for a run.

They got a single, the sacrifice worked the runner to second base, and the Blues lead-off man singled sharply against the right field wall to score the run. Rafferty closed the door on the next batter, and Bill threw the runner out at third base on the attempted steal, the lead-off man's speciality and something Bill had been watching for. He whipped that peg through the middle on the waste pitch as Rafferty dove off the mound, for Bill's pegs never rose over four feet above the ground. That should answer another question, I thought. Bill's arm was better than ever.

The Eagles threatened in the seventh, and Bill was the goat, grounding out weakly on another inside pitch with a runner on second base. The eighth was scoreless despite the Eagles scaring Skimanski with two singles and drawing a walk to fill the bases before he retired the side on fast balls . . . nothing but fast balls down the middle, the way old Dizzy used to pull himself from the holes. And I was feeling worse with every pitch. Bill had shown his old form behind the plate, but the kid was giving him goose eggs. The Blues were riding high, you could feel it in the air, and with three outs remaining I almost lost hope.

The first Eagle in the top of the ninth worked up a three-two count and grounded out. The next man flied to center field, and the Blues stood one out from the big win. I heard the door open behind us and knew who had entered the press box. He couldn't stay upstairs with so much happening; he had to come down and give us that knowing grin and a few kind words. Walter Jonas sat beside me and grinned broadly, and said, "Well, Stan?"

"Well," I said.

"Where's all the base hits from Malloy?" he asked.

"He's still a fine catcher," Jocko McCune said.

"Sure," Jonas said. "Behind the plate. But he won't last the season on that ankle. And the kid is feeding him that bad medicine. He's slowed up, and it's plain to see."

"He's still my boy," I said.

"All right," Jonas smiled. "I won't argue, Stan."

He got up and slapped my back and moved down the line speaking to the other writers. I bent over my typewriter and tried to do something with words—because you've got to write the words no matter how you feel—and a short step away in the adjoining chairs on my left, the Eagle writers were talking.

I heard them vaguely and while they talked the Eagle cleanup batter, Andy Harriss, waited out the kid to a full count, fouled off three pitches, and drew his walk. That was smart baseball on the kid's part. Harriss could break up ball games, and it was foolish to give him anything good with two away. The Eagle fifth place man fouled off half a dozen pitches while running up a full count, but the Blues weren't worried and I knew why, and so did Jocko. The kid was pitching carefully to Dobbins, giving him nothing good to hit. If they walked him, all right, Bill Malloy was the next batter, and the kid had his number if ever a pitcher in the league had the sign on another man. I watched Dobbins draw the walk on a fast ball that missed the outside corner, putting base runners on first and second.

Watching Bill step from the circle into the box, I heard the Eagle writer say to his associate, "The kid must be faster than we can tell tonight. Bill sure practiced enough to do better than this."

"Do what?" I asked.

He turned in his chair and said, "It's no secret, Stan. From the first day of spring training, Bill practiced on pulling the ball down the left field line. Half an hour every day at least. Got so he was driving them out of the park. He asked all of us not to say anything about it; after all, he was trying to overcome that right-centerfield hitting of his. But I guess he just can't pull the ball."

"He practiced that much?" I said.

"Over two months now."

I stood up then, and Jocko McCune stood up with me. I suppose they thought we were crazy, but we looked down at Bill Malloy, just settling himself in the box, and I wanted to shout, pound Jocko's back, do something, because Bill was betting everything on the odds. He was a smart ballplayer, he was perhaps even more than that. I could feel it coming in that moment, and I remembered his first three trips to the plate.

Three times while the crowd booed a little, the Blues chuckled up their blue-striped sleeves; the kid felt great, and Walter Jonas did a jig on the roof. Three times, I thought to myself. Build your mousetrap, Bill, and bait it with your very life.

"Jesus Christ!" Jocko McCune whispered. "You got it?"

"I got it," I said.

We leaned forward as the kid wound up and poured that fast ball down the alley, a white streak on the inside corner, not too high but still that inch above the wrists. A blazing fast ball, but after nine long innings, not quite so fast, or alive, as in the start.

I saw Bill stride out toward third base with one thick leg, the way Al Simmons did it in bygone years, foot in the bucket; saw Bill's shoulder drop as he came around, no longer close to the plate but a foot farther back, his bat flashing and his cap jumping from his bald head as he met the pitch squarely on the fat wood.

The ball cleared the Blues third baseman like a shot, then it began climbing. We watched it go, up and over, over the forty-foot wall, above the lower tier, going into the roof shadows and bouncing like a child's rubber ball high in the last row of seats just under the scoreboard. Three hundred and eighty feet from home plate, up and gone, hit so hard the roar didn't start until Bill dropped his bat and began his jog around the bases.

I didn't watch Bill then. I looked down at the kid. He had turned to follow the ball, it was gone now, and he stood with his head low, his shoulders dropping slack. He was a smart kid, and he was just beginning to think it out. He watched Bill all the way around, until Bill touched third base, and then the kid did something that took real courage.

He walked off the mound toward the line and as Bill trotted past, the kid grabbed his hand and give it a quick, hard shake. Bill said something and the kid nodded, and then Bill was at the plate and the Eagles were lifting him on their shoulders—something you never saw during the season—and carrying him back to their dugout.

For it was no ordinary home run. It was everything we knew it meant—to us, the Eagles, the Blues, and everybody in that park. I stood until Bill disappeared into the dugout, and then I stared at my typewriter and tried to write my lead for tomorrow's story.

The Eagle writer touched my arm. "I see it now, Stan. You knew, didn't you, when I told you?"

"I knew," I said. "So did Jocko. Bill had to take the long chance."

"All I can say," he said softly, "is that the Blues lost something we're not about to give up."

Bill had fooled the kid, had fooled everyone. The man who caught those final games and the series on a broken ankle was not the man to quit. He'd worked all spring until he had the gambler's chance of making good on his bet. He had fooled the kid, all the Blues, who had pitched to his known weakness. They fed him those inside pitches, and he played the sucker; and then he came through in the tightest clutch spot of his career. He hadn't tried anything new in baseball. Good hitters—like Paul Waner for instance—had pulled such tricks for years in various ways, but never in such a situation. As the next Eagle batter fanned and the Blues came in to hit, I knew how this game would end. And I knew, too, with sadness, what losing tonight could mean.

I watched Bill come out and take the warm-up throws from Rafferty, make his peg to second base, and crouch behind the plate. I watched him, and I knew his thoughts. He was happy inside, a man had to feel happy. But he was sad, too, for the kid. He was sad because he knew what that home run had done to the Blues; it might not show up for a few weeks, but down the home stretch, if the Blues ever rallied and got back in the race, that one home run, clinging in their minds like poison, might make the difference: Bill felt all that, but mostly, I feel sure, that home run wiped out all his anger toward the Blues' front office, wiped the slate clean and gave him a fresh start.

Because I knew him, I can tell those thoughts. He was thinking subconsciously, much as every good catcher thinks when he crouches behind the plate day after day, year after year. You can't write those thoughts in a daily story, beside the base hits and box scores, but they form the philosophy of men like Bill, and in his mind, and in mine, they go something like this:

This was the time, Bill Malloy was thinking, the thousandth

and what time, yet it stayed fresh each day like a bright new penny from your grandfather. Each day you went out in the sun and felt the strain on your legs, all the old scars and cuts and sprains and broken bones, and you knew that just once more you were good for one more time. You didn't hear the crowd roar because that was part of your life, heard and absorbed from the very beginning, down the gone, lost stairway of the years that climbed upward toward today. You felt the shin guards against your bones, the elastic straps holding those red plastic shields in place. You hitched up the serrated chest protector that lay snug and hot on your body, the long tail sliced off years ago, for you didn't need the tail with those modern inventions guarding you so well. You lifted your right hand in the gesture people knew by heart, pushed the mask atop your head until the steel bars peered emptily at the sky and you smelled the acid, wet odor of your own sweat and dirt and grease just above your ears in the thinning fringe of gray hair. And then you were crouching—they never thought how many years had gone into the making of that crouch—behind the plate and the batter was waiting, and the umpire's breath was soft against the nape of your neck as he adjusted his body to fit yours. You gave the first signal and dabbed with the mitt, and the pitcher moved out there, fifteen inches higher on his curried hill of earth. The leg went up, the long arm dropped back, then swung above and came on down, and the ball was a blur of white as you forgot whatever you might be thinking. You took the pitch and then the tenseness shattered—you were on the way, the game was moving and nothing could return it to the unfilled pages of the scorebook where your name, this day, was written on the vis-iting side, or return it to the home dressing room, the home dugout, where you would not sit again. The game would run its course, and you with it, for no matter where you played, the game was everything. You had never learned a different way. You ran, and fought, and gave everything for your team, and last year, nursing the bad ankle, you wanted more than ever to help them come back, for you loved that team. And they traded you for that!

L ong after the lights had darkened and the crowd filtered away into the sleeping city, I stood waiting on the curb. Across the street in the parking lot reserved for the home team cars, I had watched the Blues leave by twos and threes, not talking much, just pulling away from the paint-marked stalls and driving slowly from sight into the darkness. It was past midnight when I heard his steps in the corridor and saw him come from the doorway and pause, drawing deeply on his cigar that glowed redly in the night. He saw me and moved to my side, and we stood together for a moment, smiling, before he spoke.

"The kid's better this year, Stan."

"He pitched a great game," I said. "You pitched a better one, Bill."

"That's so," he said quietly. "I sure was sweating that last one out, Stan. But I know him pretty well. He was sure to come in with it."

"He did," I said.

"Yes," he said softly. "He sure as hell did, Stan."

"Feel better?" I asked.

"Feel good," he said. "It's okay now. Sometimes a guy has to wait a long time, Stan, but now it's okay."

I said, "I wrote a nice lead for my game story."

He chuckled. "Glad you could, Stan."

"Shortest lead sentence I ever wrote," I said. "Don't you want a preview before the paper comes out?"

"Sure," he said.

"'Bill Malloy came home tonight,'" I said. "That's all I wrote. Five words."

"Five nice words, Stan," he said. "Let's get a steak. Want to tell you about the family."

The Manager

H e thought that night, and rightfully so, of his boyhood, a very long time ago in the total accumulation of spent years, dulled about the bright edges by that relentless passage of time. Eighteen was a good age to revive memories, for the ragged pieces of a boy's life at eighteen did stick in the mind.

He earned his first baseball pay that summer while other boys were more deeply concerned with girls and cars and college. Even at eighteen his goal was baseball despite his father's protests and a painful awareness of his own handicaps. But a boy of eighteen was stubborn, barriers were erected only to be overcome. It was later in life, tied down by family and responsibilities, that men discovered fear. He had not believed the odds against him, and like the bumblebee who cannot fly in scientific theory, he stumbled along until he rose from the hard earth of mediocrity.

He pitched that summer of 1928 for a semi-pro team in his corner of Minnesota, already judged in local circles as possessed of mature cunning, rather than the overpowering and noticeable assets of speed and curve balls. He was small for a pitcher, weighing one hundred and seventy pounds, standing five-ten, with narrow shoulders that belied their long, flat muscles, and large feet that appeared awkward but gave him the priceless advantage of good balance.

He pitched twenty low-hit games that summer and struck out the magnificent total of thirty-two batters, for he was a control pitcher who made his fielders work behind him. He played batters as a Swede squeezed a concertina, moving them forward and back from the plate, pitching through a needle's eye to their weaknesses, feeding them bad balls that resulted in easy grounders and high, lazy flies.

He might have gone on pitching in small, unknown parks all his life, but luck brought his name to the attention of an old man with red cheeks and unexcelled judgment of raw material.

The old man, Ike Kilean, was a beloved figure in the state. Kilean owned the Double A club in the state capital, had come up through the ranks in the hardest possible way, and was noted for his discoveries among unknown youngsters. A chance word to Kilean, from a friend who saw Art Cassidy pitch one of those low-hit games, brought the telephone call and subsequent bus ride to the city.

Art Cassidy worked out that afternoon while Kilean watched from a third base box, and signed his first contract in organized baseball at five o'clock. The season had a month to run, very little time for a raw country boy in the best league below the majors, but Kilean started him against Kansas City the following day.

He was touched for twelve hits and lost the game 4-2, but Kilean had trouble hiding his pleasure in Art Cassidy's work. Eleven of those hits were singles, one a blooper double, against a power-hitting Kansas City team. Art Cassidy showed fine control and a dinky, sneaky little curve, and best of all, a flat refusal to elbow under pressure. He was raw with men on base—no one had really taught him how to stretch—and his fielding of bunts and slow grounders lacked the professional touch, but Kilean saw the future promise of a fine pitcher.

Art Cassidy started four games in the last month, split even, and during that time absorbed baseball from Kilean and the old-timers on the club with the limitless capacity of an eager sponge. In later years, old Ike Kilean enjoyed talking of Art Cassidy, telling how the boy never forgot or made the same mistake twice, and worked at the job with the zeal of a fanatic. If only, Kilean said regretfully, Art had possessed the color of Dean or Mungo, there was no telling what salary he might have commanded. But the truth was, Art Cassidy was colorless, quiet and calm and even-tempered.

He pitched the following three years for Ike Kilean; in the spring of 'thirty-one he had a total record of forty-five games won and forty-seven games lost. He was an accredited fixture on the team, classified by the writers as a steady Association pitcher who just lacked the speed and curve and size to make the big show. But Art Cassidy did not share that opinion, although he said nothing about his desires. He continued to work at his trade under Kilean's sharp eye, and that fourth season his cumulative knowledge and unnoticed assortment of pitches paid his first big dividend.

He won twenty-seven games that summer, while losing eight, and no matter a man's size or lack of color, that many wins could not be ignored by the majors. Kilean sold him to the highest bidder for twenty-five thousand dollars—big money in those depression days—plus six good ball players. And all this, as many players growled, without a fast ball or a decent curve. But his record was in the book: an ERA of 2.65 and an average of eight hits allowed per game.

He joined the Eagles in the spring of 1932. He was twenty-four years old and, among the usual crop of gaudy rookies, he went unnoticed through spring training. The morning glories hogged the headlines, but Art Cassidy had complete confidence in himself, and long after the morning glories had faded, he was firmly established on the Eagles and pitching with the best of them.

He made the transition from Double A ball to the majors

with a minimum of worry and fuss, and set himself immediately to memorizing every hitter in the league. He applied those lessons from his first start, and he was not too proud to sit in the dugout between innings and study his notebook and refresh his mind.

He was colorless and quiet. His name in the lineup—as compared to most good pitchers—attracted no more attention than a John Doe listing in a local column. But he was a manager's pitcher, a team player, he stayed in constant shape and caused no trouble. He was effective in relief, and did not object when called out of turn. He pitched steady ball against all clubs, top or bottom, and did not become that manager's bugaboo, the good pitcher who could win only against three or four teams in the league.

He became known as old dependable. He made good money, but never the big money, and he remained in the league until 1946. He won twenty games just once, but he never won less than fifteen. He pitched many clutch games in the years with his club, but the Eagles were—unhappily—the steady also-ran of the league, in second place five times during his career, and never lower than fourth, but he did not pitch in a Series and retired at the close of the 'forty-six season to begin his second career in baseball.

He was a tactician, a master at the difficult science of baseball, a man respected by everyone in the game. He returned home that fall and counted his blessings, and discovered them fairly rich. He was married, with three children all growing up, he had purchased a fine farm from his savings over the years; he had twenty thousand dollars in bonds and cash, and upon retiring, with his arm still good, he was offered lucrative jobs for the next summer, by no less than six fast semipro clubs in his state, at one thousand dollars a month, offers worth considering seriously.

But he took a job as pitching coach with the Eagles, and stayed in the league to work with the young pitchers in wonderfully effective fashion. Following the 1948 season he was approached by the Blues to manage their Triple A farm club. After a long talk with old Ike Kilean, in which he reviewed his capabilities and received Kilean's unqualified recommendation, he accepted the job.

The Blues were staging a comeback in baseball, with unlimited funds and dozens of newly signed boys. Art Cassidy's primary purpose, as he well knew, was to develop those young pitchers, give them the final year or two of Triple A polish that so often spelled the difference in the big show.

He had never dreamed of managing a major-league club. He was too modest and introspective, he had never been considered as potential big-league material as a manager. He could take a boy after others failed, and bring that boy to the highest possible degree of ability; he could handle problem players with patience or harshness; he was thoroughly rounded in all departments of the game; but no one had ever mentioned his name as a big-league manager. He worked from, and with, a twenty-year supply of knowledge, he knew baseball as well as any man in the game, but had someone asked if he desired to manage a club, he would have said honestly, "Who'd want me?"

And if the questioner was a close friend, he might add with a knowing, sober wink, "And besides, only a damned fool takes that job."

For he knew every step in that rough road, and he wanted no part of such an uncertain existence.

So the years passed, the summer of 1953 . . . midnight, replaying the afternoon's game.

A t midnight, long after his wife was asleep, he lay in the soft darkness of the cool bedroom and replayed the game. The Blues had lost, and he rode the treadmill of frustration, following a set pattern that pushed him through the entire game.

All the second-guessing and doubts and self-accusation; all this was routine and must be done before he slept. And with the game, the thoughts of past years, until sleep came.

And then, waking at his wife's call, washing and dressing, his mind prowled ahead through the unspent day, already playing the game that would not start until afternoon, juggling his batting order, wondering over his pitching choice, asking himself the never-ending questions:

Should he change the line-up, switch pitchers, do this, do that, seize the one tiny change that might tip the scale in his favor?

He was never sure which part was worse, the night—before sleeping—or the morning, after waking. On the road or home, it made no difference, he had lived this way through four years of play. And this morning, on a bright August day, with the Blues in fifth place and yesterday's loss to the Giants rancoring in his mind, he would complete a cycle begun four years ago.

"Breakfast," his wife called. "Two minutes."

Art Cassidy answered, "Be right down."

He yanked a tie from the closet door rack and knotted it carelessly, facing himself in the mirror. In a fine house, he thought, where they had lived almost four fine years. A house paid for with part of his life, and now he felt like a stranger in his own bedroom. But that was because other strangers would soon inspect these rooms and make an offer; and he'd be on the road again . . . if he was lucky enough to land on his feet. He gave the tie a jerk and turned away, thinking of the day ahead.

The news wasn't official yet, but everything fitted the familiar pattern. Steve McKay had visited in town last week and spent an evening with the front office; the writers had dropped their hints for three weeks; he was home off their worst road trip in years, and the finish was just hours ahead. Art Cassidy remembered an old ditty that went:

My name is Yon Yonson,
I come from Wisconsin,
I vork in the lumberyard there.

Three years ago during spring training, sitting in his private office adjoining the main dressing room, one of his players—an old-timer about to go down—sang that song, paused in sweaty reflection, and spoke to the room at large:

"That's about a square-headed dumbbell of a Swede. Supposed to be the Swede telling the world how happy he is to be dumb, because that way he'll never know enough to appreciate all the fine things he misses. That Swede is like us fine, upstanding ball players. We're so goddamned dumb in many ways, we'll never miss what we don't know."

Art Cassidy remembered that bitter speech and decided the long-gone player was right in one respect. Ball players were dumb . . . but managers were the dumbest of all. If they weren't, they'd never ask for the job, and his own past seemed to bear out that truth.

Four years ago he was managing a Triple A club, rocking along in third place with an outside chance at the pennant, unworried about his job because they didn't fire a man in Triple A when he lost the flag. The parent club had raided his roster during the season, the hometown writers and fans sympathized with his difficulties, and Triple A was blessed with that bastard invention—the four-team playoff—which swelled the final gates and removed the firing threat if a man did his job decently.

He was happy, Ida was happy, they'd soon go home for the winter and relax. Then—it was the third week in August—the front office called and told him to catch the next plane.

He knew why. The Blues were in sixth place, their manager was in hot water with the front office and the players. The manager was an old pro with a blunt tongue and no time to pamper the new-style kid up from some campus with a degree, a bonus and good grammar. His type was on the way out of baseball, but everyone in the trade felt he'd finish the season, then be eased out gracefully with that sweet talk about ill health and resigning for the good of the team.

Ida had kidded Art Cassidy about getting the big job, but

that was only their own private joshing. After so many years, he had no illusions. Then came the phone call that, in effect, was an order.

Art Cassidy caught the plane, arrived in the city that night, and received the velvet-carpet treatment. Baseball was great with the velvet when a man was coming up. They whisked him into town, upstairs into the owner's walnut-paneled office. They were all waiting: the general manager, the farm-club director, the chief scout, the owner's cousin who was down on the books as assistant to the farm-club director, and had as much business in the job as a jackass.

Art Cassidy accepted a drink and discussed, with them, his chance of copping the Triple A flag, while they patted his butt for doing such a fine job after they'd wrecked his team by recalling his ace pitcher, shortstop, and right fielder. Then they got down to business.

They asked him point-blank if he could handle the Blues. It was the only time a man ever got the direct question . . . coming up. After that all words were couched in double-entendre, the language baseball spoke more effectively than diplomats. Could he handle the Blues?

He had his chance to step back, but every man was human and that gold-plated saddle had a fine smell. He knew exactly what they were offering; his eyes were open; he knew that managing a major-league club was the worst job in the world. You were a hero one year, a bastard the next, and you rarely got a second chance. You won within a time limit or out you went. There was no middle course.

Art Cassidy sat facing them, the glass cold between his long fingers. "Sure," he told them. "I can handle the Blues."

"When can you take over?" the general manager asked.

He was still thinking in terms of next spring. He said, "When do you want me?"

"In three days," the general manager said. "Okay?"

Again he had the chance to hedge. He could make the usual

protest that now, so late in the season, was the wrong time, he should begin next spring with an even break. But he didn't.

"All right," he said, and put his head in the lion's mouth.

The general manager, Jack Graham, acquired that pseudo-sad expression as he said, "We hate to do it, Art. You've known Joe for years"—Joe was the present manager about to lose his head—"but you can appreciate our position."

The first law in baseball was: Watch your own skin. Nobody gave quarter, and the knives were always sharp.

"Sure," Art Cassidy said. "I understand."

The general manager was a trader, a buyer, a bargainer supreme. In bygone years he might have been a successful slave dealer. He had to come out on top in every deal. Logic proved that fact an impossibility, somebody had to lose, but general managers were very good with the tongue, and Jack Graham was one of the best.

"Baseball has changed," Graham said. He had put his glass aside and leaned forward, his face very sober and intelligent; the proper mood for one beginning what amounted to a sermon. "Joe can't seem to move with the times. The kids won't play for him, and we've spent a million dollars on these kids. They don't like his cursing, his personal habits, the way he handles pitchers. Frankly, neither do we. We've given him ample time to change; now for his own good and the team's, we've got to make a switch. And we think it's wiser to start now, give you a chance to settle the kids down. Most of them have played for you, Art; they all trust you. This season is shot, down the crapper, so don't worry about the standings. Just get the kids back to normal."

"What about next year?" Art Cassidy said. "You want me back with the Triple A club?"

Graham said firmly, "Not if you show us you can handle this job, Art."

Art Cassidy maintained his quiet, sober face. For Graham had made a funny statement. A dozen managers in the minors could go up and handle any major-league club with the best of them; but nobody wanted to admit that truth and remove some of the gilt from a long-maintained fable. Baseball seemed to suffer from a bad case of the blinkers. Managers deemed worthy of handling the sixteen teams had gradually evolved into a small, closed group of men who moved from job to job, and rarely did an outsider come up and make the grade. Art Cassidy knew he could handle the Blues—knew that without doubt—but even so he was frightened deep inside.

"If I don't cut the mustard," he said, "do I get my old job back?"

"Yes," Graham said. "Of course you do, Art."

And that was even funnier. Any promise given in baseball, unless signed and notarized and witnessed by eighty preachers, was worthless. But Art Cassidy was on the spot. If he demanded a written promise, he betrayed doubt in their honesty. Jack Graham smiled—and no one smiled as guilelessly as men in baseball—and waited.

And behind Graham's smooth, thin-skinned face, behind the owner's fat jowls, was everything that beckoned to a man, egged him into taking the big gamble: the stadiums and the players, the natural urge of any man who had spent all his adult life in the game to climb to the top in his chosen profession, the big money that brought more of the good things to a man of his family, one good season and the first big raise, another lucky year, maybe a Series cut, and the sky for a limit; until a man smelled the five-figure bank account, the new house, all the security that money could buy.

"All right," Art Cassidy said. "That's fair enough."

"Joe goes out tomorrow," Graham said. "We'll let Sammy run the team one day, then you take over on Sunday."

Sammy, Art Cassidy thought, good old Sammy! Pitching coach, bullpen coach, in solid with the owner and the cousin's wife, one of the fat-gutted millstones hung around the manager's neck. Too busy to help the kid pitchers in the right way because he had to tell them about the great days of the 'twenties when men were men, by Christ, and so on and on, while the bullpen pitchers threw to Sammy and another varicose-veined catcher who didn't know when a man was hot or cold. Good old Sammy!

"Sure," Art Cassidy said. "Fine with me."

"Can your wife move here alone, Art?"

"No need," he said. "She'll go home for the winter."

"Better not," Graham said. "We'll be busy, Art, all of us, straight through the winter, getting ready for next year. Have her move here; we'll pay the bill."

"All right," he said. "How about me then, until Sunday?"

"We've got a nice quiet suite for you," Graham said. "You'd better lie doggo."

Then he shook hands and the big car took him across the city to a quiet apartment hotel, and he settled down for the three-day wait, while Graham gave Joe a polite kick in the ass and paved the way for the official arrival of Art Cassidy. Time passed, Sunday came, he took over the Blues; and that was the beginning of four years.

Four years running swiftly, like quicksilver, through the cities and stadiums and seasons, with the endless pressure—that he had asked for, knowing what it did to a man—until time brought him to this morning, on another August day, his last with the Blues.

B reakfast," Ida called again.

"Keep your shirt on."

Art Cassidy went downstairs and kissed his wife, and drank his orange juice while she brought his bacon and eggs. She sat across the table and opened the sport pages of the morning paper and said quietly, "Today?"

They had no foolishness in their minds concerning baseball.

Not after twenty-five years. Ida was no brave, smiling wife who talked of her garden and her roses, and gave her failing husband that brave front while she hid a broken heart. That was for the birds, as Ida said, not for the old pros.

"I think so," Art Cassidy said. "Everything points that way."

"Look," Ida said, and turned the paper around.

Art Cassidy glanced at the headline. No need to read the story; he could write it himself. He'd been three long months on the griddle, and now the writers were jumping the official gun and making their forecasts so that all fans, young and old, would read their exclusive stories and remember, when Art Cassidy was fired, how the writers had predicted it from the very first. And only proper, he thought, for those writers were all old friends of his and had to live too.

This was one of three major papers in the city, and the other two would carry similar stories in the morning editions. Worded a little differently but saying the same thing. After yesterday's defeat by the Giants, following directly on the heels of a disastrous road trip which saw the Blues slip into a bad fifth place, after so many patient months of watching Art Cassidy lose his grip with a team that should be leading the league . . . after all that, it was sad but unquestionably true that the Blues were contemplating an immediate change. Rumor had mentioned several candidates for the position—here the writers simply listed all the major-league managers currently out of work—but Steve McKay, that genial old pro, seemed to have the inside track. The writers predicted that Steve would don a Blues' uniform within three days. It was all there, and all true, and Art Cassidy knew it by heart.

"Today for sure," he said.

"When?"

"After the game."

"What'll we do," Ida said. "Sell this place?"

"Might as well," Art Cassidy said. "But no hurry."

Ida smiled. "Next year's salary?"

Art Cassidy shared her smile. His contract had another year to run, at thirty thousand dollars per year. The Blues had to pay him off, and it could be handled in two ways: either he stayed on in some capacity, or they paid him off in full, very soon, and released him. It was embarrassing to have an ex-manager hanging around while the new skipper ran the old team.

"They'll pay off," Art Cassidy said. "Not right away, but soon. You know Graham, Ida. He likes it sweet and clean. I'm resigning but still a valuable part of the Blues, and a position will always be found for me so they won't lose my sage advice and keen eye."

Oh sure, he thought, my sage advice. Graham would ask him to sit tight until mid-fall, so that once football was started and baseball on the back pages, they could pay him in full and announce that Art Cassidy was going into private business, was dying of Chinese rot, or considering an offer from another club. They would pay off, write his year's salary into the tax-loss column, and forget him.

But Jack Graham would never forget how Art Cassidy had diddled him into giving that two-year contract. It wasn't the money; nobody gave a damn about money, it was just that in the deal Graham had gathered unto himself a black mark by making a mistake in judgment. Not that Graham need worry. They'd given him the contract two years ago after he won the pennant, and Graham could always say it had been the only fair thing to do, and how could they guess that Art Cassidy would lose his touch so fast.

"Well," Ida said. "We've done pretty good."

"No kicks?" he asked.

"No kicks. Money in the bank, never look back."

"And time to go," Art Cassidy said. "You be there today?"

Ida Cassidy grinned. "Today? Wouldn't miss it if I had to come on a stretcher."

He went around the table and kissed her and said, "Good girl; see you then."

Backing down the drive, turning north for the twenty miles into the city, he waved at Ida and lit his morning cigar. The last time, he thought, and a damned good time it was. And Ida was coming in after lunch to sit behind the dugout and smile at all the wives who knew exactly what was happening. That took guts. But Ida had it, all the way, and she'd give them back smile for smile, and if anybody wanted to turn catty, fine! Ida had come up when baseball was really tough. She'd be there behind him, and they'd finish it and walk away heads up. Hell, he thought, how else could a man take it? Others before him had walked away with a grin, and he knew a dozen others who died inside while they kept that smile plastered on their faces. He wouldn't die inside, at least he never had; but now, approaching the city, following the route by instinct, he knew just how tough this day would be. He had to begin and carry through every part of an ordinary day, another game, and do it exactly right.

A rt Cassidy turned down the bumpy street with the car tracks dividing the worn paving blocks; he made the next turn and saw the light towers above the housetops; he entered the parking lot where the smiling, uniformed boys waved him into his reserved stall; he spoke to them as he passed through the side gate and wondered what they were thinking behind the customer smile. For they knew, too, everybody knew. He crossed the sheet and spoke to the guard at the players' door and walked along the corridor into the cavernous passageway beneath the rumpside of the rising stands and turned left toward the home dressing room. So far, he thought, so good. No trembling in the knees, no tears in the eyes, none of that crap. He opened the door and faced the empty length of the dressing room and heard, from the trainer's room beyond the archway, the trainer's voice humming a tuneless little song.

Art Cassidy walked forward and saw the man's shadow and heard his husky voice, "Hey, Art?" and answered in kind, "How are you, Skinny?" and saw the trainer appear in the archway, smile and wave. Then Art Cassidy pushed into his office, closed the door, and carefully took his seat behind the desk. He lit his second cigar of the day and closed his eyes, for he was thinking funny little thoughts.

How many lots had he parked in during the past four years?

Well, he thought, he'd parked on the hot street beside the high broad fence in Clearwater, in the scant shadow of the palm trees and the creaky wooden stands. He'd parked on the fine paved strip behind Al Lang Field in St. Petersburg on many a blistering hot March day. He'd parked near the Tampa Terrace in Sarasota and walked to the nearby field. He'd parked in Tampa and Miami and Orlando and Lakeland; once in New York, under the backstands of the Polo Grounds in the dirty shadows of the El; he'd parked downtown here in this city, and all around the pleasant countryside attending all the fine parties given by the owner's friends. He'd parked in all those places, and each year he'd driven a bigger car; and perhaps that had something to do with having such funny thoughts. Started with a Ford, now the boys across the street were dusting his Cadillac and wondering if—hoping—Steve McKay would be as good a tipper as Art Cassidy.

And dressing rooms! How many had he seen? Not counting his own playing days. Well, he thought again, there was the clubhouse at spring training, down the third baseline from the stands and the press box, one big, low building with the main room, the trainer's corner, the showers and toilets, his own cubbyhole, and the two back rooms where the extra equipment was stored and the clubhouse attendant slept; and anyone in the know brought a woman late at night if arrangements uptown or on the beach had fallen through. He'd remember that one, all right, like a mother remembered her first baby. Some pleasure, some fear, and a good deal of pain.

And Al Lang Field, and Sarasota, all the dressing rooms in Florida, hot and sweaty and slightly moldy in a faint tropical way, not so much from body odors and rubbing solutions and sulphur water, as from the smells of ambition and hope and pride and age and finally—never so sweet and lastly lingering— the smell of last-year-up good-bye. One step slow good-bye. Middle-age spread good-bye.

And all the others: under the right field stands at Ebbets, down the drafty walkway on the brown-yellow clay walk, into that room; and Sportsman Park in St. Louis, a lousy little room with everything jammed together; Wrigley Field in Chicago, and he wondered if they'd ever get rid of the fellow who peddled knickknacks on the catwalk just outside the door; and the Polo Grounds, up the outside steps into side-by-side rooms, home and visitors, and down the broad steps directly onto the center field grass facing the entire grinning oval of the eternally shadowed stands, not to mention the ghost of old McGraw who undoubtedly pushed Leo to those histrionic outbreaks. And all the others. Of course the one in Yankee Stadium, big as a dancehall with about as much feeling, holding all the essentials and little luxuries of life, exuding confidence and money and power and continued luck . . . except that all those qualities belonged to the Yankees and he and forgotten others had felt that; oh, yes, he had felt it keenly during the series while the Yankees took his team apart. Yes, he'd remember that dressing room. And finally, for no good reason, he'd remember one more, far away from all these, buried twenty-odd years in the past. A little place under wooden stands in the southwest corner of Minnesota, with three lopsided benches and two faulty showers and broken duckboards and a cast-iron stove and one drunken attendant who showed up for the biweekly games as a labor of love. Yes, he'd remember that one, for he started there so long ago and that one was the great-grandfather, the progenitor, of all these fine rooms he had learned to know so well. Baseball, in the last few years, seemed to have forgotten those little dressing rooms and what they really meant, and what came from them.

And why did he think these funny things today? Perhaps because every man like himself had to fall back upon some device to pass the time, to keep his mind loosely occupied while the clock ticked and the players—he heard them now—entered the big room outside his door and began dressing for the game. He had to pass the time before he faced them, and innocent thoughts were the best . . . and then, thinking back and knowing too much, and smoking his cigar too fast as he began undressing, Art Cassidy knew he could never think innocent thoughts about baseball. Nothing was innocent when a man was in the game all his adult life. Every thought, no matter if it came easily and without pain, carried a barbed spear under the smoothness. Like a rose, he thought, or the joyous platitude of a general manager's smile.

A rt Cassidy was stripped down to his shorts, standing barefoot on his thick rug, when the knock sounded. He said, "Come in," and turned to the clothes rack that held the clean uniform; and heard the door open and one of the bright young men from the ticket office say,

"Art . . . Mr. Graham wondered if he could see you after the game."

Art Cassidy unslung his supporter and undersocks, and slapped them against his thigh.

"Sure, son," he said. "Where's the meeting?"

"Down here," the young man said. "Mr. Graham said to tell you he'd be down right after the game."

"All right," Art Cassidy said. "Tell Garcia I got the message."

"Who, Art?"

"Forget it." Art Cassidy laughed. "Tell him I'll be here."

"Well," the young man said. "Good luck today."

Art Cassidy pulled the supporter over his knees and said, "Thanks, son," and heard the door close softly.

He sat on his chair and pulled the undersocks smooth, rolled the woolen blue outer socks up and reached for his pants. He thrust his left foot through the webbed bottom, then his right, and stood as he yanked the pants upward and began slipping on his undershirt, then the light woolen team shirt, white with the blue stripes and the name etched across the front. He finished buttoning and belting and zipping, and gave the cap a slap against his desk corner and settled it squarely on his balding head. He was dressed now, into the armor, braced against the world, ready to go. Outside, in the big room, men were talking and whistling and singing, raising that steady conglomerate hum of sound. When the second knock came, his coaching staff arrived, dressed, and waiting for the pregame meeting. Art Cassidy gave his cap a final jerk, lit a fresh cigar, and called,

"Come in . . . all right, come in!"

Yes, he thought, by all means get your butts in here. My brave and brilliant assistants. Steeped in the game's ancient lore, gray-eared with hoary knowledge of all plays and circumstances as handed down through the ages by Mother McGraw and Lydia Pinkham Mack and a few other old, wise witches. Always ready in the clutch, my faithful men. Come, all four, and rest your weary butts on these soft leather cushions and woolgather of the roaring 'twenties when men were men and outfielders batted .300 or died in the minors. Smile with me, discuss today's strategy, and wonder how long your jobs will last when Steve McKay takes over. My friends of four long years, coaching our boys, watching my every astute move, helping me guide this team with consummate skill . . . like hell! Art Cassidy smiled at the empty walls. People had an idea big-league managers and coaches were supermen who saw everything on the field. Called every pitch, foresaw and forestalled every enemy move, knew when a pitcher was faltering, when a batter could not deliver, which fireman had the stuff, which rookie was ripe, which Sadie in St. Louis was sneaking up on the tenth floor. Did all manner of jobs bordering on the impossible, simply because they were big leaguers and, as such, had become infallible. What a lot of manure! Good men, yes, of course they were. But how could they see everything that happened? They were human, just that, and today they were a little less than human in their own eyes. For one of their tiny society had failed—and now all were suspect—and they hated him for endangering their jobs. Art Cassidy swallowed the words and thoughts they could not understand and said, more quietly, "Well, another day."

"Another dollar," his first base coach said.

"No changes," Art Cassidy said. "I guess they're pitching Maglie."

"He'll go," Sammy said wisely. "Right kind of day for him."

"Same lineup," Art Cassidy said. "Same signals. We'll switch in the third if they catch. Ken pitches."

"He's ready," Sammy said. "Had good stuff yesterday, Art, warming up."

"Then that's it," Art Cassidy said.

"That's it," they answered, eager to get out of this room.

"Okay," he said. "See you upstairs."

They crowded through the door, leaving the office. They had to get up on the field and breathe fresh air, and hope that his failure had not touched them. Because they knew today was his last—the old grapevine never failed—and already they had pushed him from their minds while they tried to remember how genial Steve McKay ran a ballclub, what signals he used, how he liked his hitters, how he ran his bullpen, how he did everything . . . everything but how he might fire one or all of them and bring in his own men. McKay had his own men; they always did, those incoming managers, their own men from past days as bitter and sad as this; past days when genial Steve had gotten the boot and walked away from a lost cause.

So they went upstairs, and the players were beginning to move out. It was time for Art Cassidy to make his appearance. He stepped into the dressing room and saw his men in their various, half-sculptured attitudes of dress and undress, talk and sudden, tight-mouthed silence; and it wasn't just today with their faces carefully averted or studiously bland, but four years of it, from the time he came here. From the day he took over and gained their confidence, made them into a fighting team, down through the seasons until he lost them, one by one, so that they had become total strangers to him as he faced them in the big room.

T hey were all strangers, no one name impinged upon his memory. That was how a man got after so many years in the game—he saw so many come and go that faces and names blurred together, with only a few well remembered, even loved, and not forgotten. And the older a man grew in the game, the harder it became to form young friendships, for a man grew into a certain mold against which youngsters had nothing new to offer.

This team was now a stranger, observed in the abstract, twenty-five players going through the motions, hoping he'd get the brush today so McKay could step in with the new deal; and not only these men, but others now traded away or sent down to the minors because he could not abide quitters and had cut them off for the benefit of those who stayed. But twenty-five of them were still here, hoping he'd be gone soon.

He had put this team together, won a pennant with them, then watched them fall apart a year later. And who took the blame? Why, nobody but Art Cassidy. Shrewd, canny, smart, experienced old Cassidy who knew all the answers . . . and absorbed all the blame which, as everyone knew, was the fault of nobody in the world but the players themselves, luck or the sudden drouth of it, and a few left-handed assists from the front office. A few trades by the general manager, who foresaw Art Cassidy's finish and prepared himself for the killing.

Yes, this was the team he'd lost a year ago when he stopped the kid-glove treatment and got tough, like Joe and other old pros, got tough when his team developed the swellhead after winning the pennant. The pattern was as old as money in the bank, and certainly not typical only of young teams: they won the pennant, demanded and received salary hikes, got complacent, became fat cats. So he got tough and tried to show them, as a team and individually, that laying down was not only betrayal of the body but the mind and the heart, and once you turned on that road it was rough coming back. He'd lost them last year; he even remembered the exact moment, one hot afternoon in Chicago. And then he faced the issue squarely, and got tough. Like all the old pros, he re-proved that baseball hadn't changed since those past days, that you still had to come down to brass tacks if you wanted to win.

So he clamped down the balance of last season, and during spring training, and he proved something to himself and other men of his own age and experience: that it wasn't so much the widely discussed change in players, it was the widely misunderstood change in front-office philosophy. There was the real change, all that wise talk about college degrees and smarter boys, no more cussing and all the rest. . . . There was the change, the application of the soft pedal, and when a man got tough and knew, within days, that he was doing the right thing, had a chance to bring his team back, and at that moment the front office hedged, protested, yelped about bad publicity and all that psychological stuff, and let the players themselves know in an underhanded backyard way that nobody need take that sort of punishment from a tyrant . . . and there were always a few bastards on any team, a few soft-hearted fools who believed that front-office line and spread the good word among the others. When all that happened, what chance did a man have? The writers had to get on the bandwagon and start the insinuations in their columns; and soon the snowball was rolling downhill, getting bigger, aimed at just one man—the manager—and if he was lucky the season's end brought temporary reprieve. But this spring everyone knew, from the first day of training, that he'd lost this team.

And how did you know a team was lost? What were the signs, the predictions, the forecast of the future? Well, like sunrise, death, and taxes, those signs hadn't changed appreciably in fifty years. Art Cassidy banned wives from spring training because that was one way to make kids and even older men grow up; and that started a fine undercurrent of bitching and protests against his damned foolishness. They talked in the showers, in the hotel, on the beach; these individual protests balled together until the writers, probing about delicately, knew exactly how the team felt. They wrote the first stories and that let the wives at home know how things stood; and the wives, preparing for the annual move to the city, built up their own hatred against the manager for keeping them from their loved ones during that fine, warm Florida vacation with pay. That, in truth, was why the wives were angry; it had nothing to do with the team's winning. The wives missed that beach, that sun, that chance to wear new clothes and take it easy. And all because of one man, one flint-hearted old bastard, who issued an edict they dared not disobey. So the talk began, the writers took it up, the wives started brewing their particular brand of poison; and that was just one spike driven into his coffin.

Just one. . . . There were others.

A few players had given their best; mostly they had come from other organizations, men he hadn't managed in the minors. But the kids he'd known all the way, now regulars on this team, how easily they forgot all the years he'd spent with them. Teaching them the facts and tricks he had amassed through the years, often in the same way, learning from someone older. But they forgot, and he could not blame them in one sense, for so often the body grew much faster than the mind, and in some cases the mind seemed to be a complete void.

And the trades made by the front office against his wishes. To strengthen the team, they announced, when no sane man would make those trades. First his catcher, the real old pro on the club, traded to another team for a second baseman, to improve their infield—and the general manager actually caught him pants-down there, for he'd kicked the second baseman off the team last summer. He fought that trade, for he needed the catcher as a man needed air and blood, but the catcher was gone, the trade was made, and if the deal went sour, who took the blame? Not the front office—there'd be some fast sluffing off then—but just one man.

Then, the harsh words he'd used on them last season, remembered this year, words that bit under their hide with truth concerning lack of spirit and empty heads. And the poker games last season. He'd tried to stop that, failed, put a curfew into effect and watched that fail. Yes, there were several reasons, stacked neatly as cordwood, and they bounced on him when the season opened. Everything had piled up, he was licked before the first game, but even then he'd shaken off the inevitable and tried his best. And now it was all over.

He walked from the dressing room into the corridor and up the tunnel to the dugout. He looked upon the field, heard the murmur of the stands, blinked his eyes against the bright sun, the grass, the rising tiers of bleacher seats beneath the scoreboard in left field. The Giants were batting, talking it up as they hit, a tough club playing good, tough baseball, moving through this season in close pursuit of the Dodgers and Phillies. Playing tough baseball for a real old pro who stood over there on his dugout step, arms folded, watching his team. Art Cassidy saw Durocher look up and lift one hand in greeting. Durocher was a throwback to the bygone days, but it came to Art Cassidy that Durocher was right and he was wrong. And if some bright boy wanted to know why Durocher was right, well, Art Cassidy now considered himself eminently qualified to explain.

He—Art Cassidy—was wrong because he'd come up the old way, then changed with the supposed times and tried to play this new kind of baseball that everyone said was so necessary, what with the different players and so forth. But Durocher hadn't changed, not a bit, no matter what the papers said about softening up. Durocher came up the hard, rough, no-quarter way, playing every game for keeps, trusting no one and fighting every man. Durocher still played it that way, unchanged, and he'd never change. They'd piled the hard knocks on old Leo's skull until the scars and bumps covered even older scars and bumps, but he hadn't faltered. He'd wrecked one team, getting his kind of club, and now he had it and that team was playing ball. Sure, Durocher took his lumps. He couldn't keep his mouth shut, but at least he spoke his mind. He was a ham, the worst kind, with that third-base hokum and the folded arms and the big jaw shoved up the umpire's ass, but never once had he broken faith with himself. Stankey crawled out from under that callused wing and made good; and Hornsby was proving that baseball hadn't changed. And while they did that—at least, while Stoneham and Paul stood firm— where was old Art Cassidy?

The gong sounded, and the Giants moved off the field. Art Cassidy watched his team take over the cage and knew, about two years late, how wrong he had been. What he should have done . . . easy to say it now . . . was pass among his prima donnas with a pisselm club and a blacksnake whip, and instill a little pride and guts in their hides. And go to the front office, take that general manager by the wattles, and let it be known that one man ran this team, and he was that man. Sure, it was easy to look back and explain everything away, tell how it should be done. But inside him, not openly for he could never whine, and make excuses. Not if he wanted to keep faith with himself.

He stood on the dugout step and heard the talk in the boxes behind. He saw Ida and smiled, and felt richer for her return grin. There she was, surrounded on all sides, and holding her own. Art Cassidy watched his team move through batting practice until the gong rang. Sammy puffed up to grab a fungo and hit infield, his first-base coach hit to left field, one of his pitchers batted the fly balls to right. His bullpen coach went down the line with the stable of high-priced talent. And he stayed on the dugout step, looking down on the catcher's equipment dropped just beneath the bat rack. He smelled the dugout and the grass and the stands, waiting for the game to start, wondering if he could last. When infield was nearly finished, he moved into the dugout shade and tacked his lineup on the front roof board and spoke to Sammy, "Everybody downstairs," and went into the tunnel, walking steadily toward his last meeting with this team.

He had no real desire to face them, but that small bit of cruelty was part of the ritual. They expected it; he had to complete the farce. He entered the dressing room and stopped at the water cooler for a drink, and stood with the paper cup in his hand, watching the trainer in the other room. He heard them coming down the tunnel, crossing the corridor, then inside and fanning out and taking seats on the scarred benches. He waited until Sammy—last man, like a hen with chicks—closed the door; then he turned from the cooler, wiped his sweaty forehead, and faced them in the silent room.

He knew what they expected. They waited for him to show, in words, just how tough he really was, how getting fired would never change his toughness. But that display of character wasn't necessary today. He had already made them feel that he wasn't licked, that it was just the reverse; they were shamed deep inside because he hadn't quit on them, for the very reason he'd tried to prove—that you can't be a fool forever, that someday you've got to grow up. They knew it now, but they waited to hear the last harsh words before going out to play the last game under him. Art Cassidy crumpled the empty paper cup between his fingers and spoke quietly:

"Same signals. Remember, Thomson's in a streak, play him deep. Beat Maglie today, you can take the odd game tomorrow. All right, let's get at it."

They didn't move, just sat there, hands dangling over their thighs, waiting for the harsh words, unable to comprehend that he was all done talking, but he had no more words and he didn't care who knew it. He looked up and jerked his cap farther down on his balding head and said, "Well . . . are you here to play ball or sit on your ass? Get at it!"

That brought them up, moving quickly into the doorway. Nobody glanced back as they filed toward the tunnel, leaving the big room empty and still. Art Cassidy let the last man clear the corridor before starting his own walk. Behind him, carrying bag and towels, the trainer spoke with false brightness, "We'll get that Maglie today, Art."

"Why, yes," Art Cassidy said curtly. "This is the day they can get anybody—emancipation day."

He heard the trainer's sharp intake of breath, then he was through the tunnel and headed for the home-plate meeting, eager to get it finished. Dascoli, behind the plate today, went through the humdrum repetition of well-known ground rules. Durocher presented his lineup card, Art Cassidy handed over his. Dascoli finished and Durocher said, "Well . . . good luck, Art," and thrust out his hand abruptly. Art Cassidy shook hands and met Durocher's sober gaze, knowing the words had nothing to do with luck in today's game. He said, "Thanks, Leo," and turned away before it became embarrassing for the umpires. Dascoli had come up the same year Art Cassidy started with the Blues, both rookies in a sense that spring, but Dascoli had made good and rode down all the talk concerning his loudness and gestures. Dascoli had made the grade; Art Cassidy hadn't; and it was a funny thing to consider. He reached the dugout and said, "Let's go," and watched them trot across the field. Just a couple of hours, he thought, not too much time to suffer. And he'd bet his year's pay check that today the Blues would win this game by five runs. It always happened when a man was going out; he left a team that suddenly rose up and played as they could. . . . And how many

ways were there of interpreting that little gesture? Just one . . .
and everybody knew the answer.

T his game, he thought, as the first pitch glinted yellow-
white in the sun, was a tiny bead added to the endless neck-
lace looped around his neck, the total of the years spent and
forgotten. Three thousand games, more or less, and every game
had counted, he had pitched and played and managed every
game to the best of his ability, fighting always to win. And today
he felt nothing, had lost the desire. But even as he walked toward
the third-base coaching box when the Blues came in to hit, old
habit stood above anger, the habit of all those years that made a
man give his best. The habit that made a man kick the third-base
bag into line, and exchange a few words with the Giant third
baseman, and take up that position in the coaching box, on the
front corner with his toes touching the lines. Old habit making
him study Maglie closely as the right-hander toed the rubber and
made the first pitch.

Old habit and memory, and every game the same, with the
fine machinery on the field meshing into the mental gymnastics
in the dugouts and on these coaching lines. And the ever-present expectancy that something new might happen and make
the game what it was at best—something always clean and
bright and honest. Whatever happened in the offices and off the
field, down here it was unchanged, it was still good, and a man
could not lie to himself about that truth.

Art Cassidy gave his signals and watched his team, and closed
his ears to the voices from the stands. The innings marched, the
scoreboard remained virgin, the scoreless duel went on three . . .
six . . . eight innings. Art Cassidy stood on his dugout step as they
retired the Giants in the first of the ninth, and now it was time for
the last walk while everyone watched him. He wanted no more of
it, no more of it for a long time. He watched his team enter the

dugout and spoke no words, only turned and made his walk and stood alone in the coaching box. And now, he thought, give me the good-bye present, the big kiss, show them how you'll do it for Steve McKay.

His lead-off man was the first batter, and watching that boy—now a man—Art Cassidy had the strange feeling of watching a boy six years younger. He wanted to say, "Remember when you came up to me on the Triple A club six years ago? Remember that, son, how green you were? Who taught you how to play your field, and make that good throw, and swing that bat as you're swinging it now? Remember all that? No, you don't remember—and why should you? Now give me the good-bye present, son." Art Cassidy stood stiff-legged while his lead-off man hit the clothesline single into center and rounded the bag and danced back, pulling at his cap and watching Art Cassidy for the sacrifice which was now in order.

Art Cassidy turned and walked in his allotted space, and gave the next batter the signal to hit away, giving him the green light, saying without words, "Go on, let's see you do it." And turned, sober-faced, to watch that second-place batter wiggle hips and wait loosely for the pitch. And thought, again, how he had met that boy five years ago and explained how a bat was an implement of finesse and not a club to batter fences, so that the batter was now, if he tried, the best second-place hitter in the league. Art Cassidy watched that man single into center field, followed the ball flight and the incoming rush of the Giant center fielder, and gave the leading runner the holdup sign as the throw came to third base, hard and true.

Durocher stepped from the Giant dugout and studied Maglie, rubbed his long jaw, and sat down. Maglie pinched the rosin bag and twitched his long nose, and faced the third-place batter, the young gentleman Art Cassidy had taken so long ago on the Triple A club, and through patience and teaching, brought along to his present eminence in the league, that of the steady .300 hitter, the twenty-thousand-a-year contract, and the ability—after three years of covert suggestion—to buy and wear decent sport coats and shirts on the road trips. Such a small point, Art Cassidy thought, but how much did such a nicety really mean to the player's over-all confidence. The count ran up and the hit was into left field, a smashing single taken on the first hop and rammed back, so that Art Cassidy held the runner, filling the bases, setting it up for the finish. The runner kicked his spikes against the bag and eyed Art Cassidy furtively and said, "Watch the fly ball, Art."

"Sure, son," Art Cassidy said. "Be awake."

Then Maglie was pitching to the clean-up hitter, the pride and joy of the Blues, running up the count as Art Cassidy gave the hit-away sign, building it up to two and two, the big man waiting at the plate, huge shoulders relaxed, feet spread wide, bat held like a matchstick in those thick, strong hands. Then the pitch went down and the bat swung, and the ball was going, all the way into the darkening stands beneath the scoreboard, and Art Cassidy felt no surprise, only a miserable sort of reverse vindication in his own teaching. He turned before the ball struck and began his walk.

The crowd was up, applauding, the Blues were trotting around the bases, and Maglie stepped off the mound, his game lost, and began his own dreary walk. His path crossed Art Cassidy's near home plate and he paused to let Art Cassidy pass in front. Art Cassidy saw Maglie's thin, dark face for a moment and wanted to say, "I know how you feel," and then saw Maglie's eyes and thought, "No, that's wrong. You know how I feel," and went on through his players to the tunnel, with a quick look at Ida, and across the corridor into the dressing room. He closed the office door that shut off the sound, and rubbed one hand across his face that now felt stiff and cold.

He lit his after-game cigar and began undressing, shedding the uniform, standing at last in his undershirt, feeling the damp warmth of his own sweat clinging to the shirt and beading on his body. The uniform lay on the chair and he wanted to let it lie, but he smiled at his own childishness and hung each piece carefully on the hangers. And then he sat behind the desk, smoking his cigar, waiting patiently for the final words.

They had won a tough ball game, but the noise outside was below normal. He heard faintly the hiss of showers and the low hum of talk, and knew they were rushing to dress and get away before it happened. He sat, unmoving, until the shower sound had stilled and the last men hurried from the big room. And then it was still and he heard the steps on the aisle carpet, and the knock. Art Cassidy ashed his cigar and said, "Come in."

G raham stepped inside and closed the door. At least he sent no other man to do the dirty work. Graham called the turn and came himself, and now he said formally, "Good game, Art."

"Yes," Art Cassidy said. "Come down for that?"

Graham had the grace to smile. "Not exactly, Art. Wish I had."

"Get on with it," Art Cassidy said.

"This comes hard," Graham said. "I want you to know that, Art."

Art Cassidy looked up, and suddenly believed that Graham was sincere. Every man to his own last, and Graham walked a lonely road himself. Art Cassidy said, "When do you want me out of here?"

"Well," Graham said. "We—"

"Look, son," Art Cassidy said. "Don't make such a job of it. Today?"

Graham said, "Yes, today. About next year's salary, Art. Would you mind waiting until the season ends, we can get it arranged at that time. We don't want you to leave the organization; there's always a place for you."

Art Cassidy remembered a conversation of four years ago. He said, "Then I get my old job back?"

"Old job?" Graham said. "I don't understand, Art."

"With the Triple A club," Art Cassidy said. "Remember, you promised it if I flopped here."

He did not crack the smile now touching his mouth, and watched Graham's face betray a very exact memory of that night and the promise.

"But, Art," Graham said. "We can't—"

"Forget it," Art Cassidy said. "I was only fooling. Now you'd better run along, Jack. Ida's waiting, and I want to shower."

He saw the intense relief flood Graham's face. Graham fumbled for the doorknob, opened the door a foot, and then said, "Thanks, Art, and the best of luck to you."

Standing, stripping off the damp undershirt, the last piece of material allegiance to this team, Art Cassidy said, "Sure, Jack. It wasn't so tough after all, was it?"

"No," Graham said. "I hoped—"

"Not for you," Art Cassidy said quietly. "It never is for you, Jack. That's why you'll never know."

Frank O'Rourke
1916–1989

Born in Colorado, Frank O'Rourke attended school in Nebraska and Missouri. In a career spanning five decades, he published more than one hundred short stories and sixty book-length works of fiction. The versatility which became a hall-mark of O'Rourke's writing was demonstrated in the stories that appeared during the 1940s and 1950s (the period of his baseball short stories and novels) in the leading magazines of the day. His first book, *"E" Company*, was introduced by Simon and Schuster in 1945 as the work of a "fresh and outstanding talent."

A restless soul, O'Rourke threatened to top the record among writers for non-stop travel. He and his wife, artist Edith Carlson, lived in California, Mexico, Texas, Minnesota, Florida, New Mexico, Arizona, Switzerland, Washington, Maine, Nevada and Utah, all places in which he soaked up history and background until he exhausted its inspiration in a frenzy of cre-ative activity and moved on.

In the years following the early sports stories, westerns and mysteries, came novels of Midwest America, contemporary satires, and a spy-suspense series under the pseudonym Patrick O'Malley, one of several pseudonyms he used. O'Rourke was presented the Southwestern Library Association's 1958-59 Award for his historical novel of New Mexico, *The Far Moun-tains*, in recognition of "literary excellence and contribution to the culture and heritage of the Southwest" given by the natu-ralist Joseph Wood Krutch. Among the motion pictures made from his books are the classic films *The Professionals* and *The Bravados*.

In 1988, O'Rourke began to write his children's books. The first, *Burton and Stanley*, was published posthumously by David R. Godine in 1993, and was the recipient of a Parent's Choice Award.

Books by Frank O'Rourke

"E" Company, 1945

Action at Three Peaks, 1948

Flashing Spikes, 1948

The Team, 1949

Thunder on the Buckhorn, 1949

The Best Go First, 1950
(writing as Frank O'Malley)

Blackwater, 1950

The Greatest Victory and Other Baseball Stories, 1950

Bonus Rookie, 1950

Football Gravy Train, 1951

The Gun, 1951

Gold Under Skull Peak, 1952

Gunsmoke Over Big Muddy, 1952

Never Come Back, 1952

Nine Good Men, 1952

The Heavenly World Series and Other Baseball Stories, 1952

Concannon, 1952

The Catcher and The Manager, 1953

Gun Hand, 1953

Latigo, 1953

Ride West, 1953

Violence at Sundown, 1953

High Dive, 1954

High Vengeance, 1954

Thunder in the Sun, 1954

The Big Fifty, 1955

Car Deal, 1955

Dakota Rifle, 1955

The Last Round, 1956

The Diamond Hitch, 1956

Hard Men, 1956

Battle Royal, 1956

The Last Chance, 1956

Segundo, 1956

The Bravados, 1957
(released as a film in 1957)

Legend in the Dust, 1957

The Man Who Found His Way, 1957

The Last Ride, 1958

A Texan Came Riding, 1958

Ambuscade, 1959

Desperate Rider, 1959

The Far Mountains, 1959

Violent Country, 1959

The Bride Stealer, 1960

Window in the Dark, 1960

Bandoleer Crossing, 1961

Gunlaw Hill, 1961

The Springtime Fancy, 1961

The Great Bank Robbery, 1961

The Affair of the Red Mosaic, 1961
(writing as Patrick O'Malley)

New Departure, 1962
(writing as Kevin Connor)

The Affair of Swan Lake, 1962
(writing as Patrick O'Malley)